# MICRO

**HARPER**

*An Imprint of* HarperCollins*Publishers*
www.harpercollins.com

# MICHAEL CRICHTON

## MICRO

A NOVEL

AND
RICHARD PRESTON

MICRO. Copyright © 2011 by The John Michael Crichton
Trust. All rights reserved. Printed in the United States of
America. No part of this book may be used or reproduced in
any manner whatsoever without written permission except in
the case of brief quotations embodied in critical articles and
reviews. For information, address HarperCollins Publishers,
10 East 53rd Street, New York, NY 10022.

HarperCollins books may be purchased for educational,
business, or sales promotional use. For information,
please write: Special Markets Department, HarperCollins
Publishers, 10 East 53rd Street, New York, NY 10022.

FIRST EDITION

*Designed by Lucy Albanese*
*Illustrated maps © 2011 by Rodica Prato*
*Running-head insect illustrations by Kevin Lass*

Library of Congress Cataloging-in-Publication Data
has been applied for.

ISBN: 978-0-06-087302-8 (Hardcover)
ISBN: 978-0-06-209141-3 (International Edition)

11 12 13 14 15  OV/RRD  10 9 8 7 6 5 4 3 2 1

For Jr.

MINUTE CREATURES swarm around us . . . objects of potentially endless study and admiration, if we are willing to sweep our vision down from the world lined by the horizon to include the world an arm's length away. A lifetime can be spent in a Magellanic voyage around the trunk of a tree.

—E. O. WILSON

# Introduction

# What Kind of World Do We Live In?

I n 2008, the famous naturalist David Attenborough expressed
concern that modern schoolchildren could not identify common
plants and insects found in nature, although previous generations
identified them without hesitation. Modern children, it seemed,
were cut off from the experience of nature, and from play in the
natural world. Many factors were held up to blame: urban living;
loss of open space; computers and the Internet; heavy homework
schedules. But the upshot was that children were no longer being
exposed to nature and no longer acquiring a direct experience of
nature. It was ironic that this should be happening at a time when
there was in the West an ever greater concern for the environment,
and ever more ambitious steps proposed to protect it.

Indoctrinating children in proper environmental thought was a
hallmark of the green movement, and so children were being in-
structed to protect something about which they knew nothing at
all. It did not escape notice that this was exactly the formula that
had led to well-intentioned environmental degradation in the past—

the deterioration of American national parks being a prime example, and the American policy of forest fire prevention, another. Such policies would never have been instituted if people really understood the environments they were trying to protect.

The problem was that they thought they did. One can argue that the new generation of schoolchildren will emerge even more certain. If nothing else, school teaches that there is an answer to every question; only in the real world do young people discover that many aspects of life are uncertain, mysterious, and even unknowable. If you have a chance to play in nature, if you are sprayed by a beetle, if the color of a butterfly wing comes off on your fingers, if you watch a caterpillar spin its cocoon—you come away with a sense of mystery and uncertainty. The more you watch, the more mysterious the natural world becomes, and the more you realize how little you know. Along with its beauty, you may also come to experience its fecundity, its wastefulness, aggressiveness, ruthlessness, parasitism, and its violence. These qualities are not well-conveyed in textbooks.

Perhaps the single most important lesson to be learned by direct experience is that the natural world, with all its elements and interconnections, represents a complex system and therefore we cannot understand it and we cannot predict its behavior. It is delusional to behave as if we can, as it would be delusional to behave as if we could predict the stock market, another complex system. If someone claims to predict what a stock will do in the coming days, we know that person is either a crook or a charlatan. If an environmentalist makes similar claims about the environment, or an ecosystem, we have not yet learned to see him as a false prophet or a fool.

Human beings interact with complex systems very successfully. We do it all the time. But we do it by managing them, not by claiming to understand them. Managers interact with the system: they do something, watch for the response, and then do something else in an effort to get the result they want. There is an endless iterative interaction that acknowledges we don't know for sure what the system will do—we have to wait and see. We may have a hunch we know what will happen. We may be right much of the time. But we are never certain.

Interacting with the natural world, we are denied certainty. And always will be.

**How then can** young people gain experience of the natural world? Ideally, by spending some time in a rain forest—those vast, uncomfortable, alarming, and beautiful environments that so quickly knock our preconceptions aside.

NOT FINISHED

MICHAEL CRICHTON

August 28, 2008

# MICRO

# THE PALI

TANTALUS CRATER

Tantalus
Base

Great
Boulder

NUNQUAM  OBLIVISCEMUR  MICHAELIS  CRICHTONIS

Kilo

Golf

Waipaka
Arboretum

Foxtrot

Delta

FERN GULLY

Echo

Shuttle to
Nanigen

Bravo

Alpha

Nanigen Bioprospecting
Zone

Charlie

## THE SEVEN GRADUATE STUDENTS

**Rick Hutter**    *Ethnobotanist studying medicines used by indigenous peoples.*

**Karen King**    *Arachnologist (expert in spiders, scorpions, and mites). Skilled in martial arts.*

**Peter Jansen**    *Expert in venoms and envenomation.*

**Erika Moll**    *Entomologist and coleopterist (beetle expert).*

**Amar Singh**    *Botanist studying plant hormones.*

**Jenny Linn**    *Biochemist studying pheromones, the signaling scents used by animals and plants.*

**Danny Minot**    *Doctoral student writing a thesis on "scientific linguistic codes and paradigm transformation."*

# PART I

# TENSOR

# Prologue

## NANIGEN
## 9 OCTOBER, 11:55 P.M.

West of Pearl Harbor, he drove along the Farrington Highway past fields of sugar cane, dark green in the moonlight. This had long been an agricultural region of Oahu, but recently it had begun to change. Off to his left, he saw the flat steel rooftops of the new Kalikimaki Industrial Park, bright silver in the surrounding green. In truth, Marcos Rodriguez knew, this wasn't much of an industrial park; most of the buildings were warehouses, inexpensive to rent. Then there was a marine supply store, a guy who made custom surfboards, a couple of machine shops, a metalworker. That was about it.

And, of course, the reason for his visit tonight: Nanigen Micro-Technologies, a new company from the mainland, now housed in a large building at the far end of the facility.

Rodriguez turned off the highway, drove down between silent buildings. It was almost midnight; the industrial park was deserted. He parked in front of Nanigen.

From the outside, the Nanigen building appeared like all the others: a single-story steel façade with a corrugated metal roof; in effect, nothing more than an enormous shed of crude, cheap construction. Rodriguez knew there was more to it than that. Before the company erected that building, they dug a pit deep into the lava rock, and had filled it with electronic equipment. Only then did they erect this unprepossessing façade, which was now covered in fine red dust from the nearby agricultural fields.

Rodriguez put on his rubber gloves, and slipped into his pocket his digital camera and infrared filter. Then he got out of his car. He wore a security guard uniform; he pulled his cap down over his face, in case there were cameras monitoring the street. He took out the key that he had taken from the Nanigen receptionist some weeks before, after her third Blue Hawaii had put her out cold; he had had it copied, then returned it to her before she woke up.

From her he had learned that Nanigen was forty thousand square feet of labs and high-tech facilities, where she said they did advanced work in robotics. What kind of advanced work, she wasn't sure, except the robots were extremely small. "They do some kind of research on chemicals and plants," she said vaguely.

"You need robots for that?"

"They do, yes." She shrugged.

But she also told him the building itself had no security: no alarm system, no motion detectors, no guards, cameras, laser beams. "Then what do you use?" he asked her. "Dogs?"

The receptionist shook her head. "Nothing," she said. "Just a lock on the front door. They say they don't need any security."

At the time, Rodriguez suspected strongly that Nanigen was a scam or a tax dodge. No high-technology company would house itself in a dusty warehouse, far from downtown Honolulu and the university, from which all high-tech companies drew. If Nanigen was way out here, they must have something to hide.

The client thought so, too. That's why Rodriguez had been

hired in the first place. Truth be told, investigating high-tech corporations wasn't his usual line of work. Mostly he got calls from lawyers, asking him to photograph visiting husbands on Waikiki cheating on their wives. And in this case, too, he had been hired by a local lawyer, Willy Fong. But Willy wasn't the client, and he wouldn't say who was.

Rodriguez had his suspicions. Nanigen had supposedly spent millions of dollars on electronics from Shanghai and Osaka. Some of those suppliers probably wanted to know what was being done with their products. "Is that who it is, Willy? The Chinese or the Japanese?"

Willy Fong shrugged. "You know I can't say, Marcos."

"But it makes no sense," Rodriguez had said. "The place got no security, your clients can pick the lock and walk in any night and see for themselves. They don't need me."

"You talking yourself out of a job?"

"I just want to know what this is about."

"They want you to go and find out what's in that building, and bring them some pictures. That's all."

"I don't like it. I think it's a scam."

"Probably is."

Willy gave him a tired look as if to say, But what do you care? "At least nobody's going to get up from the dinner table and hit you in the mouth."

"True."

Willy pushed back his chair, folded his arms over his ample belly. "So tell me, Marcos. Are you going, or what?"

**Now, walking toward** the front door at midnight, Rodriguez felt suddenly nervous. They don't need any security. What the hell did that mean? In this day and age, everybody had security—lots of security—especially around Honolulu. You had no choice.

There were no windows on the building, just a single metal door. Next to it, a sign: NANIGEN MICROTECHNOLOGIES, INC. And beneath it, BY APPOINTMENT ONLY.

He put the key in the lock and turned it. The door clicked open.

Too easy, he thought, as he glanced back at the empty street, and slipped inside.

**Night lights illuminated** a glass-walled entry area, receptionist's desk, and a waiting area with couches, magazines, and company literature. Rodriguez flicked on his flashlight, moved to the hallway beyond. At the end of the hallway were two doors; he went through the first, and came into a new hallway, with glass walls. There were laboratories on both sides, long black benches with lots of equipment, stacks of bottles on the shelves above. Every dozen yards there was a humming stainless refrigerator and something that looked like a washing machine.

Cluttered bulletin boards, Post-its on the refrigerator, whiteboards with scribbled formulas—the general appearance seemed messy, but Rodriguez had the overwhelming sense that this company was real; that Nanigen was actually doing scientific work here. What did they need robots for?

And then he saw the robots, but they were damned strange: boxy silver metal contraptions, with mechanical arms and treads and appendages; they looked like what they send to Mars. They were various sizes and shapes: some the size of a shoebox, and others much bigger. Then he noticed that beside each one was a smaller version of the same robot. And beside that was a still smaller version. Eventually they were the size of a thumbnail: tiny, highly detailed. The workbenches had huge magnifying glasses so the workers could see the robots. But he wondered how they could build anything so small.

Rodriguez came to the end of the hall, and saw a door with a small sign: TENSOR CORE. He pushed it open, feeling a cool breeze. The room beyond was large and dark. To the right, he noticed rows of backpacks, hanging on hooks on the wall, as if for a camping trip. Otherwise the room was bare. There was a loud AC hum, but no other sound. He noticed the floor was etched with deep grooves in a hexagonal shape. Or perhaps they were big hexagonal tiles; in this low light he couldn't be sure.

But then . . . there was something beneath the floor, he realized. An enormous, complex array of hexagonal tubes and copper wires, dimly visible. The floor was plastic, and he could look through it to see the electronics that had been buried in the ground.

Rodriguez crouched down to look more closely, and as he peered at the hexagons below, he saw a drop of blood spatter on the floor. Then another drop. Rodriguez stared curiously, before he thought to put his hand to his forehead. He was bleeding, just above his right eyebrow.

"What the—?" He'd been cut, somehow. He hadn't felt anything but there was blood on his gloved hand, and blood still dripping from his eyebrow. He stood. The blood was dripping onto his cheek, and chin, and onto the uniform. He put his hand to his forehead and hurried into the nearest lab, looking for a Kleenex or a cloth. He found a box of tissues, and stepped to a washbasin with a small mirror over it. He dabbed at his face. The bleeding had already begun to stop; the cut was small but razor-sharp; he didn't see how it had happened but paper cuts could look like that.

He glanced at his watch. It was twelve twenty. Time to get back to work. In the next moment, he saw a red gash open across the back of his hand, from his wrist to his knuckles, the skin spreading and starting to bleed. Rodriguez yelled in shock. He grabbed more tissues, then a towel hanging from the sink.

He ripped a strip off, and wrapped it around his hand. Then he felt a pain in his leg, and looking down saw that his trousers had been sliced halfway up his thigh, and he was bleeding from there, too.

Rodriguez wasn't thinking anymore. He turned and ran.

Staggering down the hallway, back toward the front door, dragging his injured leg, aware he was leaving enough evidence to identify him later, but he didn't care, he just wanted to get away.

**Shortly before one a.m.,** he pulled up alongside Fong's office. The light on the second floor was still on; Rodriguez stumbled up the back stairs. He was weak from loss of blood, but he was all right. He came in through the back door, not knocking.

Fong was there with another man Rodriguez had never seen before. A Chinese man in his twenties, wearing a black suit, smoking a cigarette. Fong turned. "What the hell happened to you? You look horrible." Fong got up, locked the door, came back. "You get in a fight?"

Rodriguez leaned heavily on the desk. He was still dripping blood. The Chinese guy in black stepped back a bit, said nothing. "No, I did not get into a fight."

"Then what the hell happened?"

"I don't know. It just happened."

"What you talking?" Fong said angrily. "You talk stink, man. What just happened?"

The Chinese kid coughed. Rodriguez looked over and saw a red arc was sliced beneath his chin. Blood flowed down his white shirt. The kid looked shocked. He put his hand up to his throat, and the blood seeped between his fingers. He fell over backward.

"Holy crap," Willy Fong said. He scurried forward, looking at the kid on the floor. The kid's heels were drumming on the ground; he was in spasm. "Did you do that?"

"No," Rodriguez said, "that's what I'm telling you."

"This is a fucking mess," Fong said. "You have to bring this back to my office? Did you think about it? Because cleaning this up is—"

Blood sprayed up the left side of Fong's face. The cut artery in his neck pumped in spurts. He threw his hand over the wound, but it spurted through his fingers.

"Holy crap," he said, and sagged into his chair. He stared at Rodriguez. "How?"

"No damned idea," Rodriguez said. He knew what was coming. He just had to wait. He barely felt the slice at the back of his neck, but the dizziness came quickly, and he fell over. He was lying on his side, in a sticky pool of his own blood, staring at Fong's desk. Fong's shoes under the desk. And he thought, Bastard never gave me my money. And then darkness closed around him.

**The headlines read** THREE DEAD IN BIZARRE SUICIDE PACT. It was splashed all over the *Honolulu Star-Advertiser*. Sitting at his desk, Lieutenant Dan Watanabe tossed the paper aside. He looked up at his boss, Marty Kalama. "I'm getting calls," Kalama said. Kalama had wire-framed spectacles and blinked a lot; he looked like a teacher, not a cop. But he was an *akamai* guy, knew what he was doing. Kalama said, "I hear there's problems, Dan."

"With suicide?" Watanabe nodded. "You bet, big problems. Makes no sense at all, if you ask me."

"So where'd the papers get it?"

"Where they get everything," Watanabe said. "They made it up."

"Fill me in," Kalama said.

Watanabe didn't have to consult his notes. Days later, the scene remained vivid in his mind. "Willy Fong has an office on the second floor of one of those small buildings on Puʻuhui Lane, off of Lillihi Street north of the freeway. Wooden building, kind of ratty, got four offices in it. Willy's sixty, probably you knew him, defends

DUIs for locals, small stuff, always been clean. Other people in the building complain of a smell coming from Willy's offices, so we go up there and find three deceased males. ME says dead two to three days, can't estimate closer than that. Air-conditioning was off, so the room got ripe. All three died of knife wounds. Willy got a cut carotid, bled out in his chair. Across the room is a young Chinese guy, no ID yet, he might be a national, throat cut both jugulars, bled out quick. Third vic is that Portugee with the camera, Rodriguez."

"The one who photographs guys out cheating with their secretaries?"

"That's him. Kept getting beat up. Anyway, he's there too, and he's got cuts all over his body—face, forehead, hand, legs, back of the neck. Never seen anything like it."

"Test cuts?"

Watanabe shook his head. "No. Examiner says no, too. The injuries were done to him, and done over some period of time, maybe an hour. We got his blood on the back stairs, and his bloody footprints walking up. Blood in his car parked beside the building. So he was already bleeding when he walked in the door."

"Then what do you think happened?"

"I got no idea," Watanabe said. "If this is suicide, it's three guys without notes, and nobody ever heard of that. Plus no knife, and we turned the place upside down looking, I can tell you. Plus it was locked from the inside, so nobody could have left. Windows were closed and locked, too. We dusted around the windows for prints anyway, just in case somebody entered by a window. No fresh prints around the windows, just a bunch of dirt."

"Somebody flush a blade down the toilet?" Kalama asked.

"No," Dan Watanabe answered. "There wasn't any blood in the bathroom. Means nobody went in there after the cutting started. So we got three dead guys slashed to death in a locked room. No motive, no weapon, no nothing."

"Now what?"

"That Portugee PI came from somewhere. He already got cut up somewhere else. I figure try to find out where that happened. Where it started." Watanabe shrugged. "He had a gas receipt from Kelo's Mobil in Kalepa. Filled the tank at ten p.m. We know how much gas he used, so we can get a radius of where he could drive from Kelo's to his destination and then back to Willy's."

"Big radius. Must cover most of the island."

"We're chipping away. There's fresh gravel in the tire treads. It's crushed limestone. Good chance he went to a new construction site, something like that. Anyway, we'll run it down. It may take us a while, but we'll get that location." Watanabe pushed the paper across the desk. "And in the meantime . . . I'd say the papers got it right. Triple suicide pact, and that's the end of it. At least for now."

# Chapter **|**

DIVINITY AVENUE, CAMBRIDGE
18 OCTOBER, 1:00 P.M.

In the second-floor biology lab, Peter Jansen, twenty-three, slowly lowered the metal tongs into the glass cage. Then, with a quick jab, he pinned the cobra just behind its hood. The snake hissed angrily as Jansen reached in, gripped it firmly behind the head, raised it to the milking beaker. He swabbed the beaker membrane with alcohol, pushed the fangs through, and watched as yellowish venom slid down the glass.

The yield was a disappointing few milliliters. Jansen really needed a half-dozen cobras in order to collect enough venom to study, but there was no room for more animals in the lab. There was a reptile facility over in Allston, but the animals there tended to get sick; Peter wanted his snakes nearby, where he could supervise their condition.

Venom was easily contaminated by bacteria; that was the reason for the alcohol swab and for the bed of ice the beaker sat on. Peter's research concerned bioactivity of certain polypeptides in cobra venom; his work was part of a vast research interest that included snakes, frogs, and spiders, all of which made neuroactive toxins. His experience with snakes had made him an "envenomation specialist," occasionally called by hospitals to advise on exotic bites. This caused a certain amount of envy among other graduate students in the lab; as a group, they were highly competitive and quick to notice if anyone got attention from the outside world. Their solution was to complain that it was too dangerous to keep a cobra in the lab, and that it really shouldn't be there. They referred to Peter's research as "working with nasty herps."

None of this bothered Peter; his disposition was cheerful and even-handed. He came from an academic family, so he didn't take this backbiting too seriously. His parents were no longer alive, killed in the crash of a light plane in the mountains of Northern California. His father had been a professor of geology at UC Davis, and his mother had taught on the medical faculty in San Francisco; his older brother was a physicist.

Peter had returned the cobra to the cage just as Rick Hutter came over. Hutter was twenty-four, an ethnobotanist. Lately he had been researching analgesics found in the bark of rain-forest trees. As usual, Rick was wearing faded jeans, a denim shirt, and heavy boots. He had a trimmed beard and a perpetual frown. "I notice you're not wearing your gloves," he said.

"No," Peter said, "I've gotten pretty confident—"

"When I did my field work, you had to wear gloves," he said. Rick Hutter never lost an opportunity to remind others in the lab that he had done actual field work. He made it sound as if he had spent years in the remote Amazon backwaters. In fact, he had spent four months doing research in a national park in Costa Rica. "One porter in our team didn't wear gloves, and reached down to move a rock. Bam! *Terciopelo* sunk its fangs into him. Fer-de-lance, two meters long. They had to amputate his arm. He was lucky to survive at all."

"Uh-huh," Peter said, hoping Rick would get going. He liked Rick, but the guy had a tendency to lecture everybody.

The person in the lab who really disliked Rick Hutter was Karen King. Karen, a tall young woman with dark hair and angular shoulders, was studying spider venom and spiderwebs. She overheard Rick lecturing Peter on snakebite in the jungle, and couldn't stand it. She had been working at a lab bench, and she snapped over her shoulder, "Rick—you stayed in a tourist lodge in Costa Rica. Remember?"

"Bullshit. We camped in the rain forest—"

"Two whole nights," Karen interrupted him, "until the mosquitoes drove you back to the lodge."

Rick glared at Karen. His face turned red, and he opened his mouth to say something, but didn't. Because he couldn't reply. It was true: the mosquitoes had been hellish. He'd been afraid the mosquitoes might give him malaria or dengue hemorrhagic fever, so he had gone back to the lodge.

Instead of arguing with Karen King, Rick turned to Peter: "Hey, by the way. I heard a rumor that your brother is coming today. Isn't he the one who struck it rich with a startup company?"

"That's what he tells me."

"Well, money isn't everything. Myself, I'd never work in the private sector. It's an intellectual desert. The best minds stay in universities so they don't have to prostitute themselves."

Peter wasn't about to argue with Rick, whose opinions on any subject were strongly held. But Erika Moll, the entomologist who'd recently arrived from Munich, said, "I think you are being rigid. I wouldn't mind working for a private company at all."

Hutter threw up his hands. "See? Prostituting."

Erika had slept with several people in the biology department, and didn't seem to care who knew. She gave him the finger and said, "Spin on it, Rick."

"I see you've mastered American slang," Rick said, "among other things."

"The other things, you wouldn't know," she said. "And you won't." She turned to Peter. "Anyway, I see nothing wrong with a private job."

"But what is this company, exactly?" said a soft voice. Peter turned and saw Amar Singh, the lab's expert in plant hormones. Amar was known for his distinctly practical turn of mind. "I mean, what does the company do that makes it so valuable? And this is a biological company? But your brother is a physicist, isn't he? How does that work?"

At that moment, Peter heard Jenny Linn across the lab say, "Wow, look at that!" She was staring out the window at the street below. They could hear the rumble of high-performance engines. Jenny said, "Peter, look—is that your brother?"

Everyone in the lab had gone to the windows.

Peter saw his brother on the street below, beaming like a kid, waving up at them. Eric was standing alongside a bright yellow Ferrari convertible, his arm around a beautiful blond woman. Behind them was a second Ferrari, gleaming black. Someone said, "Two Ferraris! That's half a million dollars down there." The rumble of the engines echoed off the scientific laboratories that lined Divinity Avenue.

A man stepped out of the black Ferrari. He had a trim build and expensive taste in clothes, though his look was decidedly casual.

"That's Vin Drake," Karen King said, staring out the window.

"How do you know?" Rick Hutter said to her, standing beside her.

"How do you not know?" Karen replied. "Vincent Drake is probably the most successful venture capitalist in Boston."

"You ask me, it's a disgrace," Rick said. "Those cars should have been outlawed years ago."

But nobody was listening to him. They were all heading for the stairs, hurrying down to the street. Rick said, "What is the big deal?"

"You didn't hear?" Amar said, hurrying past Rick. "They've come here to recruit."

"Recruit? Recruit who?"

**"Anybody doing good** work in the fields that we're interested in," Vin Drake said to the students clustered around him. "Microbiology, entomology, chemical ecology, ethnobotany, phytopathology —in other words, all research into the natural world at the micro- or nano-level. That's what we're after, and we're hiring now. You don't need a PhD. We don't care about that; if you're talented you can do your thesis for us. But you will have to move to Hawaii, because that's where the labs are."

Standing to one side, Peter embraced his brother, Eric, then said, "Is that true? You're already hiring?"

The blond woman answered. "Yes, it's true." She stuck out her hand and introduced herself as Alyson Bender, the CFO of the company. Alyson Bender had a cool handshake with a crisp manner, Peter thought. She wore a fawn-colored business suit with a string of natural pearls at her neck. "We need at least a hundred first-rate researchers by the end of the year," she said. "They're not easy to find, even though we offer what is probably the best research environment in the history of science."

"Oh? How is that?" Peter said. It was a pretty big claim.

"It's true," his brother said. "Vin will explain."

Peter turned to his brother's car. "Do you mind . . ." He couldn't help himself. "Could I get in? Just for a minute?"

"Sure, go ahead."

He slipped behind the wheel, shut the door. The bucket seat was tight, enveloping; the leather smelled rich; the instruments were big and business-like, the steering wheel small, with unusual red buttons on it. Sunlight gleamed off the yellow finish. Everything felt so luxurious, he was a little uneasy; he couldn't tell if he liked this feeling or not. He shifted in the seat, and felt something under his thigh. He pulled out a white object that looked like a piece of popcorn. And it was light like popcorn, too. But it was stone. He thought the rough edges would scratch the leather; he slipped it into his pocket and climbed out.

One car over, Rick Hutter was glowering at the black Ferrari, as Jenny Linn admired it. "You must realize, Jenny," Rick said, "that this car, squandering so many resources, is an offense against Mother Earth."

"Really?" Jenny said. "Did she tell you that?" She ran her fingers along the fender. "I think it's beautiful."

**In a basement** room furnished with a Formica table and a coffee machine, Vin Drake had seated himself at the table, with Eric Jansen and Alyson Bender, the two Nanigen executives, placed on either side of him. The grad students clustered around, some sitting at the table, some leaning against the wall.

"You're young scientists, starting out," Vin Drake was saying. "So you have to deal with the reality of how your field operates. Why, for example, is there such an emphasis on the cutting edge in science? Why does everybody want to be there? Because all the prizes and recognition go to new fields. Thirty years ago, when molecular biology was new, there were lots of Nobels, lots of major discoveries. Later, the discoveries became less fundamental, less groundbreaking. Molecular biology was no longer new. By then the best people had moved on to genetics, proteomics, or to work in specialized areas: brain function, consciousness, cellular differentiation, where the problems were immense and still unsolved. Good strategy? Not really, because the problems remain unsolved. Turns out it isn't enough that the field is new. There must also be new tools. Galileo's telescope—a new vision of the universe. Leeuwen-hoek's microscope—a new vision of life. And so it continues, right to the present: radio telescopes exploded astronomical knowledge. Unmanned space probes rewrote our knowledge of the solar system. The electron microscope altered cell biology. And on, and on. New tools mean big advances. So, as young researchers, you should be asking yourselves—who has the new tools?"

There was a brief silence. "Okay, I'll bite," someone said. "Who has the new tools?"

"We do," Vin said. "Nanigen MicroTechnologies. Our company has tools that will define the limits of discovery for the first half of the twenty-first century. I'm not kidding, I'm not exaggerating. I'm telling you the simple truth."

"Pretty big claim," Rick Hutter said. He leaned against the wall, arms folded, clutching a paper cup of coffee.

Vin Drake looked calmly at Rick. "We don't make big claims without a reason."

"So what exactly are your tools?" Rick went on.

"That's proprietary," Vin said. "You want to know, you sign an NDA and come to Hawaii to see for yourself. We'll pay your airfare."

"When?"

"Whenever you're ready. Tomorrow, if you want."

**Vin Drake was** in a hurry. He finished the presentation, and they all filed out of the basement and went out onto Divinity Avenue, to where the Ferraris were parked. In the October afternoon, the air had a bite, and the trees burned with orange and russet colors. Hawaii might have been a million miles from Massachusetts.

Peter noticed Eric wasn't listening. He had his arm around Alyson Bender, and he was smiling, but his thoughts were elsewhere.

Peter said to Alyson, "Would you mind if I took a family moment here?" Grabbing his brother's arm, he walked him down the street away from the others.

Peter was five years younger than Eric. He had always admired his brother, and coveted the effortless way Eric seemed to manage everything from sports to girls to his academic studies. Eric never strained, never seemed to sweat or worry. Whether it was a playoff game for the lacrosse team, or oral exams for his doctorate, Eric always seemed to know how to play things. He was always confident, always easy.

"Alyson seems nice," Peter said. "How long have you been seeing her?"

"Couple of months," Eric said. "Yes, she's nice." Somehow, he didn't sound enthusiastic.

"Is there a but?"

Eric shrugged. "No, just a reality. Alyson's got an MBA. Truth is, she's all business, and she can be tough. You know—Daddy wanted a boy."

"Well, Eric, she's very pretty for a boy."

"Yes, she's pretty." That tone again.

Feeling around, Peter said, "And how're things with Vin?" Vincent Drake had a somewhat unsavory reputation, had been threatened twice with federal indictments; he had beaten back prosecutors both times, although no one knew quite how. Drake was regarded as tough, smart, and unscrupulous, but above all, successful. Peter had been surprised when Eric first signed on with him.

"Vin can raise money like nobody else," Eric said. "His presentations are brilliant. And he always lands the tuna, as they say." Eric shrugged. "I accept the downside, which is that Vin will say whatever he needs to say to get a deal done. But lately he's been, well . . . more careful. More presidential."

"So he's the president of the company, Alyson's the CFO, and you're—?"

"Vice president in charge of technology," Eric said.

"Is that okay?"

"It's perfect. I want to be in charge of the technology." He smiled. "And to drive a Ferrari . . ."

"What about those Ferraris?" Peter said, as they approached the cars. "What're you going to do with them?"

"We'll drive them down the East Coast," Eric said. "Stop at major university biology labs along the way, and do this little song-and-dance to drum up candidates. And then turn in the cars in Baltimore."

"Turn them in?"

"They're rented," Eric said. "Just a way to get attention."

Peter looked back at the crowd around the cars. "Works."

"Yes, we figured."

"So you really are hiring now?"

"We really are." Again, Peter detected a lack of enthusiasm in his brother's voice.

"Then what's wrong, bro?"

"Nothing."

"Come on, Eric."

"Really, nothing. The company is underway, we're making great progress, the technology is amazing. Nothing's wrong."

Peter said nothing. They walked in silence for a moment. Eric stuck his hands in his pockets. "Everything's fine. Really."

"Okay."

"It is."

"I believe you." They came to the end of the street, turned, headed back toward the group clustered around the cars.

"So," Eric said, "tell me: which one of those girls in your lab are you seeing?"

"Me? None."

"Then who?"

"Nobody at the moment," Peter said, his voice sinking. Eric had always had lots of girls, but Peter's love life was erratic and unsatisfactory. There had been a girl in anthropology; she worked down the street at the Peabody Museum, but that ended when she started going out with a visiting professor from London.

"That Asian woman is cute," Eric said.

"Jenny? Yes, very cute. She plays on the other team."

"Ah, too bad." Eric nodded "And the blonde?"

"Erika Moll," Peter said. "From Munich. Not interested in an exclusive relationship."

"Still—"

"Forget it, Eric."

"But if you—"

"I already did."

"Okay. Who's the tall, dark-haired woman?"

"That's Karen King," Peter said. "Arachnologist. Studying spider web formation. But she worked on the textbook *Living Systems*. Kind of won't let anybody forget it."

"A little stuck-up?"

"Just a little."

"She looks very buff," Eric remarked, still staring at Karen King.

"She's a fitness nut. Martial arts, gym."

They were coming back to the group. Alyson waved to Eric. "You about ready, honey?"

Eric said he was. He embraced Peter, shook his hand.

"Where now, bro?" Peter said.

"Down the road. We have an appointment at MIT. Then we'll do BU later in the afternoon, and start driving." He punched Peter on the shoulder. "Don't be a stranger. Come and see me."

"I will," Peter said.

"And bring your group with you. I promise you—all of you—you won't be disappointed."

# Chapter 2

BIOSCIENCES BUILDING
18 OCTOBER, 3:00 P.M.

Returning to the lab, they experienced that familiar environment as suddenly mundane, old-fashioned. It felt crowded, too. The tensions in the lab had been simmering for a long time: Rick Hutter and Karen King had despised each other from the day they had arrived; Erika Moll had brought trouble to the group with her choice of lovers; and, like so many grad students everywhere, they were rivals. And they were tired of the work. It seemed they all felt that way, and there was a long silence as they each returned to their lab benches and resumed work in a desultory way. Peter took his milking beaker off the ice block, labeled it, and put it on his shelf of the refrigerator. He noticed something rattling around with the change in his pocket, and, idly, he took the object out. It was the little thing he'd found in his brother's rented Ferrari. He flicked it across the bench surface. It spun.

Amar Singh, the plant biologist, was watching. "What's that?"

"Oh. It broke off my brother's car. Some part. I thought it would scratch the leather."

"Could I see—?"

"Sure." It was a little larger than his thumbnail. "Here," Peter said, without looking at it closely.

Amar put it in the flat palm of his hand, and squinted at it. "This doesn't look like a car part to me."

"No?"

"No. I'd say it's an airplane."

Peter stared. It was so small he couldn't really make out details, but now that he looked closely, it did indeed appear to be a tiny airplane. Like something from a model kit, the kind of kits he'd made as a boy. Maybe a fighter jet to glue onto an aircraft carrier. But if so, it was like no fighter jet he had ever seen. This one had a blunted nose, an open seat, no canopy, and a boxy rear with tiny stubby flanges: no real wings to speak of.

"Do you mind . . ."

Amar was already heading for the big magnifying glass by his workbench. He put the object under the glass, and turned it carefully. "This is quite fantastic," he said.

Peter pushed his head in to look. Under magnification, the airplane—or whatever it was—appeared exquisitely beautiful, rich with detail. The cockpit had amazingly intricate controls, so minute it was hard to imagine how they had been carved. Amar was thinking the same thing.

"Perhaps laser lithography," he said, "the same way they do computer chips."

"But is it an airplane?"

"I doubt it. No method of propulsion. I don't know. Maybe it's just some kind of model."

"A model?" Peter said.

"Perhaps you should ask your brother," Amar said, drifting back to his workbench.

...

**Peter reached Eric** on his cell phone. He heard loud voices in the background. "Where are you?" Peter said.

"Memorial Drive. They love us at MIT. They understand what we're talking about."

Peter described the small object he had found.

"You really shouldn't have that," Eric said. "It's proprietary."

"But what is it?"

"Actually, it's a test," his brother said. "One of the first tests of our robotic technology. It's a robot."

"It looks like it has a cockpit, with a little chair and instruments, like someone would sit there . . ."

"No, no, what you're seeing is the slot to hold the micro-power-pack and control package. So we can run it remotely. I'm telling you, Peter, it's a bot. One of the first proofs of concept of our ability to miniaturize beyond anything previously known. I was going to show it to you if we had time, but—listen, I'd prefer you keep that little device to yourself, at least for now."

"Sure, okay." No point in telling him about Amar.

"Bring it with you when you come to visit us," Eric said, "in Hawaii."

**The head of** the lab, Ray Hough, came in and spent the rest of the day in his office, reviewing papers. By general agreement it was considered poor form for the graduate students to discuss other jobs while Professor Hough was present. So around four o'clock they all met at Lucy's Deli on Mass Ave. As they crowded around a couple of small tables, a lively discussion ensued. Rick Hutter continued to argue that the university was the only place where one could engage in ethical research. But nobody really listened to him; they were more concerned with the claims that Vin Drake had made. "He was good," Jenny Linn said, "but it was a sales pitch."

"Yes," Amar Singh said, "but at least one part of it was true. He's right that discoveries do follow new tools. If those guys have the equivalent of a new kind of microscope, or a new PCR-type technique, then they're going to make a lot of discoveries quickly."

"But could it really be the best research environment in the world?" Jenny Linn said.

"We can see for ourselves," Erika Moll said. "They said they'd pay airfare."

"How's Hawaii this time of year?" Jenny said.

"I can't believe you guys are buying into this," Rick said.

"It's always good," Karen King said. "I did my tae kwon do training in Kona. Wonderful." Karen was a martial arts devotee, and had already changed into a sweat suit for her evening workout.

"I overheard the CFO say they're hiring a hundred people before the end of the year," Erika Moll said, trying to steer the conversation away from Karen and Rick.

"Is that supposed to scare us or entice us?"

"Or both?" Amar Singh said.

"Do we have any idea what this new technology is they claim to have?" Erika said. "Do you know, Peter?"

"From a career standpoint," Rick Hutter said, "you'd be very foolish not to get your PhD first."

"I have no idea," Peter said. He glanced at Amar, who said nothing, just nodded silently.

"Frankly, I'm curious to see their facility," Jenny said.

"So am I," Amar said.

"I looked at their website," Karen King said. "Nanigen Micro-Tech. It says they make specialized robots at the micro- and nano-scale. That's millimeters down to thousandths of a millimeter. They have drawings of robots that look like they're about four or five millimeters long—maybe a quarter of an inch. And then some that are half that, maybe two millimeters. The robots seem very detailed. No explanation how they could be made."

Amar was staring at Peter. Peter said nothing.

"Your brother hasn't talked to you about this, Peter?" Jenny asked.

"No, this has been his secret."

"Well," Karen King continued, "I don't know what they mean by nano-scale robots. That would be less than the thickness of a human hair. Nobody can fabricate at those dimensions. You'd have to be able to construct a robot atom by atom, and nobody can do that."

"But they say they can?" Rick said. "It's corporate bullshit."

"Those cars aren't bullshit."

"Those cars are rented."

"I have to get to class," Karen King said, standing up from the table. "I'll tell you one thing, though. Nanigen has kept a very low profile, but there are a few brief references in some business sites, going back about a year. They got close to a billion dollars in funding from a consortium put together by Davros Venture Capital—"

"A billion!"

"Yeah. And that consortium is primarily composed of international drug companies."

"Drug companies?" Jenny Linn frowned. "Why would they be interested in micro-bots?"

"The plot thickens," Rick said. "Big Pharma behind the curtain."

"Maybe they expect new delivery systems?" Amar said.

"Nah, they have that already, with nano-spheres. They don't need to spend a billion dollars on that. They must be expecting new drugs."

"But how . . ." Erika shook her head, puzzled.

"There's more," Karen King said, "from the business websites. Not long after they got the funding, Nanigen was challenged by another micro-robotic company in Palo Alto, saying Nanigen had made false representations to raise money and they didn't really have the technology they said they did. This other company was also developing microscopic robots."

"Uh-huh . . ."

"What happened?"

"The threatened lawsuit was withdrawn. The Palo Alto company declared bankruptcy. And that was the end, except the head of their company was quoted as saying Nanigen did have the technology, after all."

"So you think this is real?" Rick said.

"I think I'm late for class," Karen said.

"I think it's real," Jenny Linn said. "And I'm going to Hawaii to see for myself."

"I am, too," Amar said.

"I don't believe this," Rick Hutter said.

**Peter walked down** Mass Avenue with Karen King toward Central Square. It was late afternoon, but the sun still felt warm. Karen carried her gym bag in one hand, keeping the other hand free.

"Rick gives me a pain," she said. "He acts like he's being ethical when he's really just lazy."

"How do you mean?"

"Staying in the university is safe," Karen said. "A nice life, comfortable and safe. Except he won't admit that. Do me a favor," she added, "and walk on the other side of me, okay?"

Peter moved to Karen's left side. "Why?"

"So my hand is free."

Peter looked at her right hand. She held her car keys in her fist, the key shaft protruding from between her knuckles like a knife blade. Hanging from the key chain was a canister of pepper spray, close to her wrist.

Peter couldn't help smiling. "You think we're at risk here?"

"The world is a dangerous place."

"Mass Ave? At five in the afternoon?" They were in the heart of Cambridge.

"Colleges don't report the actual number of rapes in their communities," Karen said. "It's bad publicity. Wealthy alumni won't send their daughters."

He kept looking at her clenched fist, the key poking out. "What will you do with the keys you're holding that way?"

"Straight hit to the windpipe. Instant crippling pain, maybe puncture the trachea. If that doesn't take him down, spray full in the face close-range. Kick down hard on the kneecap, break it if you can. By then he's down, and he's not going anywhere."

She was serious, almost grim. Peter suppressed an urge to laugh. The street before them was familiar, mundane. People were getting off work, heading home for dinner. They passed a harried-looking professor in a wrinkled corduroy jacket, clutching a stack of blue exam papers, followed by a little old lady with a walker. A group of joggers up ahead.

Karen reached into her purse, pulled out a small folded knife, flipped open the thick serrated blade. "Got my Spyderco knife, I can gut a bastard if it comes to that." She glanced up, saw his expression. "You think I'm ridiculous, don't you?"

"No," he said. "It's just—you'd really gut someone with a knife?"

"Listen," she said. "My half-sister is a lawyer in Baltimore. She's walking to her car in the garage, two o'clock in the afternoon, and she's attacked by some guy. Knocked down, hits the concrete, loses consciousness, beaten and raped. When she comes to, she has retrograde amnesia, she can't remember anything about the attacker, how it happened, what he looks like. Nothing. One day in the hospital and they send her home.

"So there's a guy in the firm, a partner, he has scratches on his throat, and she thinks maybe it's him. Some guy in her own firm, followed her out and raped her. But she doesn't remember, she can't be sure. And she's just so uncomfortable. Eventually she leaves the firm, moves to DC, has to start again at a lower-paying job." Karen held up her fist. "All because she didn't carry her keys like this. She was too nice to protect herself. Bullshit."

Peter was trying to imagine whether Karen King would really stab someone with the key, or gut them with a knife. He had the uneasy feeling that she would. In a university setting, where so many people just talked, it seemed she was ready for action.

They came to the storefront martial arts studio, the windows papered over. He could hear shouts in unison from inside. "Well, this is my class," she said. "I'll see you later. But listen: if you talk to your brother, ask him why drug companies put up so much money for micro-botics, okay? I'm curious." And she went through the swinging door, into the class.

**Peter returned to** the lab that evening. He had to feed the cobra every three days, and he usually did it at night, since cobras were by nature nocturnal. It was eight p.m., and the lab lights were low, when he lowered a squirming white rat into the cage and slid the glass shut. The rat scampered to the far side of the cage, and froze. Only its nose twitched. Slowly the snake turned, uncoiled, and faced the rat.

"I hate to see that," Rick Hutter said. He had come up behind Peter.

"Why?"

"So cruel."

"Everybody's got to eat, Rick."

The cobra struck, burying its fangs deep in the rat's body. The rat shivered, stayed on its feet, then collapsed. "That's why I'm a vegetarian," Rick said.

"You don't think plants have feelings?" Peter said.

"Don't start," Rick said. "You and Jenny." Jen's research involved communication among plants and insects via pheromones, chemicals released by organisms to trigger responses. The field had made enormous advances over the last twenty years. Jenny insisted that plants had to be seen as active, intelligent creatures, little different from animals. And Jenny enjoyed annoying Rick. "It's ridiculous," Rick said to Peter. "Peas and beans don't have feelings."

"Of course not," Peter answered, with a smile. "It's because you've already killed the plant—heartlessly dispatched it for your own selfish meal. You just pretend the plant didn't scream in agony when you killed it, because you don't want to face the consequences of your cold-blooded plant murder."

"Absurd."

"Speciesism," Peter said. "And you know it." He was smiling, but there was truth to what he was saying. Peter was surprised to see that Erika was in the lab, and so was Jenny. Few of the graduate students worked at night. What was going on?


**Erika Moll stood** at a dissecting board, carefully cutting open a black beetle. Erika was a coleopterist, meaning an entomologist with a special interest in beetles. As she said, that was a conversation-stopper at cocktail parties. ("What do you do?" "I study beetles.") But, in fact, beetles were very important to the ecosystem. A quarter of all known species were beetles. Years ago, a reporter had asked the famed biologist J. B. S. Haldane what could be deduced about the Creator from the creation, and Haldane had answered, "He has an inordinate fondness for beetles."

"What have you got there?" Peter said to Erika.

"This is a bombardier beetle," she said. "One of the Australian Pheropsophus that sprays so effectively."

As she spoke, she returned to her dissection, shifting her body so she was touching his. It seemed to be an accidental contact; she gave no indication that she had even noticed. But she was a notorious flirt. "What's special about this bombardier?" Peter said.

Bombardier beetles got their name from their ability to fire a hot, noxious spray in any direction from a rotating turret at the tip of their abdomen. The spray was sufficiently unpleasant that it stopped toads and birds from eating them, and it was toxic enough to kill smaller insects immediately. How bombardier beetles accomplished this had been studied since the early 1900s, and by now the mechanism was well understood.

"The beetles produce boiling-hot benzoquinone spray," she explained, "which they make from precursors stored in the body. They have two sacs in the rear of the abdomen—I'm cutting them open now, there, you see them? The first sac contains the precursor hydroquinone along with the oxidant, hydrogen peroxide. The second sac is a rigid chamber, and contains enzymes, catalases, and peroxidases. When the beetle is attacked, it muscularly squeezes the contents of the first sac into the second, where all the ingredients combine to produce an explosive blast of benzoquinone spray."

"And this particular beetle?"

"It adds something more to its armamentarium," she said. "It also produces a ketone, 2-tridecanone. The ketone has repellent properties, but it also acts as a surfactant, a wetting agent that accelerates the spread of the benzoquinone. I want to know where the ketone is made." She rested her hand lightly on his arm for a moment.

Peter said, "You don't think the beetle makes it?"

"Not necessarily, no. It might have taken on bacteria, and let the bacteria make the ketone for it." That was a fairly common event in nature. Making chemicals for defense consumed energy, and if an animal could incorporate bacteria to do the work on its behalf, so much the better.

"This ketone is found elsewhere?" Peter said. That would suggest it was of external bacterial origin.

"In several caterpillars, yes."

"By the way," he said, "why are you working so late?"

"We all are."

"Because?"

"I don't want to fall behind," she said, "and I assume I'll be gone next week. In Hawaii."

**Jenny Linn held** a stopwatch while she watched a complex apparatus: leafy plants under one large flask were being eaten by caterpillars, while an air hose connected the first flask to three more flasks, each with more plants but no caterpillars. A small pump controlled air flow among the flasks.

"We already know the basic situation," she said. "There are 300,000 known species of plants in the world, and 900,000 species of insects, and many of them eat plants. Why haven't all the plants vanished, chewed down to the ground? Because all plants long ago evolved defenses against insects that attack them. Animals can run away from predators, but plants can't. So they have evolved chemical warfare. Plants produce their own pesticides, or they generate toxins to make their leaves taste bad, or they release volatile chemicals that attract the insect's predators. And sometimes they release chemicals that signal other plants to make their leaves more toxic, less edible. Inter-plant communications, that's what we are measuring here."

The caterpillars eating the plants in the first flask caused the release of a chemical, a plant hormone, that would be carried to the other flasks. The other plants would increase their production of nicotinic acid. "I'm looking to measure the rate of response," she said. "That's why I have three flasks. I'll be cutting leaves from various places to measure nicotinic acid levels in them, but as soon as I cut a leaf from the next plant . . ."

"That plant will act like it's under attack, and it will release more volatiles."

"Right. So the flasks are kept separate. We know the response is relatively rapid, a matter of minutes." She pointed to a box to one side. "I measure the volatiles with ultra high-speed gas chromatography, and the leaf extraction is straightforward." She glanced at her stopwatch. "And now if you'll excuse me . . ."

She lifted the first flask, and began cutting leaves from base upward, setting each aside in careful order.

**"Hey, hey, hey,** what is going on here?" Danny Minot entered the lab, waving his hands. Red-faced and rotund, he was dressed in a tweed sport coat with elbow patches, a rep tie, and baggy slacks, and looked for all the world like an establishment English professor. Which was not far wrong. Minot was getting a doctorate in science studies, a mélange of psychology and sociology, with liberal doses of French postmodernism thrown in. He had degrees in biochemistry and comparative literature, but the comparative literature had won out; he quoted Bruno Latour, Jacques Derrida, Michel Foucault, and others who believed that there was no objective truth, only the truth that's established by power. Minot was here in the lab to complete a thesis on "scientific linguistic codes and paradigm transformation." In practice it meant he made a pest of himself, bothering people, recording conversations with the other grad students as they did their work.

They all despised him. There were frequent discussions about why Ray Hough had let him in the lab in the first place. Finally somebody asked Ray about it, and he said, "He's my wife's cousin. And nobody else would take him."

"Come on, people," Minot said, "nobody works this late in this lab, and here you all are." Waving his hands again.

Jenny snorted disdainfully. "Hand-waver."

"I heard that," Minot said. "Meaning what?"

Jenny turned her back on him.

"Meaning what? Don't turn your back on me."

Peter went over to Danny. "A hand-waver," he said, "is somebody who hasn't worked out his ideas and can't defend them. So when he presents at a colloquium, and he comes to the parts he hasn't worked out, he starts waving his hands and talking fast. Like the way someone waves their hands and says, 'Et cetera, et cetera.' In science, hand-waving means you don't have the goods."

"Not what I am doing here," Minot said, waving his hand. "The semiotics are completely garbled."

"Uh-huh."

"But as Derrida said, techno-translation is so difficult. I am attempting to indicate all of you in a gestural mode of inclusiveness. What's going on?"

"Don't tell him," Rick said, "or he'll want to come."

"Of course I want to come," Minot said. "I am the chronicler of life in this lab. I must come. Where are you going?"

Peter briefly told him the entire story.

"Oh yes, I am definitely coming. The intersection of science and commerce? The corruption of golden youth? Oh definitely—I'll be there."


**Peter was getting** a cup of coffee from the machine in the corner of the lab when Erika walked over. "What are you doing later?"

"I don't know, why?"

"I thought maybe I could stop by tonight."

She was staring right at him. Something about the directness of her manner put him off. "I don't know, Erika," he said, "I might be working here late." Thinking: I haven't seen you for three weeks, since the last time.

"I'm almost finished, myself," she said. "And it's only nine o'clock."

"I don't know. We'll see."

"It doesn't appeal to you, my offer?" She was still staring at him, scanning his face.

"I thought you were seeing Amar."

"I like Amar, very much. He is very intelligent. I like you too. I always have."

"Maybe we'll talk later," he said, pouring milk in his coffee, and moving away so quickly that it spilled a little.

"I hope so," she said.

**"Trouble with your** coffee?" Rick Hutter said, glancing up at Peter and grinning. Under a halogen lamp, Rick was holding a rat upside down, measuring its swollen rear paw with a small caliper.

"No," Peter said, "I was just, uh, surprised at how hot it was."

"Uh-huh. I'd say, surprisingly hot."

"Is that a carageenen prep?" Peter said, changing the subject. Carageenen was the usual method to produce edema in the paw of a lab animal. It was a standardized animal model for edema, employed in labs around the world to study inflammation.

"Correct," Rick said. "I injected carageenen, making the paw swollen. Then I wrapped the foot in an extract from the bark of Himatanthus sucuuba, a medium-size rain-forest tree, and now we are—hopefully—demonstrating its anti-inflammatory properties. I already demonstrated it for the tree's latex. Himatanthus is an extremely versatile tree, it heals wounds and cures ulcers. The shamans in Costa Rica say this tree also has antibiotic, anti-fever, anti-cancer, and anti-parasite qualities, but I haven't tested those claims yet. Certainly the bark extract has reduced this rat's swelling remarkably fast."

"You determined what chemicals are responsible for the anti-inflammatory response?"

"Researchers in Brazil attribute it to alpha-amyrin cinnamate and other cinnamate compounds, but I haven't verified that yet." Rick finished measuring the rat, set it down in the cage, and typed in a measurement and time in his laptop. "Tell you one thing, though: extracts from the tree appear to be completely nontoxic. One day you might even be able to give this to pregnant women. Huh, look at that." He pointed to the rat as it moved around the cage. "It's not limping at all anymore."

Peter slapped him on the back. "Better be careful," he said, "or you'll have some pharmaceutical company beating you to your results."

"Hey, I'm not worried. If those guys were really in the business of developing drugs, they'd already be working on this tree," Rick said. "But why should they take the risk? Let the American taxpayer fund the research, let some graduate student spend months to make the discovery, and then they swoop in and buy it up from the university. And then they sell our discovery back to us, at full price. Sweet deal, huh?" He was starting to wind up for one of his tirades. "I tell you, these Goddamned pharma—"

"Rick," Peter said, "I've got to go."

"Oh sure, yeah. Nobody wants to hear it, I know."

"I have to spin down my naja venom."

"No problem." Rick hesitated, glanced over his shoulder at Erika. "Listen, it's none of my business—"

"That's right, it's not—"

"But I hate to see a good guy like you fall into the clutches of somebody who is . . . well . . . Anyway, you met my friend Jorge, who does computer science at MIT? If you want to know what's really going on with Erika, call this number—" he handed Peter a card—"and Jorge will access her phone records, including voice and text messages, and you can find out the truth about her, uh, promiscuous ways."

"Is that legal?"

"No. But it's damn useful."

"Thanks anyway," Peter said, "but—"

"No, no, keep it," Rick insisted.

"I won't use it."

"You never know," Rick said. "Phone records don't lie."

"Okay." It was easier to keep the card than argue. He slipped it in his pocket.

"By the way," Rick said, "about your brother . . ."

"What about him?"

"You think he's on the level?"

"About his company?"

"Yeah, Nanigen."

"I think so," Peter said. "But to be honest I don't know a lot about it."

"He didn't tell you?"

"He's been pretty secretive about the whole thing."

"But you think it's innovative?"

**Yes, I think** it's innovative, Peter thought, peering through the scanning microscope. He was looking again at the white pebble, or micro-bot, or whatever the thing was. Trying to account for his brother's explanation that it wasn't a cockpit but just a slot for a micro-power-pack, or a control unit. It didn't look like a slot for anything. It looked like a seat facing a tiny, highly detailed control panel.

He was still puzzling over this when he became aware that the lab around him had become absolutely silent. He looked up, and saw that the microscope was also displaying on a large flat-panel screen mounted on the wall. Everybody in the lab was staring at it.

"What the hell is that?" Rick said.

"I don't know." Peter flicked off the monitor. "And we're not going to find out, unless we go to Hawaii."

# Chapter 3

## MAPLE AVENUE, CAMBRIDGE
## 27 OCTOBER, 6:00 A.M.

One by one, all seven of the graduate students decided to take Vin Drake up on his offer. They collected data, they wrote out descriptions of their research, and they sent letters and information to Alyson Bender at Nanigen. One by one, they were informed that Nanigen would fly them to Hawaii; and for simplicity they would travel as a group. As October ran to its end, their days were devoted to preparations for departure. All seven had a lot to do—finishing experiments, getting their research projects in shape to leave them for a while, and, of course, packing. They planned to leave early on a Sunday morning out of Boston's Logan Airport, with a connection through Dallas, arriving in Honolulu that same afternoon. They would, by general agreement, stay four days, returning toward the end of the week.

Early on a gray, cold Saturday morning, the day before the flight, Peter Jansen was in his apartment working at his computer. Erika Moll was there, too, cooking bacon and eggs and singing

"Take a Chance on Me." Peter abruptly realized that he had forgotten to turn on his phone that morning—he'd turned it off the night before, when Erika had unexpectedly shown up. He turned on the phone and placed it on his desk. A minute later, the phone buzzed. It was a text message from his brother, Eric.

> **dont come**

He stared at the message. Was this a joke? Had something happened? He typed back:

> **why not?**

He watched the screen, but there was no answer. After a few minutes, he dialed Eric's number in Hawaii, but got his voice mail. "Eric, it's Peter. What's up? Call me."

From the kitchen, Erika said, "Who are you talking to?"

"Nobody. Just trying to get my brother."

He scrolled to the message from his brother. It had come in at 9:49 p.m. So it had arrived last night! Which had been afternoon in Hawaii.

Peter dialed his brother again, but again got voice mail. He hung up.

"Breakfast is almost ready," Erika said.

He brought the phone to the table, set it beside his plate. Erika wrinkled her nose; she didn't like phones at meals. She was scooping eggs onto his plate, saying, "I followed my grandmother's recipe, with milk and flour—"

The phone rang.

He grabbed it. "Hello?"

"Peter?" A woman's voice. "Peter Jansen?"

"Yes, speaking."

"It's Alyson Bender," she said. "From Nanigen." He had an image of the blond woman with her arm around Eric's waist. "Listen," she said, "how soon can you get over here to Hawaii?"

"We're scheduled to fly tomorrow," he said.

"Can you come today?"

"I don't know, I—"

"It's important."

"Well, I can check the flights—"

"Actually, I took the liberty of booking you on one that leaves in two hours. Can you make it?"

"Yes, I think—what's this about?"

"I'm afraid I have some disturbing news, Peter." She paused. "It's about your brother."

"What about him?"

"He's missing."

"Missing?" He felt dazed; he didn't understand. "What do you mean, missing?"

"Since yesterday," Alyson said. "There was a boating accident. I don't know if he told you that he bought a boat, a Boston Whaler? Anyway, he did, and he was out yesterday, on the north side of the island, and he had mechanical difficulties . . . there was big surf, crashing against the cliffs. The engines lost power, the boat drifted in . . ."

Peter felt light-headed. He pushed the plate of eggs away. Erika was watching him, her face pale. "How do you know this?" he said.

"There were people on the cliffs, they saw the whole thing."

"And what happened to Eric?"

"He tried to start the engines. He couldn't. The surf was high, the boat was going to be smashed on the cliffs. He dived into the ocean and swam . . . for shore. But the currents . . . he never made it to shore . . ." She took a breath. "I'm very sorry, Peter."

"Eric's a good swimmer," Peter said. "Strong swimmer."

"I know. And that's why we continue to hope he'll return," she said. "But, uh, the police have told us that, well . . . The police would like to talk to you, and go over everything with you, as soon as you get here."

"I'm leaving now," he said, and hung up. Erika had gone to the bedroom and brought his bag, already packed for the following day.

"We'd better go," she said, "if you're going to make that flight." She put her arm around his shoulder, and they headed downstairs to the car.

# Chapter 4

## MAKAPU'U POINT, OAHU
## 27 OCTOBER, 4:00 P.M.

I
t was said to be a tourist spot: Makapu'u Point, high cliffs on the
northeastern tip of Oahu, with a spectacular view of the ocean
in all directions. But once there, Peter was not prepared for the
barren desolation of the place. A harsh wind whipped the scrubby
green brush at his feet, and tugged at his clothes, forcing him to
lean forward as he walked. He had to speak loudly: "Is it always like
this?"

The policeman beside him, Dan Watanabe, said, "No, sometimes it's very pleasant. But the trades kicked up last night." Watanabe wore Ray-Bans. He pointed to a lighthouse off to the right.
"That's Makapu'u Lighthouse," he said. "Automated years ago. Nobody lives there anymore."

Directly ahead, they looked down the black lava cliffs at surging
ocean two hundred feet below. The surf boomed, smashing against
the rocks. Peter said, "Is this where it happened?"

"Yes," Watanabe said. "The boat ran aground over there—" he

pointed to the left—"but the Coast Guard got it off the rocks this morning, before it broke up in the surf."

"So his boat was somewhere offshore when it got into trouble?" Peter looked out at the ocean, which was rough, high swells and whitecaps.

"Yes. He was drifting in the water for a while, witnesses said."

"Trying to start the engine . . ."

"Yes. And drifting toward the surf."

"And what was the mechanical difficulty?" Peter said. "I understand it was a new boat."

"Yes. Couple of weeks old."

"My brother was experienced with boats," Peter said. "My family always had a boat on Long Island Sound, we were out there every summer."

"These waters are different," Watanabe said. "You're looking at deep ocean." He pointed. "Nearest land out there is three thousand miles away, the mainland. But that's not the point. It's pretty clear what got your brother in trouble was ethanol."

"Ethanol?" Peter said.

"State of Hawaii puts ten percent ethanol into all the gas that's sold here, but the ethanol screws up small engines. There's cut-rate gas dealers who put way too much ethanol in their gas—up to thirty percent. It clogs fuel lines, and anything rubber or neoprene can turn to gunk. It's caused a hell of a mess on boats. People have to put in new steel fuel tanks and lines. Anyway, we think that's what happened to your brother. The carburetors were clogged, the fuel pump might have failed. Whatever it was exactly, he couldn't restart the engines in time."

Peter was staring down at the water below. Greenish nearest the shore; then, farther out, deep blue, with whitecaps blown by wind.

"How are the currents here?" he said.

"Depends," Watanabe said. "A good swimmer can manage on most days. The problem is finding a place to get out of the water without getting cut up on lava. Ordinarily you'd swim west, try to make it to Makapu'u Beach over there." He pointed to a sandy strip half a mile away.

"My brother was a strong swimmer," Peter said.

"So I heard, but the witnesses said they couldn't see him after he dived in the water. There was big surf that day, and he disappeared into the foam. They lost sight of him right away."

"How many people saw him?"

"Two. There was a couple picnicking, right by the edge of the cliff. There were some hikers, too, and some other people, but we haven't been able to locate them. What do you say we get out of this wind?" He started back up the hill; Peter followed. "I think that finishes our work here," Watanabe said. "Unless of course you want to see the video."

"What video?"

"The picnicking couple shot some video, once they realized the boat was in trouble. They recorded about fifteen minutes of tape, including the jump from the boat. I didn't know if you wanted to see that or not."

"I want to see it," Peter said.


**They were on** the second floor of the police station, looking at a tiny screen on a video camera. It was noisy in the station, and busy, and Peter had difficulty focusing on the screen. The first images showed a man of about thirty, sitting on the green grassy hillside, eating a sandwich; then a woman of roughly the same age, drinking a Coke and laughing, waving the camera away.

"That's the couple," Watanabe said. "Grace and Bobby Choy. First part is them horsing around. Goes about six minutes." He pushed the fast-forward button, then paused the video and said, "It's time-stamped." The stamp in the screen showed the time was 3:50:12 p.m. "Now here, you see Bobby pointing offshore—he's spotted the boat in trouble."

The camera panned to show the ocean. The white hull of the Boston Whaler bobbing against the blue horizon. The boat was still a hundred yards offshore, too distant for him to make out his brother. The camera panned back to Bobby Choy, who now was looking through binoculars.

When Peter next saw the boat, it was much closer to the shore. Now he could make out the figure of his brother, bent over, intermittently appearing, then disappearing again. "I think he was trying to clear the clogged lines," Watanabe said. "That's what it looks like."

"Yes," Peter said.

The camera now showed Grace Choy, shaking her head, trying to place a cell phone call.

Then it panned back to the boat, closer now to the white surf.

Then back to Grace Choy, shaking her head as she talked on the phone. "You don't have good cellular reception up there," Watanabe said. "She called 911 but couldn't get through for a while. The call kept breaking up. If she'd gotten 911, they would've called the Coast Guard right away."

The camera work was jerky, but Peter saw something that— "Hold it!"

"What?"

"Pause it, pause it," Peter said quickly. As the image froze, he pointed to the screen. "Who's that in the background?"

The screen showed a woman, dressed in white, standing on the hill a few yards above the Choys. The woman stared intently offshore, and seemed to be pointing at the boat.

"That's one of the other witnesses," Watanabe said. "There were three joggers as well. We haven't been able to identify any of them yet. But I doubt they would give us more information than we already have."

Peter said, "Does that woman have something in her hand?"

"I think she's just pointing at the boat."

"I don't know," Peter said, "I think she has something in her hand."

Watanabe said, "I'll get the AV evidence guys to look at it. You might be right."

"What does this woman do next?" Peter said.

The tape started again.

"She leaves right away," Watanabe said. "Goes up the hill and out of sight. You see: there she goes now. She's hurrying, looks like maybe she's going for help, but nobody ever saw her again. And there were no more calls logged to 911."

**Moments later on** the tape, Eric jumped from the Boston Whaler into the roiling surf. It was difficult to be sure, but he appeared to be about thirty yards offshore at the time. He didn't dive, but rather jumped feet-first, vanishing into white foam.

Peter watched closely to see if he emerged, but he did not seem to. And Eric had done something jarring, even disturbing: he had not put on a life jacket before he jumped. Eric knew enough to put on a life jacket in an emergency. "My brother wasn't wearing a life jacket," Peter remarked.

"I noticed," Watanabe commented. "Maybe he forgot to bring it on the boat. It happens—you know—"

"Did he send out a mayday call on the radio?" Peter asked the police officer. Eric's boat had certainly been equipped with a VHF marine radio. Eric, as an experienced boater, would have sent out a distress call on channel 16, the channel always monitored by the Coast Guard.

"Coast Guard didn't hear anything."

That was very strange. No life jacket, no distress call. Had Eric's radio broken down? Peter continued to stare at the heave and pulse of the blank ocean in the video . . . an ocean that showed no trace of his brother. After another minute, he said, "Turn it off."

Watanabe stopped the camera. "He was lost in the boneyard."

"The what?"

"The boneyard. It's that churning wash after the waves break. Where all the foam slick is boiling. He may have hit rocks in the boneyard. There are some outcrops that are only five, six feet below the surface. We just don't know." He paused. "Do you want to see any of it again?"

"No," Peter said. "I've seen enough."

Watanabe flipped the screen shut, turned the camera off. "That woman on the hill," he said casually. "Do you know who she is?"

"Me? No. She could be anybody."

"I wondered . . . You had such a strong reaction."

"No, sorry. I was just surprised by—it was like she just suddenly appeared, that's all. No idea who she is."

Watanabe was very still. "You'd tell me, if you knew," he said.

"Sure, of course. Yes."

"Well, thanks for your time." Watanabe gave him his card. "I'll get one of the detectives to drop you at your hotel."

Peter said little on the drive back. He wasn't inclined to talk, and the detective didn't press him. It was true the images of his brother vanishing in the surf were disturbing. But not as disturbing as the woman on the hill, the woman in white pointing at the boat with some object in her hand. Because that woman was Alyson Bender, the CFO of Nanigen, and her presence at the scene changed everything.

# Chapter 5

In his hotel room, Peter Jansen lay down on top of the bed, experiencing a sense of unreality. He didn't know what to do next. Why hadn't he told Watanabe who Alyson Bender was? He felt exhausted, but couldn't rest. The video kept running through his mind. He saw Alyson holding something in her hand in the video, while watching Eric's death as if it meant nothing to her. And then she had hurried away. Why?

He began thinking about something Rick Hutter had said to him about Erika Moll. How to check up on somebody. He took out his wallet and began going through it, pulling out cards, money. There it was—the card Rick had given him, back in the lab, more than a week ago. It had Rick Hutter's handwriting on it. Just the word JORGE and a number.

The guy who could access telephone records. The MIT phone hacker.

It was a Massachusetts area code. He called the number. It rang for a while. And rang some more. There was no voice mail, so

Peter just let it ring. Finally it was answered, sort of, with a grunt: "Yuh?"

Jansen identified himself and explained what he wanted. "I'm a friend of Rick Hutter. Can you get me a list of recent calls to and from a certain phone number?"

"Yuh? Why?"

"Rick told me you could do it. I'll pay whatever you ask."

"Money doesn't work. I only do something if it's . . . intriguing." A faint Latino accent, a soft voice.

Peter explained the situation. "A woman may be involved in my brother's . . . my brother's . . . death." Death. It was the first time he'd used the word in connection with Eric.

There was quite a long pause.

"Listen—I have the phone number that the woman used to call me. Can you find out who else she talked to on that phone? I'm assuming it's her phone." He read out Alyson's number.

There was an emptiness on the line, a silence that extended. Peter held his breath. Finally Jorge said, "Give me—" pause—"a couple of hours."

Peter lay back on the bed, his heart pounding. He could hear traffic going past on Kalakaua Avenue, for his room faced *mauka*— inland, across the city and toward the mountains. The day lengthened; the sun began to go down; the room filled with shadows. Maybe Eric had reached shore; maybe he was suffering from amnesia and would turn up in some hospital; maybe there had been some terrible mistake . . . Peter had to hope, had to believe, that maybe Eric would turn up, somehow, somewhere—there was always a faint chance. Or had Eric been . . . murdered? Finally he couldn't stand being in his room any longer, and he went outside.


**He sat on** the beach in front of his hotel, watching the red streaks of the setting sun darken to black over the ocean. Why hadn't he told the police officer that he recognized her in the video? It had been a kind of instinct to say nothing. But why? What had made him do it? When he and Eric had been younger, they had looked out for each other. Eric had covered for him. He had covered for Eric . . .

"There you are!"

He turned to see Alyson Bender approaching in the evening light. She wore a blue Hawaiian print dress and sandals, looking quite different than she had in Cambridge, when she'd worn a business suit and pearls. Here, she looked like an innocent young girl.

"Why didn't you call me? I thought you were going to call me right after you were done with the police. How did it go?"

"It went okay," Peter said. "They took me to that point—Makapu'u Point—and showed me where it happened."

"Uh-huh. And is there any news? I mean, about Eric?"

"They still haven't found him. Or the body."

"And the boat?"

"What about it?"

"Did the police check the boat?"

"Oh, I don't know." He shrugged. "They didn't say."

She sat on the sand beside him, put her hand on his shoulder. Her hand was warm. "I'm so sorry you had to go through that, Peter, it must have been awful for you."

"It was difficult. The police had a videotape."

"Videotape? Really? Did you see it?"

"Yes."

"And? Was it helpful?"

Had she really not seen the video camera in the hands of the couple seated just below her on the hillside? Was it possible she was only looking at the boat? Her eyes scanned his face in the twilight. He said, "I saw Eric jump . . . but he never came up."

"How awful," she said softly.

Her hand moved to squeeze his shoulder, rub it. He wanted to tell her to stop, but he didn't trust himself to speak. The whole thing was incredibly creepy.

"And what do the police think?" she said.

"About what?"

"About what happened? I mean, on the boat."

"They think it was a clogged—"

His cell phone rang. He fished it out of his shirt pocket, flipped it open. "Hello."

"This is Jorge."

"One moment." He stood, said to Alyson, "Excuse me a moment, I have to take this." He walked some distance down the beach. Stars were starting to come out in the darkening sky above. "Go ahead, Jorge."

"I have the information you want for the phone number you gave me. The number is registered to the Nanigen MicroTechnologies Corporation of Honolulu. Attached to the number is the employee name Alyson F. Bender."

He looked back along the beach; Alyson was a dark shape on the sand. "Go on," he said.

"At three forty-seven p.m. yesterday afternoon local time, she called the number 646-673-2682 three times in a row."

"Whose number is that?"

"It's an unassigned number, for one of those junk phones you can buy and use until the prepayment runs out."

"She called three times?"

"Yes, but very briefly—three seconds, then two seconds, then three seconds."

"Okay . . . Meaning she didn't think she was getting through?"

"No, she clearly got through, no answering message, it went right to the beep. She knew she connected. Two possibilities. Either she kept calling because she was expecting the person to pick up, or she was triggering a device of some kind."

"A device . . . ?"

"Yup. You wire a cell phone to set off some device when there's an incoming call."

"Okay, so three calls in a row. What then?"

"At three fifty-five she called another number at Nanigen, assigned employee name Vincent A. Drake. You want to hear that call?"

"Sure."

**Ringing, then the** click of a pick-up.

VIN: Yes?

ALYSON: (breathless) It's me.

VIN: Yes?

ALYSON: Listen, I'm worried, I don't know if it worked or not. There should have been smoke or something—

VIN: Excuse me.

ALYSON: But I'm worried—

VIN: Let me stop you there.

ALYSON: You don't understand—

VIN: Yes, I do understand. Now listen. You are on the phone. I need you to speak . . . more exactly.

ALYSON: Oh.

VIN: You understand what I am saying?

ALYSON: (pause) Yes.

VIN: Okay. Now. Where is the object?

ALYSON: (pause) Not available. Vanished.

VIN: Okay. Then I don't see a problem.

ALYSON: I am still worried.

VIN: But the object did not reappear?

ALYSON: No.

VIN: Then I suggest there is no problem. We can discuss
this further in person but not now. Are you coming
back now?

ALYSON: Yes.

VIN: All right. See you soon.


Click.


**Jorge said, "There are** two other calls. Want to hear them?"

"Maybe later."

"Okay. I've e-mailed them to you as .wav files. You should be able to listen to them on your computer."

"Thanks." Peter looked back at Alyson, and shivered. "Can I take this to the police?"

"No way in hell," Jorge said. "You need a court order to access this stuff. You take it to them, you ruin any chance of prosecution. Illegal search and seizure. Also—you'll, uh, put me in a jam."

"Then what should I do?"

"Hm—yuh," Jorge grunted. "I don't know—get them to confess."

"How?"

"Sorry, can't help you there," Jorge said. "But if you need more phone records, call any time," and he hung up.


**Peter walked back** to Alyson, feeling a cold sweat on his body. It was getting dark now, her expression impossible to read. She sat very still on the sand. He heard her say, "Is everything all right?"

"Yes, fine."

In fact, Peter felt as if he was drowning, overwhelmed by on-rushing events. All his life he had been a student, and until now, he felt his life experiences had given him a clear—even cynical—sense of his fellow human beings and what they were capable of. Over the years, he'd had to deal with cheating students, students dispensing sexual favors in exchange for grades, students falsifying their results, and with professors who appropriated student work. In one bizarre instance, there'd been a thesis advisor on heroin. He felt, at the age of twenty-three, like a man who had seen it all.

Not anymore. The idea of murder, that someone would, with calculation, try to kill his brother, left him shaken and sweating and cold. He didn't trust himself to speak to this woman, who was supposed to be his brother's girlfriend but who had evidently plotted against him. No tears from this girlfriend—she didn't seem upset at all.

She said, "You're awfully quiet, Peter."

"It's been a long day."

"Buy you a drink?"

"No, thanks."

"Mai tais are famous here."

"I think I better call it a night."

"Have you had dinner?"

"Not hungry."

She got up from the sand, brushed herself off. "I know you must be upset. I am, too."

"Yes."

"Why so cold toward me? I'm just trying to—"

"I'm sorry," he said quickly. He didn't want her to suspect anything. That would be unwise, even dangerous. "It's all been such a shock."

She put her hand up, touched his cheek. "Call me if I can do anything."

"Thanks. Okay."

They walked back inside the hotel. "All your friends are arriving tomorrow," she said. "They're upset about what happened to Eric. But the tour of the facilities is all arranged. Do you want to go on it?"

"Absolutely," he said, "I can't just sit around . . . feeling like this. Waiting."

"The tour will start at the Waipaka Arboretum, in Manoa Valley, in the mountains near here," she said. "That's where we get a lot of our rain-forest materials for research. Four o'clock tomorrow. Should I pick you up?"

"That's not necessary," Peter said. "I'll take a cab." He somehow managed to give her a kiss on the cheek. "Thanks for coming by, Alyson. It means a lot."

"I just want to help." She looked at him doubtfully.

"And you are helping," he said. "Believe me. You are."


**Unable to sleep,** unable to eat, tormented by Jorge's information, Peter Jansen stood at the balcony of his room. The view looked away from the ocean, across the city, and up into a jumble of mountain peaks, wild and black, without lights, outlined only by stars in the night sky. Alyson Bender had made three brief calls to a phone number. The time of these calls, 3:47 p.m., stuck in his mind. Late afternoon. He remembered that the video shot by the couple had been time-stamped. He tried to recall the time stamp. He had a head for numbers; he used numbers constantly in his data sets. The time stamp rose in his mind's eye: 3:50 something. Just three minutes after Alyson made those calls, Eric's boat was stalled in the video.

Wait. What about that text message from Eric? When did that come in? He went indoors and got his phone, and scrolled through the call log. The text—dont come—had arrived at 9:49 p.m. Eastern time. There was a six-hour time difference between the East Coast and Hawaii. It meant . . . it meant that Eric had sent the text at 3:49 p.m. He had sent it just two minutes after Alyson Bender had made three calls to a disposable cell phone. It was only a two-word text, "dont come." That was because Eric had been in a life-or-death crisis and had not had any time to send a longer text. Eric had sent the text from his boat while he was struggling to get the engine started, moments before he had jumped overboard. Peter's hands were clammy, and his phone almost slipped from his fingers. He stared at the words: *dont come.* He was reading his brother's last words.

# Chapter 6

Akamai Boat Services was right on Ala Moana Boulevard, next to the Ala Wai Boat Basin, at the end of Waikiki Beach. The taxi dropped Peter off at eight in the morning, but the boat yard was already busy at work. It wasn't a large yard, perhaps ten or twelve hulls out of the water, and it took him no time to locate the Boston Whaler.

He was here because of Alyson's question the night before: Did the police check the boat?

Why would she ask that? Supposedly she was concerned about her boyfriend, yet she seemed to care more about the boat. He jumped off the boat.

Peter walked around the boat now, looking closely.

Considering the pounding it had taken in the surf, the Boston Whaler seemed surprisingly intact. True, the white fiberglass hull was scratched all over, as if it had been clawed by giant hands; a jagged rip ran several feet along the starboard hull, and a chunk had

been whacked out of the bow. Whalers were famous for their ability
to float even if the hull was broken into pieces. His brother had had
years of experience with Whalers. Eric would have known the boat
hadn't been in danger of sinking. Certainly, the damage to the boat
did not justify Eric's abandoning it. Plainly, his brother shouldn't
have jumped. He would have been safer staying on board.

So why did he jump? Panic? Confusion? Something else?

There was a wooden ladder on the far side of the boat, and he
climbed up onto the stern. All hatches and the door to the cuddy
cabin were sealed with yellow CRIME SCENE tape. He wanted to look
at the outboard engines, but they were sealed as well.

"Can I help you?" A man below, shouting up. Heavyset, griz-
zled, streaks of grease on his work clothes. Dirty baseball cap
shaded his eyes.

"Oh hi," Peter said. "My name is Peter Jansen. This is my brother's boat."

"Uh-huh. What're you doing here?"

"Well, I wanted to see—"

"You illiterate?" the man said.

"No, I'm—"

"Well it seems like you must be, because that sign over there
says plain as day, all visitors register at the main office. Are you a
visitor?"

"I guess."

"Why didn't you register?"

"I just thought I could—"

"Wrong. You can't. Now what the hell you doing up there?"

"This is my brother's—"

"I heard you the first time. Your brother's boat. You see all that
yellow tape? I know you do, and I also know you can read it, 'cause
you told me you're not illiterate. Isn't that right?"

"Yes."

"So that's a crime scene, and you got no business up there. Now you get the hell down right away, and go to the office and register, and show us some identification. You have identification?"

"Yes."

"Okay then. Get down off of there, and stop wasting my time." The man stalked off.

Peter climbed down the ladder on the far side of the boat. As he came near the ground, he heard a gruff male voice say, "Can I help you, Miss?" And a woman's voice answered, "Yes, I'm looking for a Boston Whaler the Coast Guard brought in."

It was Alyson's voice.

He paused, hidden from view by the hull of the boat.

"Goddamn," the man said. "What is it about that fricking boat? Gets more visitors than a rich uncle on his deathbed."

"How's that?" she said.

"Well, yesterday some guy shows up, claiming it was his boat, 'cept he had no identification, so I told him to get lost. The things people try! Then this morning we have some young guy, claiming it was his brother's boat, I had to get him out of the cockpit, and now we got you. What is it about that boat?"

"I really couldn't say," Alyson said. "Myself, I just left something on the boat, and I wanted to get it back."

"No chance of that. Not unless you got a letter of authorization from the police. Do you?"

"Well, no . . ."

"Sorry. That's a crime scene, like I told the young guy."

"Where is this guy?" she asked.

"He was coming down the ladder. Probably still on the other side of the boat. He'll be along. Want to come inside the office?"

"Why would I do that?"

"We can call the police, see if they'll give you a waiver to get your stuff off the boat."

"That seems like a lot of trouble. It's just my, well, it's my watch. I took it off my wrist . . ."

"No trouble."

"I guess I could buy another one. It did cost a bit—"

"Uh-huh."

"I thought it would be easy."

"Well, suit yourself. But you still better sign in."

"I don't see why."

"You're supposed to."

"I don't think so," she said. "I don't want to get mixed up in any police thing."

Peter waited a few minutes, then heard the man say, "You can come out, son."

He came out from behind the hull. There was no sign of Alyson in the yard. The heavyset man looked at him quizzically, head cocked to one side. "Didn't want to run into her?"

"We don't get along," Peter said.

"I figured."

"You want me to sign in?"

The man nodded slowly. "Yes, please."

So Peter went into the office and signed in. He couldn't see what difference it made. Alyson Bender already knew he had gone to the boat, and therefore she already knew he suspected something. From this point on, he would have to move fast.

By the end of the day, he thought, he had to be finished.


**He went back** to his hotel room, where he found an e-mail from Jorge on his laptop, with no text. Instead there were three .wav files, sent as attachments. One was a recording of Alyson Bender's call to Vin Drake. And there were two new files. He listened to them. They were recordings of two phone calls Alyson had made from her cell phone in the hours after Eric had disappeared. Both calls seemed fairly routine. In the first call, Alyson had phoned somebody, perhaps in a Nanigen purchasing department, and asked for a new budget breakdown. In the second call, she had spoken briefly with another person, a man, perhaps an accountant, on the subject of expenses.

ALYSON: Omicron has lost two more, uh, prototypes.
OTHER PERSON: What happened?
ALYSON: They didn't tell me. Vin Drake wants you to
    account for this as an ordinary research expense, not
    a capital write-down.
OTHER PERSON: The loss of two Hellstorms? But that's
    a big cost—the Davros people—
ALYSON: Just call it research, okay?
OTHER PERSON: Of course.

Peter saved the files after listening to them, but they didn't make sense or reveal anything he could use. He also saved the telephone conversation between Alyson and Vin, however, which would be very useful. He downloaded it onto a flash memory stick and slipped the stick into his pocket, and then burned a CD of the same conversation. Then he took the CD to the hotel business center and had them print a professional label that said "NANIGEN DATA 5.0 10/28." When he was finished, he checked his watch. It was shortly after eleven in the morning.

He went down to the terrace to have a late breakfast and sit in the sun. Over coffee and eggs, he realized he was making a lot of assumptions. The most important assumption was that Nanigen would have a conference room equipped with the usual electronic equipment. That seemed a safe enough bet. All high-tech companies had such rooms.

Second, he assumed that the tour would move all the graduate students together en masse, instead of breaking them into smaller groups or taking them around individually. But he suspected that Vin Drake would give the tour himself, and Vin liked an audience—the bigger the better. Also, if everybody stayed together, it would be easier for Nanigen to control exactly how much information they were given.

For Peter, it was important that the students be kept together, because he felt he needed as many witnesses as possible for what he was planning to do. Or should he try to stage it in front of just one or two witnesses? No . . . his mind raced . . . no, try to provoke a blowup in front of many people. That might be the best way, he thought, to get Drake's façade to crack, and perhaps reveal what Drake and Alyson had done to his brother. Finally, he had to hope that Drake would lose his cool, or at least that Alyson would, especially if they were primed in a way that made them nervous. And he thought he knew how to do that. If he pulled it off, Drake or Alyson might get very upset in front of the grad students. And that was what he wanted.

# Chapter 7

The taxi drove away from the ocean, and soon was climbing steeply into the hills. Broad acacia trees shaded the road.

"That's the university, on both sides," the driver said. He pointed to featureless gray buildings that looked like condominiums. Peter saw no students.

"Where is everybody?"

"Those are dorms. They're at class now."

They passed a baseball field, a surrounding residential area, small homes, bungalow-style. But as they drove on, the houses thinned and the trees grew larger. Now they were heading toward a green mountain wall, heavily forested, rising two thousand feet into the air in front of them.

"That's Ko'olau Pali," the driver said.

"No houses up there?"

"No, you can't build nothing there, that's straight-up, crumbly volcanic rock, can't climb it or nothing. You come way back here like we do now, you leave the city, you in wilderness now. Too much rain *mauka* side, near the mountain. Nobody live back here."

"What about the arboretum?"

"Half mile up this road," the driver said. The road was now a single lane, dark beneath a heavy covering of towering, dense trees. "Nobody come here, neither. Folks go to Foster or the other pretty arboretums. You sure you want come here?"

"Yes," Peter said.

The road narrowed and climbed, zigzagging along a steep, jungle-clad mountainside.

A car came up behind them on the twisting road, and honked, and roared past them, people in the car waving and yelling. He blinked: the grad students from the lab were crammed into the car, a midnight-blue Bentley convertible sedan. The taxi driver muttered something about crazy lobsters.

"Lobsters?" Peter asked.

"Tourists. Way they burn."

Soon the road arrived at a security gate, steel, massive, new. It stood open directly in front of a tunnel. A sign warned unauthorized persons to keep out.

The driver slowed the taxi, brought it to a stop before the gate and tunnel. "They've been doing some changes up here. Why you want to go in this place?" he said.

"It's business," Peter said. Even so, looking at the tunnel, he got an uneasy feeling. With the steel gate in front of it, it seemed like a tunnel of no return. Peter wondered if the gate was to keep people out—or was it to lock people in?

The driver sighed, and took off his sunglasses, and drove into the tunnel. It was a narrow, single-lane passage cored through a shoulder blade of the mountain. The road emerged into a pocket valley. The valley was deeply forested and walled in by the slopes and cliffs of the Koʻolau Pali. Waterfalls trailed from misty jungle mountains. The road descended, and they came into a clearing, dominated by a large, glass-roofed shed. In front of the shed were a few parking spaces in a muddy area. Vin Drake and Alyson Bender were already there, standing next to a red BMW sports car. They both wore boots and hiking clothes. The students were piling out of the Bentley. They became less boisterous when Peter stepped from the taxi.

"Sorry, Peter . . ."

"Sorry about your brother . . ."

"Yes, sorry . . ."

"Any news?" Erika kissed his cheek, took his arm. "I'm so sorry."

"The police are still investigating," Peter said.

Vin Drake shook his hand with a firm grip. "I don't have to tell you this is a great, great tragedy. If it proves true, and I hope to God it does not, it's a dreadful loss to all of us personally. To say nothing of a terrible setback to our company, which Eric was such a part of. I am so sorry, Peter."

"Thank you," Peter said.

"It's good the police are investigating."

"Yes," Peter said.

"They haven't given up, lost hope . . ."

"Quite the contrary," Peter said. "It seems they're taking a new interest in Eric's boat. Something about a missing cell phone? One that may have broken up inside the engine compartment? I didn't really follow what they told me."

"A cell phone in the engine compartment?" Vin frowned. "I wonder what that could—"

"As I said, I didn't really follow," Peter said. "I don't know why they would think there was a phone there. Perhaps my brother dropped his . . . I don't know. But they're also going to check phone records."

"Phone records. Ah yes. Good, good. No stone unturned."

Had Vin turned paler? Peter couldn't be sure.

Alyson licked her lips nervously. "Were you able to sleep, Peter?"

"Yes, thanks. I took a pill."

"Oh good."

"Well." Vin Drake rubbed his hands, turned to the others. "At any rate, welcome to the Manoa Valley. What do you say we get to the business at hand? Gather round, people, and I will give you your first insight into how Nanigen works."

**Drake led them** from the parking lot toward the forest. They passed a low shed housing earth-moving machinery, although, as Drake said, "You've probably never seen machines like this before. Notice how small they are." To Peter, the machines looked like tiny golf carts fitted with a miniature backhoe, with an antenna drooping over the top. "These diggers," Drake went on, "are specially manufactured for us by Siemens Precision AG, a German company. The machine is able to precision-dig soil with millimeter accuracy. Which is then placed in the flats you see in the back of the shed. Those flats are thirty centimeters square—about a foot square— and either three or six centimeters deep."

"And what about the antenna?"

"As you see, the antenna hangs directly over the backhoe. The antenna enables us to locate precisely where to dig and to keep a record in our data files of the exact place where the sample of soil came from. This will all be clear as the day goes on. Meanwhile let's look at the site."

They plunged into the forest itself, the ground suddenly uneven beneath their feet, the trail narrow and twisting among the giant trees overhead. The massive trunks were wrapped with broad-leaf vines; the ground was covered with plants and bushes to knee height, and the overall impression was of a thousand shades of green. The light filtering through the tree canopy overhead was pale yellow-green.

Drake began, "This may look like a natural rain forest . . ."

"It doesn't," Rick Hutter said. "And it's not."

"That's correct. It's not. This area has been cultivated since the 1920s, when it was an experimental station for Oahu farmers, and more recently for ecological studies run by the university. But in recent years nobody has bothered with this tract, and the land reverted to a more natural state. We call this area Fern Gully." He turned and walked down the trail while the students followed him, going slowly and looking at things, occasionally stopping to examine a plant or flower.

"Moving along now," Drake went on, speaking briskly, "you'll notice a profusion of ferns. Prominently around us you see the big tree ferns, Cibotium and Sadleria, and lower down to the ground, the smaller Blechnum, Lycopodium, and of course—" he indicated the mountainside with a swipe of his hand—"up there, the uluhe ferns, which cover the mountain slopes over much of Hawaii."

"You missed that uluhe fern right at your feet," Rick Hutter broke in. "It's called Dicranopteris, also known as false staghorn."

"I believe so," Vin Drake said, barely concealing a flash of irritation. He paused, and bent down on one knee. "The pe'ahi ferns line this path, the larger ones are maku'e ferns, which spiders like to live on. You will notice the large number of spiders here. Some twenty-three species, in all, are represented in this small area alone." He stopped in a clearing, where trees opened into views of the mountainsides around the valley. He pointed up to a peak on a ridge overlooking the valley. "That peak is called Tantalus. It's an extinct volcanic crater that looks down on this valley. We've been conducting research at Tantalus Crater, as well as here in the valley."

Alyson Bender fell into step alongside Peter Jansen. "Did the police contact you today?" she said.

"No," he said. "Why?"

"I wondered how you knew they were searching the boat . . . and the phone records."

"Oh." In truth, he had made that up. "Well. It was on the news."

"Was it? I didn't hear. What channel?"

"I don't remember. Five, I think."

Rick Hutter came over and said, "Really sorry, Peter. Really sorry, man."

Jenny Linn had been walking close behind Vin Drake, and she said to him, "But I don't understand your research program—like what you're actually doing here in this forest."

Drake smiled at her and said, "It's because I haven't explained it yet. In simple terms, we're planning to collect samples from a cross-section of the Hawaiian ecosystem, from Tantalus Crater down into the Manoa Valley, where we're standing."

"Collect what kind of samples?" Rick Hutter said, hands on his hips. He was wearing the usual Rick outfit, jeans and an outdoor shirt, sleeves rolled up and now damp with sweat, looking as if he was on a bushwhack through deep jungle. He had the usual combative look on his face, too, his jaw set, eyes narrowed.

Drake smiled and answered, "Essentially we will collect samples from every species of living thing in this ecosystem."

"What for?" Rick went on. He stared straight at Vin Drake.

Drake stared right back at Rick. A cold look. Then smiled. "A rain forest is the greatest repository of active chemical compounds in nature. We are standing in the middle of a gold mine full of potential new drugs. Drugs that could save uncounted human lives. Drugs worth uncounted billions of dollars. This forest, Mr., uh—"

"Hutter," Rick said.

"This lush forest, Mr. Hutter, contains keys to the health and well-being of every person on this planet. And yet this forest has barely been explored. We have no idea what chemical compounds actually exist here, in the plants, in the animals, in the microscopic life-forms. This forest is terra incognita, absolutely unknown terrain. It's as vast, as full of riches, and as unexplored as the New World was for Christopher Columbus. Our goal, Mr. Hutter, is simple. Our goal is drug discovery. We're searching for new drugs on a vast scale beyond anything imagined. We have begun a total screening of this entire forest for bioactive compounds, from Tantalus to the bottom of this valley. The payoff will be huge."

" 'The payoff,' " Rick echoed. " 'Gold mine.' 'New World.' So it's a gold rush you're talking about, isn't it, Mr. Drake? It's all about money."

"That's much too crude," Drake answered. "First and foremost, medicine is about saving lives. It's about ending suffering and helping every person reach their human potential." He switched his attention to the others, and began walking along the trail, getting himself away from Rick Hutter, who obviously annoyed him.

Rick, now standing with his arms folded, murmured to Karen King, "The guy is a modern Spanish conquistador. He's looting this ecosystem for gold."

Karen gave him a scornful look. "And just what are you doing with your natural extracts, Rick? You're boiling the hell out of tree bark looking for new drugs. Why is that any different?"

"The difference," he said to her, "is the huge sums of money involved. And you know where the money in all this is, right? It's in patents. Nanigen will take out thousands of patents on the compounds they find here—and giant drug companies will exploit the patents, earning billions—"

"You're just jealous 'cause you don't have any patents." Karen turned away from Rick, while Rick glared at her.

He called after her, "I'm not doing science to get rich. Unlike you, apparently . . ." He realized she was ignoring him. Pointedly.

Danny Minot struggled at the tail end of the group. For some reason, Danny had brought his tweed jacket to Hawaii, and he was wearing it now. Sweat poured down Danny's neck and drenched his button-down shirt, and he skidded from place to place on the trail in tassel loafers. He blotted his face with a pocket square and pretended to ignore his misery. "Mr. Drake," he said, "if you happen to be familiar with post-structuralist theory—uh—you might be aware of how—ugh—whoof!—how we can't actually know anything about this forest . . . For you see, we create meaning, Mr. Drake, when really there is no meaning in nature . . ."

Drake seemed unfazed by Danny. "My view of nature, Mr. Minot, is that we don't need to know the meaning of nature in order to make use of it."

"Yes, but . . ." Danny went on.

Meanwhile, Alyson Bender drifted back a few paces, and Peter ended up walking with Rick. Rick nodded toward Vin Drake. "Do you believe this guy? He's like Mr. Biopiracy."

"I've been listening to your remarks, Mr. Hutter," Drake said, twisting his head around suddenly, "and I have to say it's completely false. Biopiracy refers to the taking of indigenous plants without compensating the country of origin. The concept is attractive to the ill-informed do-gooder but fraught with practical difficulty. Take the example of curare, a valuable medicinal drug, used in modern medicine today. Surely someone should be compensated? Yet there are dozens of different recipes for curare, developed by many tribal groups stretching across Central and South America—a vast area. The curares differ in ingredients and cooking time, depending on what is meant to be killed, and on local preferences. How, then, do you compensate native medicine men? Did the shamans of Brazil do more valuable work than the shamans of Panama or Colombia? Does it matter that the trees used in Colombia migrated—or were transplanted—from native Panama? What about the actual formula? Is the addition of strychnos important or not? How about the addition of a rusty nail? Is there any consideration for public domain? We allow a drug company twenty years to exploit a drug, then make it public. Some say Sir Walter Raleigh brought curare back to Europe in 1596; certainly it was well known in the 1700s. Burroughs Wellcome sold curare tablets in the 1880s for medical purposes. So by all odds, curare belongs in the public domain. And finally, modern surgeons no longer use curare from native plants anyway. They use synthetic curare. You see the complexities?"

"This is all corporate evasiveness," Rick said.

"Mr. Hutter, you seem to enjoy being the devil's advocate against my points," Drake said. "I don't mind. It helps me sharpen my arguments. The truth is, using natural compounds for medicine is just the way of the world. The discoveries of every culture are valuable, and all other cultures borrow from one another. Sometimes discoveries are traded for a price, but not always. Should we license the horse stirrup from the Mongols who invented it? Should we pay the Chinese for domesticated silk production? For opium? Should we track down the modern descendants of Neolithic farmers of ten thousand years ago who first domesticated food crops in the fertile crescent, and pay them? How about the medieval Britons who learned to smelt iron?"

"Let's move on," Erika Moll said. "We take your point even if Rick doesn't."

"Okay, the point is that claims for biopiracy of plants really can't occur in Hawaii because there are, strictly speaking, no indigenous plants. These are mid-Pacific volcanic islands that rose from the surface of the ocean as barren, hot lava plains, and everything growing on them now has been brought from elsewhere—by birds, by wind, by ocean currents, by Polynesian warrior canoes. Nothing's indigenous, although some species are endemic. The legalities of the situation are one reason why, in fact, we have located our company in Hawaii."

"Evading the law," Rick mumbled.

"Obeying the law," Drake said. "That's the point."

They were coming to an area of chest-high green leaves, and Drake said, "Now, we call this area Ginger Lane, with white, yellow, and kahili ginger. Kahili has those foot-long red stems. The trees above us here are mostly sandalwood, with the typical deep-red flowers, but there are also soapberry and milo trees, with large dark green leaves."

The students were turning, looking in all directions.

"I assume you're all familiar with this, but in case you're not, this spiky, striped leaf is oleander, and it will kill a human being. One local man died from grilling meats over a fire on an oleander stick. Children sometimes eat the fruits and die. In addition, the very large tree off to your left is a strychnine tree, originally from India; all parts are fatal, the seeds most of all.

"Next to it, that tall shrub with the star-shaped leaf is the castor bean plant, also fatally toxic. But at very low doses, castor bean compounds may have medicinal properties. I assume you know that, Mr. Hutter?"

"Of course," Rick said. "Castor bean extracts have potential to improve memory function, as well as antibiotic properties."

Drake turned at a fork, following a path that went down to the right. "Finally, here we have Bromeliad Alley," he said. "About eighty varieties of this plant family, which as you know includes the pineapple. Bromeliads harbor a great range of insect life as well. The trees around us are primarily eucalyptus and acacia, but further on we have the more typical rain-forest trees—ohia, and koa, as you will see from the curved leaves littering the trail."

"And why are we being shown all this?" Jenny Linn asked.

Amar Singh joined in. "Exactly. I'm curious about the technology, Mr. Drake. How do you take samples from so many different living things? Especially when you consider that almost all living things are very small. Bacteria, worms, insects, and so forth. I mean, how many biosamples are you collecting and processing per hour? Per day?"

"Our laboratory sends a truck to this rain forest every day," Drake said, "to pick up precision-cut flats of earth, or a selection of plants, or whatever else our researchers have asked for. So you can expect to have fresh research materials brought to you daily, and in general to be provided with whatever you ask for."

"They come here every day?" Rick said.

"That's right, about two p.m., we just missed them."

Jenny Linn crouched down. "What's this?" she said, pointing to the ground. It seemed to be a small tent, about the size of her palm, covering a small concrete box. "I saw another one just like it, a short distance back."

"Ah yes," Drake said. "Excellent observation, Ms. Linn. Those tents are scattered throughout the rain forest in this area. They're supply stations. I'll explain that to all of you later. In fact, if you are ready to leave, I think it's time you learned what Nanigen is all about."

They began to circle back toward the parking lot, skirting a small brownish pond with overhanging palm fronds and small bromeliads lining the edges. "This is Pau Hana Pond," Drake said. "Means 'work is done.'"

"Strange name for a duck pond," Danny said. "Because that's what it is. I saw three or four families of ducklings here before."

"And did you see what happens?" Drake said.

Danny shook his head no. "Is this going to upset me?"

"That depends. Look in the fronds about three feet above the water."

The group paused, stared. Karen King saw it first. "Gray heron," she whispered, nodding. A dusty-gray bird, standing about three feet tall, with a spiky head and dull eyes. It looked unkempt and lazy. It was absolutely motionless and it blended perfectly into the shadows of the palm foliage.

"It can stay that way for hours," Karen said.

They watched for several minutes, and were about to leave when one of the duckling families began to skirt around the edge of the pond. They kept their bodies half-hidden in the overhanging waterside grasses, but to no avail.

In a swift motion, the heron left its perch, splashed among the ducks, and resumed its perch, this time with tiny duck feet protruding from its jaws.

"Ewwww!" Danny.

"Yuch!" Jenny.

The heron threw back his head, looking straight up, and in a single flip motion gulped down the remains of the duckling. It then lowered its head, and turned motionless again in the shadows. It had all taken place in a few seconds. It was hard to believe it had happened at all.

"That's disgusting," Danny said.

"It's the way of the world," Drake said. "You'll notice the arboretum is not overrun with ducks, and that's the reason why. Ah! If I am not mistaken, here are our cars, waiting to take us back to civilization."

# Chapter 8

On the way back to the Nanigen headquarters, Karen King drove the Bentley convertible and the other students crammed themselves into it, while Alyson Bender and Vin Drake went in the sports car. They hadn't gone far when Danny Minot, the science studies student, cleared his throat. "I think," Minot said, speaking above the rush of the wind, "that Drake's arguments about poisonous plants are subject to dispute."

"Subject to dispute" was one of Minot's favorite phrases.

"Oh? How's that?" Amar said. Amar in particular loathed Minot.

"Well, this notion of poison is slippery, isn't it," Minot said. "Poison is what we call any compound that does us harm. Or we think does us harm. Because it may not, in reality, be so harmful. After all, strychnine was once dispensed as a patent medicine in the 1800s. It was thought to be a restorative. And it's still administered for acute alcohol poisoning, I believe. And the tree wouldn't go to the trouble of making strychnine unless it had some purpose, self-defense most likely. Other plants make strychnine, like nightshade. There must be a purpose."

"Yes," Jenny Linn said, "to keep from being eaten."

"That's the plant's view."

"It's our view, too, because we don't eat it either."

"But for humans," Amar said to Minot, "are you arguing that strychnine is not harmful? Not really a poison?"

"That's right. As a concept, it's slippery. One might even say it's indeterminate. The term 'poison' doesn't really refer to anything fixed or specific at all."

This brought groans throughout the car.

"Can we change the subject?" Erika said.

"I'm simply saying the idea of what is poison is subject to dispute."

"Danny, with you everything is subject to dispute."

"In essence, yes," he said, nodding solemnly. "Because I have not adopted the scientific worldview of fixed verities and immutable truths."

"Neither have we," Erika said. "But some things are repeatedly verifiable and therefore justify our belief in them."

"Wouldn't it be pleasant to think so? But that's just a self-serving fantasy that most scientists have about themselves. In reality, it's all power structures," Minot said. "And you know it. Whoever has the power in society determines what can be studied, determines what can be observed, determines what can be thought. Scientists fall in line with the dominant power structure. They have to, because the power structure pays the bills. You don't play ball with the power structure, you don't get money for research, you don't get an appointment, you don't get published, in short you don't count anymore. You're out. You might as well be dead."

There was silence in the car.

"You know I'm right," Minot said. "You just don't like it."

"Speaking of playing ball with power," Rick Hutter said, "look over there. I think we're coming to the Kalikimaki Industrial Park, and Nanigen headquarters."

**Jenny Linn took** a small insulated Gore-Tex case the size of her hand and carefully clipped it to her belt. Karen King said, "What's that, show and tell?"

"Yes," Jenny said. "If they're really going to offer us jobs, well, I thought . . ." She shrugged. "These are all of my extracted and purified volatiles. What did you bring?"

"Benzos, baby," Karen said. "Benzoquinones in a spray container. Blister the skin, burn your eyes—it may come from beetles, but it's the ideal personal-defense chemical. Safe, short-lasting, organic. It'll make an excellent product."

"Of course, you would bring a commercial product," Rick Hutter said to Karen.

"That's because I just don't have your scruples, Rick," Karen said. "Why? You going to tell us you didn't bring anything?"

"No, no."

"Liar."

"Well, okay." He tapped his shirt pocket. "There's a latex extract from my tree. You daub it on and it kills any burrowing parasites under your skin."

"Sounds like a product to me," Karen said, swinging the wheel, and the Bentley slipped around a hairpin turn, glued to the road. "Maybe you'll make a billion dollars from it, Rick." She took her eyes off the road for a second and flashed him a wicked smile.

"No, no, I'm just studying the underlying biochemical mechanism—"

"Tell it to the venture capitalists." Karen glanced at Peter, who sat in the front seat beside her. "And what about you? You've got a lot on your mind. Did you bring something?"

"Actually," Peter said, "I did."

■ ■ ■

**Fingering the CD** in his jacket pocket, Peter Jansen felt a nervous shiver pass through his body. Now that he was going into the Nanigen building, he realized he hadn't fully worked out his plan. Somehow he had to get Bender and Drake to confess in front of the group, and playing Jorge's recording of the phone call between Alyson Bender and Vin Drake would provoke that, he hoped. And if all the graduate students heard a confession, then Drake would be unable to retaliate. There were seven of them; he couldn't attack them all at once.

At least that was the idea.

Lost in his thoughts, Peter stayed with the group as they moved into the building, led by Alyson Bender. "This way, please, and ladies and gentlemen . . ." They stopped first at the elegant black-leather reception area. "I will need your cell phones, your cameras, and any other recording devices in your possession. You will leave those here, to pick up when you depart. And please sign nondisclosure agreements at this time."

She passed out the legal documents; Peter signed absently, not bothering to read it. "Anybody doesn't want to sign, you can wait here until the tour is over. No? Everybody wants to go? Very well then. Follow me."

She led them down a corridor to a series of biological laboratories, where Vin Drake was waiting. The glass-walled labs ran along both sides of a central corridor, and they were up-to-date in the extreme. Peter noticed that several of the labs contained a surprising amount of electronic equipment, almost like an engineering laboratory. It was quiet at Nanigen, the end of the work day, and most of the labs had emptied out, though a few researchers remained, doing work that would run on into the night.

Walking down the hallway, Vin Drake rattled off bits of information about each lab: "Proteomics and genomics . . . chemical ecology . . . Phytopathology, including plant viruses . . . stochastic biology . . . electrical signaling in plants . . . insect ultrasound lab . . . phytoneurology, that's plant neurotransmitters . . . Peter, here's venoms and toxins . . . Arachnid and coleoptid volatiles . . . behavioral physiology, that's exocrine secretion and social regulation, ants primarily . . ."

"What're all the electronics for?" someone asked.

"For the robots," Drake said. "They need to be reprogrammed or repaired, after each trip in the field." He paused, looked at the group. "I see a lot of puzzled faces. Here, come inside, let's take a closer look."

They filed into the laboratory to the right. It smelled faintly of earth, decaying plant matter, desiccated leaves. Drake led them to a table where several foot-square flats of earth were laid out. Above each square was a suspended video camera on a jointed arm. "Here are examples of the material we bring back from the rain forest," he said. "We are working on different projects for each, but in every case the robots are at work."

"Where?" Erika asked. "I don't see—"

Drake adjusted the light, and the video camera. On side monitors, they saw a tiny white object in the soil, magnified many times. "As you see, it's a burrowing and collecting machine, working on a microscopic scale," Drake said. "And it has much to do, because a flat of soil like this holds a vast and interconnected world that is yet unknown to man. There's trillions of microorganisms, tens of thousands of species of bacteria and protozoa, nearly all of them uncatalogued. There can be thousands of miles of wispy fungal hyphae threads in a patch of soil this big. There can be a million microscopic arthropods and other tiny insects, too small for the naked eye to see. There are dozens of earthworms of various sizes. In fact, there are more small living things in this little square of earth than there are large living things on the entire surface of our planet. Think about it. We humans live on the surface. We think that's where the life is. We think in terms of people and elephants and sharks and forests of trees. But our perceptions are wrong. The truth of life on our planet is very different. The real bedrock fundamental life—teeming, burrowing, breeding, continuously active—is down here, at this level. And this is where the discoveries are going to be made."

It was an impressive speech; Drake had given it before, and audiences were always awed into silence. But not this group; Rick Hutter immediately said, "And what's this particular robot discovering?"

"Nematodes," Vin Drake said. "Microscopic roundworms that we think have important biological properties. In a flat of soil like this, there are about four billion nematodes, but we want to collect only those which have not yet been discovered."

Drake had turned to a line of windows that looked into a laboratory where a handful of researchers were working at banks of machines. Complicated machines. "What we're doing in that room," Drake said, "is screening. We're screening thousands of compounds, very rapidly, using high-speed fractionation and mass spectrometry—those are the machines you see. We've already found dozens of totally new drug candidates. And they're natural. Mother Nature's best."

Amar Singh had been quite impressed by the technology, but there were still things he didn't understand. One of them was the robots. The robots were really small. Too small, he thought, to have much of a computer in them. Amar said, "How can those robots sort through the worms and pick them out?"

"Oh, they do it easily," Drake said.

"How?"

"The robot has the intelligence to do it."

"But how?" Amar indicated a flat of soil, where a tiny robot was rooting feverishly in the dirt. "This machine can't be more than eight or nine millimeters in length," Amar said. "It's the size of my little fingernail. You can't put any computing power in such a small dimension."

"Actually, you can."

"How?"

"Let's go to the conference room."


**Four huge flat-panel** screens glowed behind Vin Drake. The screens showed images in deep blue and purple that looked rather like waves on the ocean, as seen from an airplane. Drake paced in front of the screens, his voice amplified by the lapel microphone clipped to his jacket. He gestured to the purple screens. "What you are looking at," he said, "are convection patterns in magnetic fields approaching sixty Tesla in strength. These are the highest magnetic fields generated by man. To give you some perspective, a sixty Tesla magnetic field is two million times greater than the strength of the earth's own magnetic field. These fields are created by cryogenic superconduction using niobium-based composite materials."

He paused to let this sink in. "It's been known for fifty years that magnetic fields affect animal tissues in various ways. You're all familiar with magnetic resonance imaging, or MRIs. You also know that magnetic fields can promote bone healing, inhibit parasites, change platelet behavior, and so on. But it turns out that those are all minor effects arising from exposure to low-intensity fields. The situation is entirely different under extremely high field strengths of the kind we have only recently been able to generate—and until recently nobody had any knowledge of what happened under those conditions. We call such magnetic fields tensor fields, to distinguish them from ordinary magnetic fields. Tensor fields have ultra-high field strengths. In a tensor field, dimensional changes can become evident in matter.

"But we did have a hint—a clue, if you will. It came from research conducted in the 1960s by a company called Nuclear Medical Data, which studied the health of workers at nuclear facilities. The company found workers were generally in good health, but they also noted that over a ten-year period workers exposed to high magnetic fields lost a quarter of an inch in height. This conclusion was considered a statistical artifact, and ignored."

Drake paused again, waiting to see if the assembled students understood where this was going. They didn't yet seem to suspect. "It turns out that it was not a statistical artifact. A French study in 1970 found that French workers in a high magnetic field area lost about eight millimeters in height. But the French study also discarded the finding, calling it 'trivial.'

"However, we now know that it was nothing of the sort. DARPA, the Defense Advanced Research Projects Agency, took an interest in these studies and apparently tested small dogs under high strength fields—the strongest that could be generated at that time, at a secret lab in Huntsville, Alabama. There are no official records of these tests, except for some faded Xeroxes of faxes, which make reference to a Pekingese dog the size of a pencil eraser."

That caused a stir. Some of the students shifted in their chairs. They glanced at one another.

"It seems," Drake continued, "that the dog squeaked pitifully and died after a few hours, exsanguinating with a tiny drop of blood. In general the results were unstable and inconclusive, and the project was abandoned by order of then Secretary of Defense Melvin Laird."

"Why?" one of the students asked.

"He was worried about destabilizing U.S.-Soviet relations," Drake said.

"Why would it do that?"

"That will be clear in a minute," Drake said. "The important point is that we can now generate extremely high magnetic field strengths, these so-called tensor fields. And we now know that under the influence of a tensor field, both organic and inorganic matter undergo something analogous to a phase change. The result is that material in the field experiences rapid compression by a factor of ten to the minus one to ten to the minus three. Quantum interactions remain symmetrical and invariant, for the most part, so that shrunken matter interacts in a normal way with regular matter, at least most of the time. The transformation is metastable and reversible under inverse field conditions. Are you with me so far?"

The students were paying close attention, but their faces registered a wide range of reactions: skepticism, outright disbelief, fascination, even some confusion. Drake was talking about quantum physics—not biology.

Rick folded his arms and shook his head. "So what are you getting at?" he said quite loudly.

Unruffled, Drake answered, "It's good you asked, Mr. Hutter. It's time you see for yourselves." The giant screens behind Drake went dark, then the central panel lit up. They were watching an HD video.

It showed an egg.

The egg sat on a flat black surface. Behind the egg there was a folded yellow backdrop, like a curtain.

The egg moved. It was hatching. A small beak poked through the eggshell; a crack lengthened; the top of the egg broke off. A baby chicken struggled out, cheeping, and stood up, wobbly, and flapped its little stubby wings.

The camera began to pull back.

As the scene widened, the chick's surroundings came into view. The yellow backdrop, it turned out, was actually the huge, clawed foot of a bird. The foot of a chicken. The baby chick now tottered by a monstrously large chicken foot. As the camera drew back farther, the entire adult chicken became visible—it seemed gigantic.

As the camera pulled fully back, however, the chick and the pieces of eggshell became nothing but specks of dirt under the grown bird.

"Get out . . ." Rick began, then stopped. He couldn't take his eyes off the screen.

"This," Drake said, "is Nanigen's technology."

"The transformation—" Amar began.

"Can be done to living organisms. Yes, we shrank that egg in a tensor field. The chicken fetus inside the egg wasn't affected by the dimensional change. It hatched normally, as you can see. This proves that even highly complex biological systems can be compressed in a tensor field and still carry on the normal functions of life."

"What are those other things in the picture?" Karen asked.

In the video, the floor under the giant chicken appeared to be splattered with tiny dots. Some of the dots were moving, some not.

"Those are the other chicks. We dimensionally shifted the whole brood," Drake said. "Unfortunately they're so small the mother has stepped on some of her babies without knowing it."

There was a brief silence. Amar was the first to speak. "You've done this to other organisms?"

"Of course," Drake answered.

"That means . . . people?" Amar said.

"Yes."

"Those little robot diggers we saw in the arboretum," Amar went on. "You're telling us you don't actually program intelligence into them."

"We don't need to."

"Because you have human beings run them."

"Yes."

"Human beings who have undergone a dimensional change."

"Holy shit," Danny Minot burst out. "Are you fucking kidding me?"

"No," Drake said.

Somebody burst out laughing. It was Rick Hutter. "Scam," Rick muttered. "Guy's selling worthless stock to fools."

Karen King didn't believe it, either. She said, "This is bullshit hype. No way. You can do anything with video."

"It's existing technology," Drake said calmly.

Amar Singh said, "So you're saying you can cause a dimensional change in a human being as great as ten to the minus three."

"Yes."

"Which means that someone six feet tall would be, uh, seventy-two inches . . . seven-hundredths of an inch tall."

"That's correct," Drake said. "Slightly less than two-tenths of a millimeter."

"Jesus," Rick Hutter said.

"And at ten to the minus two," Drake said, "the person is approximately half an inch tall. Twelve millimeters."

"I would actually like to see this for real," Danny Minot said.

"Of course," Drake said. "And you will."

# Chapter 9

**W**hile Drake was talking with the students, Peter Jansen had taken Alyson Bender aside. "Some of us brought samples and compounds to show Mr. Drake."

"That's good," Alyson said to him.

"I've got a CD with some of my, uh, research on it," Peter said. She nodded in response. "It's a recording. It involves my brother," Peter added. He hoped to start winding her up, making her nervous. She nodded again and left the conference room; did he see a flicker of alarm in her eyes?

After she'd left, while Drake was still talking, Peter slipped behind the service door and went to the audio panel. He needed some equipment; something to magnify his voice; he did not want Drake or anyone to be able to shut him up or shout him down. Behind the service door there were some drawers; he began opening them, and he found what he wanted. It was a lavalier, a wireless microphone device that would transmit his voice to a loudspeaker. The lavalier was identical to a unit Drake had used during his slide show and talk. The device consisted of a transmitter unit and a throat mike with a wire that ran to the transmitter. He slipped the transmitter into his pants pocket, stuffed the wire and mike in after it.

Drake concluded his presentation on the screens, and the lights went up in the meeting room. "Some of you have brought things to show us," Drake said, "and we are very eager to see them. Now if— yes, what is it?"

Alyson Bender had come back into the room. She leaned close to Drake, whispered in his ear. Drake stared at Peter as he listened, then looked away. He nodded twice, but said nothing. Finally he turned back to Peter.

"Peter, you have a recording?"

"A CD, yes."

"What is on that recording, Peter?" Drake didn't seem upset at all.

"Something that will interest you." Peter's heart was pounding.

"Related to your brother?"

"Yes."

Drake seemed unruffled. "I know this is a difficult matter for you," he said, placing his hand on Peter's shoulder. Gently, he added, "Wouldn't it be easier to talk privately?"

Drake wanted to get him off alone, where nobody could hear what was said. Peter balked. "We can talk here," he answered. In the conference room with everybody else.

Drake looked concerned. "If I might have a private word with you Peter—Eric was a friend of mine, too. I've suffered a loss my- self. Let's step into the next room."

Peter shrugged and got up, and walked with Vin Drake and Alyson Bender into a smaller adjacent room—it was a prep booth for the conference room. Drake closed the door behind them and with a smooth gesture flipped the door's lock. Then he spun around, and in the blink of an eye his face had been transformed: it was contorted with rage. He viciously clamped his hand around Peter's throat and slammed him against the wall. With his other hand, he took Peter's arm and bent it, holding it in a lock. "I don't know what your game is, you little bastard—"

"No game—"

"The police aren't looking for a phone on the boat—"

"No?"

"No, you little bastard. Because they haven't been to the boat yard all day."

Peter's mind was racing. "The police didn't need to go to the boat yard," he said, "because they can find the phone just by looking at the GPS tracking signal—"

"No they can't!" Drake let go of his arm and punched him in the stomach, hard. Peter gasped and doubled over, and Drake grabbed his arm and bent it behind him, and got Peter in a neck lock, immobilizing him. "Don't lie to me. They can't, because I disabled the GPS before I ever put that phone on the boat."

Alyson said nervously, "Vin . . ."

"Shut up."

"So," Peter said, "you disabled the GPS and rigged up the phone to clog my brother's gas line?"

"No. To kill the fuel pump, you little asshole . . . I killed the radio, too . . ."

Alyson: "Vin, listen . . ."

"Alyson, keep out of this—"

"Why'd you do it?" Peter said, coughing, pulling at Drake's fingers. Drake's grip was strong on his throat. "Why?"

"Your brother was a fool. You know what he wanted? He wanted to sell this technology. Turns out there's some legal issue about ownership, who really owned it. So Eric thought we should sell. Can you imagine: sell this technology. Eric betrayed Nanigen. He betrayed me personally."

"Vin, for God's sake—"

"Shut up—"

"Your mike!" Alyson pointed to the lavalier microphone on Drake's lapel. "It's on."

"Ah, shit," Vin Drake hissed. He punched Peter brutally hard in the solar plexus, and let him crumple to the floor on his knees, gasping. Very deliberately, Drake pulled back his jacket, revealing the transmitter clipped to his belt. He tapped a switch: the light was off. "I'm not stupid."

Peter knelt on the floor and retched and coughed, unable to get a breath. He realized that the small clip microphone had come out of his pocket, and dangled on its cord. Drake might see it. Groping around, he tried to stuff it back in his pocket, and his hand hit the transmitter. He heard a loud popping noise coming over the loudspeakers in the conference room.

Drake looked toward the conference room. He had heard the sound. His eyes followed Peter's hand, and he saw the little microphone. He took a step backward and lashed out with his boot, kicked Peter on the side of the head. Peter collapsed. Drake tore the lavalier's cord out of Peter's pocket, disconnecting the mike, and tossed it away. Peter rolled on the floor and groaned.

"What do we do now?" Alyson said to him. "They've heard it—"

"Shut up!" He paced. "God damn it. None of them have cell phones, right?"

"Right, they left them at the front . . ."

"Okay then."

"What are you going to do?" she said, trembling.

"Just stay out of my way."

He flipped open a security panel, and hit a red SECURITY button. A loud, rising and falling alarm began to sound. He hauled Peter up under the armpits and dragged him to his feet, where he swayed, unsteady and in pain, groggy from his beating. "Suck it up, sport," Drake said. "Time to clean up your mess."

■ ■ ■

**Drake unlocked the** door and burst into the conference room, supporting Peter. He had to shout over the alarm. "We've had a security breach," he said. "Peter has been injured. The security robots have been released. These bots are extremely dangerous. Come quickly this way, all of you. We need to get to the safety room." He led them out into the hallway, holding on to Peter while Alyson Bender took Peter's other arm.

In the hallway, a few researchers were running toward the entrance. "Get outside!" somebody shouted, running past, heading for the building's main exit. Most employees had gone home for the day.

Drake, however, turned and led the students deeper into the complex.

"Where the hell are you taking us?" Rick Hutter said to Drake.

"It's too late to get outdoors. We need to get to the safety room."

The students were in a state of confusion. What safety room? What did that mean?

"What are you doing?" Alyson said to Drake.

Drake didn't answer.

They came to a heavy door marked TENSOR CORE. Drake punched a keypad and the door swung open. "This way, come on now . . ."

The students entered a large space with hexagonal tiles on the floor. The floor was almost transparent; they could see machinery below, complex machinery, going deep into the ground. "All right, everyone," Drake said, "I want you all to stand in the center of one of the hexagons. Each hexagon is a safety spot. It's robot-proof. Do it now, that's it—hurry, hurry—we don't have much time." Drake touched a security pad and they heard bolts slamming home. They were locked inside the room.

Erika Moll had gotten extremely frightened. She uttered a cry, and made a run for the exit door.

"Don't!" Danny Minot screamed after her.

The exit door was locked, and Erika couldn't get out.

Drake had shut himself in a control room, where he looked in on the students through a window. An instant later, he went out of sight. The control room door opened, and a man, a stranger, was flung into the big room; he was a Nanigen employee. "Get in there and help them!" Drake's voice roared after the man.

The man followed Drake's order. Looking shocked, he stood in the center of a hexagon among the students.

The students were all positioning themselves; Erika had come back. Peter Jansen toppled and fell to his knees; Rick Hutter grabbed him and tried to support him but Peter stayed on his knees. Karen King noticed a row of backpacks hanging along the wall, and she ran and grabbed one and slung it over her shoulder. Meanwhile Drake had become visible in the window again, and they saw him punching buttons in a rapid sequence. Alyson was by his side.

"Vin, for God's sake," Alyson said, standing beside him.

"No choice," Vin Drake said, and he hit the final button.

**For Peter Jansen,** groggy from his beating, everything happened fast. The hexagonal floor sank beneath him, and he descended some ten feet into the multiple jaws of some huge electronic apparatus that was all around him, and very close, almost touching his skin. The jaws were actually wired armatures, painted at intervals with red and white stripes. The air smelled strongly of ozone and there was a loud electronic hum. The hairs on his skin were raised up. A synthesized voice said, "Don't move, please. Take a deep breath . . . and hold it!" There was a loud *clank!*, unnerving and mechanical, and then that electronic hum returned. A brief wave of nausea. He sensed he had shifted somehow, within the apparatus.

"You may breathe normally. Stand by."

He took a breath, let it out slowly.

"Don't move, please. Take a deep breath, and hold it!"

Another *clank!* Another hum. A ripple of nausea, stronger than before.

He blinked his eyes.

Now he was sure things had changed. Before, he had been looking at stripes at about the midpoint of the jaws. But now he was looking at stripes much lower down. He was shrinking. The jaws buzzed and moved closer toward him. Of course they would do that, he thought, the magnetic field would be strongest at small distances. The smaller the better.

The synthetic voice: "Take a deep breath, and hold it!"

When he looked upward again, he saw that he was really very much smaller. The top of the jaws, ten feet above, seemed now as high as a cathedral ceiling. How tall was he?

"Don't move, please. Take a deep breath, and—"

"I know, I know . . ." Peter's voice was shaking.

"Don't speak. You risk serious injury. Now: take a deep breath and hold it!"

One final *clank*, a grinding sound, a final spasm of dizzying nausea—but now the jaws moved away from him, and he felt the floor beneath his feet begin to vibrate as it rose upward. He saw light from above shining down, and felt a cool breeze.

And then he was flush with the rest of the floor, and the vibration stopped. He was standing on a polished black expanse stretching away in all directions. In the distance he saw Erika and Jenny, both looking around, dazed. And still farther away, Amar and Rick, and Karen. But how far away were they, actually? Peter couldn't be sure, because he himself was no more than half an inch tall. Dust motes and flecks of dead cellular debris rolled across the floor, came to rest against his knees, like tiny tumbleweed.

He looked down at this tumbleweed in stupefaction. He felt

slow, dull-witted, stupid. The reality of the situation gradually dawned on him. He looked across the floor at Erika and Jenny. They seemed as shocked as he felt. Half an inch tall!

A crunching sound made him turn; he faced the tip of an enormous boot, the sole as tall as he was. Peter looked up and saw Vin Drake crouched down on one knee, looming above him, his face enormous, his exhalations a stiff, noxious wind. And then Peter heard a deep rumbling that reverberated throughout the room like thunder.

It was the sound of Vin Drake laughing.


**It was difficult** to hear, with all the echoes and reverberations from these two enormous people. The sounds made his ears ache. They seemed to move and speak slowly, almost in slow motion. Alyson Bender crouched down alongside Drake, and together they stared at Peter. Alyson said, "What—are—you—doing—Vin?" The words boomed and rolled, and seemed to slur together into a mishmash of sounds, too deep to make out without difficulty.

Vin Drake just laughed. Apparently he found the situation amusing. But the man's laughter propelled gusts of stinking breath toward Peter, and he recoiled from the odor of garlic, red wine, and cigars.

Drake glanced at his watch. "It's—after—hours," he said, and smiled. "*Pau—hana,*—as—they—say—here—in—Hawaii.—Means—work—is—done."

Alyson Bender stared at him.

Drake tipped his head from side to side, as if he had gotten something stuck in his ear; it seemed to be a habit. The students heard his voice, rolling out: "After—work—comes—play."

## Chapter 10

Vin Drake produced a clear plastic bag. With surprising gentleness, he picked up Peter Jansen and dropped him in the bag. Peter slid down the plastic surface, came to rest at the bottom. He got to his feet, and watched as Vin went around the room, picking up each of the graduate students in turn, dropping them in the bag. Last of all he picked up the Nanigen man from the control room. They heard the man call out, "Mr. Drake! What are you doing, sir?"

Drake didn't seem to hear the man, and didn't seem to care.

As each person tumbled down among the others in the bag, nobody got hurt. Apparently they now had too little mass to cause damage. "We're almost weightless," Amar commented. "We must weigh no more than a gram or so. Like a tiny feather." Amar's voice was cool, composed. But Peter thought he detected a tremor of fear.

"Well, I don't care who knows it, I'm scared," Rick Hutter blurted.

"We all are," Karen King admitted.

"I think we're in shock," Jenny Linn said. "Look at our faces. Circum-oral pallor." Blanched skin around the lips was a classic sign of fear.

The Nanigen man kept saying, "There's been some mistake." He couldn't seem to believe what Drake had just done.

"Who are you?" someone asked him.

"My name is Jarel Kinsky. I'm an engineer. I operate the tensor generator. If Mr. Drake would just—just give me a chance to talk with him—"

"You've seen too much." Rick Hutter cut him off sharply. "Whatever Drake does to us he's going to do to you as well."

"Let's take an inventory," Karen King snapped. "Quick—what weapons have we got?"

But they got no further; the bag was tossed around, throwing them into a tangle.

"Uh-oh," Amar said, struggling to sit up. "What's happening now?"

Alyson Bender pushed her face very close to the plastic bag; she was looking carefully at the individuals inside, apparently worried about them. Her eyelashes flicked against the plastic. The pores in the skin of her nose were alarmingly large, great pink pockmarks.

"Vin—I—don't—want—them—harmed—Vin."

That drew a smile from Vin Drake. Speaking slowly, he said, "I—wouldn't—dream—of—harming—them."


**"You realize,"** Karen King said, "that that man is a psychopath. He is capable of anything."

"I realize it," Peter said.

"That's just not true about Mr. Drake," Jarel Kinsky said. "There is a reason for this."

Ignoring him, Karen said to Peter, "We should have no illusions about what Drake intends at this point. We're witnesses to his confession, that he killed your brother. Now he's going to kill us all."

"Do you think so?" Danny Minot said plaintively. "We shouldn't jump to—"

"Yes, Danny, I do think so. Maybe you'll be first."

"It's just so hard to imagine—"

"Ask Peter's brother about—"

At that moment, Vin picked up the plastic bag and walked quickly into the hallway. He was simultaneously arguing with Alyson Bender, but their words were too difficult to decipher; it just sounded like thunder rumbling.

They walked past several labs, and then Drake entered one. Even inside the plastic bag, they could immediately detect the difference in this lab.

A sharp, acrid odor.

Wood chips and feces.

Animals.

"This is an animal lab," Amar said. And they could see, through the distortion of the plastic bag, that there were rats, hamsters, and lizards and other reptiles.

Vin Drake set the bag down on top of a glass tank. Now he was talking, apparently directing his remarks at them, but they could not understand what he was saying. They looked from one to another. "What's he saying?" "I don't understand." "He's crazy." "I can't make it out."

Jenny Linn had turned her back on the group; she was entirely focused on Drake. She turned to Peter and said, "It's you."

"What do you mean?"

"He's going to kill you first. Wait just a minute."

"What . . . ?"

She unzipped her belt pack, revealing a dozen slender glass tubes, with rubber bumpers at each end. "My volatiles." It was impossible to miss the devotion; these tubes represented years of work. She pulled one out. "I'm afraid it's the best I can do."

Peter shook his head, not understanding. She uncorked the tube and in a single quick motion, poured it over his head and down his body. There was a pungent odor; then nothing. He said, "What is it?"

Before she could answer, Vin Drake thrust his hand into the bag, and gripping Peter by the leg, lifted him out upside down. Peter yelled and waved his arms.

"It's hexenol," she said. "From wasps. Good luck."

"Now—now—young—Master—Peter," Drake said, his voice booming. "You've—caused—me—a—great—deal—of—trouble." He held Peter close to his face, squinted at him. "Worried? Bet—you—are."

Drake turned on his heel; the quick movement was dizzying for Peter; and then he slid the glass top of a tank open a fraction of an inch, and dropped Peter through the slot. He slid it shut, leaving the bag with the people in it on top of the tank.

Peter fell, landing in sawdust.

**Alyson Bender said,** "Vin, I didn't agree to this, this wasn't what we discussed—"

"The situation has changed, obviously—"

"But this is unconscionable."

"Tell me about your conscience," Drake said scornfully, "later."

She had agreed to help him eliminate Eric, after Eric had threatened to destroy Nanigen. She had thought she loved Vin Drake and maybe she still did love him. Vin had been incredibly good to her, advanced her career, paid her unlimited amounts of money, while Eric had acted so badly toward Vin . . . Eric had betrayed Vin. But the others were only students . . . this situation was going out of control. Even so, she felt paralyzed. The situation had developed too fast. She didn't know how to stop Drake.

"There is nothing cruel about a predator," Drake said, standing before the snake tank. "It is extremely humane. That black-and-white striped creature on the other side of the glass is a banded krait from Malaysia. Its bite, for a creature Peter's size, will be almost immediately fatal. He'll hardly feel a thing. Slurred speech, difficulty swallowing, paralysis of the eyes, and then complete paralysis of the body in a matter of moments. He may possibly still be alive when the snake ingests him but, ah, he probably won't care . . ."

Drake placed his index finger against his thumb, and flicked the plastic bag. It caused the micro-humans inside the bag to be flung around. Shouting and swearing with terror and confusion, they tumbled upon one another, while Drake peered at them. "They're quite lively," he commented to Alyson. "I assume the krait will accept them. If not, there's also the cobra and the coral snake."

She looked away.

"It's essential, Alyson," he said. "Their bodies have to be ingested. There can't be any . . . evidence."

"But that's not all of it," she said. "What about their car, their hotel rooms, plane tickets—"

"I've got a plan for all that."

"Do you?"

"Trust me. I do." He stared at her. "Alyson," he said, after a long moment, "are you saying you don't trust me?"

"No, of course not," she said quickly.

"I hope not. Because without trust, we're nothing. We are in this together, Alyson."

"I know."

"Yes, I know you do." He patted her hand. "Ah, I see young Peter has dusted himself off, and here comes the krait, looking for his meal." Slithering black and white stripes, partially hidden in the sawdust. Black tongue flicking in and out.

"Now watch closely," Drake said to her. "It happens fast."

Alyson had turned away. She couldn't watch.

**Peter got to** his feet and brushed himself off. The fall hadn't hurt him, but he still felt the effects of Drake's punches and kicks, and his shirt was stuck to his chest with drying blood. He was waist-deep in sawdust, in a glass cage. The cage had a small branch with some leaves on it, otherwise it was empty.

Except for the snake.

From where he stood, he could only see a few dark-gray and white bands. Probably a banded krait, Bungarus candidus. From Malaysia or Vietnam. As a rule, kraits ate other snakes, but he could not count on this one to be fussy. He saw the coils of black and white move and, with a soft hissing sound, disappear. The snake was sliding forward.

He couldn't see the head, or even very much of the body. He was too small to really grasp the layout of the cage, unless he climbed the branch, which didn't seem like a good idea. All he could do was wait for the snake to come to him. Helpless, defenseless. He patted his pockets, but they were empty. His body began to shake uncontrollably: was it shock from his beating? Or fright? Probably both. He backed into a corner, glass on both sides. Maybe he would make a reflection that would disturb the snake. Maybe he would—

He saw the head. It emerged from the sawdust, tongue flicking rapidly. It came so close to Peter that the tongue almost brushed his body. He closed his eyes, unable to watch. He was trembling so hard he thought he would collapse in sheer terror.

He took a breath, held it, trying to stop the trembling. He opened one eye slightly, hazarding a look.

The snake was right there, just inches from his torso, and the black tongue continued to flick in and out, but something was wrong. This snake seemed confused, or hesitant—and then, to his utter amazement, the animal raised its head and slithered backward, pulling away from Peter.

Disappearing into the sawdust.

And gone.

And then he did collapse, falling to the ground, shaking with fear and exhaustion, unable to control his body, and one thought remained fixed in his mind—what the hell happened?

**"God damn it,"** Vin Drake said, looking down through the glass. "What the hell was that? What just happened?"

"Maybe it wasn't hungry."

"Oh, it's hungry alright. God damn it! I can't have these mishaps. I'm on a schedule, a tight schedule."

The intercom clicked. "Mr. Drake, you have a visitor. Mr. Drake, visitor at the front desk."

"Oh for Christ's sake," Drake said, throwing up his hands. "I'm not expecting anybody today." He dialed reception. "What is it, Mirasol?"

"I'm sorry, Mr. Drake, but I was in the parking lot after the alarm, and someone from the Honolulu police came to see you. So I brought them in."

"Oh. All right." He hung up. "Great. The police."

Alyson said, "I'll go see what they want."

"No, you won't," he said. "I'll deal with the police. You go back to your office and stay out of sight until they are gone."

"All right, if that's what—"

"It is, yes."

"All right, Vin."

. . .

**Jenny Linn watched** as Vin Drake and Alyson Bender left the animal room. She noticed that Drake was careful to lock the door as he left. The plastic bag was lying on top of the snake's tank. The top of the bag was twisted lightly. But it was loose. Jenny wriggled herself up in the neck of the bag, pushing, and she managed to get it open. "Come on," she said. "We can at least get out." The others followed Jenny, climbing out of the bag, until they were standing on the clear glass lid that covered the tank.

Jenny looked down into the tank. Peter was getting to his feet, obviously shaken. She shouted, "Can you understand me?"

He shook his head at Jenny: Not really.

Rick Hutter said, "Why didn't the snake strike?"

Jenny got down on her hands and knees, cupped her hands around her mouth, and said, "Peter, can you hear now?"

He shook his head.

"Try bone conduction," Amar said.

Jenny lay flat on the surface, putting her cheek against the glass. She spoke loudly: "Peter? Now?"

"Yes," he said. "What happened?"

"I doused you with volatiles from a wasp," she said. "Principally hexenol. I figured there were very few things that would put off a poisonous snake, but a wasp sting would be one of them."

"Damn clever," Amar said. "Snakes rely more on smell than sight anyway. And the krait's nocturnal . . ."

"It worked. It thought I was a wasp."

"Yes, but the substance is very volatile, Peter."

"Meaning it will evaporate."

"It is, as we speak."

"Great. I'm not a wasp anymore."

"Not for long."

"How much time would you say?" he said.

"I don't know. Minutes."

"What can we do?"

Karen King said, "How are your reflexes?"

"Shot." He held out his hand; it was shaking.

"What's your idea?" Amar said.

"Do you have any of the spider silks we worked on?" For about six months, Amar and Karen had been synthesizing spider silks with various properties—some were sticky, some strong, some flexible like a bungee cord. Some could turn from smooth to sticky from the addition of a chemical at one end.

"I have several, yes," Amar said.

"Okay, you see that plastic tube beside the cage, closed at one end?"

"It looks like it's part of a little water dispenser."

"Right. That's the one. Can you grab that tube with sticky silk and hoist it up?"

"I don't know," Amar said doubtfully. "It probably weighs an ounce or two. We'd all have to help haul it up—"

"That's fine because we all have to help, anyway. To open the cage."

"Open the cage." The top of the krait cage was a double piece of glass; one slid over the other. "I don't know, Karen, that means shifting the glass piece."

"Just an inch or so. Just enough—"

"To lower the tube."

"Right."

"Peter, are you following this?" Amar said.

"I am, and it sounds impossible."

"I don't see an alternative," Karen said. "We have only one shot at this, and you can't miss."

Amar had opened up a plastic case, which he'd had in his pocket, and he was already uncoiling his sticky silk from an armature in the case. He lowered the silk over the edge, and hooked the plastic tube. It was surprisingly light. Amar and Rick Hutter were able to raise it easily.

They tried sliding the glass plate to get it open, but that proved to be a much greater challenge. "We have to be coordinated," Karen said. "Everybody on the count of three, one . . . two . . . three!" The glass moved, just a few millimeters, but it moved. "Okay, again! Hurry!"

And the krait was becoming more active. Whether from seeing all the little people walking around on top, or because the volatile was wearing off, the snake began twisting and coiling, moving toward Peter, getting ready to try another approach.

"Get that thing down here," Peter said. His voice was tremulous.

"Lowering it now," Amar said.

The thread scraped over the glass edge, making a strange squeaking sound.

"That going to be okay?" Karen said. "Will it hold?"

"It's strong," Amar said.

"Come lower, a little lower," Peter said. "Okay . . . Hold it there." The tube was chest-high. He stood behind it, holding it in position with both hands at the back. But his hands were sweating, slippery. His grip unsure.

The snake was moving. Hissing through the leaves and sawdust.

"What if it strikes from the side?" Peter said.

"Adjust," Karen said. " 'Cause it looks like—"

"Yeah, it is—"

"Here it comes, damn it—"

"Oh shit," Peter said. The snake struck with blinding speed—unimaginable speed—unthinking, he swung the tube to meet it—the full impact of the krait's head slammed against his chest—the silk snapped, and Peter fell backward, with the krait on top of him, writhing and coiling angrily, pinning Peter's body down. But the krait's head was lodged tightly inside the tube, and it would be difficult for him to get free.

"How did you do that?" Karen said, her voice full of admiration. "The snake was so fast."

"I don't know," Peter said. "I just . . . reacted." It had all happened faster than thought. Now, Peter struggled to push the snake away. So close to him, the smell of the animal was nauseating. Finally he kicked free, and staggered to his feet.

The snake stared up at him with baleful eyes. It shook the tube hard, and banged it repeatedly against the glass, but did not dislodge it. Its furious hiss was magnified, reverberating inside the tube.

"That's great," Rick said. "But we better get you out of there."

**Vin Drake gritted** his teeth. Mirasol, the receptionist, was beautiful but she was an idiot. The muscular man in the blue uniform standing before him was not a cop but a Coast Guard ensign; and what he wanted was information about ownership of Eric's Boston Whaler, because the boat yard wanted to move it to another location, and they needed permission of the owner to do that.

"I thought the police were still inspecting the boat," Vin said irritably. He might as well try to get some information from this numbskull.

"I wouldn't know about that," the ensign said. The police hadn't come to see him, he explained; it was the boat-yard owner.

"I heard they were looking for a phone."

"Not that I'm aware. I think the police have finished their investigation."

Drake closed his eyes, gave a long sigh. "Christ."

"At least," the ensign said, "as soon as they complete their inspection of his office."

Drake's eyes snapped open. "Whose office?"

"Jansen's office. His office here, in this building. He was vice president of this company, right? I know they went to Jansen's apartment today, and that they're coming to look at his office here—" the ensign glanced at his watch—"any minute now, actually. In fact, I'm surprised they haven't already shown up."

"Christ," Vin Drake said.

He turned to Mirasol. "The police are going to be arriving soon," he said, "and someone needs to show them around."

"Should I page Ms. Bender?"

"No," Vin said. "Ms. Bender will be—she will be busy working with me. I have some lab work to ship out. It can't wait."

"Who should I call?"

"Get Don Makele, the head of security," he said. "He can show the officers around. They'll want to see Mr. Jansen's office."

"And wherever else he worked," the ensign added. He was staring fixedly at the receptionist.

"And wherever else he worked," Drake repeated. Cars were pulling up in the street outside. He repressed an urge to bolt, and instead calmly shook the ensign's hand. "You're welcome to go along with the police," he said. "And Mirasol, why don't you accompany the officers, see that they get coffee, whatever."

"All right, Mr. Drake."

"I believe I will stay," the ensign said.

"Then you must excuse me for the moment," Drake said. He turned and walked down the hallway. The moment he was out of sight, he began to run.


**Alyson Bender sat** in her office and bit her lip. The monitor on her desk showed the reception area; she could see Drake talking to the uniformed kid, and see Mirasol flirting, fussing with the flower in her hair.

As usual, Drake was impatient, quick, aggressive in his movements. Almost hostile, really. Of course he was under pressure, but seeing the way he moved—no words, just the body language—made it clear how angry he was. He was an angry, angry man.

And he was going to kill all of those kids.

It was only too clear what he intended to do. Peter Jansen had trapped him, and Vin was going to escape the only way possible, by leaving no witnesses. Seven young people, bright students with their lives before them, he didn't seem to care. It didn't seem to matter to him.

They were merely in the way.

It frightened her. Her hands trembled even when she pressed them flat against the desk. She was afraid of him, and terrified of the situation she found herself in. She could not confront him directly, of course. He'd kill her if she did.

But she had to stop him from killing those kids. Somehow, she had to do that. She knew what she had done. She knew her involvement in Eric Jansen's death, knew it only too well. Making those calls to the trigger phone. But to be involved in the murder of seven more people—no, eight, including the Nanigen employee who'd had the bad luck to be in the control room when Drake came in—she wasn't sure she could do it. It would be homicide on a grand scale. But she might have to do it . . . to save herself.

On the monitor, Drake was telling the receptionist what to do. The ensign was grinning. Drake would soon leave.

Alyson stood up, and hurried out of her office. She didn't have much time. He could return to the lab looking for the students at any moment.

**In the lab,** the students had gotten out of the bag, and they stood on the transparent top of the krait cage, looking down at Peter Jansen. Alyson Bender burst into the room. She bent down and stared at them, her face looming over them. "I—won't—hurt—you," she said. Her eyes were wide and frightened. She put out her hand, palm flat, and picked up Jenny Linn very gently, and placed her on her palm. She gestured to the others. "Hurry. I—don't—know—where—he—is."

"Ms. Bender! Let me talk with Mr. Drake!" Jarel Kinsky shouted at her, waving his arms.

She didn't seem to hear or understand.

The others, seeing no other option, climbed onto Alyson's palm. She lifted them into the air, and the room spun around, the wind blew, knocking them off their feet—she carried them swiftly to a desk, and placed them down on it. Then she went over to the snake cage, opened it, and lifted Peter out, and put him on the desk with the others. She stared at them, seeming not to know what to do with them. Her breathing was ragged and loud.

Karen King said, "We should try to talk to her."

"I don't know if it will do any good," Peter said.

Alyson moved away. They saw her go across the room. She threw open a cabinet, looked inside, took out a small brown paper bag, and hurried back to the desk. "Hide—in—this," she said, speaking slowly. "You—can—breathe." She opened the bag and laid it down on the desk with its mouth facing them, and gestured to them to get in. They scrambled into the bag. Last of all was the Nanigen man, who couldn't seem to accept the reality of their desperate situation. He kept shouting, "Ms. Bender! Ms. Bender, please!"

Alyson folded the top of the bag tightly and hurried out of the room. She carried the bag into her office and placed it gently inside her purse, which sat on the floor by her desk. She snapped the purse shut and pushed it with her toe underneath her desk, and ran back to the animal lab, arriving just as Vin Drake walked in.

"What the hell are you doing?" he said.

"I was looking for you."

"I told you to stay in your office." Drake went over to the snake's cage and saw the empty plastic bag. "They've escaped," he said. He spun around and swore, and turned around again, and lunged at a shelf full of chemicals. With one movement he swept everything to the floor, sending broken glass and liquids splashing. "Where are they?"

"Vin, please, I don't know—"

"The hell you don't," he snarled, and peered into the snake tank, where he saw the snake with its head stuck in the plastic tube, and no sign of Peter. "What the—? That Jansen kid is dead, anyway. Snake got him." He shot Alyson a violent look. "We're going to find the rest of them. And I swear to God, Alyson, if you've been screwing with me it will be the last thing you ever regret."

She cringed. "I understand."

"You'd better." At that moment, two police officers came down the hallway, visible through the lab windows, led by Don Makele. They were both young, not in uniform, which meant they were detectives. *Shit.*

Drake straightened up and suddenly composed himself, a shift that happened so quickly it seemed eerie. "Hi there, Don," Drake said, crossing the room and easing out into the hallway with a warm smile on his face. "Introduce me to our guests. We don't often have visitors to Nanigen. Officers? I'm Vin Drake, I'm the president of this company. How can I be of service to you?"

**The paper bag** was scrunched up inside Alyson's purse, and it was pitch-dark. The students and the Nanigen man sat huddled.

"I can't tell if she means to help us or not," Karen King said.

"She's obviously terrified of Drake," Peter said.

"Who wouldn't be?" Amar said.

Rick Hutter sighed. "I told you Drake was a corporate slime. Nobody listened."

"Shut up, damn you!" Karen yelled at him.

"Hey, please," Amar said in a very calm voice. "Not now."

"Sorry," Karen said. Then she added, "But we're not dealing with an ordinary slime. We're dealing with a very sick man." She fingered her knife. It was useless as a defense; it might not even break Drake's skin.

There came a banging, thunderous noise, and the bag shook, and light suddenly glowed through the bag. The purse had been opened. Then, with a slamming noise, everything went dark again. They waited, wondering what would come next.

**The students, Alyson Bender** knew, had to be put back in the generator and restored to full size, and quickly. But she didn't know how to operate the generator herself. The workday was long over, and almost all the employees had gone home, leaving Nanigen deserted.

She found Drake back in the animal room. He had finished talking with the police officers, and now he was searching the animal room carefully, looking into every corner and cabinet, peering into every cage.

He stared at her, his eyes hard. "Did you let them go?"

"No. I swear, Vin."

"I'm going to have this lab cleaned tomorrow. The animals put to death, the whole room sterilized with gas, then washed with bleach."

"That's . . . that's good, Vin."

"We don't have any choice." He touched her arm. "Go home and get some rest. I'm going to stay here for a while."

She gave him a grateful look. Then she hurried into her office, picked up her purse, and headed outdoors. Mirasol had gone home; the reception area was empty. A fat moon drifted in stars dusting the sky, a beautiful night if only her mind hadn't been in turmoil. She got into the BMW—it was a corporate car for her use. She put the purse on the seat next to her and sped off.


**Vin Drake went** into the deserted lobby, keeping himself in the shadows. When he heard Alyson's car start and go down the street, he ran outdoors to the Bentley and started it. Where were her taillights? He got to the Farrington Highway. Left or right? He swung left: the way to Honolulu, the most likely way she'd go. He pulled out into traffic and accelerated, feeling his body pressed into the seat with a surge of power.

There it was, the red BMW, traveling fast. He dropped back, watching her taillights. Her car turned onto the entry ramp to the H-1 Freeway. The midnight-blue Bentley faded into the night: he was just another set of headlights behind her in the flow of traffic.

He had not been able to find the students. There was only one possibility: Alyson had taken them with her in her car. He couldn't be completely sure of it, but his instincts told him so.

She might have to go. He certainly couldn't trust her. That was obvious. The woman had lost her nerve. But it was getting complicated, all these people disappearing. Alyson Bender was Nanigen's chief financial officer, and if she disappeared now, it would provoke a very thorough investigation.

He didn't want that. An investigation of Nanigen would, sooner or later, turn up something he had done. It was inevitable. Enough time, enough checking . . . they would find out.

No, no, he didn't want an investigation.

He began to realize he had made a terrible mistake. He couldn't kill her. He couldn't afford to kill her—at least not right now. He needed her on his side for a little while.

How could he get her on his side?

. . .

**Alyson followed the** freeway around Pearl Harbor, trying not to look at her purse on the seat. Maybe Vin was right. Maybe there was no choice. She exited into downtown Honolulu, not certain where to go. She drove to Waikiki. There, she went slowly along Kalakaua Avenue, caught in traffic. The crowds of tourists were thick, people out for the evening. Then she turned onto Diamond Head Road and circled past the Diamond Head Lighthouse. She would take the paper bag to a beach somewhere on the windward side of Oahu or maybe to the North Shore. She would drop the bag in the surf somewhere . . . no evidence . . . no survivors . . .

Drake stayed back, watching her car. She went past Makapu'u Point and through Waimanalo, and Kailua. But then she turned and picked up the freeway and headed back toward Honolulu. Where in hell was his CFO going, he wondered.

Having driven around the eastern edge of Oahu and doubled back into Honolulu, Alyson finally found herself following the Manoa Valley Road, winding up into the rain-forested valley among the mountains.

She arrived at the steel gates and the tunnel. The gates were locked. She punched the security code and went through. The tunnel emerged into a velvet dark valley.

The place was deserted, the greenhouses glinting faintly in the moonlight. She opened her purse and took the bag out of it, and got out of the car. She didn't dare open the bag. They were probably dead by now, crushed or suffocated. But what if they weren't, what if they started pleading with her? That would be worse than if they were dead. She stood in the parking lot.

Headlights. Coming out of the tunnel.

Somebody had followed her.

She stood there, holding the bag, frozen in terror, caught in the headlights of the corporate Bentley.

# Chapter 11

W hat are you doing here, Alyson?" Drake said, getting out of the Bentley. He kept the headlights burning on her.

She blinked in the glare. "Why did you follow me?"

"I'm worried about you, Alyson. Very worried."

"I'm fine."

"We have a lot to do." Approaching her.

"What?" She shrank back.

"We have to protect ourselves."

Sharp intake of breath. "What are you planning?"

He couldn't allow the blame to fall on himself. On her, but not on himself. He had begun to form an idea. There was a way to get this done. "There is a reason for their disappearance, you know," he said to her.

"What are you talking about, Vin?"

"A plausible reason why they vanish. A reason other than you and me."

"What's the reason?"

"Alcohol."

"What?"

He grabbed her hand and dragged her toward the greenhouse, saying, "They're penurious students. No money. Always trying to save their pennies. They want to have a party, get wasted, but they don't have any money. So where do poor science students go when they want to get wasted for free?"

"Where?"

"The lab, of course." He unlocked the door, flicked on the lights. The bulbs came on in banks overhead, one after another, down the long expanse of the lab, revealing benches of exotic plants, potted orchids beneath hanging mist-makers; and in the corner, shelf after shelf of bottles and jugs full of reagents. He pulled out a plastic gallon jug labeled 98% ETHANOL.

"What's that?" she said.

"Lab alcohol," he said.

"Is that your idea?"

"Yes," he said. "You buy vodka or tequila at a store, you get seventy, eighty, ninety proof. This stuff here is double that: it's a hundred and ninety-six proof. It's almost pure alcohol."

"And?"

Vin was picking up plastic cups, handing them to her. "Alcohol causes car accidents. Especially among young people."

She groaned. "Uhh, Vin . . ."

He was watching her carefully. "Okay, let's call a spade a spade," he said. "You don't have the stomach for it."

"Well, no—"

"And neither do I. That's the truth."

She blinked, confused. "You don't?"

"No, I don't. I can't stand this, Alyson. I don't want to go through with this," he said. "I don't want this on my conscience."

"Then . . . What will we do?" she said.

He allowed a look of doubt, of uncertainty, to fill his face. "I don't know," he said, shaking his head mournfully. "Probably we never should have started this, and now . . . I just don't know." He hoped his expression of uncertainty was convincing. He knew he could be convincing. He paused, then reached down and took her hand, and held it up to the light; in her hand was the paper bag, rolled up. "They're in there, aren't they?"

"What do you want me to do?" Her hand was shaking.

"Go outside and wait for me," he said. "I need a few minutes to think. We have to come up with a solution to this, Alyson. No more killing."

Let Alyson kill them. Even if she doesn't know she's killing them.

She nodded silently.

"I need your help, Alyson."

"I will," she said. "I'll help you. I will."

"Thank you." Heartfelt.

She went outside.


**He entered the** greenhouse and went to a storage cabinet, where he found a box of nitrile safety gloves. Tough lab gloves, stronger than rubber. He pulled out two gloves and stuffed them in his pocket. Then he hurried into a side office, and turned on the surveillance monitor overlooking the parking lot. It was a night-vision camera, flaring green and black. Of course everything was recorded. He watched as Alyson went outside and stood near the cars.

Looking at the bag and pacing.

He could almost see the idea forming in her mind.

"Do it," Vin whispered.

The field teams had had horrendous problems. Four employees had died in Fern Gully alone. And they had been heavily armed . . . And there was the problem of the bends. These kids wouldn't last an hour in this biological hell. After that, it would be a matter of getting Alyson on his side—temporarily.

She was walking away from the cars.

Yes.

Toward the forest.

Yes.

She went downhill, following the trail down into Fern Gully.

Good. Keep going.

On the monitor, her shape faded into the blackness. She was going downslope, down into the depths of the forest. He lost track of her.

Then a starlike point of light came on.

She had a flashlight; she'd turned it on. Now he watched the light as it went back and forth, getting fainter. She was zigzagging on a switchback trail.

The deeper into biological hell the better.

Suddenly, he heard a scream. Panicked shrieks coming from the darkness of the forest.

"Christ."

He turned away from the monitor and ran outdoors.


**Even though the** moon was up, in the depths of the rain forest it was so dark it was hard to see her. He hurried down the trail, stumbling and slipping, heading toward her flashlight, and heard her saying, "I don't know, I don't know," her voice soft in the gloom. She was shining the beam around.

"Alyson." He paused, waiting for his eyes to adjust. "What don't you know?"

"I don't know what happened."

She was a dark shape holding the bag out in front of her. As if it was an offering from a dark god. "I don't know how they got away. Here: look."

She shone the flashlight on the bag. He saw a jagged cut running along the bottom of the bag. It was a fine cut.

"One of them had a knife," he said.

"I guess."

"And they jumped. Or fell."

"I guess, yes."

"Where?"

"Right around here. I first noticed it here. I haven't moved since. I didn't want to step on them."

"I wouldn't worry about that. They're probably dead already." He took her flashlight, crouched down, swung it along the tops of the ferns. He was looking for disturbances in the shimmering dew that coated the ferns. He saw nothing.

She started to cry.

"It's not your fault, Alyson."

"I know." Sobbing. "I was going to let them go."

"I figured."

"I'm sorry, but I was going to do it."

Vin put his arm around her. "Not your fault, Alyson. That's what matters."

"Did you see any sign of them? With the flashlight?"

"No." He shook his head. "It's a big fall, and they don't have much mass. They could have been blown a considerable distance."

"Then they might still be . . ."

"They might, yes. But it's doubtful."

"We should look for them!"

"But at night, Alyson, we might step on them by accident . . ."

"We can't just leave them here."

"You know, the fall almost certainly killed them. Now, I believe you, Alyson, when you tell me that you didn't cut the bag open and dump them out—"

"What are you saying—?"

"But the police may not believe your story so readily. You could already be implicated in Eric's death, and now this—dumping those kids in the most dangerous place—intentionally. That's murder, Alyson."

"Well, you'll tell the police the truth!"

"Of course," he said, "but why should they believe me, either? The fact is, Alyson, we have only one way to go here, and that is to continue on the plan we started. Their disappearance has to be explained as an accident. Then if they reappear miraculously later on—well, Hawaii is a magical place, wonderful place. Miracles happen here."

She stood very still in the darkness. "We should just leave them?"

"We can look tomorrow, in daylight." He squeezed her shoulder, pulled her close to him. He shone the flashlight down. "Here. Let's follow the path, we can see what's ahead, and we can leave safely. Then we'll come back tomorrow. But right now we have to deal with the car. Okay? One thing at a time, Alyson."

Still sobbing, she allowed herself to be led out of the forest, back to the parking lot. Vin Drake checked his watch: it was 11:14 p.m. There was still time to carry out the next stage of his plan.

# Chapter 12

The students were jostled inside the paper bag, every movement of Alyson's magnified and accompanied by a loud rasping sound as they scraped back and forth across the paper. Peter never realized that ordinary brown paper was so rough: it felt almost like sandpaper to his skin. He saw that the others had all managed to face inward, so they didn't abrade their faces as they slid back and forth. They had been driven somewhere, and it had taken a long time, but where were they? And what would be done to them? It was hard to talk as they fell this way and that, and difficult to come up with a plan when everybody was talking at the same time. The Nanigen man, Jarel Kinsky, kept repeating that there had been some mistake. "If there was some way I could talk with Mr. Drake," Kinsky said.

"Get over it," Karen King snapped at him.

"But I can't believe Mr. Drake would just . . . kill us," Kinsky said.

"Oh, really?" Karen said.

Kinsky didn't answer.

The bigger problem was that they didn't know what Vin or Alyson were up to. They had been driven around in a car, but where had the car ended up? It made no sense. Then Vin and Alyson seemed to reach an agreement (their exact conversation was impossible to follow) and Alyson carried the bag outdoors. Into darkness.

"What's this?" Karen King said, alarmed, as they were carried along. "What's going on?"

They heard a booming sound. It was a snuffle. Alyson Bender.

"I have the feeling she wants to save us," Peter Jansen said.

"Vin will never allow it," Karen said.

"I know."

"I think we better take things into our own hands," Karen said. She produced her knife, unfolded it.

"Now hold on," Danny Minot said. "This is a decision we have to reach together."

"I don't know about that," Karen said. "'Cause I've got the knife."

"Don't be a child," Minot said.

"Don't be a coward. We act, or they act on us and they kill us. Which is it?" She didn't wait for Danny to answer. She turned to Peter. "How far above ground do you think we are, right now?"

"I don't know, maybe four and a half feet . . ."

"Hundred and thirty-seven centimeters," Erika Moll said. "And what's our mass?"

Peter laughed. "Not very much."

"You're laughing," Danny Minot said, amazed. "You people are insane. Compared to our normal size, a drop of four and a half feet is the equivalent of, uh—"

"Four hundred and fifty feet," Erika said. "Say, the height of a forty-five-story building. And no, this would not be the equivalent of a fall from a forty-five-story building."

"Of course it would," Danny said.

"Isn't it great when the science studies people don't know any science?" Erika said.

Peter explained, "It's a little issue of air resistance."

"No, that doesn't matter," Danny said through clenched teeth, clearly stung by the criticism, "because objects fall in a gravitational field at the same rate irrespective of mass. A penny and a piano fall at the same rate, hit the ground at the same time."

"Nothing can be done for him," Karen said. "And we have to make a decision now."

The jostling in the bag had slowed; Alyson was making up her mind to do something.

"I don't think the distance we fall matters very much," Peter Jansen said. He had been trying to figure out the physics of being very small.

It was all about gravity. And inertia.

Peter said: "What's important is Newton's equation for—"

"Enough! I say we jump," Karen interrupted.

"Jump," Jenny said.

"Jump," Amar said.

"Oh God," Danny moaned. "But we don't know where we are!"

"Jump," Erika said.

"This is our only chance," Rick Hutter said. "Jump."

"Jump," Peter said.

"Okay," Karen said. "I'm going to run along this seam at the bottom, and cut it open. Try to stay close together. Imagine you're skydivers. Arms and legs wide, a human kite. Here we gooo—"

"But just a minute—" Danny yelled.

"Too late!" Karen shouted. "Good luck!"

Peter felt her brush past him, the knife in her hand, and a moment later the paper bag tilted beneath his feet, and he fell into darkness.

. . .

**The air was** surprisingly cool and wet. And the night was brighter, now that he was outside the bag: he could see the trees around him, and the ground below as he fell toward it. He fell surprisingly fast—alarmingly fast—and for a moment he wondered if they had collectively made a calculation error, out of their shared dislike for Danny.

They knew, of course, that air resistance was always a factor in the speed of falling objects. In daily life, you didn't think about it, because most things in life presented similar air resistance. A five-pound barbell and a ten-pound barbell would fall at the same rate. Same thing for a human being and an elephant. They'd fall at pretty much the same rate.

But the students were now so small that air resistance did matter, and they had collectively guessed that the effect of air resistance would overcome the effect of mass. In other words, they would not fall at their full-size speed.

They hoped.

Now, with the wind whistling in his ears, tears blurring his eyes as he fell downward, Peter clenched his teeth and wiped his eyes and tried to see where he was headed. He looked around and could not see any of the others falling through the air, though he heard a soft moan in the darkness. Looking back to the ground, he saw he was closing in on a broad-leafed plant, like a giant elephant ear. He tried to spread his arms wide and shift his position so he would hit the leaf in the center.

He hit it perfectly. He smacked into the elephant ear—cold, wet, slippery—and he felt the leaf bend beneath him, then rise back up and in a swift movement toss him back into the air, like a tumbler on a trampoline. He yelled in surprise, and when he came down again he landed near the edge of the leaf, spun, and slid on the water-slick surface down to the far tip.

And fell.

In darkness, he hit another leaf beneath, but it was hard to see down here, and he again rolled down toward the tip of the leaf. He clawed at the green surface, trying to halt his inevitable descent. It was to no avail—he fell—hit another leaf—fell—and finally landed on his back in a bed of wet moss where he lay, gasping and frightened, staring up at the canopy of leaves high above, which blotted out the sky.

**"You just going** to lie there?"

He looked over. It was Karen King, standing over him.

"Are you hurt?" she said.

"No," he said.

"Then get up."

He struggled to his feet. He noticed she didn't help him. He was unsteady standing in the wet moss, which leaked through his sneakers. His feet were cold and wet.

"Stand over here," she said. It was as if she was talking to a child.

He moved to stand beside her, on a patch of dry ground. "Where are the others?"

"Somewhere around here. It may take some time."

Peter nodded, looking at the jungle floor. From his new perspective half an inch above the ground, the jungle floor was incredibly rugged. Moss-covered stumps of rotted limbs rose like skyscrapers, and fallen branches—twigs, really—made ragged arcs twenty or thirty feet above the ground. Even the dead leaves on the floor were larger than he was, and whenever he took a step, they shifted, moving around him and beneath his feet. It was like trying to move through a rotten organic junkyard. And of course everything was wet; everything was slippery, and often slimy. Where, exactly, had they landed? They had been driven around for a long time. They could be anywhere on Oahu—anywhere there was a forest, at least.

Karen jumped up on a large twig, nearly fell off, got her balance, and sat on it, her legs dangling down. Then she put her fingers in her mouth and gave a piercing whistle. "They should all hear that." She whistled again.

Just then something bulky and dark in color crunched out of the undergrowth. At first they couldn't see what it was, but the moonlight revealed a gigantic beetle, jet black, moving past in a sure-footed gait. Its compound eyes gleamed faintly. It was covered with jointed black armor, and had spiky hairs bristling from its legs.

Karen drew her legs up respectfully as the beetle crawled below the twig she was perched on.

Erika Moll pushed her way out through a spray of plant stems, dripping wet. "Well," she said. "It's probably a Metromenus. A ground crawler, it doesn't fly. Don't disturb it—it's a carnivore, it's got jaws, and I'm sure it's got a nasty chemical spray, too."

They didn't want to get drenched with chemicals or become the beetle's next meal. They stopped talking and became very still while the beetle poked along, evidently hunting. Suddenly the beetle charged forward, running remarkably fast, and seized something small in its jaws, which struggled, thrashing around. In the darkness they couldn't see what the beetle had caught, but they could hear crunching sounds as it chopped up its prey. They got a whiff of something sharp and very nasty.

"We are smelling the beetle's defensive chemicals," Erika Moll commented. "It's acetic acid—that's vinegar—and maybe decyl acetate. I believe the bitter stench is benzoquinone. The chemicals are stored in sacs in the beetle's abdomen, and may circulate in the beetle's blood, too."

They watched the beetle move off into the night, dragging its prey. "That's a superior evolutionary design. Better than ours, at least for this place," Erika added.

"Armor, jaws, chemical weaponry, and lots of legs," Peter said.

"Yeah. Way more legs."

Erika said, "Most animals that walk the earth have at least six legs." As she knew, those additional appendages made maneuvering over rough terrain easier. All insects had six legs, and there were close to a million named insect species. Many scientists suspected that another thirty million insects were just waiting to be named, which made the insects the most varied life form on earth, apart from microscopic organisms such as viruses and bacteria. "Insects," Erika said to the others, "have been incredibly successful at colonizing the land areas of the planet."

"We think they look primitive," Peter said. "We think fewer legs is a sign of intelligence. Because we walk on two legs, we think it makes us smarter and better than an animal that walks on four or six legs."

Karen pointed to the underbrush. "Until we face this. And then we want more legs."

They heard a scratching sound and a rotund shape emerged from under a leaf. It looked like a mole, and was rubbing its nose with both hands briskly. "This sucks," it said, spitting dirt. It still wore its tweed jacket.

"Danny?"

"I never agreed to be half an inch tall. Okay, size matters. I already knew that. What are we going to do?"

"For starters, you could stop whining," Karen said to Danny. "We have to formulate a plan. We have to take stock."

"Take stock of what?"

"Our weapons."

"Weapons? What's the matter with you two? We don't have any weapons!" Danny said, starting to shout. "We have nothing."

"That's not true," Karen said calmly. She turned to Peter. "I've got a backpack." She jumped off the twig and grabbed the pack on the ground, lifted it up. "I took it just before Drake shrunk us."

"Did Rick make it?" somebody asked.

"You bet," came a voice from the darkness, somewhere to their left. "This doesn't faze me. And neither does the jungle at night. When I was doing research in the field, in Costa Rica—"

"That's Rick," Peter said. "Anyone else?"

From above, there was a thwap! and the splatter of water droplets. And Jenny Linn slid down a leaf and landed at their feet.

"You took your time," Karen said.

"Got caught on a branch. About ten feet up. Had to work myself free." Jenny sat cross-legged on the ground, and immediately jumped to her feet. "Whoa. Everything's wet."

"It's a rain forest," Rick Hutter said, emerging from foliage behind them. His jeans were drenched. "Everybody okay?" He grinned. "How you doing, Danny boy?"

"Fuck off," Danny said. He was still rubbing his nose.

"Oh come on," Rick said, "get into the spirit of the thing." He pointed to the moonlight, streaking down through the canopy of trees overhead. "We're talking science studies! Isn't this the perfect Conradian moment? An existential confrontation of man facing raw nature, the real heart of darkness unfettered by false beliefs and literary conceits—"

"Somebody tell him to shut up."

"Rick, leave the guy alone," Peter said.

"No, no, not so fast," Rick said, "because this is important. What is it about nature that is so terrifying to the modern mind? Why is it so intolerable? Because nature is fundamentally indifferent. It's unforgiving, uninterested. If you live or die, succeed or fail, feel pleasure or pain, it doesn't care. That's intolerable to us. How can we live in a world so indifferent to us. So we redefine nature. We call it Mother Nature when it's not a parent in any real sense of the term. We put gods in trees and air and the ocean, we put them in our households to protect us. We need these human gods for many things, luck, health, freedom, but one thing above all—one reason stands out—we need the gods to protect us from loneliness. But why is loneliness so intolerable? We can't stand to be alone—why not? Because human beings are children, that's why.

"But those are all disguises we create for nature. You know how Danny loves to tell us that the science narrative privileges the balance of power. How there's no objective truth, except for who's got the power. Power tells the story and everyone accepts it as truth, because power rules." He took a breath. "But who's got the balance of power now, Danny? Can you feel it? Take a deep breath. Feel it? No? Then I'll tell you. The balance of power lies in the hands of the entity that always holds the balance of power—nature. Nature, Danny. Not us. All we can do is go for the ride and try to hang on."

Peter threw his arm around Rick, and steered him away. "That's okay for now, Rick."

"I hate that fucking guy," Rick said.

"We're all a little scared."

"Not me," Rick said, "I'm cool. I love being half an inch tall. That's bite size for a bird, and that's what I am. I'm a freaking hors d'oeuvre for a mynah bird and my chances of surviving another six hours are about one in four, maybe one in five—"

"We must make a plan," Karen said, her voice calm.

Amar Singh appeared around a log to the left, covered with mud, his shirt torn. He seemed remarkably calm. Peter asked, "Everybody okay?"

They said they were.

"The Nanigen guy," Peter said. "Hey Kinsky! Are you around?"

"All along," Jarel Kinsky answered softly, close by. He had been sitting underneath a leaf, his legs drawn up, motionless and saying nothing, watching and listening to the others.

"Are you all right?" Peter asked him.

"You want to keep your voices down," Kinsky said, speaking to the students as a whole. "They can hear better than we can."

"They?" Jenny said.

"Insects."

Silence fell over the group.

"That's better," Kinsky said.

**They began talking** in whispers. Peter said to Kinsky, "Any idea where we are?"

"I think so," Kinsky answered. "Look over there."

They turned and looked. A distant light was shining in that direction, buried in the trees. The light cast a glow down along the corner of a wooden building, just visible through the foliage, and the light reflected off panes of glass.

"That's the greenhouse," Kinsky went on. "We're at the Waipaka Arboretum."

"Oh, God," Jenny Linn said. "We're miles from Nanigen." She sat down on a leaf, and felt something moving under her feet. The movement went on and on, ceaselessly, nudging and bumping at her feet, and then something small crawled up her leg. She plucked it off and tossed it away. It was a soil mite, an eight-legged creature, and harmless. She realized that the soil was full of tiny organisms, all going about their business. "The ground is alive under our feet," she said.

Peter Jansen knelt down, brushed a small worm from his knee, and faced Jarel Kinsky. "What do you know about being shrunk like this?"

"The term is 'dimensionally changed,'" Kinsky answered. "I've never been dimensionally changed, until now. Of course I've talked with the field teams."

Rick Hutter broke in, "I wouldn't trust anything this guy says. He's loyal to Drake."

"Wait," Peter said calmly. "What are the 'field teams'?" he asked Kinsky.

"Nanigen has been sending teams into the micro-world. Three people on a team," Kinsky answered in a whisper. He seemed very afraid of making noise. "They're dimensionally changed, half an inch tall. They operate the digging machinery and collect samples. They live in the supply stations."

Jenny Linn said, "You mean those tiny tents we saw?"

"Yes. The teams never stay here for more than forty-eight hours. You begin to get sick if you stay changed for much longer than that."

"Sick? What do you mean?" Peter asked.

"You get the micro-bends," Kinsky said.

"Micro-bends?" Peter said.

"It's an illness that develops in people who are dimensionally changed. The first symptoms appear in about three to four days."

"What happens?"

"Well—we have some data on the disease, not much. The safety staff began testing animals in the tensor generator. They shrank mice, at first. They kept the shrunken mice in tiny flasks and studied them with a microscope. After a few days, all the shrunken mice died. The mice were hemorrhaging. Next, they shrank rabbits and finally dogs. Again, the animals died with hemorrhages. Necropsies of the animals, after they'd been restored to normal size, showed that there was generalized bleeding at sites of injury. Small cuts bled profusely, and there was internal bleeding, as well. It was discovered that the blood of the animals lacked clotting factors. Essentially, the animals had died of hemophilia—that's the inability of the blood to form clots. We think that the size-change disrupts enzymatic pathways in the clotting process, but we don't really know. But we also found that an animal could live for a short while in a shrunken state, as long as the animal was brought back to normal size within a couple of days. We began calling the illness micro-bends, because it reminded us of the bends in scuba diving.

As long as an animal's time in the shrunken state was limited, the animal seemed to be healthy.

"Next, there were several human volunteers, including the man who'd designed the tensor generator. His name was Rourke, I think. Humans could live for a few days in the micro-world with no ill effects, it seemed. But then there was . . . an accident. The generator broke down and we lost three scientists. They got trapped in the micro-world and couldn't be returned to normal size. One of the fatalities was the guy who designed the generator. Since then, we've had other . . . problems. If a person is stressed or suffers a major injury, the micro-bends can come on very suddenly, and sooner than usual. So we have lost . . . more . . . employees. That's why Mr. Drake halted operations while we try to learn how to keep people from dying in the micro-world. You see, Mr. Drake really does care about safety . . ."

"What's the disease like in humans?" Rick interrupted.

Kinsky went on. "It begins with bruises, especially on your arms and legs. If you have a cut you can bleed endlessly. It's like hemophilia—you can bleed to death from a small cut. At least that's what I'm hearing. But they're keeping the details pretty quiet," Kinsky said. "I just run the generator."

"Is there any treatment?" Peter asked.

"The only treatment is decompression. Get the person restored to full size as soon as possible."

"We're in trouble . . ." Danny murmured.

"We need to do an inventory of our assets now," Karen said decisively. She laid the backpack she'd grabbed in the generator room on top of a dead leaf. With only the moonlight to see by, she opened the pack and spread various things out on the leaf as if it were a table. They gathered around and checked the contents carefully. The backpack contained a first-aid kit, including antibiotics and basic medications; a knife; a short length of rope; a reel, rather like a fishing reel, which was attached to a belt; a windproof lighter; a silver space blanket; a thin waterproof tent; a water-backpacker's headlamp. There was also a pair of headsets with throat mikes attached to them.

"Those are two-way radios," Kinsky said. "For communicating with headquarters."

There was also a very-fine-mesh ladder; and keys or starter controls for some kind of machine not present. Karen put everything but the lamp back into the pack and zipped it shut.

"Pretty useless," Karen said, getting to her feet and putting on the headlamp. She switched it on, casting the light around, playing it over the plants and leaves. "We really need weapons."

"Your light—please turn it off—" Kinsky muttered. "It attracts things—"

"What kind of weapons do we need?" Amar asked Karen.

"Say," Danny interrupted, as if something had just occurred to him. "Are there poisonous snakes in Hawaii?"

"No," Peter said. "There are no snakes at all."

"Not many scorpions, either, certainly not in the rain forest. It's too wet for them here," Karen King added. "There is a Hawaiian centipede that can deliver a nasty sting to a human being. It could certainly kill us at our present dimension. In fact, a great many animals can kill us. Birds, toads, all sorts of insects, ants, wasps, and hornets—"

"You were talking about weapons, Karen," Peter said.

"We need some kind of projectile weapon," Karen said, "something that can kill at a distance—"

"A blowgun," Rick broke in.

Karen shook her head. "Nah. It would be a tenth of an inch long. No good."

"Wait, Karen. I could use a hollow piece of bamboo, I could use it full-size, half an inch long."

Peter said, "And a wooden dart to fit in it."

"Sure," Rick said. "The dart sharpened by—"

"Heat," Amar said, "as the tempering agent. But for poison—"

"Curare," Peter said, getting up, looking around. "I bet lots of plants around here have—"

Rick interrupted, "That's my specialty. If we could make a fire, we could boil bark and plant materials, and extract poison. And especially if we can find some piece of metal, iron . . . to make a dart point . . ."

"My belt buckle?" Amar said.

"And then what?"

"Boil the stuff. Then test it."

"That takes a long time."

"It's the only way."

"What about using the skin of a frog?" Erika Moll said. In the night, they heard the croaking of what seemed to be bullfrogs all around them.

Peter shook his head. "We don't have the right kind here. What you're hearing are bufos, large toads. They're the size of your fist. Well, your old fist. They're gray, not brightly colored. They do manufacture unpleasant skin toxins, they're called bufotenins, not curare-based compounds of the Central American—"

"All right, for Christ's sake!" Danny snapped.

"Just explaining . . ."

"We get the picture!"

Erika put her arm around Peter's shoulder, nodded to Danny. He was still fussing with his nose, scratching at it with both hands, holding them curved as if they were little paws.

As if he were a mole.

"Cracking up?" Erika whispered fearfully.

Peter nodded.

Amar said, "To continue, the poison you recommend . . ."

Watching Danny, Peter said, "Bark scrapings of Strychnos tox-ifera tree, add oleander, sap not leaf, include Chondrodendron to-mentosum if it's available, boil the mixture for at least twenty-four hours."

"Let's get started," Karen King said.

"We could find these plants a lot more easily in the morning light," Jenny Linn said. "What's the rush?"

"The rush," Karen said, "is those halogen lamps back at the en-trance. Right now Vin Drake could be heading here to kill us." She swung the pack over her shoulders and tightened the straps. "So let's get started."

# Chapter 13

## ALAPUNA ROAD
## 29 OCTOBER, 2:00 A.M.

In bright moonlight, they hadn't much cover. The dense hau bush that clung to the cliff side stopped at the level of the dirt road, and it was only too easy to see the two cars driving along the narrow volcanic ridge. To the left, the land sloped down gently to agricultural fields. To the right, a steep cliff ended at crashing surf on the north shore of Oahu.

Alyson drove the first car, the Bentley convertible. Whenever she hesitated, Vin Drake waved her on from the second car, the BMW. They still had a distance to go to reach the washed-out bridge. Finally he could see it in the moonlight, cream-colored concrete from the 1920s; amazing it had lasted that long.

Alyson stopped and started to get out of the car. "No, no," he said, waving her back in. "You have to dress it."

"Dress it?"

"Yes. The students are all jammed into the Bentley, remember? They're partying." He was carrying a laundry bag full of clothes and other items he'd collected from what the students had left in the front office and in the Bentley parked at Nanigen: several phones, shorts, T-shirts, bathing suits, a towel, a couple of rolled-up issues of *Nature* and *Science*, a tablet computer—she started tossing the things at random around the car.

"No, no," he said. "Alyson, please. We have to decide where everyone was sitting."

"I'm nervous."

"Very well, we still have to do it."

"It'll all get messed up when you push it over the cliff."

"Alyson. We still have to do it."

"But the police . . . the bodies will be missing. They won't be in the car . . ."

"The water is full of rip currents. And sharks. The sea swallows the dead. That's why we're doing it this way, Alyson."

"Okay, okay," she answered wearily. "Who's back rear?"

"Danny."

She got out a sweater and a well-thumbed Conrad novel, *Chance*. "Are you sure, Vin? Seems like a setup."

"Has his name in it."

"All right. Who's next to him?"

"Jenny. She feels sorry for him."

A delicate printed scarf, a belt of white python, shoved back.

"Expensive. Isn't that illegal?"

"Python? Just in California."

Then Peter Jansen's glasses, a pair he was always losing; Erika Moll's bathing suit; and a pair of board shorts.

They went on to finish dressing the front seat, with Karen King driving. Then Vin Drake splashed lab alcohol over the back of the car, cracked the bottle, dropped it in the front, where it would catch under the dashboard.

"Don't want to overdo it." He looked around, at the fleecy clouds in dark blue, the white surf far below. "Beautiful night," he said, shaking his head. "Beautiful world we live in." He walked to the left side of the car and surveyed it from a distance. "There's a downslope just ahead," he said. "Drive a few yards until you hit the downslope, and then you can get out and we can push the rest."

"Hey." Alyson held up her hands. "I, uh . . . I don't want to get in there again, Vin."

"Don't be silly. We're talking ten feet of driving. Just ten feet."

"But what if something—"

"Nothing will happen."

"Why don't you drive to the downslope, Vin?"

"Alyson." A firm eye in the darkness. "I'm taller, I'd have to move the seat back, it would look suspicious in a police investigation."

"But—"

"We agreed." He opened the door for her. "Come on, now."

She hesitated.

"We agreed, Alyson."

She got behind the wheel, shivering despite the evening warmth.

"Now put up the top," he said.

"The top? Why?" she asked.

"To keep everything in the car."

She turned on the engine, pressed a button, and the Bentley's top rose and folded over. Vin stood some distance away, and with his hand indicated for her to move the car forward. The car tilted downward, slid a few feet—she yelped—then it skidded to a stop.

"Okay, perfect," Vin said, reaching into his pocket for the nitrile lab gloves. "Keep it there. In park, engine on."

He came forward, and she started to get out. She didn't hear the snapping sounds as he drew on the gloves. In a swift movement he slammed the door shut, locked it, reached in through the window, and grabbed her by the hair with both hands. He slammed her head against the metal of the windshield frame, where there was less padding. She started to scream but he pounded her head again and again. Then he banged her forehead on the steering wheel a few times to be sure. She was still conscious but that wouldn't matter for long. He reached across her back and jerked the car into drive. It was awkward. He fell backward as the Bentley rolled past him, over the broken bridge, and then twisting, dropping six hundred feet to the river and ocean below.

Drake scrambled to his feet. He was too late to see the impact. Yet he heard it, the rending of metal against stone. The convertible had landed upside down, and he watched for a while, to see if there was any movement from beneath. One wheel spun loosely, but otherwise nothing. "Trust is everything, Alyson," he said softly, and turned away, peeling off the gloves.


**He had left** his own car a hundred yards back, and the dirt path was rock-hard, dry, and would take no tire impressions. He got in his car and backed slowly down the narrow path—no mistakes now!— until he found a space wide enough to turn his car around. Then he headed south, back to Honolulu. It would be several days before the police discovered the fallen car, and he should probably hurry things along. He'd call in the morning to report that his graduate students were missing and he was worried about them. They'd been taken for a night on the town by the lovely Ms. Alyson Bender.

As for wider publicity, reaching back to Cambridge and Boston, Vin Drake had few fears. Hawaii would be helpful in this regard. Hawaii was a tourist destination, traditionally reluctant to report how many visitors died from rogue waves, strong surf, crumbling hiking trails, and the other attractions of the beautiful outdoors. The Cambridge story would play for a few days, particularly since several of the kids were attractive, but inevitably it would be replaced by juicier fare: Austrian princess dies in helicopter skiing on Mount Rainier; divers lost off Tasmania; Texas millionaire dies at Khumbu base camp; freak CinqueTerra accident; tourist eaten by giant Komodo lizard.

There was always juicier news. It would pass.

Of course, there would be difficulties inside the company itself. This visit was to have been a major addition to Nanigen staffing, a very needed addition, too, because of the recent losses of staff. And therefore it would have been a major boost to his company. He would have to finesse this matter with skill.

The sports car scraped and lurched along the dirt road; he gripped the wheel firmly. He was heading south to Kaena Point ("where souls leave the planet") and the surf raged up on both sides of the trail. He made a mental note to wash the salt water off his car and tires. Better to take it to a standard car wash over in Pearl City.

He checked his watch. Three thirty a.m.

Oddly enough, he felt no urgency, no nervousness. There was time enough to get back to the other side of the island, to Waikiki, near Diamond Head. And time enough to check the kids' hotel rooms for artifacts, scientific *objets* they had brought with them.

And then plenty of time for Vin to drive back to his own luxurious apartment on the Kahala side, and slide into bed. So he could awaken shocked to learn of the absurd behavior of his chief financial officer and the talented students she had led astray.

# PART II

# A BAND OF HUMANS

# Chapter 14

The seven students and Kinsky walked through the forest single-file, listening, watching, steeped in darkness and deep shadow, and enveloped in alien sounds. As Rick Hutter moved along, stumbling his way among leaves on the ground and scrambling under dead branches that seemed bigger than fallen redwoods, he held a homemade grass spear across his shoulder. Karen King wore the backpack, and kept her knife gripped in her hand. Peter Jansen led the group on point, peering around, trying to pick a route. Somehow, in his quiet way, Peter Jansen had become the leader. They were not using the headlamp, for they didn't want to attract any predators. Peter couldn't see much of the terrain in front of him. "The moon has gone down," he said.

"Dawn must be—" Jenny Linn began.

A terrible cry drowned her out. It began as a low wail and rose into a series of throaty shrieks, coming from the depths somewhere above. It was an eerie sound, dripping with violence.

Rick spun around, holding his spear up. "What the hell was that?"

"A bird singing, I think," Peter said. "We're hearing sounds at a lower pitch." He looked at his watch: 4:15 a.m. It was a digital watch. It was running normally, even when shrunk. "Dawn's coming," he said.

"If we could find a supply station, we could try to call Nanigen on the radio," Jarel Kinsky suggested. "If they heard our signal, they would rescue us."

"Drake would kill us," Peter said.

Kinsky didn't argue, but it was clear he didn't agree with Peter.

Peter went on, "We have to get ourselves into the tensor generator, so that we can be restored to full size. To do that, we have to get back to Nanigen. Somehow. But I think it would be a mistake to ask Drake for help."

"Can we call 911?" Danny broke in.

"Great idea, Danny. Just tell us how," Rick said scornfully.

Jarel Kinsky explained that the radios in the supply stations only had a range of about a hundred feet. "If somebody from Nanigen is nearby and listening at the right frequency, they can communicate with us. Otherwise nobody will pick up our signal." And the radios, he explained, didn't broadcast on any frequency that the police or emergency services used, anyway. "The Nanigen micro-sized radios broadcast at around seventy gigahertz," Kinsky explained. "That's a very high frequency. It works well for the field teams over short distances, but it's useless for long-distance communication."

Jenny Linn said, "When Drake was showing us around the arboretum, he mentioned there's a shuttle truck that goes to Nanigen from here, from Manoa Valley. We could stow away on the truck."

Everybody fell silent. Jenny had come up with what sounded like a good idea. Indeed, as they thought about it, Vin Drake had mentioned a shuttle truck. But if the field teams had been withdrawn from the micro-world, would the shuttle still be running?

Peter turned to Jarel Kinsky. "Is the shuttle truck still making runs to Nanigen, do you know?"

"I don't know."

"What time does the truck normally arrive at the arboretum?"

"Two o'clock," Kinsky answered.

"Where does it stop?"

"The parking lot. Next to the greenhouse."

Everybody absorbed that, thinking about it.

"I think Jen's right. We should try to get on that truck," Peter said. "Get ourselves back to Nanigen, then try to get into the tensor generator—"

"Wait—how the hell are we going to climb up onto a truck when we're this small?" Rick Hutter demanded. He faced Peter Jansen. "It's a crazy plan. What if there's no truck? Nanigen is fifteen miles from here. We're a hundred times smaller than we used to be. Think about it. It means that one mile is like a hundred miles for us. If it's fifteen miles from here to Nanigen, that's really like *fifteen hundred* miles for us. Basically we have to do what Lewis and Clark did. And we have to do it in less than four days or we'll die of the bends. It's a shitty bet, guys."

"Rick's idea is to wring his hands and give up," Karen said.

Rick turned on her angrily. "We need to get practical—"

"You're not being practical. You're whining," Karen said to him.

Peter tried to defuse the argument. He put himself between Rick and Karen, figuring he could make himself a target of their wrath rather than let them continue to pick at each other. "Please," he said, putting his hand on Rick's shoulder. "Arguing isn't going to help anybody. Let's take things one step at a time."

The group set off again, walking in silence.

**Half an inch tall** on the forest floor, they had difficulty seeing much of anything, even as the sun rose. Ferns, thick and abundant, grew everywhere, and were especially difficult to deal with, for they blocked the view and created deep shadows. They lost sight of the greenhouse building, and couldn't find any recognizable landmarks. Still, they kept moving. The sun broke forth, and beams of light slanted through the forest canopy.

In the daylight, they saw the soil more clearly. It was churning with small organisms—nematode worms, soil mites, and other little, abundant creatures. This is what Jenny Linn had felt wriggling against her feet in the dark. The soil mites were very small, spiderlike creatures of many different species, crawling around or hiding in cracks in the soil. The mites would have been almost invisible to the naked eye of a normal-size person, but in relation to the micro-humans the soil mites were much larger. To the micro-humans, the mites appeared to be anywhere from the size of grains of rice up to the size of golf balls. Many of the mites had small, egg-shaped bodies covered with thick armor and spiky hairs. The mites were arachnids; Karen King, the arachnologist, kept stopping to gaze at them. She didn't recognize a single mite; they all seemed to be unknown, a vast number of different kinds of mites. She couldn't get over the richness of nature: here was biodiversity as far as the eye could see. The mites were everywhere. They reminded her of crabs on a rocky seashore: small and harmless, busy and scuttling, carrying on their small, hidden lives. She picked up a mite and set it down on the palm of her hand.

The creature seemed so delicate, so perfect. Karen felt her spirits lifting. What was going on? To her surprise, she realized that she felt happy in this strange new world. "I don't know why," she said, "but I feel like I've been searching all my life to find a place like this. It's like I'm coming home."

"Not me," Danny said.

The mite walked up Karen's arm, exploring it.

"Watch out, it could bite you," Jenny Linn said.

"Not this little guy," Karen answered. "See his mouth parts? They're adapted for sucking up detritus—dead stuff. He eats crud."

"How do you know it's a he?"

Karen pointed to the mite's abdomen. "Penis."

"A guy's a guy, no matter how small," Jenny remarked.

As they hiked along Karen grew animated. "Mites are incredible. They're highly specialized. Many mites are parasites, and they're particular about their hosts. There's a kind of mite that lives only on the eyeballs of a certain fruit bat—nowhere else. There's another mite that lives only on the anus of a sloth—"

"Please, Karen!" Danny erupted.

"Get over it, Danny, it's just nature. About half of all people on earth have mites living in their eyelashes. Many insects get mites on them, too. In fact, there are mites that live on other mites—so even mites get mites."

Danny sat down and pulled a mite off his ankle. "Little monster chewed a hole in my sock."

"Must be a detritus eater," Jenny said.

"That's not funny, Jenny."

"Anybody want to try my natural latex skin cream?" Rick Hutter said. "Maybe it'll keep the mites off."

They stopped and Rick took out a plastic lab bottle, and passed it around. They rubbed small amounts of the cream on their faces, hands, and cuffs. It had a pungent smell. And it worked. It did seem to repel mites.


**For Amar Singh,** the reality of the micro-world seemed to assault his senses. He noted that being small even changed the sensations he felt on his skin. His first impression of the micro-world involved the feeling of air flowing over his face and hands, tugging at his shirt and ruffling his hair. The air seemed thicker, almost syrupy, and he could feel every ripple of breeze as the air coiled and flowed around his body. He waved his arm, and felt the air sliding between his fingers. Moving through the air in the micro-world was a bit like swimming. Because their bodies were so small, the friction of air passing over their bodies became more pronounced. Amar staggered a little, feeling a puff of air pushing him sideways. "We're going to have to get our sea legs in this place," he said to the others. "It's like learning how to walk all over again." The others were having similar difficulties: staggering, feeling the air tugging at them, and sometimes miscalculating the steps they took. Trying to jump up on something, they would jump too far. Their bodies were clearly stronger in the micro-world, but they hadn't learned how to control their movements.

It felt like moonwalking.

"We don't know our own strength," Jenny said. She gathered herself, leaped high, and grabbed the edge of a leaf in both hands. She hung by her hands for a moment, then from only one hand—it was easy. She let go and fell back to the ground.

Rick Hutter had taken a turn wearing the backpack. Though it was loaded with gear, he discovered he could jump up and down pretty easily even with the pack on—and he got himself fairly high in the air without much effort. "Our bodies are stronger and lighter in this world, because gravity's no big deal here."

"Small has its advantages," Peter remarked.

"I don't see them," Danny Minot said.

As for Amar Singh, a feeling of dread crept over him. What lived among these leaves? Meat-eaters. They were many-legged animals with jointed armor and unusual ways to kill prey. Amar had been raised in a devout Hindu family—his parents, immigrants from India who'd settled in New Jersey, did not eat meat. He had seen his father open a window and chase a fly out rather than kill it. Amar had always been a vegetarian; he had never been able to eat animals for protein. He believed that all animals were capable of suffering, including insects. In the laboratory, he worked with plants, not animals. Now, in the jungle, he wondered if he would have to kill an animal and eat its meat in order to survive. Or whether an animal would eat him. "We're protein," Amar said. "That's all we are. Just protein."

"What's that supposed to mean?" Rick asked him.

"We're meat walking on two legs."

"You sound kind of gloomy, Amar."

"I'm being a realist."

"At least . . . it's interesting," Jenny Linn remarked. Jenny noted the smell of the micro-world: it had a smell all its own. A complicated earthy scent filled her nose, and it wasn't bad, actually quite nice, in a way. It was an odor of soil mixed with a thousand unknown scents, some sweet, some musky, drifting in the liquid air. Many of the smells were pleasant, even lovely, like exquisite perfumes.

"We're smelling pheromones, the signaling chemicals that animals and plants use for communication," Jenny said to the others. "It's the invisible language of nature." It lifted her spirits—here, she could experience the full spectrum of scents in the natural world for the first time. This revelation both thrilled her and made her feel afraid.

Jenny held a chunk of soil up to her nose and sniffed it. It was teeming with tiny nematode worms and numerous mites and several plump little creatures called water bears, and it smelled faintly like antibiotics. She knew why: the soil was full of bacteria, and many of the bacteria were different kinds of Streptomyces. "You can smell Streptomyces," Jenny said to the others. "They're one of the types of bacteria that make antibiotics. Modern antibiotics are derived from them." The soil was also laced with thin threads of fungus known as hyphae. Jenny pulled a fungal thread out of the soil: it was stiff but slightly stretchy. A cubic inch of soil could hold several miles of these threads of fungus.

Something drifted past Jen's eyes, falling downward through the thick air. It was a small nugget the size of a peppercorn, studded with knobs. "What on earth is that?" she said, stopping in her tracks to watch it. The nugget landed at her feet. Another fell slowly past. She put out her hand and caught it in her palm, then rolled it between thumb and forefinger. It was tough and hard, like a small nut. "It's pollen," she said with wonder. She looked up. There was a hibiscus tree overhead, bursting into a profusion of white flowers, like a cloud. For some reason she could not explain, her heart leaped at the sight of it. For a few moments, Jenny Linn felt glad to be very small.

"I think it's kind of . . . wonderful here," Jenny said, turning slowly around, looking up at the clouds of flowers, while a steady snow of pollen fell around her. "I never imagined this."

"Jenny, we need to keep moving." Peter Jansen had stopped to wait for her, and was shepherding people along.

As for Erika Moll, the entomologist, she did not feel happy at all. She was experiencing a growing sensation of fear. She knew enough about insects to be extremely afraid of them right now. They have armor and we don't, Erika thought. Their armor is made of chitin. It's bioplastic armor, light and super-tough. She ran her fingers over her arm, feeling the delicacy of her skin, the downy hair. We're soft, she thought. We're edible. She didn't say anything to the others, but felt a choking sense of terror seething below the surface of her calm. She was afraid her fear would betray her, that she would lose control of herself in a panic. Erika Moll compressed her lips, and clenched her hands, and, trying to keep her fear under control, kept walking.

**Peter Jansen called** for a halt. They rested, sitting on the edges of leaves. Peter wanted to pick Jarel Kinsky's brain. Kinsky knew a lot about the tensor generator, since he operated it. If they could somehow get themselves back to Nanigen, and could get themselves inside the tensor generator room, would they be able to operate the machine? How would they do it, if they were tiny? Peter asked Kinsky, "Would we need to get help from a normal-size person to run the machine?"

Kinsky looked doubtful. "I'm not sure," he said, and poked at the ground with a grass spear. "I heard a rumor that the man who designed the tensor generator put a small-size emergency control in it that a micro-human can operate. I presume this tiny control panel is somewhere in the control room. I've looked for it, but I've never found it. There's nothing in the engineering drawings, either. But if we could find the tiny control panel, I can operate it."

"We'll need your help," Peter said.

Kinsky lifted the spear from the soil and gazed at a mite that walked along the spear, waving its forelegs. "All I want is to get home to my family," he said softly, and shook his spear, tossing the mite away.

"Your boss couldn't care less about your family," Rick Hutter snapped at Kinsky.

"Rick doesn't have a family," Danny Minot whispered to Jenny Linn. "He doesn't even have a girlf—"

Rick lunged at Danny, who scrambled away, shouting, "You can't solve a problem with violence, Rick!"

"It would solve you," Rick muttered.

Peter took Rick by the shoulder and squeezed it, restraining him, as if to say, Stay cool. To Kinsky he said, "Are there any other possibilities for getting back to Nanigen? Besides the shuttle truck, which might not exist."

Kinsky bowed his head, thinking. After some time he said: "Well—we could try to get to Tantalus Base."

"What's Tantalus Base?"

"It's a bioprospecting facility in Tantalus Crater, on the mountain ridge above this valley." Kinsky pointed vaguely toward the mountain, which was only a green shape, barely visible through gaps in the tangled forest. "The base is somewhere up there."

Jenny Linn said, "Vin Drake mentioned Tantalus during the tour."

"I remember," Karen said.

"Is the base open?" Peter asked Kinsky.

"I don't think so. People died at Tantalus. There were predators."

"What kind?" Karen demanded.

"Wasps, I heard. But," Kinsky went on musingly, "there *were* micro-planes at Tantalus Base."

"Micro-planes?"

"Small aircraft. Our size."

"Could we fly to Nanigen?"

"I don't know what the range of these aircraft is," Kinsky answered. "I don't know if any of them were left at the base."

"How far above us is Tantalus Base?"

"It's two thousand feet above Manoa Valley," Kinsky answered.

"Two thousand feet up!" Rick Hutter exploded. "That's . . . impossible for people our size."

Kinsky shrugged. The others said nothing.

Peter Jansen took charge. "Okay, here's what I think we should do. First, let's try to find a supply station and take what we can from it. Then we'll try to get to the parking lot. We'll wait there for the shuttle truck. We have to get back there as soon as possible."

"It's obvious we're going to die," Danny Minot said, his voice cracking.

"We can't just do nothing, Danny," Peter said, trying to keep his voice even-sounding. He sensed Danny could break down into a panic at the drop of a hat, and that would be dangerous for the whole group.

The others went along with Peter's plan, some of them grumbling—but nobody had a better idea. They took turns drinking water from a dewdrop on a leaf, and began moving again, looking for a trail, a tent, or any trace of human presence. Small plants near the ground arched over them, sometimes forming tunnels. They wound their way through the tunnels, and wandered past the trunks of stupendous trees. But there was no sign of a supply station.

"Okay, so we're going to bleed to death if we don't get the hell out of here fast," Rick Hutter said, as they hiked along. "And we can't find a damn supply station. Plus we've got a psychopathic giant looking to kill us. And I've got a blister. Is there anything else I need to worry about?" he asked, sounding very sarcastic.

"Ants," Kinsky replied calmly.

"Ants?" Danny Minot broke in, his voice quavering. "What about ants?"

"Ants are a problem, I've heard," Kinsky answered.

**Rick Hutter stopped** in front of a large yellow fruit lying on the ground. He looked up and all around. "Yes!" he said. "That's a chinaberry tree. Melia azederach. The berry is highly poisonous, especially to insects and insect larvae. It contains around twenty-five different volatiles, principally 1-cinnamoyl compounds. This berry is absolute death to insects. It can be an ingredient for my curare." He took off the backpack and stuffed the chinaberry into it. The berry filled much of the pack, and loomed out of the top of the pack, a bright yellow ovoid, sort of like a giant melon.

Karen glared at him. "It's going to leak poison."

"Nope." Rick grinned and tapped on the yellow berry. "Tough skin."

Karen gave Rick a skeptical look. "It's your life," she said curtly. The group moved on.

**Danny Minot kept** falling behind. His face had gotten red, and he kept wiping his forehead with his hands. Finally he took off his sport coat and threw it to the ground. His tassel loafers had gotten coated with mud. He sat on a leaf and started scratching inside his shirt, and pulled out a single pollen grain, and held it between thumb and forefinger. "Does anybody know I have serious allergies? If one of these objects gets up my nose I could go into shock."

Karen gave a scornful laugh. "You aren't that allergic! If you were, you'd be dead by now."

Danny flicked it away, and the grain danced off, spinning as it drifted through the air.

Amar Singh couldn't get over the profusion of life, the small creatures that seemed to exist in every nook and cranny of the micro-world. "Gosh! I wish we had a camera. I want to document this."

They were young scientists, and the micro-world revealed a wonderland of unknown life. They suspected they were seeing creatures that had never been noticed or given names. "You could get a dissertation out of every square foot of this place," Amar remarked. He began thinking he would do just that. He could get himself one incredible PhD out of this trip. If I survive, he reminded himself.

Little torpedo-shaped creatures with jointed bodies and six legs were crawling about on the ground. They were quite small and were all over the place. Some were sucking up strands of fungus as if they were eating spaghetti. As the humans walked along, every now and then one of these creatures would get startled, make a loud snapping noise, and flip high into the air, spinning end over end.

Erika Moll stopped to examine one of them; she picked it up and held it, while it struggled, snapping its tail with vigorous clicking sounds.

"What are these things?" Rick asked, pulling one out of his hair.

"They're called springtails," Erika Moll said. In the normal world, she explained, springtails are extremely small. "No bigger than the dot over an *i* on a page of text," she said. The animal had a spring mechanism in its abdomen, she explained, that propelled it long distances, helping it escape from predators. As if on cue, the springtail flung itself off her hand, soaring into the air and out of sight beyond a fern.

Springtails kept bouncing into the air as they moved along, disturbed by their footsteps. Peter Jansen led the way. Sweat dripped from his body. He realized their bodies were losing moisture fast.

"We need to make sure we drink enough water," he said to the others. "We could dry out really fast." They found a clump of moss hung with droplets of dew, and they gathered around it. They drank from dewdrops, cupping the water in their hands. The surface of the water was sticky, and they had to swat the water to break the surface tension. As Peter lifted a bit of water to his mouth, it heaped up into a blob in his hands.

**They came to** a massive tree trunk. It soared up from a sprawling buttress of roots. As they worked their way around the roots, a sharp smell became apparent. They began to hear thrumming, tapping sounds, like rain falling. Peter, who was leading the way, climbed on top of a root and came in sight of a pair of low walls, snaking across the ground and out of sight. The walls were made of bits of dirt stuck together with some kind of dried substance.

Between the walls a column of ants was moving, streaming in both directions. The walls protected an ant highway. In one spot, the walls extended into a tunnel.

Peter crouched down and motioned to the others to stop. They moved forward cautiously, until they were lying on their stomachs and looking down on the ant column. Were the ants dangerous? Each ant was nearly as long as his forearm. Not *that* big, Peter thought; and he felt relieved, for somehow he had expected ants to be much larger than this. But there were certainly a lot of them. They flowed swiftly by the hundreds along their road and through the little tunnel they'd built.

Their bodies were reddish brown in color, and prickly with hair. Their heads were shining black, as black as coal. The odor of the ants drifted from the ant highway like exhaust coming from freeway traffic. The smell was tart and acidic, yet perfumed with a delicate fragrance. "That sharp smell is formic acid. It's a defense," Erika Moll explained, as she knelt down, watching the ants with great intensity.

Jenny Linn said, "The sweet smell is a pheromone. It's probably the colony scent. The ants use that scent to identify each other as members of the same colony."

Erika continued, "They're all females. They're all daughters of their queen."

Some of the ants were carrying dead insects or pieces of dismembered insects. The food carriers were all traveling in the same direction along the highway, toward the left. "The nest entrance is that way. It's where they're carrying the food," Erika added, pointing to the left.

"Do you know the species?" Peter asked her.

Erika searched her mind for the name. "Um . . . Hawaii doesn't have any native ants. All ants in Hawaii are invading species. They've arrived here with humans. I'm pretty sure these ones are Pheidole megacephala."

"Do they have a name in English?" Rick asked. "I'm just an ignorant ethnobotanist."

"It's called the bigheaded ant," Erika went on. "It was found originally on the island of Mauritius, in the Indian Ocean, but it's now spread all over the world. It's the most common ant in Hawaii." The bigheaded ant had turned out to be one of the most destructive invasive insects on the planet, Erika explained. "The bigheaded ants have done a lot of damage to the ecosystem of these islands," she said. "They attack and kill native Hawaiian insects. They've nearly wiped out some Hawaiian insect species. They also kill nesting baby birds."

"That doesn't sound good for us," Karen said. A baby bird, she realized, would be much larger than they were as micro-humans.

"I don't see what's big about their heads," Danny remarked.

Erika said, "These ones are minor workers. The majors have the big heads."

"Majors?" Danny asked nervously. "What are they?"

"The majors are soldiers," Erika went on. "The bigheaded ant has two castes—minors and majors. The minors are workers. They're small and plentiful. The majors are the warriors, the guards. They're large and uncommon."

"So what do the big-headed soldiers look like?"

Erika shrugged. "Big heads."

There were so many ants, and each ant seemed filled with inhuman energy. One ant by itself certainly didn't pose a danger, but thousands of them . . . excited . . . hungry . . . Despite the threat, the young scientists couldn't help gazing at the ants with fascination. Two ants stopped and tapped their antennae together, and then one of the ants began wagging its rear end and making a rattling sound. The other ant obligingly vomited a droplet of liquid into the other's mouthparts. Erika explained what was going on: "She was begging food from her nest-mate. She wagged her rear end and made those scratchy sounds to say she was hungry. It's the ant's version of a dog's whine—"

Danny interrupted. "I fail to see the joy of watching an ant blow lunch into another ant's mouth. Let's go, please."

The ant highway wasn't very wide. They could have easily jumped over it, but they decided to avoid the ant column rather than risk trouble. As Peter put it, "We don't want an ant to latch on to someone's ankle."

Jarel Kinsky had stopped, and he was staring up at the branches of the great buttressed tree, which soared over their heads. "I know this tree," he said. "It's a giant albesia tree. There's a supply station on the other side of it, I'm pretty sure." He clambered up onto a root, and walked along the root for a distance, and hopped down. "Yes," he said. "I think we're getting close." Kinsky took over the lead from Peter, and began heading toward the left around the albesia tree, pushing his way through dead fern leaves, striking at things with a grass-stem spear, knocking leaves and plants aside.

Peter Jansen dropped back to the rear. He had not liked the look of the ants and wanted to keep an eye on them as the group moved along. Rick Hutter was the last in line, moving slowly with the pack on his back, carrying the chinaberry, and holding his spear. "Hey Rick, can I take your spear for a while? I'll bring up the rear," Peter said.

Rick nodded, handed him the spear, and kept walking.

Kinsky, meanwhile, dragged a leaf aside, and said loudly, "If we can get back to Nanigen, we'll have to find the hidden console so we can operate the generator, even if Mr. Drake doesn't want—" At that moment Jarel Kinsky froze in his tracks. Ahead in the distance, beyond the roots of the tree, stood the peak of a tent.

"A station! A station!" Kinsky shouted, and he started running toward the tent.

He didn't see the entrance of the ant nest.

It was an artificial tunnel, fashioned from bits of glued dirt, emerging from the base of a palm tree. Kinsky ran right past the tunnel mouth. Standing around the tunnel, in guard positions, were dozens of bigheaded soldier ants. The soldiers were two to three times larger than the workers. Their bodies were dull red, covered with sparse, bristly hair. Their heads were gleaming black and massively oversized, packed with muscles and plated with armor, and fitted with mandibles designed for fighting. Their eyes were black marbles.

They spotted Kinsky as he ran toward the tent.

Instantly all the soldiers charged. Kinsky noticed the giant ants running toward him, and he swerved. But the soldiers had fanned out. They converged on Kinsky, coming from different directions, a strategy that cut off his escape. Kinsky stopped running and backed up inside a closing ring of ant soldiers, holding his grass spear over his head. "No!" he shouted. He slashed at a soldier with the spear, but the ant grabbed the spear in its mandibles and broke off its point. Several soldiers darted in and began to pull Kinsky to the ground, while one ant closed its mandibles around Kinsky's wrist. He shouted and shook his hand, whirling the ant around, trying to make it let go. But the ant had clamped on his wrist and was shaking its head, bulldogging Kinsky. His hand came off, and the ant flew away and hit the ground running, with the hand in its mandibles. Kinsky screamed and went down on his knees, cradling his severed wrist, which spouted blood. A soldier climbed up Kinsky's back, fastened its jaws behind his ear and began tearing off Kinsky's scalp. Kinsky fell to the ground writhing. Within moments the soldiers had him spread-eagled and were pulling on his arms and legs from different directions; they were drawing and quartering the man, attempting to tear him limb from limb. A soldier got its mandibles fastened under his chin, and his screams ended with a guttural noise as blood spurted from his throat and drenched the ant's head. Smaller workers joined the attack, and Kinsky seemed to disappear under a pile of frantic ants.

Peter Jansen had run forward, waving a spear, shouting at the ants, trying to drive them off Kinsky, but it was too late. Peter stopped and stood his ground before the mass of struggling soldiers, holding the spear and watching the horror. He could buy time for the others to get away, he thought, and he started advancing toward the ants. Then he noticed that Karen King stood beside him, holding her knife. "Get out of here," Peter said to her.

"No," she said to him. She crouched, facing the ants, holding her knife in front of her. She could delay the ants, maybe, give the others time to escape. Meanwhile, more soldiers poured out of the nest. They began hunting around, seeking enemies. A soldier raced toward Peter and Karen, its mandibles wide.

Peter thrust his spear at the ant. The ant dodged it and went for him, moving extremely fast.

"Leave me, Peter!" Karen King shouted. She backed away from the ants. Then she leaped into the air, soaring far higher than a normal human could ever jump, and landed catlike away from the ants. At the same time, she pulled from her belt the spray bottle of defensive chemicals that she'd planned to show to Vin Drake. Benzos. Ants didn't like benzos, she was pretty sure of that. She sprayed the stuff toward an advancing ant. The ant stopped instantly, turned around . . . and ran away.

"Yeah!" she yelled. The spray worked. It made them run like rabbits.

Out of the corner of her eye, she could see the others running away from the ant nest. Good. Buying them time. She kept spraying, and the spray held the ants back, stopped their attacks. But the bottle had contained only a small amount of the liquid. And still more soldier ants were breaking out of the nest. The nest had gone into full alarm. An ant leaped up onto Karen, landing on her chest, tearing her shirt, and it began snapping at her neck.

"Hai!" she shouted and grabbed the ant behind its head, held it up in the air, and with her other hand slammed her knife into the ant's head. The blade punched through the ant's head, and a clear liquid squirted out—it was hemolymph, insect blood. Instantly she flung the ant away. It landed on the ground and went into convulsions, its brain destroyed. But the ants had no fear, no sense of self-preservation, and there seemed to be no end to their numbers. As the ants closed in on her, Karen jumped away, soaring head over heels backward like a circus tumbler, and again landed on her feet.

And then she ran.

Ahead of her, she saw the other humans running explosively fast, driven by fear, leaping over leaves and fern stems, dodging things, fleeing like gazelles. How can I run this fast? I've never run so fast in my life . . . Karen thought. Clearly their bodies were much stronger and faster in the micro-world. It gave Karen a feeling of superhuman power and exhilaration. She leaped over obstacles like a hurdle runner, clearing things in a series of incredible jumps. She realized she was sprinting at about fifty miles an hour, in the scale of the micro-world. I killed an ant. With a knife and my bare hands.

They soon got out of the visual range of the ants. Ahead, in the distance, stood the tent.

Worker ants continued to butcher Kinsky's body. They bit off the arms and legs and cut the torso into chunks, making cracking sounds as they sheared through the ribs and spine, yanking out the man's viscera. The ants drank the spilled blood, making sucking noises. A welter of torn clothing, blood, and intestines was strewn about, while the ants began transporting the meat underground.

Karen King stopped running for a moment to look back, and she saw the ants carry Kinsky's head down the hole. The severed head stared back as it went down, pulled by workers. It seemed to hold a look of surprise.

# Chapter 15

NANIGEN HEADQUARTERS
29 OCTOBER, 10:00 A.M.

It was a sunny day in central Oahu, and the view from Nanigen's meeting room swept across half the island. The windows looked over sugar-cane fields to the Farrington Highway, then to Pearl Harbor, where Navy ships floated like gray ghosts, and to the white towers of Honolulu. Beyond the city, a ragged line of peaks extended along the horizon, painted in misty greens and blues. These were the Ko'olau Mountains, the Pali of Oahu. Clouds had begun to build over the range.

"It will rain on the Pali today. It usually does," Vincent Drake murmured to nobody in particular, while he thought, *The rain will solve the problem. If the ants haven't solved it already.* Of course, if there were any survivors, they might find refuge in a supply station. He reminded himself not to overlook this detail.

Drake turned away from the window and sat down at a long table of polished wood, where a number of people were waiting for him. Seated across from him was Don Makele, the vice president for security. There was the Nanigen media officer, Linda Wellgroen, and her assistant, as well as various other people from different departments.

At the far end of the table, by himself, sat a slender man wearing rimless spectacles. Edward Catel, MD, PhD, was the chief liaison for the Davros Consortium, the group of pharmaceutical companies that had supplied capital to Nanigen. The Davros Consortium had invested a billion dollars in Nanigen; Edward Catel monitored events at Nanigen for the Davros investors.

Drake was saying, ". . . seven graduate students. We were recruiting them to do field work in the micro-world. They've disappeared. Our CFO Alyson Bender has also gone missing."

Don Makele, the security chief, said, "Maybe they went to watch the surf on the North Shore."

Drake looked at his watch. "They should have checked in with us by now."

Don Makele said, "I should file a missing-persons report."

"Good idea," Drake said.

Drake wondered just when the police would discover the corporate car with Alyson's body and the students' clothing in it. The car had fallen into a tidal inlet. He did not think the police would be able to make much sense of the crash. The cops are locals, he thought. Hawaiian locals take life easy, they go for the simple explanation, since that makes the least amount of work for them. Even so, he didn't want the police to get too interested, so he gave Don Makele and the media staff his orders: "Nanigen cannot afford any media attention right now. We are at a critical stage of our explosive growth. We need to work quietly while we smooth out the wrinkles in the tensor generator, especially the problem of the micro-bends." He turned to Linda Wellgroen, the media officer. "Your job is to stop publicity over this incident."

Wellgroen nodded. "Understood."

"If you get media inquiries, be warm and helpful but don't give out any information," Drake went on. "Your job is to be boring."

"It's in my résumé," Wellgroen said with a smile. " 'Experienced at media-diffusive ambiguation in real-time crisis contexts.' It means that when the crap is flying I can be as exciting to the media as an Episcopalian vicar discussing how to toast a crumpet."

"Those kids didn't get into the tensor generator, did they?" said Don Makele, the security chief.

Drake said firmly, "Of course not."

Linda Wellgroen jotted something on a legal pad. "Any idea what happened to Ms. Bender?"

Drake looked concerned. "Frankly, we've been worried about Alyson in recent days. She was known to be deeply depressed, possibly distraught. She had been having an affair with Eric Jansen, and when Eric tragically drowned . . . well . . . let's just say Alyson struggled with private demons."

"You think Ms. Bender took her own life?" Linda Wellgroen said.

Drake shook his head. "I don't know." He turned to Don Makele. "Tell the police about Alyson's state of mind."

The meeting broke up. Linda Wellgroen tucked her legal pad under her arm and walked out of the room, accompanied by the others—but at the last minute, Vin Drake touched Don Makele's elbow and said, "Wait."

The security chief stayed while Drake closed the door. Now only Makele and Drake were left in the room, along with the Davros advisor, Dr. Edward Catel, who had remained seated at the end of the table. He hadn't spoken a word during the meeting.

Drake and Catel had known each other for many years. They had made significant amounts of money working together on deals. Vin Drake thought that Ed Catel's greatest strength was the fact that he displayed no emotions. The man had no discernible feelings of any kind. Catel was a medical doctor, but he had not treated a patient in many years. He was all about money, deals, and growth. Dr. Catel was as warm as slate in January.

Drake waited a moment. Then he said, "The situation is different from what I just told our media people. Those kids did go into the micro-world."

"What happened, sir?" Makele asked.

"They are industrial spies," Drake said.

Catel broke in, speaking for the first time. "Why do you think that, Vin?" He had a mild, even voice.

"I caught Peter Jansen in the Project Omicron area. That zone is forbidden. He had a memory stick in his hand. When I walked in on him, he looked guilty as hell. I had to grab him and rush him out of the zone. The bots could have killed him."

Catel raised an eyebrow; he was one of those people who seem to have yogic control over their facial muscles. "The Omicron zone doesn't sound secure if a grad student can walk in there."

Drake got annoyed. "The zone is very tight. But we can't have the security bots active all the time—nobody could enter the zone. I should be asking you about security, Ed. You paid Professor Ray Hough a great deal of money to let us recruit his grad students."

"I didn't pay him a cent, Vin. He got stock in Nanigen. Under the table."

"So what? You are responsible for the behavior of those students, Ed! You manipulated the situation in Cambridge to get those students out here."

"You have not solved the problem of bends," Dr. Catel answered in a bland voice. "You planned to send them into the micro-world at considerable risk to their lives. Or am I conjecturing?"

Drake ignored him and paced the room. "The ringleader is Peter Jansen," he went on, speaking rapidly. "He's the brother of our deceased vice president, Eric Jansen. Peter seems to irrationally blame Nanigen for his brother's death. He's looking for payback. He's trying to steal our corporate secrets. He may be planning to sell our technology—"

"To whom?" Catel asked sharply.

"Does it matter?"

Catel's eyes narrowed. "Everything matters."

Drake didn't seem to hear him. "A Nanigen employee is involved in the spying," Drake went on. "A control-room operator named Jarel Kinsky."

"Why do you think so?" Catel asked.

Drake shrugged. "Kinsky has disappeared, too. I think he's in the micro-world, in the Waipaka Arboretum. Where he's serving the students as a paid guide. What they're doing, I think, is trying to find out how we operate in the field and what we're discovering."

Dr. Catel pinched his lips together but said nothing more.

"You want me to start a rescue—?" Don Makele began.

Drake cut him off. "Too late. They're dead by now." Drake gave his security chief a sharp look. "Nanigen has been attacked on your watch, Don. You didn't seem to notice. Is there anything you want to explain about that?"

Don Makele's jawline tightened. He was wearing an Aloha shirt. He had an ample belly, but his bare arms, sinewy and massive, were fatless, and Drake saw how his security man's arms went rock-tense. Don Makele was an ex-Marine intelligence officer. A security failure like this—a spy ring operating under his nose—was unforgivable. "I offer my resignation, sir," he said to Drake. "Effective immediately."

Drake smiled and stood up, and put his hand on Don Makele's shoulder, feeling the moisture soaking the man's rayon shirt. It pleased him to see how a few well-chosen words could make an ex-Marine break into a sweat. "Not accepted." Drake's eyes narrowed, and he got a careful look. He had humiliated his security chief, and now the man would be eager to please. "Go to Waipaka Arboretum and collect the supply stations, Don. All of them. Bring them back here. They need to be cleaned and refurbished."

That would prevent any survivors from taking refuge in a station.

Dr. Catel had picked up his attaché case and was moving toward the door. He glanced at Drake and gave him a nod, and left without saying another word.

Vin Drake understood exactly what Dr. Catel's nod meant. Clean up this mess quickly and the Davros Consortium won't hear about it.

He went over to the window and looked out. As always, the trade winds were blowing across the mountains, endlessly lofting into mist and showers. There was nothing to worry about. For humans without weapons and protective gear, survival time in the micro-world was measured in minutes to hours, not in days. Speaking to himself in a murmur, he said, "Nature will take its course."

# Chapter 16

STATION ECHO
29 OCTOBER, 10:40 A.M.

The seven graduate students gathered at the entrance of the tent. A sign over the tent's door said, SUPPLY STATION ECHO. PROPERTY OF NANIGEN MICROTECHNOLOGIES. They were in a state of shock, filled with horror over the brutality of Kinsky's death. They were also extremely surprised at how fast they had run. Danny Minot had lost his tassel loafers. The shoes blew off his feet while he'd made a jaw-dropping dash that would have shamed an Olympic sprinter. Danny stood there in muddy, bare feet, shaking his head. And they had seen Karen King fighting the ants. Her twists and leaps, soaring through the air.

It was clear they could do things in the micro-world they couldn't have dreamed of before.

They investigated the supply station quickly, as a raiding column of ants could show up at any moment. The tent, stocked with various boxes, sat atop a concrete floor. In the center of the floor, there was a round steel hatch. The steel hatch was operated with a wheel lock, like a bulkhead door of a submarine. Peter Jansen spun the wheel and lifted up the hatch. A ladder went down into darkness. "I'll check it out." He put the headlamp on his head and switched it on, and descended the ladder.

He ended up standing in the middle of a dark room. As he swung his headlamp around, the beam fell across bunks and tables. Then he spotted a bank of power switches on the wall. He threw them, and the lights came on.

The room was a concrete bunker. It contained spartan living quarters. Tiered bunks were stacked along two walls. There were laboratory benches, equipped with basic lab supplies. There was a dining area, with a table and benches and a cooking stove. A door led to the bunker's power source: a pair of D-size flashlight batteries, looming far above their heads. Another door led to a toilet and shower. A chest held some freeze-dried meals in pouches. The bunker was secure against predators, a sort of bomb shelter in a dangerous biological environment.

**"It's not a** Disneyland ride out there," Peter Jansen said. He sat slumped at the table in the bunker, exhausted. He felt unable to think clearly. Images of Kinsky's death ran through his mind.

Karen King leaned against the wall. She was splashed with ant blood. The blood was gooey and clear, with a slightly yellowish color, and it dried fast.

Danny Minot sat hunched at the dining table. He had resumed picking at his face and nose with his fingertips.

A computer sat on the lab bench. "We could learn something from this," Jenny Linn said, and switched it on. The computer booted, but a password screen came up. Of course, they didn't know the password. And Jarel Kinsky wasn't there to help them with things like that.

"We're not safe here," Rick Hutter remarked. "Drake could show up."

Amar Singh agreed. "I propose, let's stock up with food and gear and leave immediately."

"I don't want to go outdoors," Erika Moll said, her voice trembling, as she sat down on a bunk. Why had she ever left the university in Munich? She longed for the safe world of European research. These Americans played with fire. Hydrogen bombs, megapower lasers, killer drones, shrunken micro-people . . . Americans were demon-raisers. Americans awakened technological demons they couldn't control, yet they seemed to enjoy the power.

"We can't stay here," Karen said to her, speaking gently. She could see how frightened Erika was. "The most dangerous organism we face is not an insect. It's human."

It was a good point. Peter Jansen suggested that they stick to the original plan: go to the parking lot, try to get on a truck to Nanigen, get into the tensor generator somehow. "We have to get restored to normal size as soon as possible. We don't have much time."

"We don't know how to operate the generator," Jenny Linn said.

"We'll cross that bridge later."

Rick said, "We have some good tools for getting ourselves on the truck, including the rope ladder we found in the pack." He had been poking around in the supply boxes, and he'd pulled out something: another pair of radio headsets. This meant they now had a total of four communication radios.

"There is only one thing to do," Danny Minot murmured. "Call for help." He held up a radio headset.

"You call Nanigen," Rick said to him, "and Vin Drake will come around looking for us, and not with any magnifying glass. With the toe of his boot."

Peter suggested that they keep radio silence except in an emergency, in case Drake was listening for them.

"I don't see the point," Danny said. "We need to call for help."

Jenny Linn did not take part in the conversation. Instead, she opened all the cabinets, one by one, and went through them carefully. She found a lab notebook. She opened it and began flipping through the pages. Somebody had jotted handwritten notes on the first few pages—weather readings, logs of sample-gathering activities, mostly. It didn't seem useful, until she came to the map.

"Look at this, guys," Jenny said, spreading the notebook on the table.

On a page of the lab notebook, somebody had sketched a rough map of the Manoa Valley. The map showed the locations of ten supply stations, scattered through Fern Gully and partway up the mountain slopes toward Tantalus Peak, at increasing distances from the greenhouses and parking lot. The supply stations were designated by letters of the NATO alphabet, from Alpha, Bravo, and Charlie, up to Kilo. There was an arrow marked TO TANTALUS BASE—GREAT BOULDER. Tantalus Crater wasn't shown on the map, nor was the base.

The map, as crude and incomplete as it was, still contained valuable information. It showed the basic layout of the supply stations. The location of each supply station was indicated by landmarks around the station—trees, rocks, clumps of ferns—making it possible to find the station as long as you could locate the landmarks. There was a station next to the parking lot. It was Station Alpha, and it was located under a clump of white ginger plants, according to a note on the map.

"We could head for Station Alpha," Peter Jansen said. "Maybe not stay at Alpha, but at least we could search it for more supplies and information."

"Why should we go anywhere?" Danny said. "Kinsky was right. We have to negotiate with Vin."

"Don't you dare try!" Rick was practically shouting.

"Please, stop this!" Amar Singh said. He couldn't stand conflict. First there had been all the fighting between Rick and Karen, and now Rick was getting into a hassle with Danny. "Rick, people have different styles. You need to be more tolerant of Danny . . ."

"Cut the crap, Amar. That guy is going to be the death of us all, with his stupid—"

Peter Jansen could feel the situation spiraling out of control. The one thing that would certainly destroy them would be conflict within the group. They had to become a team, Peter thought, or they would soon be dead. Somehow, he had to get this quarrelsome, catty group of intellectuals to understand that survival required cooperation. He stood up and went to the head of the table, and waited for silence. Eventually they quieted down.

"Are you done squabbling?" he said. "Now I have something to say. We're not in Cambridge anymore. In the academic world, you guys got ahead by cutting down your rivals and proving you're smarter than everybody else. In this forest, it's not about getting ahead, it's about staying alive. We have to cooperate to survive. And we have to kill whatever threatens us or we will be killed."

"Oh, it's *kill or be killed*," Danny said dismissively. "An outmoded pseudo-Darwinian philosophy dating back to Victorian times."

"Danny, we have to do whatever it takes to survive," Peter said. "But there's more to survival than just killing. Think about who we are as humans. A million years ago, our ancestors survived on the plains of Africa by operating in teams. Bands is a better word for it—we were bands of humans, back then. A million years ago, we were not at the top of the food chain. All kinds of animals hunted us—lions, leopards, hyenas, wild dogs, crocodiles. But we humans have been dealing with predators for a very long time. We survive with brains, weapons, and cooperation—teamwork. I think we were built for this journey. Let's think of it as the chance of a lifetime to see incredible things in nature no one has ever seen before. But whatever course of action we decide on, we will have to work together or we'll die. We're only as strong as the weakest member of our team." Peter stopped, wondering if he'd gone too far, if he had sounded too preachy to these grad students.

There was a period of silence as they digested Peter's speech.

Danny Minot was the first to speak. He turned to Peter. "By 'weakest member,' I assume you mean me."

"I didn't say that, Danny—"

Danny cut him off. "Excuse me, Peter. I am not a slack-lipped hominid with a beetling brow, clutching a chunk of stone in my hairy-knuckled fist and cheerfully bashing in skulls of leopards. In fact, I am an educated person used to an urban environment. It is not Harvard Square out there. It is a green hell crawling with ants the size of pit bulls. I will stay in this bunker and wait for help." He rapped on the wall. "It's ant-proof."

"Nobody's going to help you," Karen said to Danny.

"We'll see about that." He went off and sat by himself.

Amar spoke to the others. "Peter is right." He turned to Peter. "I'm on the team." He leaned back and closed his eyes, as if he was thinking about something.

Karen said, "I'm on the team, too."

Erika Moll finally agreed. "Peter is right."

"I think we need a leader," Jenny Linn said. "I think Peter should lead us."

"Peter is the one person here who gets along with everybody in the group," Rick said, and turned to Peter. "You're the only person who can lead us."

It was confirmed quickly by a vote; Danny refused to take part.

Now it was a question of getting the team's act together.

"First we need to eat. I'm freaking starved," Rick said.

Indeed, they all felt ravenously hungry. They had been up all night, without food. And there had been that mad dash from the ants.

"We must have burned a lot of calories," Peter said.

"I have never been so hungry in my life," Erika Moll said.

"Our bodies are tiny. We probably burn calories a lot faster. Like a hummingbird, you know?" Karen said.

They took out the instant food packets, tore them open, and

devoured them, sitting at the table and sprawled around the room. There wasn't much food, and it vanished in moments. They found a giant block of chocolate, and Karen hacked it up seven ways with her knife. The chocolate disappeared quickly.

**Searching the bunker** for anything that might be useful on their journey to the parking lot, they found a number of plastic lab bottles with screw lids, and piled them on the table. The bottles could be used as canteens for water, and to store any chemical compounds they might be able to gather. "We're going to need chemical weapons, just like insects and plants have them," Jenny Linn said.

"Yeah, and I'll need a jar to hold my curare," Rick added.

"Curare," Karen said. "Right."

"It's wicked stuff," Rick said.

"If you know how to make it."

"I do!" Rick said huffily.

"Who taught you, Rick? A hunter?"

"I've read papers—"

"Papers on curare." Karen turned to something else, while Rick fumed.

In one chest she had found three steel machetes. Each machete had a belt and holster with a diamond knife-sharpener tucked into a pocket of the belt. Peter Jansen drew a blade and touched it with his thumb. "Wow, that is sharp." As an experiment, he tapped the blade on the edge of a wooden table, and saw the blade sink into the wood as if it were soft cheese. The machete was far sharper than a scalpel.

"It's as sharp as a microtome," he said. "We used one in our lab—remember—for slicing tissue."

Peter ran the diamond sharpener over the machete, whisking it along the edge. The sharpener was obviously to keep the edge in top condition. "The edge is very fine, so it probably gets dull quickly.

But we can sharpen the machete as needed." The machetes would be useful in cutting a path through vegetation.

Karen King swung a machete around her head. "Nice balance," she said. "Decent weapon."

Rick Hutter had stepped backward with alarm as Karen whirled the machete. "You could cut somebody's head off," he said to her.

She smirked at him. "I know what I'm doing. You stick to berries and blow-darts."

"Quit pushing me!" Rick burst out. "What's your problem?"

Peter Jansen stepped in. Despite their promises to work as a team, it was easier said than done. "Please—Rick—Karen—we'd all appreciate it if you didn't argue. It's dangerous for everybody."

Jenny Linn slapped Rick on the shoulder and said to him, "Karen's just showing her fear."

This didn't sit well with Karen, but she didn't say anything more. Jenny was right. Karen knew full well that the machetes wouldn't stop some predators—such as birds, for example. She had been needling Rick because she was afraid. She had revealed her fear to the others, and it embarrassed her. She climbed up the ladder and opened the hatch, and went outdoors to get herself calm. Under the tent, she began investigating the chests that were stored there. She found packets of food in one chest, and many vials and scientific samples in another, probably samples that a team had left behind. She discovered a steel rod, hidden under a tarp. The rod was longer than she was tall. It had a point at one end, while the other end had been enlarged and flattened. For a moment she couldn't figure out what this enormous metal thing was. Then the scale of the object clicked in her mind, and she knew. She climbed down the ladder and informed the others of what she'd found. "It's a pin!" she said.

It wasn't clear what the pin was doing in the tent. Possibly it had been used to pin something to the ground. In any case, the pin was made of steel. It could be shaped into a weapon. "We could use the diamond sharpeners to hone the pin, make it really sharp," Karen said. "We could put a notch in the tip—that would make a barbed point. A killing point. A barb that would grab in the prey and wouldn't come loose. A harpoon."

They had to work on the pin inside the tent, for it was too long to be brought down the ladder. Using the diamond sharpeners, they fell to work cutting and shaping the steel. First they sawed off the flattened head of the pin, which shortened it and gave it better balance, so that a person could hold it and throw it. They took turns filing the point into a notch, to create a barb; the diamond sharpeners worked quickly on the steel. After the work had been done, Peter picked up the harpoon and hefted it. It was a steel pole—massive, gleaming, balanced—yet he handled it as if it weighed almost nothing. In the micro-world, a piece of steel that size was just about heavy enough to do some damage to an insect if you threw it hard and it was sharp enough.

Danny Minot refused to help in any of the preparations. He sat on a bed in the bunker with his arms crossed and knees drawn up, and watched. Peter Jansen felt sorry for him, and went over to him, and said quietly, "Please come with us. You're not safe here."

"You said I was the weakest person," Danny replied.

"We need your help, Danny."

"For assisted suicide," he said bitterly, and refused to budge.

**Rick Hutter had** set about making blow-darts. He went a few paces outside the tent, carrying the machete for protection against ants, and cut several grass stems. Back inside the bunker, he sliced a stem lengthwise, and began stripping out the harder strands of woody material. The grass seemed as tough as bamboo. He shaped the splinters into a couple of dozen darts. The darts still needed to be hardened. He went over to the stove and switched on a coil. He carefully heated and hardened the point of a dart by holding it over the hot coil. When he was finished, he tore open a mattress and pulled out some stuffing.

He needed to fasten a "puff" of soft material to the tail of the blow-dart, so that the dart could be propelled through the tube by a person's breath. In order to attach this tail-puff to the shaft he needed thread. "Amar—is there any more of that spider silk?"

Amar shook his head. "It got used up saving Peter from the snake."

No problem. Rick rooted around and found a coil of rope. He cut a short length of the rope, then picked it apart into strands with his fingers. This produced a pile of very strong threads. He held a piece of fluff from the mattress against the end of the dart and wound a thread around it, lashing the tail-puff in place. Now he had a real honest-to-goodness blow-dart—hardened tip, tail-puff, the dart ready to be armed with poison.

Even so, no scientist would assume the dart worked. He would have to test the dart. One of the grass stems, full-length, made a blow tube. Rick fitted the dart into the blow tube, took aim at the wooden frame of a bunk, and blew. The dart zinged across the room, hit the bunk . . . and bounced off.

"Shit," he muttered. The dart couldn't penetrate wood. That meant it would never get through an insect's exoskeleton, either.

"Fail," Karen remarked.

"The dart needs a metal tip," Rick said.

Where to find the metal?

Tableware. Stainless steel tableware. Rick took a steel fork from the kitchen area and bent back one of the fork's tines. He cut off the tine using the edge of a diamond sharpener, then honed the tine into an exceedingly sharp point. He lashed the steel point to a grass dart, and fired the dart at the bunk. This time, the dart embedded itself in the wood of the bunk with a satisfying *thwock*, and stayed there, trembling. "Now that will drive into a beetle," Rick said.

One by one, he cut the tines off all the forks in the bunker, until he had created a supply of more than two dozen darts and several blow tubes. He placed the darts in a plastic box he'd found in the lab, to keep them dry and protected from damage.

Rick still had to make curare, but in order to do that he needed to collect more ingredients. Like a fine sauce, a good curare contained a variety of ingredients cooked together, a chemistry of horrors. All he had for an ingredient, at the moment, was the chinaberry, which he'd stored upstairs in the tent. Nobody wanted a toxic chinaberry to be kept inside the bunker. It might give off fumes; it might make them sick. For the same reason, he could not boil curare on the stove. He did not have the ingredients for curare, anyway, and even if he did, everybody could get poisoned if he tried to make curare inside the bunker. The fumes would probably kill them.

He would have to boil curare outdoors over an open fire.


**They also turned** up a pair of binoculars and two more headlamps, and packed them into the duffels. Amar Singh dug up a roll of duct tape. "We can't possibly survive in a super-jungle without duct tape," Amar joked.

Rick Hutter opened a chest and shouted, "A gold mine!" And he pulled out a laboratory apron, rubber gloves, and safety goggles. "This is just what I need for making curare. Excellent, excellent!" He stuffed the things in a duffel bag. He'd have to cook the curare in a vessel of some kind. In the bunker's tiny kitchen facility, at the bottom of a shelf near the floor, he found a large aluminum pot. He lashed the pot to his duffel pack and then put the pack on his back, testing its weight. He was surprised. The pack, though enormous, felt very light. "I'm as strong as an ant," Rick said.

Jenny Linn rooted through a supply box and discovered a military compass. The compass, battered and worn, was the type used by American soldiers ever since the Korean War. It could be used to keep them going in a straight line. But none of them could find a GPS unit anywhere at the station.

"It's because GPS can't tell us where we are," Peter explained. "A GPS unit is accurate to about ten meters. At our small size, that's equivalent to a one-kilometer accuracy. In other words, GPS can't tell our location more precisely than a kilometer in any direction, by our measure of things. A compass is much more accurate than GPS for us."

Suddenly, after the meal and all the work, a desire for sleep came over all of them. Peter's watch showed that the time was just before noon.

"Let's finish packing up our gear later," Karen King suggested. They hadn't slept the night before, but they were used to pulling all-nighters in the lab. Karen prided herself on her stamina, but even so, she couldn't keep her eyes open. Why am I so tired all of a sudden? she thought. Maybe it had something to do with their small bodies, all the calories they'd burned . . . but she couldn't focus . . . And she couldn't resist crawling into a bunk, where she fell instantly asleep. They all slept.

# Chapter 17

A pickup truck, black and new, swung into the parking lot by the greenhouses at the Waipaka Arboretum. Don Makele, the security director of Nanigen, got out. He put on a knapsack and clipped a sheath knife to his belt. He knelt on the ground by a clump of white ginger plants growing along the edge of the parking lot, and drew the knife blade. The knife was a KA-BAR, a combat model with a black blade. Delicately, he pushed aside plant stems with the flat of the knife, until he found the little tent: Supply Station Alpha, hidden in the gloom of the ginger leaves. He leaned into the plants to get a better look, and, with the tip of his knife, pulled aside the tiny flap of the tent.

"Anybody home?" he said.

He knew he wouldn't hear a response, even if a micro-human did answer. He didn't see any micro-humans, anyway. Station Alpha had been tidied up and battened down a month ago, when it had been abandoned by the last field team to stay there.

He plunged the knife into the soil next to the station and cut a circle around the station, rocking the blade back and forth. Then he yanked the bunker out of the earth, the soil dropping off it, the tent fluttering and shaking on top of the structure. He stood up and banged the bunker on his shoe to knock off clots of dirt, and put the bunker into his knapsack.

Don Makele took out a map and studied it. Next stop, Station Bravo. He walked swiftly along a path that led into Fern Gully. After fifty feet, he plunged off the path into the forest, not reducing his speed, moving easily through the jungle environment. According to the map, Station Bravo was at the south side of a koa tree, and the tree's trunk had been marked to make the station easy to find. A few minutes of tramping around brought him to the right tree: a reflective orange tag had been nailed to the trunk. He knelt at the spot, found the tent, and peered into it. Nobody. What about the bunker?

He straightened up and called, "Hey!" and stomped on the ground beside the tent. That would send them scurrying out if they were in the bunker. But he saw nothing, no movement, no tiny figures running. He knifed the soil and took out the bunker and put it in his pack with Station Alpha. He consulted the map again, and looked along the hillside, peering up the sloping land that rose to cliffs and eventually to the heights of Tantalus. It seemed like a waste of time to bring all the stations back to Nanigen. The microworld had swallowed the students without a trace. Still, he had to follow Drake's orders. It didn't bother him to be removing the only hope of survival for the students, since the students were dead anyway, for sure. He wasn't doing anything wrong, just cleaning up the stations.

As he hiked laterally along the hillside, he dug up Stations Foxtrot, Golf, and Hotel. He moved along quickly, at ease in the jungle. Higher on the mountainside, he located Station India and dug it up.

Higher still, he found Juliet, and knocked the mud off it. But Station Kilo seemed to have disappeared. Kilo was supposed to be embedded in the ground at the base of a cliff, among a tangle of vines, by a small waterfall. Yet he simply could not find it; eventually, Don Makele decided that Kilo had probably been washed away in a rainstorm. This happened to stations occasionally. The weather was hard on them, because they were so small.

Then he doubled back, going straight downhill into the depths of Fern Gully. He was heading for Station Echo, which lay deep in Fern Gully amid a stand of albesia trees.

**"H-E-Y!" The sound** thundered through the bunker, waking up all the students. The room jounced, and boomed, and they were flung out of the bunks and tossed around the room, as if a major earthquake had just hit. The lights went out. Crashing sounds of chests and boxes and lab equipment filled the darkness, and the room shook. Peter Jansen understood what was happening. "Someone's out there!" he shouted. "Get out! Go! Go!" He groped around for a headlamp by his bunk, found it, and switched it on.

The lights came on again. The batteries had been rattling on their contacts.

Rick Hutter grabbed his darts and started scrambling up the ladder, Karen King following him. The others frantically began to grab duffel bags, machetes, whatever they could carry.

Rick, leading the way, reached the top of the ladder. He put his hands on the hatch wheel, when suddenly the room felt like it was being yanked into the air, and he fell off the ladder, and everybody went sprawling. The room turned sideways, and a deafening noise, a hammering sound, made the bunker shake.

"—Ah—stupid—thing—" The words seemed to shake the bunker like artillery shells landing.

. . .

**He'd cut a circle** around Station Echo, gotten it out of the soil, squinted into the door of the tent. The tent had supplies scattered all around inside it. That looked unusual, so he decided to open the hatch and look inside. He pinched the hatch wheel between his thumb and forefinger, but the wheel snapped off. Now he couldn't get the hatch open. "Shit." He laid the station on its side on the ground, and knelt, and tapped on the hatch cover with the tip of his knife, but that didn't work. The hatch was tightly shut and not even the tip of his knife would get it open. So he raised his knife over his head. He would split it open.

**The KA-BAR blade,** as tall to the micro-humans as a ten-story building, plunged through the bunker with a roar, driving shattered blocks of concrete through the room. The blade continued down into the earth, opening a gaping hole in the room. The edge began to saw raggedly through the bunker while rocking back and forth.

Rick clung to the bottom of the hatch, trying to spin it, trying to open it. He got the hatch open, and thrust out his duffel bag. But then the bunker began rising up into the air: he saw the ground below. The bunker turned completely sideways, until he was lying on the ladder. People were crowding behind him. He began reaching for the others. He grabbed Amar and pushed him out through the hatch, and saw him falling away. The bunker was rising higher, tilting. Peter Jansen got next to Rick. "Help me get the others out!" Peter shouted.

They managed to get Danny out through the hatch. They heard Danny scream, and saw him falling. Erika went next.

Inside the bunker, Jenny Linn had been pinned against the giant knife blade, her arm trapped between the blade and concrete.

Karen King struggled to free Jen's arm, while the blade moved sideways, threatening to crush them both.

"My arm," Jenny whimpered. "I can't move."

A table slid up against Jenny, then a concrete fragment smashed the table and rammed into Karen. Karen kicked the concrete away, surprised at her strength, and worked frantically to free Jenny.

The bunker went down again, slammed against the ground, and the knife cut it in half, spilling Jenny and Karen out, revealing the sky above. Against the sky towered a man. A man they didn't recognize. He opened his mouth and sounds rumbled out. He raised the knife high.

Karen picked Jenny up, and got her to her feet, watching the knife wave over them. Jen's arm hung limply at a strange angle. "Run!" Karen screamed, as the great knife flashed downward at them.

# Chapter 18

The knife entered the ground between Karen and Jenny, driving them apart, and continued down into the earth for what seemed like a vast distance. Then it was withdrawn with a rumbling sound, shaking the world. Jenny was on her knees, holding her arm and moaning.

Karen scooped Jenny up with one hand, and began to run with her, heaving her across her back and sprinting at high speed. The knife plunged down again, but this time Karen had dived under a clump of ferns, still carrying Jenny on her back.

The ground thumped and bounced, and the thumping receded. The man was walking away, carrying the broken halves of the station in his hands. They saw him toss the pieces into a knapsack. He moved off, and was gone.

A silence descended. Jenny was crying.

"My arm," Jenny said. "It hurts . . . hurts so much."

Jen's arm had been broken, badly. "Don't worry, we'll get you fixed up," Karen said, trying to sound optimistic. Jen's arm looked horrible, a compound fracture of the humerus, probably. Karen found a duffel bag lying on the ground nearby, and she opened it, and took out a radio headset, and began calling on it. "You guys? Anybody? I'm with Jenny. She has a broken arm. Can you hear me?"

Peter's voice came on. "We're okay. Everybody's accounted for."

They gathered under the fern, and placed Jenny on a leaf, using it like a bed. None of them had any medical experience. Karen opened the medical kit and found a syringe with morphine. She held it where Jenny could see it. "Do you want this?"

Jenny shook her head. "No. Too groggy." She might need her wits, despite the pain. Instead, Jenny accepted a couple of Tylenol tablets, while Karen ripped up a piece of cloth and fashioned a sling. They helped her sit up. Jenny swayed, her face ashen, her lips pale. "I'll be okay," she said.

But she was not okay. Her arm was swelling dramatically, the skin darkening.

Internal bleeding.

Karen caught Peter's eye, and she knew he was thinking the same thing she was. Remembering what Jarel Kinsky had said about the bends. You could bleed to death from a small cut. And this was not a small cut.

Peter looked at his watch. It was two o'clock in the afternoon. They'd slept for two hours.

The ground was scattered with debris. It was like a shipwreck. The duffel bags and the backpack lay in various places. Many other things had fallen out of the bunker when the knife had split it open. They found the machetes and the harpoon. Rick's chinaberry rested on the ground nearby; it had fallen out of the tent. They had survival gear and supplies, at least, but where would they go? If Station Echo had been taken away, what had happened to the other stations? Had the man seen them? Did he work for Vin Drake?

They had to assume the worst.

They had been discovered. The stations had been taken away. Where to hide? Where to go? How to get back to Nanigen now?

As they stood pondering what to do, the sky grew darker. A gust of wind tugged at the leaves of a haiwale plant nearby, revealing the fuzzy undersides of the leaves. As Peter looked up, he saw the wind catching leaves overhead, flipping them over, tossing the leaves . . .

Then came a strange sound, a deep *sploosh*, and another *sploosh*. They watched in stunned surprise as a flattened sphere of water, of enormous size, fell on the ground next to them and exploded into a hundred smaller droplets flying everywhere. The afternoon rains had arrived.

"Get to high ground!" Peter shouted. "This way!" They began to run, heading upslope, grabbing whatever they could carry. Karen carried Jenny on her back, while raindrops exploded around them like bombs going off.

**At Nanigen, Vin Drake** turned away from his computer screen. He had been watching a weather-radar scan of the Ko'olau Pali. Those trade winds were so dependable. As the winds ran up against the windward side of Oahu, they dropped their moisture on the mountains. The peaks of the Ko'olau Pali were some of the wettest places on earth.

Don Makele knocked on the door. The security man entered and placed the pieces of Station Echo on Drake's desk. "The beds are rumpled, toilet's been used. And I saw a couple of them on the ground running. I ordered them to stop. I tried to stop 'em with my knife. They scattered like cockroaches."

"That's disturbing," Drake said. "Very disturbing, Don. I told you to fix this."

"What do you want me to do, sir?"

Vin Drake leaned back and tapped a gold mechanical pencil on his teeth. A portrait of him hung on the wall behind him, painted by an up-and-coming Brooklyn artist, in which Drake's face seemed to fracture into bold colors; it was an image of power, and Drake liked it. "I want you to close off the security gate at the entrance to Manoa Valley. Stop the shuttle truck. The valley is to be sealed. And bring me your two best security men."

"That would be Telius and Johnstone. I trained them in Kabul."

"They have experience in the micro-world?"

"Plenty," Makele answered. "What do you want them to do?"

"Rescue the students."

"But you're sealing off the valley—"

"Just do as I say, Don."

"Yes, sure."

"I'll meet your men outdoors. Parking lot B, twenty minutes."

**The raindrops were** pounding down, exploding, hurling gouts of water mixed with soil. Peter vanished in a cloud of spray as a raindrop hit him. The raindrop knocked Peter through the air and left him sprawled and coughing. The others ran, slipping and sliding, while more raindrops landed around them. Then came a sound like a freight train.

It was a flash flood running down a cleft in Fern Gully. It burst around a rock and past the base of a tree fern, and hit the people with a wall of brown water, sending them swimming for their lives. Karen was carrying Jenny along, when suddenly, as the flood hit, Jenny was torn from her back with a cry.

"Jenny!"

The water took Karen down. She couldn't see Jenny. She found herself clinging to a leaf, which was spinning around and around in the current. Rick was kneeling on the leaf in front of her. "Grab my hand!" he shouted to her. Rick caught Karen by one hand, and hauled her onto the leaf. She coughed and gasped. The leaf spun and ran along with the current. "I've lost Jenny!" Karen shouted, looking around frantically. With her broken arm, Jenny would not be able to swim.

Danny Minot had climbed up onto a rock. It poked out of the floodwaters ripping around it.

A drowned earthworm floated past, rolling over and over in the water. Jenny Linn struggled in the water, trying to swim, but her sling interfered and her broken arm flopped in a frightening way. Her head went under. And came up.

Rick lay flat on the leaf. "Jenny!" he shouted. "Reach out! Jenny!"

"Hang on, Rick!" Karen shouted, and she grabbed Rick's feet, and held on, trying to keep him from sliding off the leaf as he reached out to try to save Jenny.

Jenny rolled on her side, and reached out with her good hand, but she passed by Rick, her fingertips just brushing his. He lost her, couldn't get a grip on her fingers, and he shouted in frustration.

Jenny was approaching the rock where Danny huddled. "Danny, please!" she screamed, putting out her good hand. The current shook her body, threatening to drag her under.

Danny Minot reached out for her. He touched her hand. Her fingers closed around his fingers. He reached farther with his other hand, and managed to get his fingers under the sling. He pulled Jenny toward him. Then he felt himself slipping off the rock.

Jenny screamed in pain as he wrenched her broken arm. But she welcomed it. "Don't let go of me, please!" She reached with her good hand . . . caught Danny's shirt.

A drowning person will take you down with them. Danny knew about drowning people. They were very dangerous.

He looked around. Was anybody watching? Then he locked eyes with Jenny Linn. "Sorry," he said. He opened his hands and let her go. He was going to be pulled into the water and drowned by her, for sure . . .

Danny turned away. He couldn't bear that expression on Jen's face. He had done everything he could to save her. If he hadn't let her go, she would have pulled him in, certainly . . . they both would have died . . . Jenny was doomed anyway. I'm a good person . . . He huddled on the rock while the water rumbled around it. Nobody had seen what he'd done. Except Jenny. That look in her eyes . . .

Karen screamed as she saw Danny lose his grip on her. "No! Jenny! No!" They glimpsed Jen's head bob once more in the current, and she went down, and they didn't see her again.

# Chapter 19

V in Drake crossed the parking lot, moving toward Telius and Johnstone, who waited between two cars at the edge of the lot. Better to talk outdoors. Anything you said could be heard, recorded, preserved. He had to keep track of the details. Details are evidence. Evidence could escape. Evidence could fly out into the world; you could lose control of it.

"We've had a breach of security," Drake said to the two men. Telius stood with his shaved head bent, listening, a short, wiry man with fierce, restless eyes that darted over the ground as if he was searching for some small object he'd lost. Johnstone, much taller than Telius, wore sunglasses and stood at ease, with his hands behind his back. A tattoo on Johnstone's scalp shone through a fade haircut. Drake went on. "We're dealing with industrial spies. They could destroy Nanigen. We believe these spies are working for a foreign government. As you may know, there are certain classified activities at Nanigen that unfriendly governments would very much like to know about."

"We don't know anything about that," Telius said.

"That's correct," Drake said. "You don't."

Somebody drove by and parked their car, and Drake paused. He and the two men turned away, and walked along the edge of the parking lot, saying nothing for a few moments, waiting for the person to go inside the building. The trade wind rattled the seed pods of acacia shrubs growing in the empty lot nearby.

Drake turned and gazed at the metal building. "That building doesn't look like much. But in the near future, the business inside it will be worth at least a hundred billion dollars. A hundred billion dollars." He paused to let the number sink in. "Incredible wealth will be created for the lucky people who own ground-floor shares in Nanigen." He squinted into the sunlight, then looked sideways at the two men. "You know what ground-floor shares are, right? The owners of ground-floor shares can sell their shares for a spectacular profit when the company goes public in an IPO." Did they see where he was going with this? Their faces revealed precisely nothing. No thought, no emotion, nothing to be read or inferred.

Professional faces, he thought.

Drake continued. "I want you to go into the micro-world on a rescue mission to find the spies. I'll give you a full movement kit. A hexapod and weapons, anything you need. The spies were dropped . . . are believed to have been lost in an area about twenty-meters radius around Supply Station Echo. So I want you to begin your search at Echo. It's possible the missing persons are following the micro-trails, looking for supply stations in order to take refuge in them. The supply stations have all been removed—all except for Station Kilo. We couldn't find Station Kilo. You are to follow the networks of trails, moving from the site of one station to the next, searching for the spies. And . . . ah . . ." How to put this clearly, so there would be no mistake? "You will find the missing people. But here's the point: the rescue will fail. Understand? Despite your best efforts, the spies will not be found. I don't want to know anything about how you do it. The spies have to disappear, but I don't want to hear any rumors about what happened to them, either. If no trace of them is found, there will be a . . . reward." Drake put his hands in his pockets, and felt the wind kissing his face. "Failure," he added softly, "is the only option."

He turned around and looked at the two men. He saw nothing there. The men's faces held no expression. A small bird whipped past and landed in the acacia bushes.

"If the rescue effort fails, the reward for each of you will be one share of Nanigen ground-floor stock. When Nanigen goes public, a single share will be worth at least a million dollars. Get it?"

The men just looked at him with eyes as flat as the parking lot.

But they got it. He was sure of that.

"You're venture capitalists now," Drake said, slapping Telius on the shoulder as he left.

**The rain ended** as quickly as it had begun. A steamy golden glow filled the forest as the clouds broke, and the water quickly receded as the rivulets emptied, and the rain ran off into the stream that drained the Manoa Valley. They had lost a lot of their gear, scattered by the water. And Jenny had disappeared. They collected themselves together in a group, and when everyone was accounted for, they spread out looking for their gear and, most of all, for Jenny. They went downhill, following the water flow, using the two headset radios to keep in touch.

"Jenny! Are you there? Jenny!" they shouted, but there was no answer and no sign of her.

"I found the harpoon," Rick said. It hadn't traveled far. His darts had been in a plastic case inside his duffel bag, and the bag turned up wedged against a stone. Even the chinaberry was found, underneath the edge of a leaf, glowing yellow.

Karen King moved along with a sense of dread as they searched for Jenny Linn. She was shaking; she had seen the look on Jen's face when she went down that last time.

The worst horrors are the human ones. What had Jenny seen?

Then Karen spotted something pale, soft, draped under a twig. A human hand. She had found Jenny. Her body was pinned under the twig, crushed and oddly twisted, and speckled with mud, with the forsaken look of the drowned, her broken arm flung akimbo and contorted like a wet rag. Jen's eyes were open, vacant. Her body was covered with spaghetti-like threads, which crisscrossed and draped her like a veil. They were threads of fungus, already beginning to grow.

Karen knelt by the body and pulled a thread from Jen's face, and closed Jen's eyes, and wept.

The others gathered around. Rick found himself weeping, and it embarrassed him. He tried to control his tears, but it didn't work. Peter put his arm around Rick, and Rick shook him off.

"I tried so hard," Danny said, and cried. "I just couldn't save her."

Erika enfolded Danny in her arms. "You are a brave man, Danny. I never realized it until now."

There was a creaking sound. The veil of fungus threads that covered Jen's body seemed to twitch.

"What was that?" Erika said . . . and her eyes widened with horror as she saw a thread of fungus bend and wave, like a crooked finger, and the tip of the thread touched Jen's skin. It went in through the skin, making a scratchy sound, piercing the body, probing for nutrients. The fungus veil had already begun to consume the body. Erika cringed, and stood up.

Peter spoke. "We need to bury her—quickly."

Using the harpoon and the machetes, they hacked apart the soil. It was soft and rich, and alive with small creatures moving and squirming. The soil was almost a living organism in its own right. The only nonliving thing was seemingly Jenny. They lowered her into the grave they'd dug, and crossed her arms over her chest, arranging the broken arm. They tried to clear the fungus off her, but the threads had tightened, clamping themselves to the body, penetrating it everywhere.

Erika Moll wept uncontrollably. Peter cut a part of a petal from a fallen hibiscus flower lying on the ground, and he laid the piece of petal over Jenny like a white shroud. It covered the activity of the fungus beneath it.

Then Erika suggested that they say a prayer. She wasn't a religious person, at least she didn't think she was, but she had been raised a Catholic, and had been taught by nuns in a nursery school in Munich. The nuns had taught her how to say the twenty-third Psalm in German. *"Der Herr ist mein Hirte,"* Erika began, haltingly, trying to remember it.

Peter picked it up in English:

> The Lord is my shepherd; I shall not want.
> He maketh me to lie down in green pastures . . .

"Magical incantations," Danny commented. "The words have no reference to so-called 'reality,' but possibly they help us in a psychological way. I suspect praying stimulates primitive parts of the brain. Actually, it even makes me feel a little better."

Then they piled soil on top of Jenny. The body would not last long, and would soon be consumed by the fungus and nematode worms; it would be digested by bacteria, and devoured by the soil mites that crawled everywhere. Soon there would be no trace of Jenny Linn left in the soil, her remains swallowed and recycled, her body returned to the bodies of other creatures. In the micro-world, no sooner had life ended than it became life again.

Afterward, Peter gathered the group, and spoke to them, trying to rally their spirits. "Jenny wouldn't want us to give up. She went on bravely. We can honor her by looking to our own survival now."

They assembled the backpack and the two duffel bags. They

couldn't linger at Jenny's grave; they had to keep moving toward the parking lot.

The lab notebook containing the map hadn't been lost; Karen had tucked it into the backpack. They took it out; it was crumbling, mushy, soaked, but they could still read the map. It showed a trail or path running from Station Echo to Station Delta, and finally to Alpha by the parking lot. They had a lot of travel ahead of them. "We don't know if any of the stations remain. But we can still follow the trail."

"If we can find it," Karen said.

They couldn't find any sort of trail. The rain had altered the landscape, shifting debris around, cutting new channels in the soil. Peter took out the compass and, studying the hand-drawn map, he sighted a line toward the parking lot. They began walking, with Peter leading the way, cutting a path with a machete. Karen stepped along behind him, carrying the harpoon across her shoulder. Rick Hutter brought up the rear, silent and wary, holding a machete ready for action.

Danny kept stopping to rest.

"Don't your feet hurt?" Peter asked him.

"What do you think?" Danny muttered.

"We could make you some shoes."

"It's hopeless," Danny said.

"But we must try," Erika said to him.

"I tried so hard to save Jenny."

Peter cut up strips of dead grass, while Erika wrapped Danny's feet in the grass, making rough moccasins out of the grass strips. Amar remembered the duct tape he'd found at Station Echo. He dug it out of a duffel bag and began winding strips of tape around Danny's grass moccasins to hold them on his feet. Danny stood up and took a few steps in his duct-tape-grass mocs. They were surprisingly tough, and remarkably comfortable.

▪ ▪ ▪

**A thudding noise** drifted high overhead, sounding strangely like a helicopter. A mosquito appeared. It soared downward out of the trees and dodged around them. Despite its large size, the mosquito held itself effortlessly suspended in the air on its beating wings, and it seemed to be studying them. It had a black-and-white striped body and striped legs. A long proboscis hung from its head. They could see twin razor-sharp cutting blades at the tip of the proboscis; the blades were caked with dried blood. The mosquito's blood-sucking tools looked sharp enough to stab straight through the body of a micro-human.

Danny Minot lost his nerve. "Get away!" he shouted at the mosquito, and ran, waving his arms and shuffling in his moccasins.

Perhaps attracted to Danny's motion, or perhaps to his scent, the mosquito chased after him, hovering just above his neck. Without warning, it dove down, almost spearing him between the shoulders with its proboscis. Danny flung himself to the ground and rolled over on his back, kicking his legs in the air. "Get off me!"

The mosquito buzzed over him, and lunged at him again—until Karen King leaped on top of Danny, straddling him and waving her machete, trying to scare off the mosquito.

It didn't scare easily.

"Form up," Peter shouted. "Make a defensive circle."

The humans formed themselves into a defensive ring around Danny, who lay on the ground in terror. They faced outward with their machetes held ready, watching the mosquito while it circled around them. The mosquito evidently smelled their blood, and may also have sensed the carbon dioxide they gave off as they breathed. It darted in and out, seeming to stare at them with goggly eyes, its proboscis dangling.

"Uh-oh," Erika Moll said.

"What?"

"It's a female Aedes albopictus."

"Meaning?" Danny said, lurching to his knees.

"An Asian tiger mosquito. The females are aggressive, and they carry diseases."

Rick Hutter grabbed Karen King by the arm. "Gimme that harpoon—"

"Hey!" she said, whirling on him, but he'd snatched the harpoon from her. Rick advanced toward the mosquito, raising the harpoon. "Be patient, Rick," Peter said. "Wait for an opening."

The mosquito darted in toward Rick. He saw his chance. He whirled the harpoon, using it like a stick, and whacked the mosquito across the head with it. "Go pick on someone bigger than you!" Rick yelled.

The mosquito thundered off, wobbling in the air.

Karen King began to laugh.

"What's so funny?" Rick ripped at her.

"The mosquitoes ran you back to your hotel in Costa Rica. You've come a long way, Rick."

"That's not funny," he said to her.

"Give me that back," she said, grabbing the harpoon from him. They got into a tug-of-war over the harpoon. Karen won. She yanked the harpoon away from Rick, who swore at her.

Karen couldn't take that. She lost it. She stepped toward Rick, pointing the harpoon at his face. "Don't use a word like that with me."

"Whoa, now." Rick backed away, holding up his hands.

Karen flung the harpoon at Rick's feet. "Take it."

Peter stepped between them. "We're a team, hey? You two have to stop fighting with each other."

Karen smoldered. "I wasn't fighting with Rick. If I was, he'd be holding his softies and puking his guts out."

. . .

**Peter Jansen stayed** out front, picking the route, cutting tirelessly at obstacles with the machete, and pausing every now and then to sharpen the blade with the diamond sharpener. The blade could cut anything as long as its edge was maintained. He tried to keep everybody's spirits up. "Do you know what Robert Louis Stevenson said about travel?" he said, calling back to the others. "He said, 'It is better to journey hopefully than to arrive.'"

"Fuck hope, I'll settle for arrival," Danny Minot remarked.

As he marched along at the back of the line, Rick Hutter glanced at the others, studying them. He considered Karen King. He really couldn't stand her. She was full of herself, arrogant, aggressive, thinking she was such an expert in spiders and arachnids and hand-to-hand combat. She was good-looking, but beauty wasn't everything. Even so, Rick felt somewhat better that Karen was with the group. She was a fighter, you could say that much for her. Right now she seemed icy, cold, alert, on edge, weighing every move. As if she was in a fight for her life . . . well, of course she was. He despised her and yet . . . he was glad to have Karen around.

Next Rick studied Erika Moll. She walked along pale, frightened. Erika was holding herself together, on the edge of some kind of emotional crack-up. The fungus devouring Jen's body . . . this had gotten to Erika, Rick thought. If Erika didn't pull herself together, she might be doomed. But who could say just which of the humans possessed the strength and cunning to get out alive from this kingdom of tiny horrors?

As for Amar Singh, Rick thought he seemed resigned to his fate, as if he'd already decided he was going to die.

Danny Minot trudged along in his duct-tape slippers. That guy's tougher than he looks, Rick thought, watching Danny. He could be a survivor.

Rick looked at Peter Jansen. How did Peter do it? He seemed so calm, almost gentle, at peace with himself in some deep way Rick couldn't fathom. Peter Jansen had become a true leader, and it fit him well. It was as if Peter had come into his own in the micro-world.

There was Rick Hutter himself.

Rick was not a reflective person. He rarely thought about himself. But he did now. Something strange was happening to him, and he couldn't quite understand it. He felt *okay*. Why, he wondered, did he feel okay? *I should feel terrible. Jenny is dead. Kinsky got ripped by ants. Who's next?* But this was the expedition Rick Hutter had always dreamed of, yet never thought possible. A journey into the hidden heart of nature, into a world of unseen wonders.

In all likelihood, he would die on this quest. Nature was not gentle or nice. There was no such thing as mercy in the natural world. You don't get any points for trying. You either survive or you don't. Maybe none of us will make it. He wondered if he would vanish here, in a small valley on the outskirts of Honolulu, swallowed up in a labyrinth of threats almost beyond imagining.

Got to keep going, Rick thought. Be smart. Be clever. Get through the eye of the needle.

**After what seemed** like miles of walking, Rick noticed a strange, bittersweet smell drifting in the air. What was it? He looked up and saw tiny white flowers overhead, scattered like stars through a tree that had snaky limbs and smooth, silver-gray bark. The odor of the flowers resembled semen, but with a nasty edge of something harmful.

Yes.

Nux vomica.

Rick called to the others to stop. "Wait a minute, guys. I've found something."

He knelt by a gnarled root, which poked from the ground. "It's a strychnine tree," he said to the group. With his machete he began hacking at the root, until he'd revealed a strip of inner bark, which he chopped out, working carefully with the machete. "This bark," he explained, "contains brucine. It's a drug that induces paralysis. I would have preferred the seeds, because they are incredibly toxic, but the bark will do."

Handling the bark carefully, trying not to get any sap on his hands, he tied a rope to the bark and started dragging it along behind him. "We can't put this in my pack. It would poison everything," Rick explained.

"That bark is dangerous," Karen said.

"You wait, Karen, it's going to get us food. And I'm hungry."

Erika stood aside and sniffed the air, watching, keeping alert for the warning smell of ants. The air felt slightly heavy as it went in and out of her lungs. Everywhere she looked, every crack and cranny in the soil, every blade of grass, every little ground-hugging plant, teemed with small living things—insects, mites, nematode worms. And she could actually see masses of soil bacteria, tiny dots in clumps. Everything was alive. Everything was feeding on something else. It reminded her . . . she had begun to feel really hungry.

They were ravenously hungry but had nothing to eat. They drank water from a hole in a tree root, and moved on, Rick dragging the piece of bark. "We have strychnine and we have the chinaberry," he said. "But it's not enough. We need at least one more ingredient." He kept looking around, scanning the vegetation for plants he recognized, for anything toxic. And eventually he found what he was looking for. He discovered it by scent. He recognized a sharp odor coming from a mass of vegetation.

"Oleander," Rick said, and he went toward a mass of shrubbery with long, pointed, shiny leaves. "The sap is the wicked stuff." Crashing through leaf litter, he arrived at the trunk of the shrub. He drew his machete, sharpened it, and hacked into the trunk. A translucent, milky sap surged forth, while Rick backed away quickly.

"That liquid will kill you fast if it touches your skin. It's got a lethal mix of cardenolides in it. It'll stop your heart, bam. You don't want to breathe the fumes, either. The fumes could give you a heart attack." While the sap oozed down the bark, Rick rummaged in his duffel, and he put on the lab apron and the rubber gloves and goggles he'd found at Station Echo.

Amar grinned. "Rick, you look like a mad scientist."

"Madness is my style," Rick said. He opened one of the plastic lab jars and advanced toward the running sap. Holding his breath, he let the jar fill up while the sap dribbled over his gloves. He screwed on the cap, then rinsed the outside of the jar in a drop of dew. He filled a second jar the same way, and held up both jars with a triumphant smile. "Now what we need to do is cook everything into a paste. For that, we need a fire."

But the forest was soaking wet after the rain. Nothing would burn.

"No problem," Rick said. "All we need is Aleurites moluccana."

"What the hell is that, Rick?" Karen King said.

"It's a candlenut tree," he answered. "The Hawaiians call them kukui trees. There are kukui trees growing all over this forest." He stopped, and looked up, and turned around, staring upward. "Yeah! That's a kukui, right there." He pointed at a tree with large, silvery leaves. The tree stood out like a pale thunderhead, ten meters away. It was hung with greenish balls of fruit.

They pressed on toward the candlenut tree. When they reached its base, they saw pulpy fruits scattered on the ground around the tree. "Let me have a machete," Rick said. "Now watch."

He began hacking into a fruit, chopping off the pulp using the machete. Soon he reached a hard core, a nut. "That's a kukui nut," he said. "The nut is loaded with oil. The ancient Hawaiians filled stone lamps with kukui nut oil. It's a great source of light. They also put the nuts on a stick and used it as a torch. The nut burns."

The kukui nut, covered with a glossy hard shell, proved difficult to crack. However, they took turns chopping away at it with a machete. The weapon had a heavy blade and an exceedingly sharp edge, and it cut slowly into the nut's shell. A few minutes of chopping revealed the oily nutmeat. They began hacking out chunks of the nut, and they made a pile of the nutmeat on the ground. They added husks of dry grass, which Peter peeled out of the center of dead grass stems, which had stayed dry despite the rain. Rick set his metal pot on top of the nut pieces and put on his chemical equipment. He adjusted his goggles and loaded the pot with strips of strychnine-root bark, chunks of the chinaberry, the two jugs of oleander sap, and water collected from the top of a leaf.

Rick lit the fire with the windproof lighter.

The tinder began to burn, and the kukui-nut fire blazed up, yellow and bright. It was a small fire by the standards of the normal world, not much bigger than a candle flame, yet to them it seemed like a bonfire. The fire heated their faces and made them blink and shy away, and it brought the water in the pot to a boil within seconds. Two minutes of boiling time was enough to reduce the contents of the pot to a tarry goo.

"Fresh curare," Rick said. "Let's hope, anyway."

Working carefully with a splinter of wood, wearing rubber gloves, and holding his breath, Rick packed the curare into a plastic lab bottle. He could dip his darts in the stuff to arm them with poison. He hoped the goop was poisonous, but he wouldn't know for certain until he used it in a hunting situation. He screwed the top on the bottle, then lifted the goggles from his eyes and parked them on his forehead.

Peter stared at Rick's plastic bottle and the brown-colored gunk in it. "So you think that'll take down big game? Something as big as a grasshopper?" he asked.

Rick offered him a wry smile. "It's not finished."

"How so?"

"We need one more ingredient."

"Which is—?"

"Cyanide."

"What?" Peter said, while the others gathered around, listening.

"You heard me—cyanide," Rick said. "And I know where to get it."

"Where?" Peter wondered.

In answer, Rick turned his head around slowly. "I can smell it. Hydrogen cyanide. Also known as prussic acid. That whiff of bitter almonds . . . can you smell it? Cyanide—a universal poison, it'll kill practically anything, and fast. Cyanide—a favorite of Cold War spies. Get this—there's an animal around here that makes cyanide. It's probably hiding under a leaf. Probably asleep."

The others stared, while Rick set out through the super-jungle, stopping occasionally to sniff the air, following his nose. He started turning over leaves, dragging them with both hands. The smell grew stronger; it tickled their noses now, once Rick had pointed it out to them. He stuck his head under a leaf. "Got it!" he whispered.

Under the leaf, a brownish, oily, jointed carapace gleamed, along with many curved legs. "That's a millipede," Rick said. "I'm just an ignorant botanist, but I know these guys make cyanide."

Erika moaned. "Don't! It's a very big animal. It's dangerous."

Rick chuckled. "A millipede?" He turned to Karen King. "Hey— Karen! What's the behavior of this animal when it's threatened?"

Karen King smiled. "Millipedes? They're scaredy cats."

"Wait! Are you sure it's not a *centipede*?" Danny quavered, remembering that Peter had said a centipede can deliver a nasty sting.

"Nah, this baby isn't any centipede," Karen said, kneeling and looking under the leaf. "Centipedes are predators. A millipede doesn't eat meat, it eats rotten leaves," she explained. "It's a peaceful animal. Doesn't even have a sting."

"What I thought." Rick hauled the leaf off the millipede, revealing it. The millipede lay curled up and seemingly asleep. It was a cylindrical animal with segmented armor and at least a hundred legs. In relation to the micro-humans, the millipede appeared about fifteen feet long, akin to the biggest boa constrictors. It breathed gently, making whistling noises through holes in its carapace; a millipede's version of snoring.

Rick drew his machete. "Wake up!" he cried, and slapped the millipede with the flat of the blade.

The animal thrashed suddenly. The humans backed away, and the odor grew stronger. The millipede curled its body into a tight spiral, a defensive posture. Holding his nose, Rick darted forward and whacked the animal again. He didn't want to hurt the millipede, he wanted to frighten it. The trick worked. A pungent smell of almonds mixed with a nasty, bitter stench filled the air, and blobs of an oily liquid oozed from pores in the millipede's armor. Rick opened a clean plastic jar and quickly put on his gloves, apron, and goggles.

The millipede wasn't going anywhere. It remained curled up, apparently frightened.

Wearing his gear, Rick advanced and scooped some of the liquid into the jar, until he'd collected about a cup of the stuff. "It's an oil. It's full of cyanide," he explained. He dumped the oil into the jar that held his curare goo, and stirred the mess with a stick. "I scared the cyanide out of the poor bastard," he said, holding up the jar of curare, which reeked of lethal chemicals. "And now," he added, "it's time to start hunting."

# Chapter 20

Vin Drake stood before a window that looked into the tensor core. The window was bulletproof, and it gave the scene in the chamber the appearance of a fish tank. Inside the chamber, the hexagons of the size-translation tubes were set flush with the plastic floor. Two men walked around the core: Telius and Johnstone.

They were suiting up. They put on segments of lightweight Kevlar armor, vests, arm coverings, greaves for the legs. The armor was tough enough to turn away the jaws of a soldier ant. Each man carried a .600 caliber Express gas rifle. The gun was powered by a pressurized gas tank. It fired a heavy steel needle tipped with a broad-spectrum super-toxin. Long range, total stopping power. The super-toxin was equally effective on insects, birds, and mammals. The gun had been designed especially for the protection of humans in the micro-world.

"Wait for the hexapod," Drake said.

Telius nodded and searched the floor with his eyes as if he was looking for a coin he'd dropped. Telius was a man of few words.

Drake went to a door marked RESTRICTED AREA. Under the sign there was a symbol that looked vaguely like a biohazard symbol, and a word: MICROHAZARD.

This was the entry door that led from the tensor core directly to Project Omicron. No sign on the door advertised its name, of course.

Drake took up a hand controller, a device that looked a little like a video game control, and punched a code into it. This disarmed the bots inside the Omicron zone, and he entered a cluster of small, windowless labs with its own special access to the tensor core. Nobody was permitted inside Omicron except for a handful of top Nanigen engineers. In fact, few of the Nanigen employees were even supposed to know of the existence of Omicron. Inside the rooms, several lab benches stood about, and on the benches sat a series of objects draped in black cloth shrouds.

The shrouds concealed the objects. Whatever they were, they were secret. Even people permitted to enter the Omicron zone were not allowed to look at them.

Drake took a shroud off one of the objects. It was a robot with six legs, and it vaguely resembled a Mars robot lander or possibly a metal insect. It was not very big, about a foot across.

Drake carried the six-legged robot back into the tensor core, and handed it to Johnstone. "Your transportation. It's got a full charge. Quad micro-lithiums."

"We're good," Johnstone mumbled. He was chewing something.

"God damn it," Drake barked. "What's in your mouth?"

"Energy bar, sir. You get so hungry—"

"You know the rule. No eating in the core. You could contaminate the generator."

"Sorry, sir."

"It's okay. Just swallow it." Drake clapped the man on the shoulder in a friendly way. A little bit of mercy goes a long way with people who work for you.

Telius placed the six-legged device into Hexagon 3. The two

men stood in Hexagons 2 and 1. Drake went into the control room. He would operate the generator himself. He had cleared all employees out of the core. Nobody could see him shrinking these men and this equipment. That would be a loose detail. He programmed Hexagon 3 to shrink the walker somewhat less than the humans would be shrunk. Just as he had locked down and started to initiate the sequence, Don Makele came into the control room behind him.

Drake and Makele watched together as the generator hummed and the power structures under the floor ramped up, and the hexagons descended. After the men had been shrunk, Drake placed the micro-humans in a transport box, and he put the hexapod in another box. He handed the boxes to Don Makele. "Let's just hope the rescue succeeds."

"Let's hope," Makele replied.

It was dangerous enough that Peter and the rest knew he had murdered Eric. But Drake also worried that Eric might have shared with his brother a very sensitive fact about Drake's activities that could not be made public—and that Peter might have passed it on to the other students. This particular fact, if it were known, could destroy Nanigen's business.

It was just business. Nothing personal, only logic. Just what had to be done in order to keep the business moving. Had Don Makele figured anything out? Drake couldn't be sure quite what the security man thought or knew. Drake gave his security chief a sharp sidelong glance. "How many ground-floor shares do you own?"

"Two, sir."

"I'm giving you two more shares."

Makele's expression didn't change. "Thank you."

Don Makele had just made two million dollars on this conversation. The man would keep his mouth shut.

# Chapter 21

**B**e quiet and don't move. They have keen eyesight and sharp hearing." Erika Moll was speaking. She was looking up into the branches of a mamaki plant, which extended some distance over their heads, unfolding large, lobed leaves. Clinging to a leaf was an enormous creature, a winged insect. The animal shone with brilliant greens, and its body was enclosed by a pair of lacy, green wings that looked like leaves. The animal had long antennae, bulging eyes, jointed legs, and a bloated abdomen, visibly packed with fat. They could hear a faint *hiss, uhh, hiss* sound as it breathed, the air flowing in and out of a line of holes in its flanks.

It was a katydid.

Rick took one of the blowgun tubes he had made and balanced it on his shoulder. He fitted a dart into the tube. The steel tip had a glob of stinking poison smeared on it, wafting a smell of bitter almonds and nastiness: Rick's curare. A wisp of mattress stuffing, which Rick had taken from Station Echo, was fastened to the butt of the dart.

Rick knelt and brought the tube to his lips, being exceedingly careful not to get any curare in his mouth. The cyanide made his eyes water, and his throat felt tight.

"Where's the heart?" he whispered to Erika Moll, who crouched beside him. She would direct his shot, for she knew insect anatomy best.

"The heart? It's posterior dorsal to the metathorax," Erika said.

Rick grimaced at Erika. "Huh?"

Erika smiled. "Just under the top of the animal's back."

Rick shook his head. "Can't make the shot. The wings are covering the area." He aimed the tube this way and that, and finally decided on a gut shot. He took aim at the animal's lower abdomen, took a deep breath, and fired.

The dart sank deep into the katydid. The creature gasped and shivered its wings. For a moment they thought it would take off and fly, but it didn't. The animal let out a deafening shriek, an earsplitting cry. Was it a cry of alarm, of pain? Its breathing sped up, and it sagged, and slipped, and dangled from the edge of the leaf.

Amar cringed, watching this. He had never realized how the suffering of an insect could affect him. Rick's curare was very powerful.

They waited. The katydid now dangled upside down. Its breathing slowed, the *hiss, uhh, hiss* dragging out and sounding raspy. Then its breathing stopped. Shortly afterward, the katydid fell to the ground.

"Nice work, Rick!"

"Rick the hunter!"

At first the dead katydid didn't seem appealing to anyone except Erika Moll. "I ate some termites once in Tanzania. They were quite delicious," Erika said. "People in Africa consider insects a delicacy."

Danny Minot sat down on a twig, feeling sick. He felt like he might heave just looking at the dead bug. "Maybe we'll find a burger joint around here," he said, trying to make a joke.

"Insect meat is not as bad as hamburger," Amar Singh said. "Mashed muscle, blood, and connective tissue of a bovine mammal really grosses me out. I will not eat a cow. But a katydid . . . well . . . maybe."

As they stared at the dead animal, their hunger grew sharper and more insistent. Their small bodies had been burning energy at a high rate. They simply had to eat. Had to. Their hunger overcame their squeamishness.

They butchered the katydid with machetes, while Erika guided them through the anatomy. As they pulled out meat and organs, Erika insisted that everything edible be washed in water. The animal's blood, the hemolymph, was a transparent, yellow-green liquid, and it dripped out as they cracked open its armor. They removed the legs, cutting through the tough bioplastic to get at the meat inside the legs. The upper rear legs, once split open, revealed masses of lean white muscle. They sliced steaks out of the largest parts of the legs. The animal's blood might contain toxins from the dart, and so the meat had to be washed. But after they'd dipped and rinsed the flesh in dewdrops, it smelled clean and delicious. They ate the meat raw. It had a mild, sweet flavor.

"Not bad," Rick said. "Tastes like sushi."

"Really fresh," Karen said.

Even Danny began eating the meat, gingerly at first but with increasing gusto, until he was cramming katydid steak into his mouth. "Needs salt," he mumbled.

The fat of the animal, soft and yellowish, oozed out of the abdomen. "The abdominal fat is good for you, I'm sure," Erika said. When none of them would try it, she scooped some fat out with her hands, and ate it raw. "It's sweet," she said. "Slightly nutty taste."

Their bodies craved the fat, and soon they all dug into the katydid's abdomen, scooping out the fat and gulping it down, licking their fingers.

"I feel like we're lions at a kill," Peter said.

The katydid yielded far more meat than they could possibly eat. They didn't want to let it go to waste, so they gathered up bundles of moist moss, and wrapped some of the meat in the moss, as much as they could carry, and stuffed it down in the duffel bags to keep it cool. They ended up with enough katydid steaks to keep them going for a while, anyway.

Feeling much better, they consulted the hand-drawn map. Peter had been carrying the map, and had been guiding them with the compass. He pointed to features.

"We're right here, I think," he said, noting a cluster of tree ferns that appeared on the map. "We're pretty close to Station Bravo. We might make Bravo by nightfall." He looked around and up at the sky. The light was going; it was late afternoon. "Let's just hope the station is intact."

Peter sighted the compass on the distant trunk of a palm tree, and they headed out, carrying the duffel bags and stopping once in a while to smell and listen for ants. Whenever they ran into an ant, they knew there would be more. As long as they moved quickly away, the ants wouldn't get too excited. The big danger was a nest entrance. As the sun began to set, shadows deepened on the forest floor, and Peter, who was leading, became more cautious about ants and more worried about stumbling into an ant nest. But so far, so good.

"Stop!" Peter said. He examined a mark on the stem of an ilihia plant growing up from the ground like a miniature tree: the stem had been cut with three V-shaped notches, and above them was splashed an X made of orange paint.

It was a blaze.

They had come to a trail.

Peter advanced, and found another orange X sprayed on a pebble. The trail proceeded onward, a faint disturbance of the soil marked with blazes at points along the way.

Minutes later, he stopped at the edge of a large, ragged hole in the ground. The soil around it had been dug up and turned over. Around the hole, giant footprints were impressed in the ground. The footprints had filled with water, like swimming pools. Peter consulted the map. "We're at Station Bravo," he said. "But there's no station."

The footprints told a story. Somebody had dug the station out of the ground and taken it away.

"We have to assume the worst," Karen King said, taking off her backpack and sitting down by the hole. She wiped her brow. "This is Vin Drake's work. It means he knows or suspects we're still alive. He's taken away our means of survival."

"So Drake could be hunting for us," Peter said.

"But how would he find us?" Rick wondered.

It was a good question. Their bodies, less than an inch tall, would not be easily noticed by a normal-size person. "Radio silence is essential now," Peter said.

The disappearance of Station Bravo meant that they had no place to hide during the hours of darkness. The sun was setting, and night was coming on fast, as it does in the tropics.

Erika was becoming increasingly alarmed as she watched the sun go down. "Just to point out," she said to the others, "the vast majority of insects come out at night, not during the day. And many of them are predators."

"We need to make a bivouac," Peter said. "We're going to build a fort."

**Not far away,** a hexapod walker vehicle strode rapidly across the forest floor, climbing over pebbles and pushing leaves aside, its six legs working with seemingly boundless energy. Motors on the legs whined.

Johnstone was driving, his hand sunk in a glove-like device, a hand controller, while he watched the readouts. The readouts told him the levels of power the servomotors were delivering to the vehicle's six legs. Telius sat next to him in the open cockpit, his eyes tracking left and right, up and down. Both men wore full-body armor.

The walker was powered by a nano-laminate micro-lithium power pack. It had a long range and plenty of power. Regular vehicles didn't work well in the micro-world; they got stuck, the wheels spun uselessly. Wheeled vehicles couldn't climb over obstacles, either. Instead, the Nanigen engineers had copied the design of an insect. The design worked extremely well.

The walker arrived at a hole in the ground.

"Stop," Telius said.

Johnstone brought the vehicle to a halt and stared into the hole. "That's Echo."

"Was," Telius corrected him.

Both men leaped out of the vehicle in soaring jumps, their armor clattering. They landed on their feet. They had a lot of practice at physical movement in the micro-world, and they knew how to use their strength. They began circling around the hole, examining moss, crumbs of dirt. The rain earlier in the day had obliterated most traces of the students' passage across the surface, but Johnstone knew that clues remained. He could track anybody anywhere. A growth of moss on a rock attracted his attention. He went up to it and studied it. The moss stood waist-high. He touched a narrow stalk that came up out of the moss: it was a spore stalk with a broken spore capsule at the end of it. The stalk was bent at a right angle, broken, and spores had spilled out, some of them clinging to the moss. In the sticky fluff of wet spore granules Telius found the imprint of a human hand. Somebody had grabbed the spore stalk, broken it, spilled the pollen, then put their hand in it. Farther on, Telius found a confused set of human footprints, clambering over a lump of dirt, in a spot under a spreading leaf that had protected the ground underneath from rain splashes.

Johnstone knelt and examined the footprints. "There's five of them—no, six. Walking in a line. He looked off. "Heading south-east."

"What's southeast?" Telius said.

"Parking lot." Johnstone narrowed his eyes and smiled.

Telius looked at him quizzically.

Johnstone picked a mite off his shoulder plate, crushed it, flicked it away. "Fucking mites. Now we know their plan."

"What plan?"

"They're looking for a ride back to Nanigen."

He was right, obviously. Telius nodded and began walking swiftly ahead, following clues. Johnstone jumped back into the hexapod and began driving it, following Telius as he moved swiftly ahead of the walker, often leaping over things, traveling at a pace somewhere between a dogtrot and a flat-out run. Occasionally Telius stopped to examine tracks in the soft soil. The targets hadn't made any effort to cover their tracks. They didn't suspect they were being followed.

But it was starting to get dark. Telius and Johnstone knew enough about the micro-world to know they needed to go to ground for the night. You did not move after dark. Not ever.

They stopped the hexapod. Johnstone ran an electric-shock cable in a circle around the vehicle, staking the cable into the ground chest-high, while Telius dug a foxhole directly underneath the vehicle. They energized the power cable from the capacitor—it would deliver a shock to any animal that touched it—and they hunkered down in the foxhole, sitting back to back, holding their .600 Expresses propped at their sides, loaded and ready for action.

Telius leaned back and put a dip of snuff under his lip. Johnstone took the radio locator with him into the foxhole, so that he could listen for any radio transmissions during the night. Johnstone wasn't worried. This was his tenth trip into the micro-world, and he knew what he was doing. He turned on the locator and watched the screen, looking for signs of any radio transmissions in the seventy-gigahertz band—the frequency used by the Nanigen headsets. He saw no sign of radio chatter. "They might not even have radios," he said to Telius.

Telius grunted in response, and spat a jet of tobacco.

They ate packaged meals. They got up to urinate separately, one man going off a few paces while the other man kept his partner covered with a gas rifle, just in case something tried to attack through the electrified wire. Some of those bastards out there could smell you when you took a piss.

Afterward, they traded watches, one man dozing while the other stayed on lookout. The lookout wore infrared goggles, his eyes just above the level of the ground.

Johnstone couldn't get over how damn lively this world was at night. In his IR goggles he saw constant, ceaseless movements of small creatures, going about their damn business—bugs, a million bugs, crawling everywhere. He didn't even know what they were. Seen one bug you've seen 'em all. As long as they weren't some kind of predator. He watched for the warm shape of a mouse. He wanted to shoot some big game tonight. Dropping a mouse with a .600 Express was as good as shooting a cape buffalo, which he'd done a few times in Africa.

"I'd like to blow away a mouse," Johnstone said. "That would be fun."

Telius grunted.

"I just don't want to meet a fucking Scolo," Johnstone added.

# Chapter 22

The six surviving students picked a rise of higher ground at the base of a small tree. At this spot they wouldn't get flooded out if it rained during the night. The tree was an ohia, and it had gone into bloom, shining with red blossoms, which glowed in the evening light.

"We should make a palisade," Peter said.

They gathered dry twigs and stalks of dead grass. They split the twigs and grasses into long splinters, then jammed the splinters into the ground side by side. This formed a wall of sharpened stakes surrounding their campsite, with the points of the splinters facing outward. They left an opening in the palisade just wide enough for a human to slip through, with a barrier of stakes around the opening in a zigzag, to make the entrance hard to penetrate. They continued to work on strengthening the fort as long as there was any light to see by. They dragged dead leaves inside the palisade, and used the leaves to make a roof over their heads. The roof would give protection against rain, and would also conceal them from the sight of flying predators.

They spread leaves on the ground under the roof, too. The leaf-bed kept them up off the ground, which was a constantly squirming bustle of small worms. They cut the lightweight tent to make a flat tarp out of it, and they spread the tarp on top of the leaf-bed to keep the surface dry and make the bed a little more comfortable for sleeping.

They had made a fort.

Karen brought out her spray bottle. It was nearly empty—she'd used most of it during the fight with the ants. "It's got benzoquinone in it. If anything attacks us, there's a couple of shots left."

"I feel much safer now," Danny said sarcastically.

Rick Hutter took the harpoon and dipped the point in the jar of curare. He leaned the harpoon against the palisade, ready for action.

"We should stand watches," Peter reminded them. "We'll change shifts every two hours."

There was the question of whether to build a fire. If you were stranded in the wilderness at night in the normal world, you would build a fire to stay warm and drive off predators. The situation was different in the micro-world. Erika Moll summed it up: "Insects are attracted to light. If we have a fire, it could draw predators from hundreds of meters away. I suggest we do not use our headlamps, either."

It meant they would spend the night in total darkness.


**As dusk turned** into night, the world was drained of color, fading into grays and blacks. They began to hear a pattering, thudding noise, coming closer—a sound of many feet passing over the ground.

"What's that?" Danny's voice rose in a quaver.

A herd of ghostly, delicate animals appeared and wandered past the camp. They were daddy longlegs, also called harvestmen, eight-legged creatures walking on spindly legs that seemed impossibly long. From the point of view of the students, the legs spanned fifteen feet. The body of each daddy longlegs was an oval nugget perched on the legs, and the body sported two bright eyes. The creatures glided over the terrain, tapping their legs around, looking for things to eat.

"Giant spiders," Danny hissed through his teeth.

"They're not spiders," Karen King said to him. "They're Opiliones."

"Meaning what?"

"They're a cousin of spiders. They're harmless."

"Daddy longlegs are poisonous," Danny said.

"No they aren't!" Karen snapped at him. "They have no venom. Most of them eat fungus and decaying material, detritus. I think daddy longlegs are beautiful. To me, they're the giraffes of the micro-world."

"Only an arachnologist would say that," Rick Hutter said to her.

The herd of daddy longlegs moved on, and the noises of their pattering feet faded. The darkness thickened and filled the forest like a rising tide. The sounds of the forest became different. It meant that a whole new set of creatures was coming out.

"It's the changing of the guard," Karen King's voice came out of dimness. "The new shift will be hungry." They couldn't see one another clearly, now.

As the night advanced, the noises rose up and grew stronger, more insistent, swirling around them. From near and far came screeching, booming, wailing, tapping, whistling, stretched-out, growling, and pulsing sounds. The humans could feel vibrations running through the ground, too, for some insects communicated by tapping on the ground or on a surface. The students couldn't understand a word of it.

. . .

**They curled up** next to one another, while Amar Singh took the first watch. Holding the harpoon, he climbed up on the leaf-roof of the fort, where he sat bolt upright, listening, and sniffing the air. The air was thick with pheromones. "I don't know what I'm smelling," he confessed. "It's all strange to me."

Amar began to wonder how they were able to smell anything. Their bodies had been shrunken by a factor of a hundred. Presumably this meant that the atoms in their bodies were a hundred times smaller, as well. If so, how could the tiny atoms in their bodies interact with the giant atoms of the environment? They shouldn't be able to smell anything. In fact, they shouldn't be able to taste anything. In fact, how could they breathe? How could the tiny hemoglobin molecules in their red blood cells capture the giant oxygen molecules that existed in the air they breathed? "There's a paradox," Amar said to the others. "How can the tiny atoms in our bodies interact with the normal-size atoms of the world around us? How can we smell anything? How can we taste anything? In fact, how does our blood manage to hold oxygen? We should be dead."

No one could figure it out. "Maybe Kinsky would have had an answer," Rick said.

"Maybe not," Peter said. "I get the idea Nanigen doesn't understand their own technology very well."

Rick had been thinking about the micro-bends. He had been secretly inspecting his arms and hands, looking for bruises. So far he hadn't noticed anything. "Maybe the micro-bends are caused by some mismatch in the sizes of atoms," he said. "Maybe something goes wrong in the interactions between the small atoms in our bodies and the large atoms around us."

A mite crawled over Amar, and he plucked it off his shirt and dropped it, not wanting to hurt the creature. "What about our gut bacteria? We have trillions of gut bacteria inside us. Did they get shrunk, too?"

Nobody had any idea.

Amar went on, "What happens if our super-tiny bacteria get loose in this ecosystem?"

"Maybe they'll die of the bends," Rick said.

**A silvery glow** had brightened the forest slightly. The moon was up, and was climbing higher in the sky. Along with the moon came an eerie, booming cry, which echoed through the forest: *Puuu . . . eee . . . ooo . . . o-o-o-.* . . .

"My God, what was that?" someone said.

"I think it's an owl. We're hearing it at a lower frequency."

The hoot sounded again, coming from a tree top, and the cry sounded like a death threat wrapped in a moan. They felt the owl's lethal presence somewhere above them.

"I'm beginning to understand what it feels like to be a mouse," Erika said. The hooting stopped, and then a pair of sinister wings crossed the canopy in total silence. The owl had bigger prey to catch; it had no interest in anything as small as a micro-human.

A creaking, rustling tremor shook them. The ground heaved.

"There's something under us!" Danny cried, leaping to his feet. He lost his balance as the ground began to break apart and he began staggering back and forth as if on the deck of a heaving ship.

The others scrambled up off the bed of leaves, pulling out their machetes, while the earth under them groaned and trembled. Amar took up the harpoon, raised it over his head, his heart hammering in his chest. He was ready to kill. He knew it. The humans scattered, running up against the palisade, wondering if they should flee outside or wait and see the threat materialize.

And then it appeared, a pinkish-brown cylinder of stunning

size, rising up from the bowels of the earth, thrusting the dirt before it. Danny screamed. Amar almost threw the harpoon, but checked the thrust at the last moment.

"It's just an earthworm, guys," Amar said, putting down the harpoon. He wasn't going to stab an earthworm if he could help it; the gentle animal was just trying to make a living in the dirt, and was a threat to nobody.

The earthworm didn't like what it found. It withdrew, sliding back down into the earth, and it traveled on, crunching like a bulldozer, while the palisade wall jiggled and shook.

**As the moon** climbed, the bats came out. The students began to hear whistling cries, staccato sounds, and whooshing roars, crisscrossing the treetops and gulfs above them: the bats' sonar. The noise was eerie, the sound of flying predators using beams of ultrasound to probe the air for prey. A bat's sonar is too high-pitched for human hearing. But in the micro-world, the bats sounded like submarines pinging the deep.

They heard a bat zeroing in on a moth and killing it.

The kill began with a lazy chain of pings. The bat was directing pulses of sound toward a moth, identifying the prey and ranging the moth, getting its distance and the direction it was flying. Next, the bat's pings sped up and grew louder. Erika Moll explained what was happening. "The bat is 'painting' the moth with sonar. It is firing a beam of ultrasound at the moth and hearing the echoes that come back. The echoes tell the moth's location, its size and shape, and the direction it's flying. The pings get faster as the bat zeroes in on the moth."

Often, as a bat was pinging a moth, the moth would defend itself with a loud drumming noise. "Moths have very good hearing," Erika explained. The moth had heard the bat's sonar, and the moth was starting up its defensive noisemakers. The banging sounds were coming from drums on the moth's abdomen. The sounds could jam the bat's sonar, confusing the bat, making the moth invisible to the bat. As a bat closed in on a moth, there would be a crescendo of bat pings, mixed with a rising drumming sound as the moth tried to jam the bat's sonar. *Ping, ping, ping*, went a bat. *Pom-pom-pom-pom*, went a moth, trying to jam the bat's sonar. Sometimes a moth's drumming would end abruptly. "The bat ate the moth," Erika informed them.

They listened, almost hypnotized, as the bat-sounds played over their heads. And then a bat passed right over their fort, with a *whoomp* of velvet wings. The sound of the animal's sonar as it passed almost deafened them, and left their ears ringing.

"This world scares the hell out of me," Karen King said. "But somehow I'm glad to be here anyway. I must be nuts."

"At least it's interesting," Rick commented.

"I do wish we had a fire," Erika muttered.

"Can't do it. It would advertise us to every predator out there," said Peter.

Erika Moll was the person who had advised them not to build a fire. But even so, the ancient human in her longed for a fire. A simple fire, warm and bright and comforting. A fire meant safety, food, home. But only darkness and chill and weird noises surrounded her. She began to notice the sound of her heart thudding in her throat. Her mouth had gone dry, and Erika realized that she was terrified, more frightened than she had ever been in her life. The primitive part of her mind wanted to scream and run, even when the rational part of her mind knew it would be certain death to run blindly through this super-jungle at night. The rational thing was to stay silent and not move, yet her primitive fear of darkness threatened to overwhelm her.

The darkness seemed to coil around the humans and watch them.

"What I'd give for a light," Erika whispered. "Just a small light. I would feel better."

She felt Peter's hand close around her hand. "Don't be afraid, Erika," he said.

Erika began to cry silently, gripping Peter's hand.

Amar Singh sat with the harpoon across his knees. He smeared more curare on the point, working by sense of touch and hoping he wouldn't cut himself. Peter began to sharpen his machete with the diamond sharpener. They heard a *whisk, cling* sound as Peter passed the sharpener back and forth over his machete. The others slept, or tried to sleep.

**The sounds changed.** A blanket of quiet dropped around them. The quiet woke the sleepers. They listened, straining their ears. The quiet seemed worse than any noise.

"What's going on?" Rick Hutter said.

"Take up your weapons," Peter whispered urgently.

There were clinking sounds—machetes being grappled, held, poised.

Then a strange, soft whistling noise began. It seemed to come from several places at once. The whistling came closer. Something was approaching.

"What is that?"

"It sounds like breathing."

"Maybe it's a mouse."

"That's no mouse."

"It has lungs, anyway."

"Yeah—too many lungs."

Peter said, "Get your headlamps ready. Turn them on at my signal."

"What's that smell?"

An acrid, musty reek filled the air. It grew stronger, and thicker, until the smell seemed to coat their skin like oil.

"That's venom," Peter Jansen said.

"What kind, Peter?" Karen asked sharply.

Peter tried to summon from his memory the odors of different venoms. He didn't recognize it. "I don't know what—"

A very large, heavy animal began rushing toward them, making crashing sounds.

"Lights!" Peter shouted.

Several headlamps came on, and the beams crisscrossed over a vast centipede, rippling toward them. It had a blood-red head studded with four eyes. Under its head, a pair of red fangs with black tips were held open around a complicated mouth. The centipede traveled on forty legs moving in waves, and its body was encased in segmented armor the color of mahogany. It was a Hawaiian giant centipede, a Scolopendra, one of the largest centipedes on earth.

# Chapter 23

The Scolopendra burst through the wooden palisade, scattering splinters, while the people leaped and tumbled aside, screaming and shouting. The centipede had a keen sense of smell, and the humans' scent had provoked it to attempt an ambush. The centipede mistook the leaf-bed for its prey, and sank its fangs into it as the humans scattered. With astonishing speed, it coiled itself around the leaf-bed. Gallons of venom gushed from the fangs, splashing, and filling the air with a foul odor.

The individual legs of a giant centipede end in pointed fangs— foot-fangs. Each foot-fang is loaded with venom, and can deal a sting. The Scolo's forty legs hammered around, dribbling venom.

Amar had been sitting on the leaf roof of the shelter. When the centipede crushed the roof, Amar fell down among the coils. He threw himself facedown to the ground, trying to protect himself.

Karen knew something about centipede anatomy. She shouted to Amar: "Watch out for the legs! Each leg has a poison barb!"

Amar rolled over, and began writhing this way and that while the foot-fangs danced and thrust around him, dribbling venom. He was going to be pierced by one of those feet.

"Amar!" Peter shouted. He advanced with his machete and began hacking at the centipede, trying to draw the centipede away from Amar, but the machete had no effect, only bounced off the armor. Amid shouts and crisscrossing headlamp beams, the others struck at the centipede with their machetes, trying to distract it and give Amar a chance to escape. Karen sprayed the benzo spray, but the animal didn't even seem to notice.

The centipede suddenly let go of the leaf-bed and began lashing its head back and forth, opening and closing its mouth-fangs, looking to seize prey. It had poor eyesight but could detect smell with its antennae, which it now whacked around. An antenna slapped Karen, knocking her into the wall of the palisade.

The centipede swung around and faced her.

Amar, lying on his back on the ground, rolled away as the centipede turned on Karen. He struggled to his feet, still holding the harpoon, and shouted, "Hey!"

That had no effect, so Amar jumped up onto the centipede's back. He stood on the armored shell, trying to keep his balance as it heaved around, holding the harpoon, uncertain where to thrust it.

"Aim for the heart!" Karen shouted.

He had no idea where the heart was; the creature's body was divided into many segments. "Where?" he shouted.

"Segment four!"

Amar counted four segments down from the head and raised the harpoon, but then hesitated. There was something magnificent about the creature. In that moment of hesitation, the centipede heaved its back. Amar drove the harpoon down deep into the centipede's back, but was thrown off. He tumbled to the ground, the harpoon still lodged in the centipede's back. The centipede whirled around, twisting and writhing, and its fangs snapped shut, the point of one fang slashing across Amar's chest, tearing apart his shirt and covering him with squirting venom. The venom drenched Amar.

Amar curled up, moaning in pain. He felt as if his chest had been dipped in flames. The centipede went into a flurry while the harpoon clanged around. Rick and Karen rushed in and dragged Amar away. The centipede uncoiled, coiled up again, hissing. The harpoon stood in its back.

"Go up!" Karen shouted. "Centipedes don't climb trees!"

They had camped at the foot of a tree, and the tree was covered with moss. They jumped up into the moss, grabbing handholds and footholds, and started to climb. Because gravity was less powerful in the micro-world, they could climb quickly and easily. Amar tried to climb, but shooting waves of pain were running through his body, and he couldn't grip anything. Peter hauled Amar up, lifting him under the arms and trying not to touch the wound on his chest. They quickly reached two feet above the ground, and they stopped in a sort of cave of moss, looking out and down, trying to see the centipede.

The centipede was crawling out of the ruins of the fort, the harpoon waving in its back. They could hear it hissing. It did not get very far. It became still, and its breathing ceased. Amar had dealt it a fatal blow with the harpoon. Rick's curare had worked.

**They were huddled** in a cave of moss, two feet above the ground, out of reach of any centipede. They had turned off their headlamps. Amar Singh seemed to be going out of his mind. Peter and Karen held him, talking to him, trying to keep him calm. Amar was in shock, sweating profusely, but his body temperature plummeted, and his skin felt cold and clammy. They wrapped him in the space blanket.

They also examined him with a light. The slash from the centipede fang had laid open his chest to the bone, and he had obviously lost a lot of blood. He had been splashed with a large quantity of venom, too, which had drenched the wound. There was no way of knowing how much venom Amar had absorbed, or what it would do to him.

Amar struggled with them, delirious. His breathing ran fast and shallow. "It burns . . ."

"Amar, listen to me. You've been envenomed," Peter said.

"We have to leave this place!"

"You need to keep still."

"No!" Amar struggled while the others held him and tried to calm him. "It's coming! It's almost here!" he moaned.

"What is?"

"We're going to die!" Amar screamed. He fought to escape.

They held him down, trying to quiet his struggling.

Peter knew that the venom of centipedes had not been studied much by scientists. There was no antivenin, no antidote, for any type of centipede venom. Peter feared Amar might go into a breathing arrest. Some of the symptoms of centipede envenomation resembled rabies. Amar was experiencing waves of hyperesthesia, feeling and sensing everything with too much intensity. Sounds were too loud, and the slightest touch on his skin made him cringe. He kept trying to pull the space blanket off his body. "It burns, it burns," he kept saying.

Peter flicked on his headlamp for a moment to get a look at Amar.

"Turn it off!" Amar screamed, swinging his arms. The light hurt his eyes. His eyes watered with tears that streamed down his face, though he wasn't crying. Above all, an unspeakable feeling of doom had gripped Amar's mind. He seemed to believe that at any moment something terrible would happen. "We have to leave this place!" he moaned. "It's coming! It's getting closer!" But he couldn't say what "it" was.

"Run!" Amar shrieked. He tried to crawl out of the moss cave and jump. Peter and the others struggled with him, and they held his arms and legs, trying to keep him from leaping from the tree into the night.

**For a long** time Amar Singh struggled and babbled, but during the early hours of the morning he grew quieter and seemed to stabilize. Or perhaps he had exhausted himself. Peter took this as a good sign. He hoped Amar was turning the corner.

"I'm going to die," Amar whispered.

"No you're not. Hang in there."

"I've lost my faith. When I was a little kid I believed in reincarnation. Now I know there's nothing after death."

"It's the venom talking, Amar."

"I've hurt so many people in my life. No way to make it up now."

"Come on, Amar. You haven't hurt anybody." Peter hoped his voice conveyed confidence.

All of this happened in darkness, for they didn't dare turn on their lights. Erika Moll had been very afraid of the dark as a small child, and her fear of the dark roared back as she listened to Amar's frightened babbling. Amar's suffering hit Erika Moll harder than the others, and she began to cry. She couldn't stop crying.

"Will somebody shut the woman up, please?" Danny Minot said. "It's bad enough with Amar going insane, but this sobbing is getting on my nerves." He began stroking his nose, running his fingertips over his face.

Peter could see that Danny wasn't doing well, either, but he turned his attention to Erika. He put his arms around her and smoothed her hair. They had been lovers, but this wasn't love, it was survival. Just trying to keep people from dying. "It will be all right," he said to Erika, and squeezed her hand.

Erika began reciting the Lord's Prayer. *"Vater unser im Himmel . . ."*

"She turns to God when science fails her," said Danny.

"What do you know about God?" Rick said to him.

"As much as you do, Rick."

The others tried to sleep. The moss was warm and soft, and they were exhausted after the harrowing fight. None of them wanted to fall asleep, but sleep took them gently in its arms anyway.

# Chapter 24

CHINATOWN, HONOLULU
30 OCTOBER, 11:30 A.M.

Lieutenant Dan Watanabe sat at a table in an eatery in downtown Honolulu, called the Deluxe Plate, holding a piece of Spam sushi in his fingertips. The sushi was a ball of fried rice wrapped in seaweed, with a chunk of Spam at the center. He took a bite. The seaweed, the fried rice, and the salty pork combined in his mouth into a taste that could be found nowhere but Hawaii.

He savored it, chewing slowly. During World War II, whole shiploads of Spam had arrived in Hawaii to feed the troops. American soldiers had basically fought the war on Spam; Spam and an atomic bomb had guaranteed American victory. At the same time, the people of Hawaii had developed a passion for the canned pork product, a love that would never die. Dan Watanabe believed that Spam was a brain food. He believed it could help him think more clearly about a case.

Right now he thought about the missing Nanigen executive. The executive, Eric Jansen, had apparently drowned off Makapu'u

Point when his boat had stalled out and flipped in heavy surf. However, his body had not turned up. Plenty of white sharks cruised the Molokai Channel, the stretch of sea between Makapu'u Point and the island of Molokai, and the sharks could have eaten the body. But more likely the body should have washed up around Koko Head, since the prevailing winds and currents would carry it that way. Instead, it disappeared. Then, shortly after Eric's disappearance, his brother, Peter Jansen, shows up in Hawaii.

And then Peter disappears.

The Honolulu Police had gotten a call from the chief security officer of Nanigen, Donald Makele, who reported that seven graduate students from Massachusetts had gone missing along with a Nanigen executive named Alyson F. Bender. One of those students had been Peter Jansen. The students had been in employment discussions with Nanigen. All eight persons, including the Bender woman, had gone out for the evening and never returned.

Don Makele's call had been taken by the Missing Persons Detail in the Honolulu Police Department. A report had been written up, and it ended up in the "Daily Highlights" bulletin that circulated through the department each morning. Watanabe, glancing over the "Highlights," had noticed it. So there were two missing Nanigen executives, Eric Jansen and Alyson Bender. Plus seven students.

Nine people tied to Nanigen. Gone.

Of course, people did go missing in Hawaii, especially young tourists. The surf could be very dangerous. Or they went on a drinking binge, or they got so high on Puna weed they seemed to forget their names. They hopped a flight to Kauai and went backpacking on the Na Pali Coast, and didn't tell anybody where they'd gone. But nine people, all linked to Nanigen, from different places, doing different things, all missing?

Dan Watanabe took a swig of black coffee, and finished off his sushi. He had an unpleasant feeling mixed with a professional curiosity. He could almost smell it. It was a whiff of probable cause. A scent of unrevealed crime.

"Refill?" the waitress, Misty, said to him, offering a coffee pitcher.

"Thanks." It was Kona coffee, strong enough to put structure in one's afternoon.

"Dessert, Dan? We got a haupia chiffon pie."

Watanabe patted his stomach. "Gosh, no thanks, Misty. I just had my ration of Spam."

Misty left the check on the table, and he stared out the window. An elderly Chinese woman passed by, hauling a wheelie basket full of her day's shopping, which included a fish wrapped in newspaper, the tail sticking out. A shadow raced down the street, darkening the people—a passing cloud—then hot sunlight flared, then another cloud-shadow. As usual, the trade winds were driving rain and sunlight across Oahu. Rain and sun, endlessly marching over the island, and when you looked into the mountains, you often saw rainbows.

He put on his sunglasses and walked back to police headquarters, taking his time, running his tongue over his teeth, trying to work out a Spam knot from between his molars. By the time he got back to his office, Watanabe had made up his mind.

He had decided to open an investigation into Nanigen.

Do it quietly.

The matter was sensitive. Nanigen was a rich company, with a high-profile CEO. The company might have political connections, who knows. The Nanigen matter would take time away from his investigation into the bizarre case involving the three dead men—the lawyer Willy Fong, the PI Marcos Rodriguez, and the unidentified Asian male. The victims had bled to death from numerous cuts while they'd been inside Fong's locked office. The Willy Fong

Mess, as he liked to call it, would have to go on hold. He wasn't getting anywhere with the Willy Fong Mess anyway.

At headquarters, Watanabe dropped by the office of his boss, Marty Kalama. "I want to look into these disappearances at Nanigen."

"Why, Dan?" Kalama said, sitting back and blinking rapidly.

Watanabe knew Kalama wasn't questioning his methods. Kalama just wanted to hear what he had in mind, his reasoning. Watanabe said, "First I want to wait a short while and see if the missing people turn up. If they don't, I'll assemble a squad. But right now, I just want to do a little poking around on my own. Low-pro."

"You suspect criminal activity?"

"I don't have probable cause. But things don't add up."

"Okay," Kalama said. "Explain."

"Peter Jansen. When I showed him a video of his brother, Eric, drowning, he seemed to recognize a female in the video who was a witness to the drowning. But then he, like, covers it up, says he doesn't know the woman. I think he was lying. Then I had a couple of my people visiting Nanigen to get info on Eric Jansen, the executive who drowned. My guys met the CEO, named Drake. Drake was polite, but. My guys said it was like a traffic stop when the subject is visibly nervous but there's no obvious reason for him to be nervous."

"Maybe Mr., uh—"

"Drake."

"—Drake was upset about losing his executive."

Watanabe said, "It was more like he had a body in the trunk of his car."

Marty Kalama squinted behind his rimless spectacles. "Dan, I'm not hearing about evidence."

Watanabe patted his stomach. "Gut. My Spam is talking to me."

Kalama nodded. "Be careful."

"About what?"

"You know what Nanigen does, right?"

Watanabe grinned. Oops. He hadn't yet looked into Nanigen's business.

"They make small robots," Kalama went on. "Really small."

"Okay, so?"

"A company like that could have contracts with the government. That's trouble."

"You know something about Nanigen?" Watanabe asked his boss.

"I'm just a cop. Cops don't know shit."

Watanabe grinned. "I'll keep you out of it."

"The hell you will," Kalama snapped. "Get out of here." He took off his glasses and polished them with a Kleenex, watching Dan Watanabe leave. The guy was quiet and smart, one of his best detectives. Those were the ones who created the worst trouble. The thing about trouble was that Marty Kalama kind of enjoyed it.

# Chapter 25

**M**orning came, and the six survivors stirred inside a pocket of moss on the trunk of a tree somewhere on a rain-forested mountainside in the Koʻolau Pali. The birds were singing, slow and deep. They sounded like whales calling to one another in the deep sea.

Peter Jansen stuck his head out of the hiding place in the moss on the side of the ohia tree and looked around. He could see the remains of the fort on the ground below, trashed by the centipede. Nearby lay the dead centipede. Ants had already begun butchering it, and had removed large portions of the carcass.

They were near the bottom of a sea, Peter reflected. It was a sea of jungle as deep as any ocean.

He craned his neck, looking up along the tree's trunk. The tree was young and small, and its crown was ablaze with red blossoms, as if the tree had burst into flame. "I think we should try to climb to the top," Peter said.

"Why?" Rick asked.

Peter looked at his watch. "I'd like to get a view of the parking lot. To make sure we're headed in the right direction. And to watch what happens in the parking lot."

"Makes sense," Rick said.

Peter and Rick pulled their heads in. The others sat huddled in the moss, with Amar between them wrapped in the silver blanket; he had finally fallen asleep. A bruise had developed on the side of his head, extending over his left temple. It might be just a bruise, or it might be a sign of the bends—in any case, they decided that Rick would remain with Amar to look after him, while the others would attempt to climb the tree. There were four radio headsets, all told. Rick would keep one radio, while the climbers would carry the others. Peter said, "We should keep radio silence, except in an emergency."

"You think somebody from Nanigen could be listening?" Karen said.

"The radio's range is only a hundred feet. But if Drake suspects we're alive, he may be listening for us. And he's capable of anything," Peter answered.

They began climbing the tree. Peter led the way up the first pitch. He put on the belt with the reel and line attached to it, and carried the rope ladder from the backpack. Karen King took along Rick Hutter's blowgun and the box of darts, and the jar of curare. Karen would serve as the expedition's hunter.

**Tree climbing proved** to be extremely easy. Mosses and lichens, as well as the rough bark, offered plenty of handholds and footholds as they climbed. They were strong enough in the micro-world to be able to hang from something with one hand, even by just a few fingers. And it didn't really matter if you fell. There was no real danger in a fall. You'd land on the ground unhurt.

They took turns lead-climbing. One person, secured by another with the reel and belt down below, would lead the way up the trunk carrying the rope ladder, which he would then secure to the tree and drop down to the others to climb.

The tree was covered with furrowed bark, and the bark was densely packed with mosses and liverworts—tiny plants, some of them almost microscopic in size, though to the micro-humans the mosses and liverworts seemed as big as shrubbery. The tree was also crusted with many kinds of lichens, frilly, lacy, and knobby. The leaves were rounded and leathery and the branches snaked around.

Eventually, Danny Minot gave up. "I can't do this," he said, and sat down and tucked himself into a lump of lichen in a sunny, warm spot.

"Do you want to stay here while the rest of us go on?" Peter asked.

"Actually, I'd prefer to be in the Algiers Coffeehouse in Harvard Square, drinking espresso and reading Wittgenstein." Danny grinned weakly.

Peter handed him a radio headset. "Call if you have an emergency."

"Okay."

Peter put his hand on Danny's shoulder. "Everything's going to be all right."

"Obviously not." Danny tucked himself down into a frilly lichen.

"We can't just give up, Danny."

Danny scowled and leaned back in the lichen, and put on the radio headset. "Testing, testing," he said into the radio. His voice crackled in their ears.

"Hey—radio silence," Peter warned him.

"Vin Drake! Help! S.O.S. We're stuck in a tree!" Danny shouted into his mike.

"Knock it off."

"I was only joking."

. . .

**"Got a transmission."** Johnstone bent over the radio locator in the cockpit of the hexapod, earphones on his head. He started laughing. "Dumb bastards—they're calling Drake for help." His eyes moved upward, searched the canopy. "They're in a tree somewhere above us."

Telius grunted. A pair of binoculars hung around his neck. Telius stood up with the binoculars and began searching through the crowns of trees all around, looking for motion, listening for voices. The spies were somewhere up there. They were not going to be easy to find.

He couldn't see anything. Then he silently pointed with one finger: go this way.

Johnstone toggled the joystick. The hexapod responded by walking swiftly and smoothly across the forest floor, making almost no sound, only a faint whine coming from the motors on the legs.

Telius was pointing to the base of a tree. A pandanus tree. Telius pointed upward along the trunk. "Up," he said.

Johnstone operated a control, and claws on the vehicle's feet were withdrawn into sheaths, revealing soft pads covered with extremely fine bristles. They were nano-bristles. The bristles, similar to the pads on a gecko's feet, could stick to virtually any surface, even glass. The hexapod began to walk straight up the trunk of the tree. Strapped in the cockpit, the two men hardly seemed to notice that the walker had gone vertical. They could barely feel gravity anyway.

**The climbers reached** the top branches of the ohia tree, and Karen King led the way up the final pitch. She crawled and walked along a high branch into a cluster of leaves that stood in bright sunlight, where she broke out into a magnificent view. The others followed her, and they ended up standing on a branch among the leaves. The branch swayed in the breeze. The ohia blossoms, red and spray-like, resembled fireworks. The flowers consisted of a radiant explosion of red stamens, and they smelled impossibly sweet.

The view from among the flowers took in the Manoa Valley and the surrounding mountain ridges. Around the valley, mountain flanks, cloaked in green and sheared by cliffs, plunged down from ridges and defiles, veiled in clouds. Waterfalls threaded through rifts in the forested mountainsides. Tantalus Peak, the curving rim of a volcanic crater, looked down on the valley from the north. To the southwest beyond the narrow mouth of the valley, the buildings of Honolulu rose, revealing how close to the city the valley was. Even so, the Nanigen headquarters, on the far side of Pearl Harbor, might just as well have been a million miles away.

Off to the southeast, they saw the greenhouse and the parking lot, a dirt expanse dotted with puddles of rainwater. The parking lot was empty and deserted; no sign of people or vehicles. At the narrow mouth of the valley the access tunnel was visible, running through a cliff area. They could see the security gate. The gate was closed.

Peter took a compass reading on the parking lot. "Parking lot is on a bearing of a hundred and seventy degrees south-southeast," he said to the others as he peered at the compass. Then he looked at his watch. It was nine-thirty in the morning. The shuttle truck wouldn't arrive until the afternoon. If indeed it did arrive. But right now the valley looked devoid of human activity.

A thundering sound passed by overhead in the leaves. Instinctively, the humans ducked, grabbing at leaves and wedging themselves down. Peter went sprawling. "Look out!" he yelled. A butterfly zoomed past. Its wings, patterned with orange, gold, and black, made booming sounds as the creature whipped and twisted through sunlight. The insect seemed to be playing. Then it hovered, wings thundering, and landed on an ohia flower.

Droplets of nectar gleamed in the blossom. The butterfly unrolled its proboscis and sent it deep into the flower, until the tip touched a droplet. They heard sucking, squishing sounds as the butterfly pumped seemingly endless gallons of nectar into its stomach.

Peter slowly raised his head.

Karen was laughing. "You should see yourself, Peter. Frightened by a butterfly."

"It's, uh, impressive," Peter said sheepishly.

The species, Erika told them, was the Kamehameha butterfly, native to Hawaii. It fed in the flower for a while, poking here and there, while the wind carried a bitter stench to the humans. The butterfly might be lovely to look at, but it gave off a nasty smell.

"It's a chemical defense," Erika Moll said. "Phenols, I think. The compounds are bitter enough to make a bird throw up."

The butterfly ignored the humans. It took off from the flower and with powerful strokes caught the wind, and soared outbound into the blue oceans of air.

The butterfly had taught the humans a lesson. The flowers dripped with liquid sugar. Just what they needed for energy. Karen King crawled into a flower headfirst. She reached a glob of nectar and began scooping it into her mouth with both hands. "You guys have to try this," her voice came out of the flower, muffled with stickiness. She could feel her body ramping up with energy almost as soon as she swallowed the nectar.

The others crawled into flowers and drank as much nectar as possible.


**While they gorged** on nectar, a movement in the distance caught Peter's eye. "Somebody's coming," he said.

They stopped drinking and watched as a vehicle approached in the distance, coming up the winding road from Honolulu. It was a black pickup truck. It followed the road along the cliff edge as it climbed, and stopped at the gate in front of the tunnel. Here the driver got out. Peter, studying the scene with binoculars, saw the man take a yellow sign from the back of the pickup truck. The man placed the sign on the gate.

"He put up a sign," Peter said.

"What does it say?" Karen asked.

Peter shook his head. "I can't see."

"Is it the shuttle truck?"

"Hold on."

The man drove the truck through the gate; it closed behind him. Moments later the truck emerged from the tunnel and descended into the valley, and stopped in the parking lot. The man got out.

Peter studied the scene through the binoculars. "I think it's the same man who dug up the supply stations. Muscular guy, wearing an Aloha shirt. There's a sign on the truck that says NANIGEN SECURITY."

"That doesn't sound like the shuttle," Karen said.

"No."

In the parking lot, the man walked around, scuffing at things, peering at the ground. Then he got down on his knees and started running his hand back and forth under a clump of white ginger plants.

"He's searching the ground around the edge of the parking lot," Peter said.

"For us?" Karen asked.

"Looks like it."

"That's not good."

"Now he's talking on a handheld radio to somebody. Uh-oh."

"What?"

"He's looking straight at us."

Karen scoffed. "He can't see us."

"He's pointing toward us. And talking on the radio. It's like he knows where we are."

"That's impossible," Karen said.

Now the man went over to the back of the truck and lifted out a spray tank of some kind. He hoisted the tank to his shoulder on a strap and walked around the edge of the parking lot, spraying the vegetation. Then he sprayed the surface of the parking lot as well.

"What is that about?" Erika asked.

"Poison, I bet," Karen said to her. "They know we're alive. They've guessed we'd try to hitch a ride on the shuttle, so they're nuking the parking lot. And I'm sure there's no shuttle now. They're trying to trap us in this valley. They're figuring we'll die here."

"Let's make them wrong," Peter said.

Karen remained very skeptical. "How?"

"We'll revise our plan," said Peter.

"How?" Karen asked.

"We'll go to Tantalus," Peter answered.

"Tantalus? That's insane, Peter."

"But why?" Erika asked.

Peter said, "There's a Nanigen base up there. There could be people at the base. They might help us, you don't know. And Jarel Kinsky talked about airplanes at Tantalus. He called them micro-planes."

"Micro-planes?" Karen said.

"Well, I've seen a very small Nanigen airplane. And you guys did too—remember? I found it in my brother's car. Amar and I magnified it. It had controls and a cockpit. Maybe we could steal some micro-planes and fly."

Karen stared at Peter. "That's completely, totally crazy. You don't know anything about Tantalus Base."

"Well, at least they won't expect us at Tantalus, so we have the element of surprise."

"But look at the mountain," Karen said to Peter, sweeping her arm. Indeed, Tantalus Peak dominated the view upward, a hulk of a volcanic cone blanketed with near-vertical super-jungle. "It's two thousand feet high, Peter." She paused and thought for a moment. "For us that's like climbing seven Mount Everests."

"But gravity won't slow us down," Peter answered calmly. He had taken out the binoculars and was sweeping across Tantalus. He found a massive boulder, sitting in an open area on the lip of the crater. "That could be the Great Boulder. The map says Tantalus Base is at the foot of it." He couldn't see the base, though—it would be only a few feet across, not visible from this distance. He took out the compass and sighted a line on the boulder. "It's on bearing of three hundred and thirty degrees from here. Just follow the compass line—"

"It'll take weeks," Karen said. "We have a couple more days, tops, before the bends hit us."

"Soldiers," Peter said to her, "can walk thirty miles a day."

"Peter, we're not soldiers," Erika groaned.

"I s'pose we could try," Karen said. "But what about Amar? He can't walk."

"We'll carry him," Peter said.

"What are we going to do with Danny? He's a pain in the ass," Karen said.

"Danny is one of us. We'll take care of him," Peter said firmly.

Just then, Peter's radio beeped and started crackling with a frantic voice. It was Danny calling.

"Speak of the devil," Karen murmured.

Peter put on the headset and heard Danny Minot shouting, "Help! Oh, God! Help me!"


**In the lower** branches of the tree, tucked in a sunny spot, Danny Minot had fallen asleep. His mouth hung open and he snored; he was exhausted after the longest and most terrifying night of his life. He didn't hear the clattering noise that approached him and hovered over him. As she helicoptered, hovering, her expressionless eyes studied him. She was a wasp.

She landed and advanced carefully. Lightly, she touched his left arm with her antennae, then tapped her antennae over his throat, his cheeks, tasting his skin. The skin, so pale, so soft, reminded her of a caterpillar. A host. From the end of her abdomen hung a long tube, like a length of garden hose. The tube had a drill bit at the end of it.

She took him gently in her forelegs and planted her drill bit in his shoulder. She thrust the bit into his flesh. It injected anesthetic. Then she activated the drill bit, and drove the tube in deep.

She began gasping, making sounds that eerily resembled a woman in childbirth.

Danny was dreaming. The dream shifted. He was holding a beautiful girl in his arms. She was naked and gasping with arousal. They kissed. He felt her tongue go down his throat . . . he looked up at her, and her eyes were compound eyes, bulging in a woman's face . . . she clutched him, wouldn't let go . . . he woke with a start . . .

"Ahhg!"

He was staring into the eyes of a giant wasp. The wasp was holding him tight, gripping him with her legs and burying her stinger in his shoulder. And he felt nothing. His arm had gone dead.

"No!" he screamed, and grabbed the stinger in both hands, and tried to pull it out. But then the wasp pulled its stinger out of his shoulder anyway, and let go of him, and flew away.

He rolled over on his back, clutching his arm. "Aah! Ay! Help!" The arm had become a nothingness hanging from his shoulder, a dead weight with no feeling in it, as if it had been pumped full of Novocaine. He noticed a small hole in his shirt, with dark wetness spreading in the cloth—blood. He tore open his shirt and stared at a hole in his shoulder. It was as neat and round as a drill hole, and it oozed blood. There was no sensation of pain, nothing.

He clutched for the headset. "Help! Oh God! Help!" he shouted.

"Danny?" Peter's voice came on.

"Something stung me . . . Oh my God."

"What stung you?"

"I can't feel it. It's dead."

"What's dead?"

"My arm. It was so big . . ." His voice ran up into whimpering terror.

Rick Hutter's voice came on. "What's happening?" He was calling from the moss cave lower on the tree, where he had stayed with Amar Singh.

"Danny's been stung," Peter said. "Danny—stay where you are. I'm coming down to you."

"I fought it off."

"Good."

Danny hunched up, not wanting to look at his shoulder. The blood oozed into his shirt. He felt his forehead. Did he have a fever? Was he getting delirious? He began muttering. "No poison . . . I'm fine . . . No poison. No poison, no poison . . ."

Peter took the first-aid kit with him. Descent was easy and quick: he let himself down hand over hand, sometimes hanging by one hand. He found Danny curled up in a fetal position, his face drained of color. His left arm seemed limp.

"I can't feel my arm," Danny whimpered.

Peter pulled open Danny's shirt and inspected the wound on his shoulder. It was a small puncture wound. He cleaned it with an iodine swab, expecting Danny to feel a sting from the swab, but Danny felt nothing.

Peter searched for signs of envenomation. He stared into Danny's eyes, looking for constriction or dilation of the pupils. His eyes seemed normal. He took Danny's pulse, noted his respiration, and looked for changes in skin color or mental state. Danny seemed very frightened. Peter inspected Danny's arm. The skin had a normal color, but the arm was limp. He pinched the arm. "Did you feel that?"

Danny shook his head.

"Nausea? Pain?" he asked Danny.

"No poison . . . No poison . . ."

"I don't think you've been envenomed." If there had been venom in the sting, then Danny would be extremely sick, with severe pain, or even dead. But his vital signs remained stable. "I think you scared it away. What was it, anyway?"

"A bee or a wasp," Danny muttered. "I don't know."

Wasps were much more common than bees. Hawaii probably had thousands of different kinds of wasps, many of them unnamed and unidentified. There was no telling what kind of wasp had stung Danny—if it had been a wasp at all. Peter opened a Band-Aid and placed it over the puncture in Danny's shoulder. Then he tore off the sleeve of his own shirt and turned it into a makeshift arm sling for Danny. He wondered how to get Danny down to the ground. "Do you feel able to jump?"

"No. Maybe."

"It won't hurt us." Then Peter called on the radio to Karen King and Erika Moll, who were still at the top of the tree. "Danny and I are going to jump to the ground. You might as well do the same."

Karen and Erika leaned out from a cluster of leaves. They couldn't see the ground. Karen glanced at Erika, who nodded. "We're cool," Karen said on the radio, and she checked to make sure the blowgun was strapped tightly to her back. "One, two, three . . ." Erika jumped first, Karen following moments later.

As she fell into space, Karen spread-eagled herself like a sky-diver. She went into a glide. "Wow!" she shouted. She could see Erika falling below her, and Erika was shouting. They were gliding, and it was controllable. Karen moved her legs and arms, and went off at a slant. She could feel the air flowing over her body, thick and soft, supporting her weight. This was like bodysurfing, except it was in air rather than water. She slammed into a branch and tumbled into space, unhurt, and spread her arms again, and surfed the liquid wind, descending through the tree. She saw Erika diving at an angle below her. Erika had gotten ahead of her, was falling faster.

Karen wanted to slow herself down. She rolled her body leftward and rightward, catching the air and using her arms and legs to slow her fall. "Whooo!" she yelled. Leaves were coming. She had lost sight of Erika . . . she heard Erika scream . . .

She burst through the leaves . . . and a spiderweb lay dead-ahead. Erika was trapped in it, bouncing up and down, thrashing her arms and legs, trying to escape. A pale green spider clung to the edge of the web . . . A crab spider . . . very poisonous . . .

Karen rolled her body sideways as she fell, her knowledge of this spider flashing through her mind. She needed to fall into the web. It was the only way to save Erika. Gotta hit the web. She had no fear. She could handle a crab spider . . . She slammed into the edge of the web and hung there, bouncing in midair.

To Karen, the web seemed maybe fifty or sixty feet across, far bigger than a safety net in a circus. Unlike a safety net, the web was sticky, its radial threads spangled with droplets of glue. She felt the glue soaking into her clothes, pinning her to the web, while Erika struggled in a blind panic, screaming for help, trapped in threads out of Karen's reach. The crab spider seemed to hesitate. Possibly it didn't recognize the humans as prey, Karen thought. But it would attack, she thought, and soon. The attack would come in a rush. "Hold still," she called to Erika. She rolled herself over until she was facing the spider, and drew her machete. "Yah!" she shouted at the spider. Her eyes moved rapidly over the web. She was looking for a trigger line, and she saw it—a thread running from one of the spider's feet across the spiral threads to the center. She flung herself across the web and cut the trigger line.

The spider used the trigger line to sense the presence of prey in the web. Cutting the trigger line was like cutting a nerve. It also alarmed the spider.

The spider suddenly fled, running away and tucking itself inside a curled-up leaf—its home.

"Most of 'em scare easily," Karen said to Erika. She cut another thread, and the two women fell free, while Karen called back to the spider, "Sorry, sweetheart."

They landed together on the ground amid a tangle of sticky silk. Erika was badly shaken. "I thought I was going to die."

Karen pulled threads of silk off her. "Nothing to worry about as long as you know the structure of the web."

"But I'm a beetle person," Erika answered.

Peter and Danny landed nearby, crashing into leaves. Finally Rick appeared, lowering Amar with the help of the rope. They gathered in a group at the base of the ohia tree, and Peter explained the change of plan. They would head for Tantalus.

**Ten minutes later,** with Rick and Peter carrying Amar between them, they entered a fern forest, a seemingly endless maze of sword ferns, tall and dripping with moisture, arching over tunnels that ran in all directions. Koa trees, olopua trees, and white kokio hibiscus trees sprang from among the ferns, twisting into the upper story of the forest.

Peter sighted with the compass. "That way," he said, and they began to walk down a long, winding passageway among the ferns. Fronds arched far overhead, covering the world in green.

Danny was stumbling along, when he stopped, stared at Amar Singh. Danny's eyes widened. "He's—he's bleeding."

Nobody had noticed. Rick lowered Amar, and Amar sank to his knees, while a rivulet of blood trickled out of one nostril and ran across his upper lip. The blood began falling to the ground in a steady drip.

"Leave me," Amar whispered. "I have the bends."

# Chapter 26

## BENEATH THE GREEN CANOPY
## 30 OCTOBER, NOON

They're hiding in there," Telius said to Johnstone, looking through binoculars into a mass of sword ferns on the forest floor. The two men were hanging upside down in their seat harnesses in the hexapod. The machine, in turn, hung upside down from a leaf in the pandanus tree, clinging to the leaf with its feet. They had been able to get a fix on the radios.

Telius stared for a while, then gestured silently with one finger: Drop us.

Johnstone hit a button and the footpads let go of the leaf, and the hexapod went into free fall. Johnstone, working the controls, folded the legs under the vehicle as it fell. It tumbled a few times, its legs tucked underneath it, and hit the ground, and bounced, and came to rest upside down. The roll cage had protected the humans inside.

Johnstone popped open the legs. They lashed out and flipped the vehicle upright, and the hexapod moved off, stalking its way around the edge of the fern forest, and went into the ferns. Telius stood up and turned his head, listening. He had heard them talking. He indicated with his finger where the people were, then directed Johnstone to drive up a fern stem.

The hexapod climbed the stem, got in among the fronds, and stopped. Telius took up the binoculars and stared through them. He had acquired the targets. Six of them, down below. Somebody was sick, had a bloody nose. Might be the bends. The others were gathered around the victim. Indian guy, looked like. Blood streamed from the guy's nose and over his upper lip and chin. Yup—the man had the bends. He was a goner. "Poor fucker's having a bend bleed-out," he murmured to Johnstone, who grunted.

As he studied the group, Telius identified the leader—slender guy, light brown curly hair, standing slightly apart and talking to the others, who listened. This was the individual who'd taken leadership of the group, Telius could see it. Telius could always tell an officer. You drop the officer first, of course.

A good setup. Telius nodded to Johnstone and took up the gas rifle and aimed it at the group's leader, while Johnstone took up spotter duty, training his binoculars on the target and speaking to Telius. Telius looked through the scope and put the crosshairs on the leader's head. The range was long, about four meters. A slight breeze stirred the fern leaf and the hexapod. Telius shook his head. Not stable. The shot was a little chancy, and Telius left nothing to chance. He would have to make several kills in quick succession on moving targets, because the moment he dropped the leader, the others would scatter like frightened rabbits. He gestured to Johnstone, meaning, get us lower.

Johnstone turned the vehicle, and it began creeping down the fern leaf, hunting for a more stable position. Then Telius signaled to Johnstone to stop. Telius unbuckled himself and fell out of the hexapod, spun once in the air, and landed on the ground on all fours like a cat, rifle on his back. He crept closer to the targets.

. . .

**Peter broke open** the medical kit and knelt over Amar, holding a compress to Amar's nose. He didn't know what to do. The nosebleed would not stop.

"I'm useless. Please go on," Amar said.

"We're not going to leave you."

"I'm just protein. Leave me."

"Amar's right," Danny said, touching his sling arm. "We have to leave him. Or we'll all die."

Ignoring Danny, Peter took the compress away from Amar's nose; it was soaked. He had lost a lot of blood, and he had become anemic. And the bruises all over Amar's arms . . . it seemed as if the centipede venom had accelerated the bends in Amar. And decompression was the only treatment for the bends, yet they were no closer to Nanigen.

"We have to call for help on the radio," Danny said, plunking himself down and glowering at the others.

"Danny could be right," Erika said. "Maybe there is some good person at Nanigen—"

"Maybe we should call," Karen said. "It might be our only chance to save Amar."

Peter stood up, holding a radio headset. "All right."


**From lower down** on the fern stem, Telius took aim. He had the leader in the crosshairs of his gas rifle, but now the leader was bending over the guy with the bends, trying to help him. Hmm. Maybe he could get both of them with one shot. The leader and the bleeder—yeah. He adjusted his aim, squeezed the trigger, and the gas rifle kicked viciously.

...

**There was a** sudden hiss. A steel needle, seemingly a foot long, zipped past Peter's neck, tearing his shirt, and entered Amar Singh, and detonated. The explosion threw metal fragments and blood in all directions. Amar jerked into the air, yanked off the ground, and his body seemed to come apart. Peter froze, a quizzical expression on his face, while Amar and pieces of Amar spattered around Peter.

Peter stood up, covered with Amar's blood. "What—?" he began.

The others watched it happen as if it wasn't real.

Karen looked around. "Sniper!" she screamed. "Get cover!" She began to dash for the nearest fern, but saw that Peter wasn't moving—he seemed paralyzed, as if he couldn't process what had just happened.

The sniper's second shot hit a leaf over Peter's head and exploded. The blast sent Peter to the ground. Karen realized the sniper was aiming for Peter. She swerved and ran toward Peter, and grabbed him. "Duck and zigzag!" she screamed at him. He needed to get away but not make any predictable movements: the sniper could pull lead on Peter, and hit him as he ran. "Go!" she yelled at Peter.

Peter understood. He began to run, left, right, left—left—stop. Run. Always heading for the cover of ferns. Karen ran, too, zigzagging, staying with Peter but not too close to him, wondering if the next shot . . .

Peter tripped, fell, and sprawled.

"Peter!" she screamed. "No!" Peter had stopped moving; he had become an easy target.

"Karen—get away—" Peter said, hauling himself to his feet.

These were his last words. In the next instant a needle flew through Peter's chest, exploding as it went. He toppled. Peter Jansen was dead before he hit the ground.

# PART III

# TANTALUS

# Chapter 27

FERN GULLY
30 OCTOBER, 12:15 P.M.

Rick Hutter felt Karen King lift him up by his shirt, dragging him out of what he thought was a good hiding place, and heard her say, "Get up—go!" He noticed his blowgun lying on the ground, picked it up, grabbed the dart kit, and sprinted for cover. He lost track of Karen; he had no idea where she had gone. He ran underneath a stick, bashed through some leaves, and began to run among fern stems looming over him. That was when he saw the insect vehicle. A six-legged truck up there on the fern, clinging to a frond and moving along it, making a faint whine, driven by a man wearing armor. It was a man just Rick's size. A micro-human. The man seemed experienced and confident.

The man stopped the vehicle, held up a strange-looking gun with a large-caliber muzzle. He loaded a metal needle in the breech, took aim through a scope, and fired. The gun kicked, giving off a hiss.

Rick had flung himself down behind a rock, where he lay on his back, panting, while he watched the man shoot. The man seemed relaxed. Comfortable with murder, Rick realized, while a hot rage welled up in him. The man had butchered Peter and Amar in cold blood. Rick was still holding the blow tube. Get off a dart at that bastard, anyway. I think Karen just saved my life. It was dumb to stay crouched like that. *She pulled my ass out of a bad place.*

He opened his dart kit and took out a dart. Looked at it with a sense of futility. It was just a splinter with a metal point made from a dinner fork. Never get through that bastard's armor. He opened the curare jar and jammed the tip into the sludge and twirled it, choking back a cough as an odor wafted from the jar. Put a hot load on the dart anyway.

He fitted the dart into the tube, and rolled over, and looked out past the rock.

The vehicle wasn't there. It had moved out of sight.

Where?

Rick crept out from behind the rock, listening, looking around. He heard a whining sound to his left. The bug truck. He got up and ran toward the sound, and when it got louder, he dove into a clump of moss and waited. The sound got closer. Carefully he looked out of the moss.

The bug truck had crawled up on the moss and stopped almost directly above him. He was looking at the bottom of the truck. He couldn't see the man from here.

There was another hiss. The man had fired again.

Rick had no idea if anyone but himself was still alive. Karen could be dead. Erika, too. They were being slaughtered.

It made him furious.

It made him want to kill. Even if it cost him his life.

The man had stopped firing, and now the truck advanced. It came to a halt a short distance away, and he heard the man talking on a radio. "There's a female at your three o'clock. Bitch has a knife."

Bitch.

Karen.

No—she was about to be shot. He started crawling frantically through the moss, then got himself wedged under a fallen leaf. He was looking right up at the man. The man wore a helmet, a breast-plate, armored plates over his arms. His chin was bare. Bare neck.

Rick aimed for the man's neck. Try to hit him in the jugular. He inhaled slowly, trying not to make a sound, and blew with all his might.

The dart missed the man's neck, but landed in the soft flesh under his chin, and drove deep, buried up to its fluff. It had entered the man's chin just above his Adam's apple and gone upward. Rick heard a choking scream and the man tumbled down into the vehi-cle, out of sight. He heard wet cough, then thrashing, thumping. The guy was seizing, flopping around like a fish inside the truck. Then silence.

Rick loaded another dart into the blowgun, and jumped up on the truck. Ready to shoot again, he looked inside. The man lay sprawled, face cherry-red, eyes popping, frothy mucus drizzling out of his mouth—cyanide poisoning, Rick realized. Only the tail puff of the dart remained visible, a wisp of cotton stuck under the man's chin. The dart had punched vertically upward through his tongue and the roof of his mouth and pierced his brain.

"That was for Peter," he said. His hands were shaking, then his whole body began to shake. He had never killed a person before; hadn't thought he was capable of it.

Off to his right, he heard another hiss.

Oh fuck, not another one, he thought—another sniper out there. Shooting at my friends. *Get the bastard.* Rick leaped from the truck and began running toward the sound, holding the loaded blowgun. As he ran, he noticed that things had gotten darker over-head, and then he saw . . . a shadow moving in the ferns. He stopped running. Suddenly he felt very, very small and completely power-less. He couldn't believe how big the damned thing was.

■ ■ ■

**Karen saw the** man rise up between two fern stems. He was a small man, agile and catlike in his movements. He wore camo armor and a glove on his right hand. His left hand was bare and was closed around the gun's trigger, and the gun was aimed at her. He was about one meter away. Close enough.

She had drawn her knife. It was no match for the gun. She glanced around. No cover.

He moved out from behind the fern stems, keeping the gun trained on her. He seemed to be playing with her, for he could make the shot easily. He spoke into a throat mike: "Found her." After a pause he added, "You copy?" Evidently he didn't get an answer. "Copy?"

He still didn't get an answer. He stepped forward.

It was then that Karen saw the shadow behind the man. At first she didn't know what it was. She saw something brown and covered with fur, buried in a cluster of fern fronds. It moved slightly, then stopped. She thought it must be a mammal, maybe a rat, because of the brown fur and because it was really big. But then a leg appeared, a long, tapering, jointed leg, an exoskeleton covered with bristly brown hair. Then a fern frond was pushed aside, and she saw the eyes. All eight of them.

It was an enormous spider, as big as a house. The spider was so vast it seemed almost unrecognizable as a spider. Karen knew the species, though. It was a brown huntsman, common in the tropics. It was a carnivore, too. Huntsmen spiders don't build webs. They are ambush predators, and they hunt on the ground. This one was holding its body close to the ground—a sign that it was hunting. It had a flattened body, protected by hair, with sickle-shaped fangs folded under bulbous appendages. This one was a female. She would crave protein, Karen knew, since she was making eggs.

Karen was struck by the stillness of the spider. Since it was an ambush predator, the fact that it wasn't moving was bad news. This meant it was hunting.

The man stood with his back to the spider, unaware of it. Its constellation of eyes stared at the man, like droplets of black glass. Karen heard a soft, moaning intake and exhalation of air flowing through the spider's lungs, located in the spider's abdomen.

"Johnstone. Do you copy?" the man said.

He paused, listening for his partner.

"What happened to your friend?" Karen whispered. Make him talk.

He just looked at her. Not a chatty one.

She kept her body very still. No sudden movements. She knew that a spider couldn't see very well, even with so many eyes, but a spider had highly accurate hearing. Ten "ears" were scattered over each leg—holes in its armor that picked up sounds. Eighty ears, all told. In addition, the thousands of hairs on its legs were also listening devices, vibration sensors. The hearing organs on its legs gave the spider a 3-D sound-image of the world.

If she made any noise or vibration, the spider would form a sonic image of her. Would recognize her as prey. The attack, she knew, would happen in the blink of an eye.

She knelt, very slowly, and picked up a rock. Raised her arm slowly.

The man smiled. "Go ahead. If it makes you feel better."

She threw the rock at him. It struck his breastplate and bounced off with a thump.

He raised his gun at her and took aim through the scope and chuckled just as the fangs closed around him and yanked him into the air, crushing his gun. He screamed.

The spider took a few steps forward and then, surprisingly, flipped itself over on its back, while Karen sprinted for safety. Lying on its back, it lifted the man into the air, sinking its fangs deeper. The razor-sharp, hollow tips punched through the man's armor, and began pumping venom into him.

His body swelled up as the venom pressurized it, until his armor began to make popping sounds, and blood mixed with venom began squirting out of the cracks in the armor. As the venom went to work, his spine curved backward and his head whipped back and forth. Neurotoxins in the venom set off a firestorm in his central nervous system. He began to writhe, and went into convulsions, a grand mal seizure. As he seized, his eyes rolled up into his head until only the whites showed. Then, abruptly, the whites turned hot-red. Blood vessels had burst in his eyes, as they were rupturing everywhere in his body, for the venom contained digestive enzymes that liquefy flesh. Internal hemorrhages flooded the man's body, until his heart stopped.

The spider venom was Ebola in thirty seconds.

The spider continued to pump poison into the body until the armor began to crack and split. The breastplate popped open, and the man's viscera peeked out, drizzling venom.

Karen had taken cover behind a fern, where she found Rick crouching, blowpipe in hand.

They watched the spider process its meal.

Having killed the prey while it lay on its back, the spider flipped over and stood upright on its eight legs again, and began cutting up the prey. It gripped the man in its palps, a pair of hand-like appendages on either side of its mouth. The fangs opened like folding knives; they had serrated inner blades. The blades macerated the body, chopping it into a bloody mash of flesh, broken bones, and intestinal contents, mixed with scraps of Kevlar and pieces of plastic. Using its palps, the spider handled the meat-mass deftly, molding and shaping it into a food ball, while squirting digestive fluid into the mass through the tips of its fangs. In a minute or two, the human remains had been turned into a spheroid of liquescent pap speckled with bone fragments and shredded armor.

"Interesting," Karen whispered, and turned to Rick. "Spiders digest their food outside their bodies."

"I didn't know."

Having digested its prey, the spider placed its mouth firmly on the food ball and began sucking fluids out of the mess, while its stomach made a steady pumping noise. The eyes gleamed with a faraway expression, Karen thought, or maybe a look of satisfaction.

"Do we need to worry?" Rick asked.

"Nah, she's busy. But we should get out of here before she starts hunting again."

They began calling for Erika and Danny. Erika had hidden herself under a hibiscus flower, and Danny had tucked himself under a tree root.

**There were four** survivors now. Rick, Karen, Erika, and Danny. They gathered themselves, put on the packs, and hurried off into the ferns, abandoning the bodies of Peter and Amar, while a sense of terrible emptiness swept over them. Amar Singh, a gentle person who loved plants, was gone. Peter Jansen, gone. It had not seemed possible that Peter could die.

The loss of Peter had devastated them. "He was so steady," Rick said. "I really thought he could bring us through."

"Peter was our hope," Erika said. She began to cry. "I believed he would save us, somehow."

"This is what I predicted," Danny said. He sat down and adjusted his arm sling, then, with his good hand, unstuck some duct tape on his grass shoe and stuck it back in place, trying to tighten his shoe. Then he put his head down between his knees. His muffled voice rose up: "The inevitable has happened . . . The catastrophe . . . We are completely, totally, utterly . . . dead."

"Actually we're still alive," Rick said.

"Not for long," Danny muttered.

Karen said, "We all had faith in Peter. He was so . . . calm. He never lost his courage." She wiped sweat from her face, and hefted her pack, adjusting it, and kept walking. Karen could hardly admit it to herself, but for the first time she had lost her nerve entirely. She was petrified. She couldn't see how they would ever get back to Nanigen. "Peter was the only person who could lead us. Now we don't have a leader."

"Yeah, and it's clear that Drake knows we're alive and is trying to kill us—sending hired killers to take us out," Rick said. "We got rid of two goons, but who knows who else is out there with orders to kill us."

"Two of them?" Karen asked him.

Rick answered her with a grim smile. "Look straight ahead." The hexapod stood crookedly on top of a mound of moss. Rick leaped into the vehicle. A moment later a body was flung out, spinning through the air, and landed with a crash at Karen's feet. She saw the man's armor, the dart embedded in the man's chin, the eyes bulging . . . the foamy tongue, thrust out . . .

She drew in her breath. There had been two snipers. Rick had said nothing about it until now. "You killed—this man . . ."

"Get in," Rick said, busying himself with the controls. "We're driving to Tantalus. And we've got a gun."

# Chapter 28

The pickup truck wound up the single-lane road leading to the Manoa Valley. It was a beat-up Toyota, spray-painted several different colors, with a surfboard rack and fat tires that seemed affected by elephantiasis. It arrived at the gate in front of the tunnel and stopped, and a man got out. He walked up to the gate and read the sign: PRIVATE. NO ADMITTANCE.

"Shit." Eric Jansen rattled the gate. He examined the lock. It was a keypad. He tried some corporate codes, but nothing worked. Fucking Vin had changed the code on the lock, for sure, Eric thought.

He backed around and drove down the road a short distance, to a turnout, where he rammed the truck into the undergrowth. If anybody from Nanigen noticed it, they'd assume he was a pot farmer gone off to tend his crop on the mountain. Not a vice president of the company, looking for his brother.

He put on a knapsack and hurried down the road, slipped underneath the gate, jogged down the tunnel. Beyond the tunnel, in the valley, he went off the road and into the forest, out of sight, where he opened the knapsack and took out a laptop computer and complicated-looking box of electronic circuits. It had a homemade look: soldered boards, an antenna. He put on a pair of headphones and began to listen, scanning around the seventy-gigahertz band. He heard nothing. He switched frequency, checking the band of Nanigen's private wireless communication network, and heard a garbled hiss. He always heard it. Intracompany chatter. The problem was to decipher it.

He waited three hours, listening, until the battery began to run down. He packed up the gear and hurried down the road, through the tunnel and back to the truck, and drove off. Nobody had noticed him; nobody had been around, anyway. He would be back tomorrow to listen again. Just in case Peter and the others were somewhere in the valley. He didn't know where they were, only that they had gone missing.

# Chapter 29

**HONOLULU**
**30 OCTOBER, 1:00 P.M.**

In his windowless office, Dan Watanabe called an officer in the Missing Persons Detail. "Let me know if any new information about those students comes up."

"Funny you should ask. You want to call Nanci Harfield. She's out in District 8 right now."

Sergeant Nanci Harfield was in the Traffic Division; District 8 covered the southwest side of Oahu.

"I'm at Kaena," she said to him. "We've got a luxury car upside down in the tidal inlet below the 1929 Bridge. The vehicle is registered to one Alyson F. Bender slash Nanigen MicroTechnologies. There's a body trapped under the vehicle. Female, by appearance. No other bodies visible."

"I'd like to have a look," Watanabe said.

He got in his brown unmarked Ford Crown Victoria and drove it at an easy ninety along the freeway around Pearl Harbor. He continued into Waianae, a town that lay on the southwest coast of Oahu. This was the leeward side of the island, dry and sunny, where the beaches were lapped by gentle waves and the smallest *keiki*s could play and paddle. It was the rougher side of the island in terms of law enforcement, though. Lots of car break-ins and petty thefts, but little or no violence, anyway. Back in the 1800s, in the days of the Kingdom of Hawaii, the leeward side of Oahu had been a violent place, a haven for bandits, who robbed and murdered people who ventured there. Now it was mostly property crimes.

At Kaena Point, a car rested upside down in shallow water. The police department's heaviest winch truck was parked on the road. A cable ran from the truck down through hau tangle to the car; it had been a nasty job getting the cable down through the brush. The car tipped as the cable yanked on it, and it flipped over, landing right side up. A dark blue Bentley convertible. Its soft top torn and crushed. Sand and water streamed out of the car, and a dead woman sat in the driver's seat, creepily upright.

Watanabe made his way down the slope. He tore his slacks, and slipped and skidded, regretting that he wore street shoes.

By the time he reached the car, the cable had winched it out on the rocks. The dead woman wore a dark business suit. Her hair swirled around her face and clogged her mouth. Her eyes were gone: reef fish had eaten them.

He leaned into the car, past the corpse, and looked around. He saw articles of clothing plastered all over the wet compartment, clinging to the seats and caught in the twisted metal of the convertible's top. Board shorts. A belt made of snakeskin, chewed by fish. A woman's underpants, lime-green. Another pair of board shorts, with a tag still on them, just purchased. A Hilo Hattie shirt. A pair of bootcut jeans with a hole in the right knee.

"Was the lady going to do laundry?" he remarked to an officer. The clothing was the sort that younger people wear. He noticed a plastic jug wedged under the dashboard and took it out and studied the label. "Ethanol. Hmm." He found a wallet in the backseat. It held a Massachusetts driver's license belonging to one Jenny H.

Linn. One of the missing students. But there were no bodies in the car other than the woman's—which might or might not be Alyson Bender. That would have to wait for the medical examiner.

He climbed back up to the road. There, Nanci Harfield and another officer had photographed and measured the tire tracks in the grit leading over the shoulder of the road.

Watanabe looked at Harfield. "So what do you think?"

"Looks like the car stopped here before it went over. Then it rolled straight off." Harfield had searched carefully around the tire tracks for any shoeprints in the gravel. The gravel was scuffed but there were no clear shoeprints. She went on, "It looks like the driver stopped right here. Then the car goes off the edge, no use of the brakes. If she'd braked, you'd see the skidmarks in the dirt. No skidmarks means no attempt to stop. She could have sat here for a while making up her mind, then touched the gas and went over."

"Suicide?" Watanabe asked her.

"That's a possibility. It's consistent with these marks."

The evidence squad took photographs and video. They bagged the body and loaded it into an ambulance, which drove off silently, lights flashing. The totaled Bentley followed, riding on the deck of the police tow truck, still dripping seawater.

**Watanabe ended up** back at his desk at headquarters, looking at the scratched metal wall he would stare at sometimes to clarify his thoughts. He couldn't get over the feeling that somebody had put the clothing in the car. Especially that wallet. People who are planning to go off don't leave their wallets behind. If Jenny Linn had gone off voluntarily, she would have taken her wallet with her. What if she hadn't gone voluntarily? Maybe kidnapped? Had this been a boating accident? A lost boat would explain so many people missing at the same time.

He called the Property Crimes Unit and asked if there were any reports of missing boats. Not lately. He stared at the wall some more. It might be time to eat an emergency Spam sushi.

But then his phone rang. It was an officer in the Missing Persons Unit. "I've got another one for you."

"Yeah? Who?"

"A Joanna Kinsky called to report her husband didn't come home from work last night. He's an engineer at Nanigen."

"Another Nanigen missing? You've got to be kidding—"

"Ms. Kinsky says she called the company. Nobody's seen her husband since yesterday afternoon."

The Nanigen security chief hadn't reported this one. There were just too many Nanigen people dropping out of sight in the quiet little Honolulu town.

Another phone call. It was Dorothy Girt, a forensic scientist in the Scientific Investigation Section. "Dan—would you come down and take a look at something? It's the Fong case. I've found something."

Shit. The Willy Fong Mess. Not what he needed right now.


**Don Makele walked** into Vin Drake's office. He had a disturbed look on his face. "Telius and Johnstone are dead."

Drake gritted his teeth. "What happened?"

"I lost radio contact with them. They had located the survivors. They had begun the, uh, rescue operation," Makele said. He was sweating again. "Right in the middle of this, they were attacked by something. I heard screaming and then—Telius—well . . . he got eaten."

"Eaten?"

"I heard it. Some kind of predator. His radio went dead. I called for a long time. There were no more transmissions."

"What do you think?"

"I think everybody's dead."

"Why?"

"My men were the best. Something got through their weapons and armor."

"So the students—"

Makele shook his head. "Not a chance."

Drake leaned back. "So there was an accident with a predator."

Makele sucked on his lips. "When I was in Afghanistan, I noticed something about accidents."

"What's that?" Drake asked.

"Accidents happen more often to assholes."

Drake chuckled. "That's true."

"The rescue—it failed, sir."

Drake realized that Don Makele understood exactly what was meant by rescue. Nevertheless, Drake had his doubts. "How can you be sure, Don, that the rescue . . . ah . . . failed?"

"There's no survivors. I'm sure of it."

"Show me the bodies."

"But there aren't—"

"I will not believe the students are dead until I see evidence of their deaths." Drake leaned back. "As long as there's hope, we will spare no effort to save them. No effort. Am I clear?"

Makele left Drake's office without saying a word. There was nothing to say.

As for Vin Drake, he felt reasonably good about what had happened to Telius and Johnstone. It meant he didn't have to pay them bonuses in valuable stock. Nevertheless, he could not assume that all the students were dead. They had shown some survival skills, surprising tenacity, and so he would continue to try to flush them out, just in case some of them were still alive.

# Chapter 30

This thing would kick ass in Boston traffic," Karen King remarked. She was driving the hexapod up a steep slope, guiding it across a jumble of rocks and grass stems. It lurched.

"Please! Watch my arm." Danny was sitting in the passenger seat, gripping his left arm, which hung like a sausage in the sling. It had become badly swollen, filling the sleeve of his shirt. The hexapod moved along steadily, its legs whining, climbing through a vast, vertical world glowing with a million shades of green. In the cargo compartment, in back, Erika sat huddled, tied in with rope. Rick walked along beside the vehicle, holding the gas rifle and looking around, alert for predators, a bandolier of needle-bullets slung over his shoulder.

The terrain had gotten very steep. The soil had given way to crumbly lava pebbles and grit with protruding masses of lava rock, everything festooned with grasses and small ferns. Koa and guava trees twisted this way and that, mixed with thin, straight shafts of loulu palms. Many of the trees were draped with vines. Branches rattled in a steady wind that blew across the mountain face, and the breeze occasionally battered the truck and the humans. A wall of mist drifted through the vegetation—a cloud—followed by brilliant sunshine.

The deaths of Peter Jansen and Amar Singh weighed on the students. Their group had been winnowed from eight people stranded in the micro-world down to four survivors. Their number had been cut in half in just two days. Fifty percent fatalities. That was a horrible statistic, thought Rick Hutter. It was worse than the life expectancy of soldiers fighting on the beaches of Normandy. Rick could see more fatalities coming—unless by some miracle they were rescued. But they couldn't reveal themselves to anyone at Nanigen now; for Vin Drake had mobilized his resources to try to find them and make them disappear. "Drake's still looking for us," Rick remarked. "I'm sure of it."

"That's enough," Karen said to him. There was no point talking about Vin Drake, since all that did was to make them feel more helpless. "Peter wouldn't give up," Karen said to Rick, more calmly, as she worked the controls, guiding the truck straight up the face of a large rock. Rick jumped on board for the ride.

They had gotten into mountain vegetation. Occasional gaps in the canopy revealed a striking vista. Cliffs and blades of the Pali plunged all around, and a waterfall roared nearby. Somewhere above them, a curving stretch of ridge formed the lip of Tantalus Crater. As the machine marched along, its feet stirred up living things. Startled springtails bounced away, flipping through the air; worms wriggled and seethed; mites scuttled here and there, sometimes climbing up the legs of the hexapod. They had to keep brushing mites off the vehicle, or the creatures would crawl around inside it and all over the gear, dropping small blobs of mite dung and getting everything dirty. And in the air all around, insects by the thousands flew, humming past, spiraling around, glittering in the sunlight.

"I can't stand all this *life*," Danny complained. He hunched forward over his bad arm, looking utterly miserable.

"If the batteries last," Rick was saying, "we might make Tantalus by nightfall."

"What then?" Karen said, working the controls.

"We do reconnaissance. Watch the base, then decide our next move."

"What if the base isn't there? Torn out, just like the stations?"

"Do you have to be such a pessimist?"

"I'm just trying to stay realistic, Rick."

"Fine, Karen. Tell me your plan."

Karen didn't have a plan, so she didn't answer Rick. Just get to Tantalus and hope something turns up. It wasn't a plan, it was a hail-Mary pass. As they moved along, Karen considered their situation. She was profoundly frightened, she had to admit it, but her fear also made her feel very alive. She wondered how much longer she had to live. Maybe a day, maybe hours. Better make the best of it, just in case your life turns out to be as short as an insect's, she told herself.

She looked over at Rick Hutter. How did the guy do it? There he was, tramping along with the gun slung over his shoulder, swaggering a little, looking like he didn't have a care in the world. For a moment, she envied him. Even though she disliked him.

She heard a moan. It was Erika, sitting in the back of the truck with her arms wrapped around her knees.

"Are you all right, Erika?" Karen asked her.

"All right."

"Are you . . . scared?"

"Of course I am scared."

"Try not to be too scared. It'll be okay," Karen said.

Erika didn't reply. She didn't seem able to handle the pressure of this journey. Karen felt sorry for Erika, and worried about her.

**Don Makele paid** a visit to the communications center at Nanigen, a small office equipped with encrypted radio gear and corporate wireless networking equipment. He spoke to a young woman who was monitoring all the corporate channels. "I want to try to get a ping from a piece of equipment we've lost in Manoa Valley," he said to the young woman. He gave her the serial number of the piece.

"What kind of equipment is it?" she asked him.

"Experimental." He wasn't going to tell her it was an advanced hexapod from the Omicron Project.

Typing commands by remote, the young woman switched on a high-power seventy-two-gigahertz transmitter on the roof of the greenhouse in the Waipaka Arboretum. It was a line-of-sight transmitter. "Where should I point it?"

"Northwest. Toward Supply Station Echo."

"Got it." Tapping a keyboard, she oriented the transmitter.

"Now ping."

The young woman entered a command and stared at the screen. "Nothing," she said.

"Start pinging in a search pattern around that location."

She worked the keys for a while. Still nothing happened.

"Now point the transmitter up the mountainside. Do sequential pings."

After she worked some more, she brightened. "Got it. It pinged me back."

"Where is the equipment?"

"Gosh. It's on the cliffs. Halfway up Tantalus." She called up an image of the terrain on her screen and pointed to a spot on the mountainside, far above the bottom of Manoa Valley. "How did the equipment get there?" she asked.

"I don't know," Makele answered.

Somebody had survived. They were now driving the hexapod straight up the mountain. Interesting.

Makele returned to Drake's office. "Just for the hell of it, I pinged the hexapod. I got a ping back. Guess what. The hexapod is halfway up to Tantalus Crater."

Drake's eyes narrowed. What the hell. Somebody had survived the predator that had eaten Telius and Johnstone. "Can we find that hexapod, retrieve it?"

"Those cliffs are really steep. I don't think we could reach the hexapod right now. Plus we can't get a tight fix on it. We can get its approximate location on the cliffs. Only good to a hundred meters."

A tiny smile formed at the corner of Drake's mouth and grew wider, until it had become a grin. "I wonder . . . maybe they're heading for Tantalus Base."

"Yeah, could be."

Drake broke into laughter. "Tantalus Base! Ha! I would like to see their faces when they see Tantalus. They're in for an ugly surprise—if they get there." He became serious. "You go up to the crater and make sure they get a surprise. I'll keep track of their progress."


**Rick was driving** when there was a beep, and the hexapod's communication panel lit up. A display flared: ANSWERBACK 23094-451.

"What the hell was that?" Rick said.

Danny slumped in the passenger seat next to him. "Turn that thing off."

"I can't. It's just doing this shit on its own." Rick began to wonder: was somebody trying to talk to them? Maybe it was Drake.

But then the panel went quiet again. He had a feeling, though, that Drake might know where they were. If so, what would they do if Drake found them? The gas rifle would have no effect on a human of normal size. Karen walked alongside.

"The radio's acting funny," he said to Karen.

She shrugged.

The terrain trended upward at a steep angle. They came to a low cliff, and the walker climbed it. At the top of the cliff they made their way around a bunch of sedge grass, and came to a rock. "Stop!" Rick said. He advanced toward the rock; he had seen something under it. Something black and shiny. "It's a beetle hiding under there," he said. "Erika, what kind?"

Erika focused her attention on the beetle. It was a Metromenus, the same kind they'd seen when they'd first arrived in the micro-world.

"Be careful," Erika said. "They have a nasty spray."

"Exactly," Rick said.

"What's up?" Karen asked him.

"It's a chemical war out there. We need chemical weapons, too."

"We don't need it," Karen said to him. "We've already got the benzo spray." She lifted the spray bottle out of her pocket—the self-defense compound that she had made in the lab, which she'd hoped to show to Vin Drake. But when she squeezed the pump, nothing came out. It had been used up spraying the centipede.

Rick was determined to reload the bottle with spray. He crept ahead with the gas rifle, took aim, and fired at the beetle. The needle penetrated the beetle's shell. There was a muffled explosion, and the beetle shuddered and sprayed chemicals around in its death throes, until the air reeked of acids.

Erika assured them there would be a lot of spray left in the beetle. Rick put on his mad scientist outfit: the rubber apron, the goggles, and the gloves, and he went to work.

First, he flipped the dead beetle over on its back. Next, with his machete, he began tapping around on the jointed segments of the abdomen, looking for an opening.

Erika gave him advice. "Cut between segment six and segment seven. Lift the sclerite plates off—gently."

Rick sliced into the beetle, working the blade along a joint between segments, then pried with his machete, lifting up the armored plates. They came off with a tearing sound, revealing fat. He started cutting into the fat carefully.

"You're looking for a pair of chemical sacs at the base of the abdomen," Erika explained, kneeling next to Rick. "Don't burst a sac or you'll be sorry."

Rick lifted out a football-shaped organ, then another one. These were the chemical sacs. They were closed—muscles clenched them shut. Following Erika's instructions, he cut the muscle, and the sac began to leak liquid. It stank.

"That's benzo," Erika said. "It's mixed with caprylic acid, a detergent. That helps the chemical stick to surfaces, which enhances its power as a weapon. Don't get it on your skin."

It pleased Karen to see Erika interested in something, for a change. Erika had gotten so quiet, so depressed. At least this would distract her.

Rick collected the liquid in a bottle and screwed on the top. Then he handed it to Karen. "There you go. For your protection."

Karen wondered at Rick. He certainly had energy. She should have thought of collecting more chemicals herself. Rick seemed quite skilled at this business of getting along in the micro-world; he even seemed to enjoy it. It didn't make her like Rick Hutter any better, but, somewhat to her surprise, she found herself glad to have him along on the journey, anyway. "Thanks," she said to him, stuffing the bottle back in her pocket.

"Don't mention it." Rick took off his outfit and stored it away, and they resumed their upward climb.

• • •

**The land grew** impossibly steep. It went almost vertical, and they arrived at the base of an endless cliff. The cliff ran upward as far as the eye could see, an expanse of bubbly volcanic rock draped with lichens and hanging moss, and dotted with clumps of uluhe ferns. There seemed to be no way around it.

"Damn the cliff, full speed ahead," Rick said.

They made sure the equipment was tied down, and then Rick jumped in back with Erika, and tied himself in. Karen drove. The truck's feet stuck to the rock beautifully, and the truck moved upward. They made excellent speed, gaining altitude fast.

But the cliff just seemed to go on forever.

The day was coming to a close, and they didn't know how far they had come, or how far they had to go. The battery readout showed that the power had been draining steadily; the vehicle had only about a third of its battery power left.

"I think we should bivouac on the cliff," Rick finally said. "It might actually be safer than anywhere else."

They found a ledge and parked the truck on it. It was a lovely spot, and it looked out over the valley. They ate the last of the katy-did steaks.

Danny spread out some things in the back of the truck, where he intended to spend the night. His arm was clearly swollen. It felt bloated and lifeless. It didn't seem to belong to him anymore, but had become a dead weight.

"Oooh," he whispered. He clutched his arm and made a face.

"What's the matter now?" Rick Hutter said to Danny.

"My arm just popped."

"Popped?

"Nothing. Just a noise in my arm."

"Let's have a look," Rick said, bending over Danny.

"No."

"Come on. Roll up your sleeve."

"It's fine, all right?"

Danny's left arm had remained paralyzed, and it hung in the sling. The arm had packed the shirt sleeve, giving the sleeve a bulging, taut appearance. The shirt was filthy, too. "You might want to roll up your sleeve to let your skin get some air," Rick said. "That arm could get infected."

"Go away. You're not my mother." Danny stuffed a rag under his neck as a pillow, and curled up in the truck bed.

Darkness fell over the Pali. The night sounds rose up again, the cryptic noises of insects.

Rick settled down in the passenger seat. "You sleep, Karen. I'll stay up."

"That's all right. Why don't you sleep, Rick? I'll do the first watch."

They both ended up wide awake, keeping watch in smoldering silence as Erika and Danny slept. The bats came out, and squeals and echoes sounded near and far, crisscrossing the sky, as the bats plucked moths and other flying insects from the air.

Danny stirred. "The bats are keeping me awake," he complained. But soon they heard him snoring.

The moon climbed high over the Manoa Valley, turning the waterfalls into silver threads falling into emptiness. Around one of the waterfalls an arc of light glimmered. Rick stared at it: what was that light around the waterfall? The light seemed to shimmer, change.

Karen had noticed it, too. She pointed the harpoon at it. "You know what that is, right?"

"No idea."

"It's a moonbow, Rick." She touched his arm. "Look! It's a double moonbow."

He hadn't even known moonbows existed. Here they were, travelers in a dangerous Eden. It would be just his luck to be stuck in

Eden with Karen King, of all people. He found himself glancing at her. Well, she was beautiful, especially in the moonlight. Nothing seemed to keep Karen down for long, nothing seemed to defeat her. Karen King made a good partner for an expedition, even if they didn't get along personally. She did not lack courage, that was for sure. It was just too bad her personality was so unruly, so contrary. He drifted off, and woke later to find that Karen had fallen asleep against him, her head nestled on his shoulder, breathing gently.

# Chapter 31

I t's strange." Dorothy Girt, senior forensic scientist with the Honolulu Police Department, kept her eyes focused on the eyepieces of a Zeiss binocular microscope. "I've never seen anything like it."

She stood up, and Dan Watanabe sat down at the microscope. They were in an open area subdivided by lab benches. The benches were stocked with testing equipment, imaging equipment, microscopes, computers. He adjusted the eyepieces, and focused.

At first, he saw . . . a small object with a metallic look.

"How big is it?" he asked.

"One millimeter."

It was somewhat larger than a poppy seed. But it was a machine. Or looked like one.

"What the hell . . . ?" he said.

"My feeling, too."

"Where'd it come from?"

"Fong's office," Dorothy Girt said. "The evidence team dusted the office for prints. They lifted this object on a print tape, from a window near the lock."

Watanabe changed the focus, and moved his gaze up and down the object. It was damaged; it appeared to be crushed, and was covered with a dark, tarlike material. The object vaguely resembled a vacuum cleaner, except that it had something that looked like a fan on it. Fan blades inside a housing. A little bit like a jet engine. There was a long, flexible neck, a gooseneck, and at the end of the neck two sharp, flat metal pieces stuck out.

"It must have fallen out of somebody's computer," he said.

Dorothy Girt was standing next to him, leaning on the lab bench. She straightened up. "Does a computer have knives in it?" she said quietly.

He looked again. What he had thought were two flat pieces of metal coming off the gooseneck now looked more like blades. Crossed daggers, gleaming, at the end of a flexible arm. "Do you think . . . ?" he began.

"I want to know what you think, Dan."

Watanabe turned the zoom knob. He went down into the view, deeper and deeper, magnifying the daggers. They became precision instruments, forged and polished. Each blade reminded him of a *tantō*, a Japanese dagger used by samurai. There was some kind of dark, dirty material smeared on the blades. And then he saw the cells. Dried red blood cells. The cells were mixed with fibrin.

"There's blood on it," he said.

"I had noticed."

"How long are those blades?"

"Less than half a millimeter," Girt answered.

"Then it doesn't work," he said. "The victims bled to death from cuts up to two centimeters deep. The cuts opened their jugulars. These blades are far too small to cut somebody's throat. It's like trying to kill a whale with a pen knife. Can't do it."

They both were silent for a moment.

"Except at birthdays," Watanabe added.

"Excuse me, Dan . . . ?"

"You're wrapping a birthday present. You cut the paper with . . . ?"

"Scissors."

"Those blades are scissors," he said. "They could have snipped large wounds in the victims."

He began scanning the device, searching for identifying marks—a serial number, a printed word, a corporate logo. He found nothing of the sort. Whoever had built the device had not put on identifying marks, or had carefully erased them. In other words, whoever had made the device didn't want it to be traced.

He said, "Did the autopsies turn up any more of these devices? In the wounds, in the blood?"

"No," Girt said. "But the examiners probably wouldn't have noticed them."

"What's the status of the bodies?"

"Fong was cremated. Rodriguez got buried. John Doe is in the fridge."

"He needs a second look."

"Will do."

Watanabe stood back from the microscope and put his hands in his pockets, and began to walk up and down the lab. He frowned. "Why was the device found on a window? If it came out of a body, how did it get to the window? How did it get into the body in the first place?" He returned to the microscope, and studied the little device's fan-like housing. Whoa—it was a propeller. "My gosh. This thing could fly, Dorothy."

"That's speculative," Dorothy Girt said dryly.

"It could swim in blood."

"Possibly."

"Can you recover DNA from the blood that's stuck on the device?"

A prim smile. "I can get DNA from a flea's sneeze, Dan."

"I'd like to see if the blood on the device matches any of the victims' blood."

"That would be interesting," Dorothy Girt said, her cynical eyes brightening a little.

"They make small robots," he murmured.

"What, Dan?"

He stood up. "Nice work, Dorothy."

Dorothy Girt gave Lieutenant Watanabe a faint smile, hardly a smile at all. What did the lieutenant think she did with her time in the forensic lab, other than nice work? With exquisite care, she picked up the tiny object with a pair of tweezers and lowered it into a plastic vial smaller than her pinky, and carried the vial into the evidence locker area. After all, she could be handling a murder weapon.

Watanabe went out thinking. Nanigen. Small robots. Now there seemed to be a link between the Willy Fong mess and Nanigen.

Time to have a chat with the CEO.

**Vin Drake had** dropped by the communications center. He had kicked the young woman operator out of the room and locked the door, and had taken over the pinger himself. Now he gazed into a screen that displayed a three-dimensional terrain map of the northwest cliffs of Manoa Valley, from the valley's bottom to the structure of Tantalus Crater, two thousand feet above. Near the top of Tantalus Cliffs, at the base of the crater, he saw a circle with crosshairs over it.

This showed the approximate location of the stolen hexapod. The survivors, he could see, had made it nearly to the lower slopes of Tantalus Crater. At the rate they were climbing, they would reach Tantalus Base maybe by tomorrow morning, unless a predator got them. He couldn't control the predators. What he could control was Tantalus Base.

Sitting in the communications room, Drake got out his en-crypted corporate phone and called Don Makele. "The hexapod is getting close."

# Chapter 32

TANTALUS CLIFFS
31 OCTOBER, 9:45 A.M.

The truck climbed up over a lip of rock and emerged into a pocket of mossy ground. A small pond gleamed, and a miniature waterfall dribbled into the pond. As the drops landed in the water, they made the water shimmer with prismatic flashes.

Rick, Karen, and Erika climbed down from the truck. They stood by the pool, gazing into it. It was crystal-clear, with a mirror-like surface.

"We're so dirty," Erika said.

"I could use a swim," Karen said.

They saw their reflections in the water; they were tired-looking and sweaty, and their clothing had become ragged and grimy. Karen knelt and touched the water. Her finger dented the water but didn't break it. She was touching the meniscus, the rubbery surface of the water. She pushed against the meniscus, putting her weight into it, and her hand broke through the surface. "It's so tempting," she said.

"Don't do it. You'll be killed," Danny said from the truck.

"There's nothing dangerous here, Danny," Karen said.

Rick wasn't so sure. He took the harpoon and probed it around in the pool, jabbing it into the bottom and stirring the water. If any nasty creature lived in the pool, he hoped the disturbance would lure it out. The water flickered with single-celled organisms drifting and corkscrewing, but none of these little creatures seemed dangerous.

The pool was small and shallow enough that they could see all of it. Nothing seemed threatening.

"I'm going for a swim," Erika said.

"I'm not," Danny said.

Rick and Karen glanced at each other.

Erika went off behind a clump of moss, and returned naked. "Is there a problem?" she said to the others, while Danny stared. "We're all biologists here." She stepped onto the surface of the pool. The water dimpled under her toes, but it supported her weight, didn't break. She pressed down harder, and suddenly she broke through and went in up to her neck. She waded over to the waterfall and stood under it. The droplets tumbled down, bursting on her head and making her gasp. "It's magnificent. Come in."

Karen began to take off her clothes in a matter-of-fact way. Rick Hutter wasn't sure what to do; he felt embarrassed to be looking at Karen while she undressed, more embarrassed to be swimming with her and Erika naked. He got his clothes off fast, and jumped into the water.

"Welcome to Eden," Erika said.

"A dangerous Eden." Rick ducked down, and began scrubbing his head.

As Karen explored the pool, she saw it was like a fish tank full of living things, but they weren't fish, they were single-celled organisms. The creatures spun and darted and drifted. A torpedo-shaped creature swam up against her.

It was a Paramecium, a pond-water animal, a protozoan consisting of a single cell. The Paramecium was covered with rippling hairs that propelled the creature through the water. It began bumping along Karen's arm, tickling her skin. She cupped her hands and picked up the Paramecium, holding it in a handful of water. She could feel the hairs beating on her palms, and the cell squirmed. It reminded her of a cat that didn't like being held. "I won't hurt you," she said to the cell, stroking it gently with a fingertip. As she touched the hairs, they reacted by reversing direction, beating against her finger. It was like stroking velvet that fought back.

Why am I talking to a cell? Karen thought. That's pretty silly. A cell is a machine, she told herself. It's just a clockwork of proteins inside a water-filled bag. And yet . . . she couldn't help feeling that the cell was also a small being, full of its own purposes and desires. A cell wasn't intelligent the way a human is, of course. A cell couldn't imagine galaxies or compose a symphony, yet it was a sophisticated biological system, perfectly adapted to survive in this environment, and bent on making copies of itself, as many as possible. "Good luck," she said out loud, opening her hands and letting the cell go free. She watched it hurry away, corkscrewing as it swam. She said to Rick, "We're not so different from these protozoa."

"I don't see the resemblance," Rick said.

"A person is a protozoan on the day the person is conceived. As the biologist John Tyler Bonner likes to say, 'A human being is a single-celled organism with a complicated fruiting body.' "

Rick grinned. "The fruiting body is the best part."

"Crude," Karen remarked. Erika smirked at him.

A shadow crossed the pool, and a scream echoed above. Instinctively they ducked their heads under the water. When they came up, Rick looked around and said, "Birds."

"What kind?" Karen said.

"No idea. They're gone, anyway." They washed their clothes

in the pool, rinsing the dust and mud out. Afterward, they spread their clothes to dry, and sunbathed for a little while on the moss. The clothes dried quickly.

"We need to get going," Rick Hutter said, buttoning his shirt.

Just then, the distant cries grew louder, and dark shapes flashed through the air above them. The humans leaped to their feet.

A flock of birds was cruising along the cliffs, landing and taking off. The birds were foraging. Their cries shattered the air.

A bird landed before them. It was enormous, with shiny black feathers, a yellow bill, and an alert gaze. It hopped around, investigating the spot, and screamed, a raspy, echoing cry. And then suddenly it took off. More birds arrived overhead, and they began circling, inspecting the scene, and landing in trees that clung to the cliff face. The humans became aware of many eyes watching them. The cries of the birds surrounded the pool.

Rick dashed for the truck, grabbed the gas rifle. "They're mynahs!" he shouted. "Get cover!"

Mynahs were carnivores.


**Danny had tumbled** out of the truck, and he cowered underneath it. Karen had thrown herself down behind a rock, while Erika wedged herself down into clumps of moss. Rick knelt in the open, holding the gas rifle, watching the black shapes as they swept past the cliff, their cries streaming in the wind.

The birds saw him. They had no fear of something so small. A mynah cruised in and landed, and hopped across the ground toward him. He fired at the bird. The gun erupted with a hiss, kicking him backward, but at that instant the mynah leaped into the air and soared away, downwind. He had missed. He reloaded frantically, slamming another pin into the chamber. The gun was a bolt-action rifle: it fired one projectile at a time.

He thought there must be twenty or thirty of them, anyway. They swirled around the cliffs, their cries deafening. "They hunt in packs," Rick said.

Another mynah landed.

He pulled the trigger. Nothing happened.

"Shit!"

A jam. He frantically worked the bolt. The bird took one hop toward him and cocked an eye at him. Then it pecked at him, and grabbed the gun. It was a shiny object; it had attracted the bird's eye. The mynah slammed the gun against a rock, crumpling it, and tossed it aside. Then it held up its head, opened its beak, and howled, letting out a cry that seemed to make the ground shake.

Rick, meanwhile, had thrown himself flat, and was crawling for the harpoon, which lay near the pool.

The mynah turned its attention to Erika, who cowered in the moss. She crouched, staring up at the bird, and suddenly lost her nerve. She broke and ran, ducking her head, whimpering.

"Don't, Erika!" Rick shouted at her.

Erika's motion drew the bird's attention, and it hopped toward her.

Karen King had been watching, and she made a sudden decision. She would sacrifice her life for Erika. She would give Erika a chance to live. It was good while it lasted, she thought, and stood up and ran toward the bird, waving her arms. "Hey! Take me!"

The bird swerved, and pecked at Karen, but missed her, and she went sprawling. Erika had now jumped into the truck and was attempting to start it. Erika had gone into a full-blown panic; she didn't know what she was doing, other than trying to get away. Danny shouted at her, "Stop! I order you to stop!" Erika paid no attention. The truck lurched off, and began climbing upward along the rocks. But it was very exposed.

She was deserting the others.

"Erika! Turn around!" Karen screamed.

Erika had gone past the point of hearing anybody.

The truck, shiny and moving up the cliff, its six legs working, must have seemed like something tasty or interesting. A mynah coasted in and plucked Erika out of the driver's seat. Packs and gear flew out of the truck as it tumbled down the cliff and bounced out into sheer air. And then it was gone.

The mynah landed, carrying Erika Moll in its beak. The bird slammed her several times against the cliff, whipping its head back and forth to kill its prey. The bird then took off, carrying the corpse. Immediately it got into a squabble with another mynah, and they fought with each other over the remains of Erika Moll, and tore the body apart in midair.


**It wasn't over.** Rick had gotten his hands on the harpoon, and he looked around: where was Karen? She was lying on the ground, out in the open, underneath a mynah. The bird, which had an unusual black streak on its bill, had landed, and was staring down at Karen. It seemed to be trying to make up its mind about her. Was this thing edible?

"Karen!" Rick shouted, and threw the harpoon at the bird.

The harpoon, a thread of metal, went into the bird's feathers. Not very far. The bird shook itself, and the harpoon dropped to the ground. The bird studied Karen.

She crouched, trying to make herself look small and unappetizing.

"Over here!" Rick shouted, and started running, hoping to distract the bird.

"No, Rick!"

The mynah cocked its eye at Karen when she spoke. It lunged for her and picked her up in its beak, threw its head back, and swallowed Karen in one gulp. Then it flew off, wings thundering.

"Damn you!" Rick yelled at the mynah. He waved the harpoon at the bird, which had become a fluttering speck in the distance. "Come back with her!" The flock in the trees chattered and roared. Now he couldn't tell which of them had eaten Karen. "Come back! Come back for a fair fight!" He jumped up and down, waving his arms, shaking the harpoon.

He felt like crying. He would have done anything to get the mynah bird to come back, the one with the streak on its bill. He couldn't give up now.

But then he remembered something he'd learned about birds. A bird does not have a stomach. It has a crop.

# Chapter 33

## EDGE OF TANTALUS
## 31 OCTOBER, 10:15 A.M.

Karen King was curled up in a fetal position inside the crop of the mynah bird, holding her breath. The muscular walls of the crop pressed in on her, clamping her in place so that she couldn't move. The walls were slimy, slick, and smelled foul. However, there were no digestive juices in the crop. It was simply a bag for storing food, before the food was passed down into the rest of the digestive system.

She knew the bird was flying, because she felt the regular thump-thump of the bird's pectoralis muscles, driving its wings. She got her arms around her face and pushed outward, and managed to open a space for her nose and mouth.

She took a breath.

The air smelled horrible, with an acid stench of rotting insects, but at least it was air. Not much air, though. Almost immediately it became stifling hot and she began to pant. A wave of claustrophobia came over her. She wanted to scream. With an act of will she tried to calm herself. If she began to scream and struggle, she would use up the air quickly and would suffocate. The only way to stay alive was to stay calm, move sparingly, and try to make the air last as long as possible. She straightened her spine and pushed her legs out. This stretched the crop and opened up a little more space. Even so, she was running out of air.

She tried to get her knife in her hand, but she'd tucked it down deep in her hip pocket. She couldn't reach the knife. The muscular walls of the bird's crop held her arm back.

Damn. Gotta get that knife.

Right then she vowed to hang her knife around her neck, in the future. If there was a future . . . she drove her right arm downward, fighting against the rubbery walls that surrounded her. She forced her fingertips into the pocket, and let her breath out with a whoosh, gulped in nasty air, and coughed. Her fingertips closed on a bottle in her pocket—what was this? It was the spray bottle. Filled with beetle spray. Rick had filled it.

A weapon.

She grimaced, and dragged the bottle out.

At that moment, the bird maneuvered in flight. The crop tightened, the muscles squeezing the breath out of her lungs with a whoosh. A sensation of weightlessness came over her, a sense of falling. Then came a lurch and a bump. The bird had landed. She lost consciousness.

**The mynah had** returned to the same spot where it had caught Karen, looking for more food. It stared at Rick Hutter, cocking its head.

Rick recognized the black streak on its bill. The same bird. It had eaten Karen; no way of knowing if she was still alive. But she might be. He waved the harpoon in front of him and advanced toward the bird. "Come and get me, you cowardly bastard."

The Masai thrust. That was what he had to do to this bird. A young Masai warrior, a boy of thirteen or fourteen, can kill a lion with a spear. It's doable, he told himself. It's all about technique.

The bird hopped toward him.

He watched, judging the distance, timing his move, planning what he would do with his body, the angle of the harpoon. He would have to use the animal's own strength and weight against itself, as Masai hunters do with lions. The Masai hunter provokes the lion to charge him, and at the last instant he plants the butt of his spear in the ground, with the point angled toward the lion, and he kneels behind the spear: the lion runs onto the spear and impales itself.

The bird struck at him with its beak. As the strike came, Rick jammed the harpoon's butt at an angle into the ground with the point aimed upward at the bird. He took his hand off the harpoon and threw himself forward, diving under the bird's chest to get out of the way.

The harpoon caught the bird in the neck as the bird pecked down at Rick. With a barbed tip honed to greater fineness than a surgical needle, and drenched with poison, the weapon pierced the bird's neck, breaking through the skin, and the barb stuck there. The bird backed off with the harpoon dangling from its neck. It shook its head, trying to dislodge the harpoon, while Rick crawled away. He sat up and drew his machete. "Come on, fight!" he shouted at the bird.

Karen heard Rick's voice. It brought her to her senses—she had passed out momentarily. She started hyperventilating, drawing air into her lungs, but she couldn't get enough to breathe. Prickles of light flashed in her eyes, a sign of oxygen starvation. She became aware of the spray bottle clutched in her fist. She pulled the trigger, and felt a horrible burning sensation as the chemicals surged out and spread around her. The muscles squeezed tighter, and the stars turned into fog and then into nothing—

**The mynah wasn't happy.** The harpoon had pricked it, and there were unpleasant sensations in its crop. It vomited.

Karen King landed in the moss and the bird took off.

She was unconscious. Rick knelt by Karen and felt her neck for a pulse, and discovered that her heart was still beating. He placed his mouth on hers and drove a breath into her lungs.

With a rasping sound, she took a breath on her own. She coughed, and her eyes opened.

"Ohh."

"Keep breathing, Karen. You're okay."

She still gripped the spray bottle; her hand was locked around it. Rick pried her hand open and released the bottle. Then he dragged her under a fern. There, he helped her to sit up, and then he cradled her in his arms. "Take deep breaths," he said. He pulled a strand of hair off Karen's face, and smoothed her hair. He didn't know where the birds were, whether they were still hunting in the area or had moved on, but their screams had grown more distant. He propped Karen against a stem and sat beside her, drawing his knees up. He kept his arms around her.

"Thank you, Rick."

"Are you injured?"

"Just a little dizzy."

"You weren't breathing. I thought you were . . ."

The cries of the birds faded. The flock had moved on.

Rick made a quick survey of their remaining gear. Their survival was in real jeopardy. The truck was gone. Erika dead. Most of their supplies had gone over the cliff with the truck. The harpoon was gone, as well, for the mynah had flown off with the barb still lodged in its neck. The backpack lay near the pool. They still had the blow-gun and the curare. A single machete lay on the ground. Danny Minot was nowhere to be seen.

But then they heard his voice coming from above. In his panic, he had climbed up a vine, and had come out at the top of the rock. They saw him crouched up there, waving his good arm. "I see the Great Boulder! We're almost there!"

# Chapter **34**

D rake had taken over the communications room. He was staring at the screen of the remote tracking system that had been pinging the hexapod truck. Right now, he was a little puzzled by what he saw on the screen. The crosshairs on the cliff face, indicating the approximate position of the truck, had suddenly shifted downward by a hundred and fifty meters—by about five hundred feet. At first he suspected a system error. But as he watched, and waited, the truck's location didn't change. It wasn't moving.

He allowed himself a modest smile. Yes. It looked like the damn truck had fallen off the cliff. That had to be it. The truck had plunged down the cliff face.

He knew that a micro-size human body could survive any fall, any distance. But the fact that the truck wasn't moving meant that, at the very least, the truck had been damaged. It might be busted.

The survivors would be in a total panic by now, he realized. They weren't getting any closer to Tantalus. And the bends would be just starting to affect them. They would not be feeling exactly chipper.

He got Makele on his phone. "Have you been to Tantalus?"

"Yes."

"And?"

"I didn't do anything. Didn't need to. It's—"

"They're not going to make Tantalus anyway. They took a tumble, poor souls."

# Chapter 35

**KALIKIMAKI INDUSTRIAL PARK
31 OCTOBER, 10:30 A.M.**

Lieutenant Dan Watanabe parked his brown Ford in the single, lone parking space marked VISITORS. The painted metal building stood next to the skeleton of a half-finished warehouse on one side and an empty lot on the other side dotted with thickets of underbrush. By the warehouse, he noticed an area covered with gravel. He walked over to it and picked up a few pieces. Crushed limestone. Interesting. It looked like the same stuff trapped in the PI Rodriguez's tires. He dropped a few pieces in his shirt pocket, for Dorothy Girt to have a look at.

The parking lot around Nanigen's building was full of cars.

"How's business?" he said to the receptionist.

"They don't tell me much."

A coffeemaker on a table diffused the sour smell of coffee that had been heating for hours.

"Would you like me to make some coffee?" the receptionist asked.

"I think you already did."

The company's security chief walked in. Don Makele was a heavyset man packed with muscle. Makele said, "Any news on the missing students?"

"Could we talk in your office?"

As they entered the main part of the building, they passed doors that were shut. Windows looked into rooms, but the windows were covered with black blinds on the inside. Why were the blinds all drawn? Why were they black? As he walked along, Dan Watanabe felt the presence of a hum, a vibration coming up through the floor. That hum meant there was a lot of AC electrical current running in the building. For what?

Makele ushered Watanabe into his office. Windowless. Watanabe noticed a photograph of a woman, must be the guy's wife. Two children, just *keiki*s. He noticed a plaque on the wall. U.S. Marine Corps.

Watanabe sat on a chair. "Nice kids."

"I love 'em to death," Makele said.

"You served in the Marines?"

"Intel."

"That's cool." Chitchat never hurts, and you can pick up things. "We found your vice president, Alyson Bender—" he began.

"We know. She was very depressed."

"What got her depressed?"

"She'd lost her boyfriend, Eric Jansen. Who drowned."

"So Ms. Bender and Mr. Jansen were romantically connected, I take it," Watanabe said. He could feel the uneasiness of the man under the surface. Cop instinct. He went on: "It's actually pretty hard for seven people to vanish in these islands. I've called around to see if the students showed up anywhere. Like Molokai. Everybody on Molokai knows everybody else on Molokai. If seven kids from Massachusetts showed up there, the Molokai folks would be talking about it."

"Don't I know. I was born on Molokaʻi," Makele said.

Watanabe noticed that he pronounced the name of the island in the old way. Molokaʻi. With the glottal stop. It made him wonder if Makele spoke any Hawaiian. People born on Molokai sometimes did speak Hawaiian; they learned it from their grandparents or from "uncles"—traditional teachers. "Molokai is a beautiful place," Watanabe remarked.

"It's the old Hawaiʻi. What's left of it."

Watanabe changed the subject. "Do you know a gentleman named Marcos Rodriguez?"

Makele looked blank. "No."

"How about Willy Fong. A lawyer up north of the freeway." Watanabe did not mention they were dead.

Makele picked it up anyway. "Sure—" He squinted, looked puzzled. "The guys who got stabbed, right?"

"Yes, in Fong's office. Fong, Rodriguez, and another man, still unidentified."

Makele seemed confused. He spread his hands out and said, "What am I missing, lieutenant?"

"I don't know." Watanabe watched Makele to see his reaction to that.

Makele seemed surprised and irritated, but he stayed calm. Watanabe was pleased to see that the security chief fidgeted in his chair. He's nervous, Watanabe thought.

"What I know about those murders," Don Makele went on, "is what I saw on the news."

"What makes you think they were murders?"

"It's what they said on the news." Makele paused.

"Actually they said it was suicide," Watanabe said. "Did you think it was murder?"

Makele didn't take it casually. "Lieutenant, is there some reason why you want to talk to me about this—?"

"Fong or Rodriguez weren't doing any work for Nanigen, were they?"

"Are you kidding? Nanigen would never hire losers like that," Makele answered.

Don Makele knew very well what had happened to Fong and Rodriguez. Nineteen security bots had disappeared on the night of the break-in. They had swarmed onto an intruder, cut into his body, and circulated in the man's bloodstream, slicing open arteries from the inside. But the bots weren't supposed to do this. They weren't programmed to kill anybody. They were supposed to photograph the intruder and cut the skin lightly, making the intruder bleed and thus leave a blood trace behind—and they were supposed to trigger a silent alarm. That was all. Nothing dangerous, certainly not lethal. But somebody had programmed the bots to kill. Vin Drake did it, Makele thought. The bots had sliced he intruder to ribbons, then had cut their way out of the man's body, and jumped from that man to the next man like fleas. Bloodthirsty, lethal fleas. A burglar and his friends had gotten themselves killed. Accidents happen more often to assholes. But what did this detective know? Makele wasn't sure, and it made him nervous.

He decided to get tough. He leaned forward and put his voice into Official Mode and said, "Is this company or any of its employees the subject of a criminal investigation?"

Watanabe let a signficant silence elapse. "No," he finally answered. Not at this time.

"I'm glad to hear that, lieutenant. Because this company is highly ethical. The founder, Vincent Drake, is known for putting his own money into cures for orphan diseases, diseases that nobody else bothers to cure because they aren't profitable. Mr. Drake is a good man who puts his heart where his money is."

Lieutenant Dan Watanabe listened to this with a neutral face. "You mean, he puts his money where his heart is."

"That's what I said," Makele answered, gazing back at Watanabe.

Watanabe placed his card on the security man's desk, and wrote a phone number on it with his pen. "That's my cell. Call it any time if anything comes up. I think Mr. Drake is expecting me."


**Vin Drake sat** behind his desk, leaning back in an executive chair. An Oriental rug covered the floor, an antique. The air held a pleasant aroma of cigar. Given the pleasance of the aroma, Watanabe concluded that the cigar had cost more than ten dollars. The office had no windows. Soft panel lighting. He noticed, through a side door, a private bathroom with marble fixtures. Interesting to see that inside a warehouse. The guy took care of himself.

"We're very distressed by the recent events," Drake said. "We've been hoping you could help us."

"We're doing our best," Watanabe said. "I just wanted to get more background on the disappearances."

"Sure."

Watanabe had been enjoying the portrait of Drake on the wall behind him. It wasn't bad. Maybe a little pretentious, but lively. "Can you tell me what your company does?"

"Basically we make small robots and use them to explore nature, as a way of discovering new drugs to save human lives."

"How small?"

Drake shrugged and put his thumb and forefinger half an inch apart.

Watanabe squinted. "You mean half an inch? Like the size of a peanut?"

"Maybe a little smaller," Drake answered.

"How much smaller?"

"Somewhat."

"One millimeter, say?"

Drake gave a crisp smile. "That's barely feasible."

"But have you done it?"

"Done what?"

"Made robots one millimeter in size."

"We're getting into proprietary areas." Drake leaned back.

"Have you had any industrial accidents with your robots?"

"Accidents?" Drake frowned, and then broke into a chuckle. "Yes—frequently."

"Anybody get hurt?"

"It's the other way around." Drake laughed. "People step on the robots by accident. The robots always lose." He sighed and looked at his watch. "I have a meeting."

"Sure. Just one thing." Watanabe would describe what he'd seen in the microscope, but he would not show Drake a photograph of the device, because a photo was evidence, and you don't flash evidence. So he kept things vague. "We've become aware of a device, pretty small, that appears to have what might be a propeller and cutting blades. It might be able to fly, or swim in somebody's bloodstream. Is this a Nanigen product?"

Drake took a moment to reply; Watanabe thought the moment lasted a beat too long. "No," Drake answered. "We don't make robots like that."

"Does anybody make them?"

Drake gave Watanabe a careful look. Where was this cop going? "I think you're describing a theoretical device."

"What kind?"

"Well, it would be a surgical micro-robot."

"A what?"

"A surgical micro-bot. Also called a surgibot. It's a very small robot used for medical procedures. In theory, a surgibot could be made small enough to circulate in a patient's bloodstream. Equipped with scalpels, a swarm of surgibots could perform microsurgery.

They could be injected into a patient, and the surgibots would swim through the bloodstream to the target tissue. Surgibots could cut arterial plaques from the inside of an artery, for example. Or a swarm of surgibots could hunt down metastasized cancer cells. The surgibots would kill the cancer cells one at a time, thus defeating the cancer. But as of now, surgibots are a dream, not a reality."

"So you're not actually building these . . . what you call . . . surgibots?"

"Not like that, no."

"I'm sorry, I don't understand," Watanabe said.

Drake sighed. "We're getting into an area that's very sensitive."

"Why?"

"Nanigen is doing research . . . for you."

"For me?" Watanabe said, looking mystified.

"You pay taxes?"

"Sure."

"Nanigen is working for you."

"Oh, so you're doing government—?"

"We can't go there, lieutenant."

They were doing secret government work, classified, something with small robots. Drake was warning him off, hinting he'd have trouble with the government if he pursued this. Fine. Abruptly, Watanabe changed gears. "Why did your vice president jump off his boat?"

"What? What do you mean?"

"Eric Jansen was an experienced boater. He knew to stay with his boat even in surf. He jumped into the surf for a reason. Why did he jump?"

Drake stood up, his face flushed. "I have no idea what you're getting at. We've asked you to find our missing students. You haven't found anybody. We've lost two key executives. You haven't given us a damn bit of help there, either."

Watanabe stood up. "Sir, we did find Ms. Bender. We're still looking for Eric Jansen." He took out his wallet and nudged out his business card.

Drake took the card and sighed as he looked at it, and an unpleasant expression flitted across his face. "To be frank, we are disappointed with the Honolulu police." He let the card flutter down to his desk. "One wonders what you actually do."

"Well, sir, the Honolulu Police Department is older than the New York Police Department—I didn't know if you knew that. We'll just keep working our cases like we always do, sir."

**"We've got five** more of them." Dorothy Girt laid the photographs out for Watanabe on her lab bench. They showed the same devices, each with a propeller inside a housing and a gooseneck with blades. "I found them in the Asian John Doe. A smelly job."

"How did you find them, Dorothy? They're really small."

Dorothy Girt flashed him a cool smile of triumph, and opened a drawer, and held up a heavy object. It was an industrial horseshoe magnet. "I swiped it over the wounds. Darned thing is heavy."

She put the magnet aside, then showed him a blowup photo of one of the robots. The bot had been split cleanly, in a perfect cutaway view. Incredibly small chips and circuitry were visible, and something that looked like a battery, a driveshaft, gears . . .

"This thing is cut perfectly in half! How did you do that, Dorothy?"

"It was simple. I mounted it in an epoxy block, just like a tissue sample. Then I sliced it with a microtome. Same thing you do with tissue samples." Dorothy's microtome, with an ultrasharp blade, had split the micro-bot right down the middle. "Note this feature, Dan."

He bent over the photo and followed her finger to a boxlike

object in the guts of the robot. A small lowercase *n* was printed on the box.

"So," he said. "The CEO lied to me." He wanted to slap Dorothy on the back, but stopped himself at the last moment. Dorothy Girt didn't seem like a person who would welcome the gesture. Instead he offered her a slight nod of the head in the Japanese mode of respect—a family habit. "Excellent work, Dorothy."

"Hmp," she snorted. Her work was never anything but excellent.

# Chapter 36

TANTALUS CRATER
31 OCTOBER, 1:00 P.M.

**M**other Fucking Nature," Danny Minot muttered. "It's nothing but monsters with insatiable appetites." He was trudging along, dragging his grass-covered feet and holding his swollen arm protectively. His arm seemed to have gotten even bigger, to the point where his shirt sleeve was beginning to show small rips and tears. Rick Hutter and Karen King walked along next to Danny, Rick wearing the backpack, Karen holding a machete bared and ready for action. They were the last three survivors. They were stumbling across a vast, curving sweep of land, covered with sand and gravel. It was the lip of Tantalus Crater. The open land extended to a bushy line of bamboo in the distance, towering to an immense height. Through a gap in the bamboo, a boulder the size of a mountain lurked, moss-covered and furrowed with gullies. The boulder seemed to be miles distant, at least for people of their size.

The sun beat down on them. No rain had passed over Tantalus in many hours. They were getting very thirsty. Their small bodies lost moisture fast.

Karen felt exposed. They were targets. In motion across a wasteland, without cover. A bird passed overhead, and she cringed and clutched her machete. But it wasn't a mynah, it was a hawk circling over Tantalus, and the humans were too small to make a decent meal for a hawk—or so she hoped.

"Are you okay, Karen?" Rick asked.

"Stop worrying about me."

"But—"

"I'm fine. Check on Danny. He looks bad."

Danny had sat down on a stone and seemed unable to keep going. He was fondling his bad arm, adjusting the sling, and his face had gone white.

"You okay, man?"

"What's the meaning of that question?"

"How's your arm?"

"There's nothing wrong!" But now Danny was staring at his arm. A muscle in his arm spasmed, tensing against the cloth, relaxing, tensing again. It looked involuntary. Danny seemed to have lost control of the muscles.

"Why is it doing that?" Rick asked, as the spasms moved in corrugated waves along Danny's arm. The arm seemed to have a life of its own.

"It's not doing anything," Danny insisted.

"But Danny, it's jerking—"

"No!" Danny shouted, pushing him away, and he picked up his arm and moved it out of Rick's reach, cradling it with his good hand and turning his back to Rick as if he were guarding a football. Rick began to suspect that Danny had lost all motor control of his arm.

"Are you able to move your arm?"

"I just did."

Suddenly there was a tearing, splitting sound. Danny started moaning, "No . . . no . . ." His shirt sleeve was finally coming apart. As the sleeve split, it revealed a horrible sight. The skin had become translucent, like oiled parchment. Beneath the skin, fat white ovoids rested, twitching slightly. They had a contented look.

"The wasp laid eggs," Rick said. "It was a parasite."

"No!" Danny screamed.

The eggs had hatched. Into larvae. Grubs. They'd been feeding on the tissues in his arm. Danny stared at his arm, holding it and moaning. The popping sounds in his arm—those were the eggs hatching . . . the grubs were digging . . . chewing through his arm . . . he whimpered, and began screaming. "They'll hatch!"

Rick tried to calm him. "We'll get you medical help. We're nearly at Tantalus . . ."

"I'm dying!"

"They won't kill you. They're parasites. They want to keep you alive."

"Why?"

"So they can keep feeding—"

"Oh, God, oh, God . . ."

Karen picked him up. "Come on. You gotta keep moving."

They resumed walking, but Danny was slowing them down. He kept stumbling and sitting down. He couldn't take his eyes off his arm, as if the grubs had hypnotized him.

Halfway across the ground they came to a round tube made of blobs of clay stuck together. The tube emerged from the ground, like a bent chimney.

Karen said, "I wish Erika was here. She might have been able to tell us what made it."

They had to assume the mud chimney held something danger-ous, probably some kind of insect. They gave the chimney a wide berth, ready to dash for cover if anything moved. As they passed it, the Great Boulder drew closer.

∎ ∎ ∎

**She was a mother.** Like a butterfly, she drank only the nectar of flowers for her sustenance. Even so, she was a predator. She hunted for her babies; they lived on meat. Like all predators she was intelligent, capable of learning, with an excellent memory. In fact, she had nine brains. They consisted of one master brain and eight minor brains, strung out along her spinal cord like beads on a string. Among insects, she was one of the smartest.

She had mated once with her husband, who had dropped dead after having sex with her. She was a queen, who lived her entire life in isolation. She was a solitary wasp.

She emerged from her chimney and looked at the sun. Her head came out first, followed by her body. Her wings normally lay folded and flat across her back, like a folded fan. She unfolded her wings and vibrated them, letting her muscles warm up in the sunlight.

As the wasp climbed out of the chimney, the humans froze. She was truly enormous, with a jointed abdomen splashed with yellow and black stripes. The wasp unfolded its wings and beat them, thundering, and took off into the air, its legs dangling beneath it.

"Get down!"

"Lie flat!"

The humans threw themselves to the ground and began crawling toward whatever sort of cover they could find, scraps of grass, pebbles.

The wasp didn't notice the humans at first. After she launched herself from her chimney, however, she began flying in a zigzag pattern, orienting herself for a hunting flight. During the orientation phase, she looked down at the ground, inspecting every detail. She kept a precise map of the terrain fixed in her memory.

She saw something new.

Three objects occupied the ground at the southeast quadrant

away from her chimney. The objects were alive. They were crawling across the ground. They looked like prey.

She immediately changed her flight path and swooped in.

**The wasp turned** and dove down very fast. It chose Rick Hutter, and landed on him.

He rolled over on his back, waving his machete, while the wasp straddled him with her legs. Her wings beat over him. She caught him lightly in her mandibles.

"Rick!" Karen shouted, running toward him, machete raised.

He couldn't breathe. The mandibles had driven the air out of his chest. But somehow they didn't cut through him. The wasp was being gentle.

Then she curled her abdomen underneath her and brought her sting forward, aimed at Rick. Armor plates at the jointed tip of her abdomen pulled apart, and two soft fingers, covered with sensory hairs, emerged, waving and wagging. These soft fingers were the sting palps. The palps dabbled over Hutter's neck and face, tasting his skin.

She liked what she tasted.

The sting happened very fast. Two stingers inside a sheath emerged from a hole beneath the taste palps. As the sheath drilled into Rick just under his armpit, the stingers lanced into him, first one and then the other, sliding back and forth in tandem as they worked inward.

Rick felt the needles go into him. The pain was extraordinary. He gasped.

Karen threw herself at the wasp, her machete swinging, but she landed too late. The wasp went airborne, carrying Rick gripped in her legs. Karen saw him kicking his legs, but then his body went limp.

The wasp landed on the chimney, then pushed Rick inside, down the shaft of the chimney, butting him forward using her head. She went down the chimney after Rick, her striped abdomen disappeared down the chimney, the sting going down last.

**Huddled in the** sandy area, Karen and Danny debated what to do.

"Rick's dead," Danny Minot said.

"How do you know?" Karen King said.

Danny rolled his eyes.

She wished desperately for Erika Moll; Erika might have information about the wasp. "He could still be alive."

Danny just groaned.

She racked her brain, trying to remember what she'd learned about wasps in Entomology 101. "That was a solitary wasp, I think."

"So what. Let's go, please."

"Wait." That college class she'd taken on insects . . . "Solitary wasps—they're female, of course. They build a nest for their young. They paralyze their prey, I think. But they don't kill their prey. They feed it to their young." She had no clue as to the exact species of wasp she was dealing with, or how it really lived.

"Come on!" Danny got to his feet and began walking away.

Karen unsheathed her machete.

"What are you doing?" Danny said.

"Rick saved my life," Karen said.

"You're insane."

She didn't answer. She pulled the sharpening stone from her belt and drew it across the blade of her machete. "That bitch has Rick."

"No, Karen! Don't!"

Karen ignored Danny. She opened the pack and took out a radio headset and a headlamp. She took out another headset and flipped it at Danny. "Put that on." She stood up and rushed over to the chimney. Then she spoke on the radio. "Copy me, Danny?"

He was lying on his stomach in the shade of a small plant. "You're crazy!" he shouted at her on the radio.

She put her ear up to the chimney again. It was made of dried clay and it smelled odd. Insect saliva glue. She could feel a slow thrumming sound under her feet—the wasp's wings beating underground. There was a nest down there. The thrumming continued for a while. Then the sound began to move up to ground level, coming closer. The wasp was climbing up the chimney out of its nest.

Karen stood in the shadowed side of the chimney, trying to blend in.

The wasp's head emerged as Karen flattened herself against the chimney. Two semicircular compound eyes looked at her. She felt sure she'd been noticed, but the wasp didn't react; instead, it took off. Airborne, the wasp flew back and forth in a Z pattern, orienting itself, and then sailed off straight into the northwest sky, aiming for distant hunting grounds of its own choosing.

When the wasp had dwindled to a point and vanished, Karen took a step backward and drove her machete into the chimney, hacking at it. She bashed the chimney to pieces, breaking it down, keeping an eye toward the northwest, fearful the wasp might reappear. But the sky remained empty. She cleared away chunks of mud and then jumped feet-first into the tunnel.

"Don't leave me!" Danny shouted.

Karen adjusted her headset and beeped him on the radio. "Can you hear me?"

"You're going to die, Karen. I'll be left with no one—"

"Call me if you see her."

"Ohhh . . ."

"Clear. Over," Karen said, and snapped off. She would have to move fast, try to find Rick and bring him out. The wasp could come back at any time.

The tunnel had round walls lined with hardened clay. It trended steeply downward. Karen descended feet-first, crab-walking on her hands and elbows. It was tight in here. Daylight filtered in through the entrance behind her, but the light dimmed as she proceeded deeper underground. She switched on her headlamp. The tunnel smelled of something pungent but not unpleasant. It was probably the mother wasp's pheromones, she figured. The smell came mixed with a rancid stench, which grew stronger as she went deeper underground.

Suddenly she came to a falloff. The tunnel turned straight downward here, plunging into a vertical shaft. Claustrophobia almost choked her as she looked down it. It was a dark hole that seemed to go down into nothingness, with no apparent bottom. Rick is down there, just my luck, she thought. Well, he saved my life. It's a debt I have to pay. And I don't even like the guy.

She twisted her body, struggling against the tight walls of the tunnel, and sat herself at the lip of the shaft, letting her feet dangle. She lowered herself into the hole and began descending the shaft, pressing her hands and knees against its walls to provide a friction grip. She definitely did not want to fall. If she got wedged in the shaft, she might not be able to get out. The thought of being trapped in a vertical shaft while a giant wasp descended upon her . . . no. Don't think about it.

**Out in the** open air, Danny Minot tore open the pack and searched it for food. He had to keep his strength up. Not that it mattered, he was dead anyway. He took off his radio headset and placed it next to him. And began inspecting his arm. It was so horrible.

The radio was talking at him. He picked it up. "What?"

"See anything?"

"No, no."

"Listen Danny. Keep a lookout. If you see the wasp, tell me so I can get out. It's in your interest."

"I will, I will." He fastened the radio on his head and propped

himself up in the shade with his back against a rock, facing northwest, where the wasp had gone.

Karen reached the bottom of the chimney. It widened slightly,
then made a sharp horizontal bend. She crawled around this bend,
and the tunnel opened into a chamber. She flashed her headlamp
around the chamber. Many tunnels—about two dozen of them—
radiated from the chamber in a starburst pattern. Each tunnel ran
into darkness.

"Rick?"

He was in one of those tunnels. Probably dead.

She crawled into a tunnel. After a short distance it ended at a
wall. The wall had been built of rubble crammed loosely into place,
plugging the tunnel—grains of sand and gravel glued with saliva,
with spaces and gaps between them. She shone her headlamp into a
gap in the rubble, trying to see what lay beyond.

She realized the gaps in the rubble were breathing holes. Because
something alive was in there, past the rubble. The rubble door was
a kind of stopper or plug with holes in it. Crunching, slurping sounds
filtered out through the holes, along with a clicking noise. A rotting
smell wafted from the holes, too. Something hungry lived in a room
beyond the rubble, something that ate continually.

"Rick!" she called. "Are you there?"

The clicking stopped for a moment, then resumed. There was
no other response.

She put her eye up to a gap and pointed her light in. It fell over
a glistening surface the color of antique ivory. The surface was
creased into segments. The segments were moving past the gap,
one by one; this went on for a while, like a subway car moving past
an opening. She could hear breathing, but it wasn't human. What
frightened her was the size of the thing in there. It seemed as big as
a walrus.

There were many more tunnels to investigate. She crawled back
into the main chamber and headed into the next tunnel, and tried

to see through the blockage of stone and dried mud that clogged it. "Rick?" she shouted. "Can you hear me?"

Danny Minot's voice came over her headset, faint and crackly, because she was so far underground. "What's happening?" he said.

"I reached a large chamber. The chamber breaks into at least twenty tunnels going off in all directions. Each tunnel leads to a cell. There's a larva in each cell, I think—"

She whacked at a rubble-door with her machete, and began chopping through mud glue. "Rick!" she shouted. "Are you in there?" Maybe he can hear me but he can't talk. Or maybe he's dead. Maybe I need to get out of here. Just give this a try. She hacked out the wall, enlarging the opening until she could get her body through it, and she crawled into the cell.

The cell held a wasp grub larger than she was, an obese blob that hissed, breathing heavily, with a blind, eyeless head. Its mouth was bracketed by twin black cutting fangs. The mother wasp had provisioned the cell with food for her infant. There were two caterpillars, a koa bug, and a miserable-looking spider. At that moment, the wasp grub was feeding on the koa bug, an insect with a shiny green carapace. The room was strewn with broken pieces of insect armor, stripped of flesh. There were also three whole heads of insects, uneaten and reeking of decay.

Karen edged her way into the cell, keeping away from the grub's wicked-looking mouthparts. It was busy rooting into the koa bug.

She listened. She heard whispers of air moving through the holes in the exoskeletons of the food items. Good. This meant the food was paralyzed but was still alive. So Rick could be alive. As for the paralyzed spider, its abdomen rose and fell as it breathed, but otherwise it remained deathly still, its eight eyes glazed over.

The grub shook its head, yanking strings of koa bug meat in its mandibles, and it sucked the flesh down like spaghetti. The koa bug was breathing, too.

Karen resisted an impulse to stab the larva. She wanted to kill the horrible thing, but she pulled back. The wasp grub was a part of nature. This was no more evil than a lion cub eating meat provided by a lioness. Wasps were the lions of the insect world. They did good things, they kept populations of plant-eating insects in check, just the way lions kept an ecosystem healthy. Even so, Karen did not like the idea of a wasp eating Rick.

**She crawled out** of the cell, and made her way into the next tunnel. She shouted into the breathing hole, then cut it open and went into the cell. Here she found a mature grub polishing off its last caterpillar, having eaten everything else.

"Rick!" she shouted. The soil deadened her voice. He could be anywhere around here, above, below, off to the side, hidden inside a cell.

Her headset crackled. "What's happening?" Danny.

"I can't find Rick. This place is a maze."

She broke into another cell. It contained a cocoon spun of silk. An unborn wasp, visible through the silk, curled up tight, soon to break out of the cocoon as an adult. As her light played over the cocoon, the wasp shivered. She got out of there, and jammed rocks back into the door. That was the last thing she needed: a newborn wasp wandering around in here, armed with a stinger, no doubt.

"Rick! It's me, Karen!" she shouted. She held her breath and listened.

No sound reached her ears except the chewing of the grubs and the beating of her very frightened human heart.

**Rick Hutter lay** inside a cell in total darkness, unable to move or speak. The sting had paralyzed him, but he possessed all his senses. He could feel lumps in the dirt floor pressing into his back and legs. He could smell rotting insect flesh. He could not see the grub that lived in the chamber, but he could hear it perfectly. It was eating something, making crunching, sucking noises. His breathing went on normally. He could blink his eyes when he wanted to—he could do that much by his own will. He tried to move one finger, and wasn't sure if the finger was moving or not, he couldn't tell.

Help. Somebody help me.

It was just a thought.

He realized that the wasp venom had paralyzed only part of his nervous system, the sympathetic nerves, the nerves that are controlled by conscious will. His autonomous nervous system, the unconscious part, continued to function normally. His heart was beating, he was breathing fine, all systems go. But he couldn't will his body to do anything. His body was like an engine stuck in idle; he couldn't seem to find the controls or press the accelerator. Something hurt, and for a little while he didn't know what it was, until a warmth spread underneath him as his bladder emptied automatically. He welcomed the relief.

The venom was a wasp's version of refrigeration. It kept the prey alive and fresh until it was eaten.

The crunching and slurping activity continued near his feet. The grub seemed to be nearly finished with its meal, because he could hear a rattling sound of broken pieces of exoskeleton being shoved around. The grub was nosing at the scraps of its meal. He could hear crackling noises, scraping sounds. So the grub had jaws. He dreaded the first touch of those jaws. He couldn't stop wondering which part of him the grub would eat first. Would it start by chewing on his face? Or would it bite off his genitals first, or burrow into his abdominal cavity?

Despite the horror of his situation, Rick Hutter felt strangely bored. Paralyzed in the dark, he had nothing to do except imagine his approaching death. He decided he'd better focus his mind on the things that had made him happy during his life. This might be his last chance for memories. He recalled wading into the surf at Belmar, on the Jersey Shore, where his family had spent a week at a motel each summer—what they could afford. His father had driven a delivery truck for a convenience store chain. He remembered standing on the driver's seat of his father's truck when he was five years old and telling everybody he was going to be a truck driver just like his dad. He saw himself opening the acceptance letter from Stanford and reading it with complete disbelief . . . a full scholarship at Stanford. Then graduate school at Harvard, again on financial support. He saw himself in Costa Rica, interviewing an old lady, a *curandera*, as she brewed a healing tea from the leaves of the Himatanthus tree.

His mind turned to the lab. One night he had been trying to extract a compound from the Himatanthus leaves. Karen King had been working late, tending an experiment with her spiders. They had been alone in the room together. They had worked side by side at the lab bench, right next to each other, without saying a word, the air thick with mutual dislike. But their hands had brushed by accident . . . Maybe I should have tried to hook up with Karen that night . . . of course, she probably would have punched me . . .

A dying man thinks mostly about missed sexual opportunities. Who said that, anyway? It might really be true . . .

He began to feel sleepy . . . drifting off . . .

"Rick!"

Her voice woke him up. It came faintly through the earth.

I'm here, Karen! he shouted, in his mind. But he couldn't make his mouth move.

"Rick! Where are you?"

Hurry up! There's a Hoover with jaws in here with me.

Karen's light flickered briefly, the first light he'd seen in a long time—and was gone. Total darkness swallowed him again. She had moved on.

Come back! he shouted in his mind. You missed me!

Silence. She had gone away.

Then, in the darkness, the horror of horrors arrived. Something moist and very heavy slid over his ankle, pressing his foot into the ground. It's not happening. Next he felt the segments of the larva bumping over his leg, bump, bump, bump. No! The segments were sliding over his stomach, now, then sliding over his chest, squeezing the breath out of him. No! Please, no! The wasp grub lay on top of him now, its weight pressing down on him, suffocating him. He could feel the grub's heart beating, thumping against his chest. He heard a moist clickety-click. Those jaws were starting to work.

Click-click. Snip-snap. Snick.

The light returned. A ray shot into the cell. It revealed the black cutter knives flicking around a queerly soft mouth like a pale anus. Right in front of his face.

Karen was shining her headlamp into the cell. She saw the scene. "Oh, my God, Rick!" She began hacking at the rubble in the doorway, flinging stones aside.

The teeth brushed against his forehead. The grub was nosing around, looking for a soft spot to begin chewing. It tapped its teeth over his shoulder, leaving a streak of drool. He felt the teeth prick his nose. And the moist mouth brushed across his lips like a kiss, spewing out drool. It made him cough and choke, automatically.

"Hang on—!"

Hurry, this bastard wants to give me a hickie.

She got through the opening and threw herself at the grub, kicking the grub with both feet, pushing it away from Rick's face. "You leave him alone!" she shouted, and thrust her machete into the grub. The grub gasped, a hiss coming out of its airholes. Karen pulled out the blade and raised the machete and swung it, beheading the grub in one blow. The blob-like head slopped away while the decapitated body went into a spasm, and began whipping back and forth in reversing *C*s. Karen continued to stab and slash at the beheaded grub, but that only seemed to intensify its thrashing.

She got her arms around Rick and dragged him out of the chamber, leaving the headless grub thumping the walls. A strange odor chased them.

That's bad, Hutter said silently. That's an alarm pheromone.

King realized it, too. The dying larva was screaming for help, wailing for its mother in the language of scent. The scent was filling the nest. If the mother detected it . . .

Danny's voice came on. "What's going on?"

"I have Rick. He's alive. Stand by, I'm bringing him out."

Rick was like a sack of potatoes, a dead load, but her strength was incredible. She had got Rick and she would fight to the death before she'd give him up now. Dragging him, she crawled through the big chamber, heading for the vertical shaft . . .

Just then, Danny's voice came on her headset: "She's back!"

# Chapter 37

The solitary wasp flew in slowly, a paralyzed caterpillar dangling between her legs. She began to fly back and forth in zigzags over her nest, then settled lower, searching for the mud chimney of her burrow.

Within moments she had registered that her chimney had been smashed. Her nest had been damaged and invaded. There was an intruder.

Danny Minot wrapped himself around the rock, hiding under the plant, trying to make himself as rocklike or plantlike as possible. "You idiot!" he whispered to Karen. He'd been left alone in the micro-world.

The mother landed, carrying the caterpillar. Vibrating her wings, she advanced to the entrance. At that moment she caught the scent of her baby's death leaking out of the hole. She began beating her wings furiously. The air filled with the thunder of her wings. She dropped the caterpillar, then charged into the hole headfirst.

Karen King heard a rumbling sound in the earth above—a buzz of wasp wings, a clatter and clash of a wasp's exoskeleton.

"Danny!" she called. "What's happening?"

There was no answer.

"Talk to me, Danny!"

The mother surged down into her nest, a toxic, armored bundle of maternal rage.

**Karen listened to** the wasp coming. She crouched in the chamber at the foot of the vertical shaft, with Rick lying on the floor behind her. The sounds were frightening—and informative. A sharp smell wafted into the room—an advance wave of the mother's fury.

Karen got out her diamond sharpener and began to frantically hone her machete, *zing, swish, zing.* "Hang on, Rick," she muttered. She worked the sharpener over the steel, bringing the blade to an extreme edge. It would have to slice through massive bioplastic armor. Then she poised herself by the opening with the blade raised over her head. "Come on, come on," she muttered.

The mother reached the bottom of the shaft. There was a pause.

And then the wasp's head, huge, black-and-yellow, appeared in the opening.

Upside down.

She swung the machete at the wasp's face with every ounce of her strength.

The blade bounced off the wasp's eye, leaving a mark. The lady had armored eyes.

The wasp thrust her head—still upside down—into the room, snapped her jaws around the machete, and tore the blade out of Karen's hands, dragging it back into the hole. Karen heard crunching metallic sounds: the wasp was cutting up her last weapon.

The room shook: the wasp was pounding her wings against the tunnel walls. Getting ready to charge. She heard the wasp gasping.

She glanced over her shoulder, and her headlamp beam passed over Rick. He looked dead—

In swinging her head around, she became aware of the little knife dangling from her neck. She'd sworn never to carry it in her pocket again. My knife. She thumbed the blade open and yanked the cord off her neck.

The wasp's head was in the room now—still upside down—and the jaws snapped at her. Karen dove down to the floor, and slid her body underneath the wasp's upside-down head. The head was covered with bristles. She gripped the bristles. The head jerked up and down, battering her against the floor. The wasp could see her: a trio of little eyes stared at her from the top of the head.

Karen clung to the head as it rotated and beat her against the tunnel, the jaws crossing and snapping. She was getting a terrible thrashing. Even so, in searching for a grip, she reached behind the wasp's head and managed to get her fingertips wedged in the occipital suture, the crack between the head capsule and the pleuron, the first armored plate of the thorax. This was the back of the wasp's neck. There was a joint in the armor at that spot. Her fingertips felt soft tissue in the crack.

The neck was so narrow that she was able to wrap her fingers entirely around the wasp's neck. She had gotten a stranglehold. Maybe she could choke the wasp.

At that moment, the wasp jerked backward into the tunnel, dragging Karen along. Now she was jammed in the tunnel, being crushed by the wasp's head, which continued to hammer against her body. The wasp curled its body, and Karen realized it was trying to bring its abdomen forward and sting her. The wasp pushed her back into the room again, and began twisting, trying to throw her off its neck. But she held her grip. Having located the neck joint, she let go of the neck with one hand, grabbed her knife, then slipped the tip of her knife into the crack. Then she quickly ran the knife blade around the neck, following the crack and sawing as she went. All the way around.

The wasp's head fell off.

It rolled on top of her, and she scrambled back into the room, followed by a spurt of blood.

The mandibles snapped twice and froze. The body exsanguinated fast, blood spewing out of the severed neck all over Karen. The wings of the headless body thumped against the walls in the tunnel, the wing-beats weakening and slowing down, until the corpse quieted and lay still.

Karen pulled herself away and knelt by Rick and took his hand. She was shaking badly. "I did it."

Out of the corner of his eye, Rick saw movement behind her. He blinked his eyes and shouted in his mind: Look out!

**The master brain** inside the severed head had lost contact with the eight minor brains in the wasp's body, but those minor brains were still sending out messages to the rest of the body. The wasp's legs went into action, dragging the headless body into the room. The abdomen curled and thrust forward, and the stinger came out.

A noise at her back made Karen whirl around. Just in time she saw the stinger coming, and jumped aside as the abdomen slammed her into the wall. She struggled, trapped, as the sting waved past her face. She saw the twin blades working against each other, inches from her eyes. The sting palps popped out and tapped her cheek, and entered her mouth. But finally the stinger went still, lightly resting on Karen's collarbone, the blades bared. A dewdrop of poison swelled from the blades and hung there. She could see her face reflected in the droplet of wasp venom.

She delicately extricated herself from under the sting, avoiding contact with the liquid and blades. Then she got down on her knees and wiped the dirt from Rick's face. "How're you doing, soldier?"

He seemed completely paralyzed. Rick's face looked like a mask. Eyes moving, blinking, but no expression. The muscles in his face had gone AWOL and he had peed his pants. At least he was breathing, and his heart was beating. The wasp venom was tricky stuff, she realized. It had disabled some of his nervous system but not all of it. Was he trying to talk? She couldn't be sure.

"Can you blink?" she asked. "If you blink your eyes, it means yes. If you don't blink, it means no. Can you understand me?"

He blinked once. Yes. Then something trembled in his face.

"Rick! Is that a smile?"

Yes. Trying to.

"That's a start. Does anything hurt?"

Yes.

"What hurts? . . . Never mind. I'm going to carry you. Will that hurt?"

He didn't blink. No.

She lifted Rick under the arms and dragged him around the dead wasp, keeping their bodies away from the big droplet of venom that still hung from the wasp's stinger. As she dragged Rick, though, she could see how dire his condition was. He would never survive unless he could move his muscles. His nervous system needed help. That fucking venom—the droplet of poison gleamed in her headlamp, suspended from the stinger—that venom had acted like a smart bomb, taking out only parts of his nervous system. Horrible poison, but sophisticated, too. Nature could do magic with chemistry that no human drug could accomplish.

Rick needed help or he would die.

Staring at that clear drop of poison, Karen got an idea. The venom that had paralyzed Rick might also help save him.

She needed to collect it. She groped at her waist, and found a water bottle suspended on a cord from her machete belt. She poured out the water, then held the open mouth of the bottle to the venom droplet, and watched as the liquid dripped into the bottle. She screwed on the top. Okay.

"I've got a plan, Rick. It's crazy but it might work."

He just stared at her.

**Jamming her knees** against the walls of the shaft, Karen pushed him up the shaft ahead of her as she climbed. She felt like Superwoman; she never could have done this in the big world. It was a long climb, accomplished in stages with rests in between, and she was glad she was as strong as an ant. Finally she arrived at the mouth of the nest.

Danny Minot had given up hope. He couldn't believe his eyes when Rick Hutter popped out of the hole, followed by a battered-looking Karen King. "I got him," she said fiercely, and hoisted him across her shoulders. She carried him across the sand and dropped him in the shade of the plant beside Danny.

She knelt by Rick and studied him. Danny huddled nearby, crouching to keep out of the wind.

"Can you stand up?" she asked Rick.

He blinked once.

"Yes? You want to try?" She helped him stand up. He swayed, tottering, and dropped to his knees, then sank and fell over.

She showed him the canteen of wasp venom. "This might save you, Rick. No guarantees. What we need to do now—" she looked at the line of towering bamboo across the open ground—"is get ourselves back into the forest."

She was thinking of the death of that sniper, how the man had gone into a grand mal seizure from the spider venom. The man's death carried information that might save Rick.

# Chapter 38

The wind blew across the ridgeline of Tantalus Crater. Karen King and Danny Minot walked along slowly, carrying Rick in a stretcher made from a space blanket. Karen wore the backpack, and the blowgun was slung across her back. They moved step by step, making their way painstakingly toward the wall of bamboo trees and the Great Boulder. Rick's breathing came hoarsely from the stretcher.

"Put him down," Karen said to Danny. She examined Rick. His face was pale and drawn, and his lips were turning blue. He wasn't getting enough oxygen. What especially worried her was his breathing: ragged, irregular, insufficient. The wasp venom might have affected the breathing center in his brain stem. If his breathing shut down, he was finished.

She opened his shirt and found a bruise on his chest. What was that? The bends coming on? Or just the result of being thrown around by the wasp? They had to get out of this open area. They were morsels for birds, food for another wasp.

"How are you doing, Rick?"

He moved his head slowly from side to side.

"Not so good? Just don't fall asleep. Okay? Please."

Karen studied the bamboo forest ahead. "We just need to get under those plants, Rick. It's not far, now." She hoped, prayed, she'd find what she needed there. In the leaves.

She heard a sigh. "How are you doing, Rick?"

Silence. Rick had lost consciousness. She shook him. "Rick! Wake up! It's me, Karen!" His eyes opened and closed. He was becoming unresponsive.

All right. Maybe she could make him angry. She had always been good at that. She slapped him in the face. "Hey Rick!"

His eyes flew open. That had worked.

"I nearly got myself killed dragging your sorry ass out of that hellhole. Don't you dare die on me now."

"We might have to leave him," Danny said softly.

She turned on Danny in fury. "Do not say that again."

Finally they got beneath the plants, and put Rick down in the cool shade. Karen gave him a droplet of water to drink, holding the water in her cupped hands and pouring it into his mouth. She looked up at the leaves. She wasn't sure of the species of plant. That didn't matter, what mattered was whether any spiders lived on the leaves.

There was a particular spider she wanted to find.

She knelt by Rick, and talked to him. "Rick," she said. "You need a swift kick in the pants."

He smiled faintly.

"What are you going to do?" Danny asked her.

She didn't answer. She rooted around in the pack and removed a clean, empty plastic lab bottle. Then she started pacing around, looking up into the leaves. She grabbed the blowgun and the dart kit, and she ran into the deeper parts of the vegetation.

"Where are you going?" Danny shouted.

"You watch him, Danny. If you let anything happen to Rick, I'll—"

"Karen!"

She ran off. She had spotted a flash of color under a leaf. Day-Glo green, red, yellow. It might be what she was looking for.

It was.

She wanted to find a spider that wasn't very poisonous. All spiders used venom to kill their prey, generally insects, but spider venom varied a lot in its toxicity to humans and mammals generally. Black-widow venom was among the worst. The bite of a black widow spider could make a horse drop dead. Yet other spiders seemed less toxic to humans.

She stood under the spider now, looking up at it. It was small, with legs as transparent as glass, and a body splashed with colorful markings. The markings formed a pattern that looked like a human face, grinning with laughter—it looked like the face of a smiling clown.

It was a happy-face spider. Theridion grallator. One of the most common spiders in Hawaii, much studied by scientists. Known to have essentially no effect when it bites a human.

The happy-face spider rested in a little cobweb, a tangle of threads strung randomly under the leaf.

These spiders were very shy. They tended to flee at the first sign of trouble. "Don't run away on me," she whispered.

She began to climb the stem of the plant. She shinnied up it a distance, and then, getting herself seated on a leaf, she took out a dart from the kit, and opened her canteen. The wasp venom had filled it almost to the neck. She dipped a dart in the venom, loaded the gun, and took aim.

The spider backed away, staring at her. It appeared to be frightened. Yes, it was scared: it scrunched itself down inside its little web.

She knew the spider could hear her, and was forming a sonic image of her with the "ears" in its legs. It had probably never encountered a human and had no idea what Karen was.

She blew.

The dart lodged in the patterned back of the spider.

The spider backed up, its legs flipping around, and it tried to run, but the venom acted swiftly, and within moments the spider stopped moving. Karen heard air whistling faintly in and out of the spider's lungs, and she saw its back rising and falling. Good. It was still breathing and its heart was beating. That was important. The animal needed to have blood pressure in order to pump out venom.

She climbed up to the web. She took a strand and shook it. "Yah!"

The spider didn't move. Karen swung herself into the web and crawled across the threads, right up to the spider, reached out to one of the legs and flicked at a sensory hair. Nothing happened.

Lying on the web, she unscrewed the top of the empty lab jar and positioned it under the fangs. Using two fingers, she lifted a fang from its base, unfolding the fang from its sheath as she stared into the spider's eyes.

How to get the venom flowing? The venom glands were located in the spider's forehead, behind its eyes. She made a fist and rapped on the spider's forehead. The spider stirred, and a few drops of liquid dribbled out of the fangs. She screwed the cap on. She hoped the spider would wake up no worse for its experience. She cut the web below her and fell to the ground.

**She bent over Rick.** "This spider venom—" she held up the jar so that he could see it—"might give your nerves a jolt. It has excitotoxins in it. You understand?"

He looked at her. Blinked once. Yes, I understand.

"Excitotoxins. They'll make your nerves fire. But there's a real danger. I don't know anything about this venom. I can't control the dose. This stuff could kill cells in your body. It could start digesting you." In her mind's eye, she saw the sniper's body going through that digestive meltdown.

She took his hand in hers, and squeezed it. "I'm afraid, Rick."

He squeezed her hand back.

She said, "You want it?"

He blinked. Yes.

She removed a blow dart from the case. A clean one, no curare on it. She dipped the tip of the dart into the spider venom. The tip came up wet, barely covered with a minuscule amount of the liquid. She held it in front of him where he could see it. "Are you sure?"

Yes.

She laid the point across his forearm. She caught the point in his skin, over a vein, and pushed it in. Not too deep. Then she gripped his hand, and leaned over him. "Rick . . ."

For a few moments, nothing happened. She was beginning to wonder if she had given him enough—but then he gasped. His breathing sped up. She touched his neck, and felt his pulse racing. The venom was hitting him hard.

There was an explosive sound: Rick gasped, and dragged air into his lungs. Then he went into a seizure. His gaze flew around wildly and he strained upward against her, eyes staring, body trembling. She lay across him, holding his arms down, but afraid to press on him too hard. He gasped, taking huge lungfuls, hyperventilating as his spine arched. She threw her weight on him, trying to pin him down, fearful that he would hurt himself.

He groaned. And then his hand whipped out and fastened around her neck. He gripped her throat, his fingers squeezing, closing her throat off.

He was trying to strangle her. He hated her that much.

But then his fingers relaxed, his grip softened. He released her throat. He ran his hand over her shoulder. The touch became a caress. His hand worked up the side of her neck and under her ear, passed lightly over her skin, and his fingers opened and ran through her hair. Now she was kissing him and the great thing was that he was kissing her back.

She broke off, finally. "Does it hurt, Rick?"

"Hurts . . . like . . . hell . . ." he croaked. "I . . . could . . . get to like it."

She helped him sit up. He was dizzy, and almost toppled over, but she held him, keeping her arms around him, talking softly to him, telling him everything would be all right. "You saved my life, Rick. You saved my life."

Danny sat there watching Rick and Karen make up to each other, feeling extremely uncomfortable. In his opinion, this kind of stuff did not advance the effort to get back to Nanigen. He needed a doctor as soon as possible. He glanced down at his arm and almost threw up. The grubs seemed fatter than ever.

In a little while, Rick was able to stand. They began to walk. They went into the bamboo forest, where stalks of bamboo soared like redwoods. They made their way through it, and broke out onto a stunning view. They were facing the Great Boulder on the lip of Tantalus Crater, and looking down into the crater.

**The crater extended** beneath them, a basin stuffed with rain forest, rimmed by bare ground and patches of stunted, wind-wracked trees. All around the crater, peaks of the Ko'olau Pali fingered into boiling clouds, and the wind pummeled the scene. At the foot of the Great Boulder lay Tantalus Base.

The base would have been virtually unnoticeable to a person of normal size. There was an aircraft runway about three feet long. At least Karen felt pretty sure it was a runway: she could see a dashed line and taxi markings. Beside the runway stood a cluster of miniature buildings made of concrete. The largest building seemed to be an aircraft hangar. The other buildings were smaller, and looked like bomb shelters. The buildings were embedded partway in the soil and were lightly covered with dead leaves and plant debris, so they blended into the micro-terrain.

Karen stopped. "Wow, Rick!" she said. "We made it!"

He turned his head and smiled, and looked at her. She rubbed his hands, his arms, to get the circulation going.

"Your hands feel warmer. You're getting better I think."

They didn't want to draw attention to themselves, because they didn't know what to expect from the inhabitants of the base, Nanigen employees who might well be following orders from Vin Drake. They decided to watch the base for a time, looking for activity. They lay down under a mamaki plant. The Great Boulder loomed above like a mountain.

There was no activity on the runway. The place seemed deserted.

The runway was strewn with stones, dried mud, plant debris. A cone of dirt had risen next to it, an ant nest. An ant trail extended across the runway and headed downslope toward the bottom of the crater.

"It doesn't look good," Danny Minot whispered.

Karen's heart fell. If no micro-humans lived here, then there wouldn't be any shuttle to Nanigen, and no chance of help. This place hadn't been tended to; it had been overrun by ants.

But there might be airplanes.


**They walked slowly** down the hillside and went into the hangar. There were tie-downs for aircraft, but no planes. While Rick sat and rested with Danny, Karen explored the base. She found a room that she guessed had once held mechanical parts and supplies, but it had been emptied out, leaving bent metal pins and bolts protruding from the walls and floor. She went into another room. Empty. The next room contained living quarters. It had been flooded by rain and was half-filled with mud.

There was no sign of human life anywhere. Tantalus Base had been abandoned. There was no sign of a road to Honolulu, either. No shuttle truck. No airplanes. Only the trade wind endlessly worrying the ground and whistling through the empty halls of Tantalus.

They emerged from the complex and sat by the runway looking down into the crater. They could see the city, too, through the gap in the crater's wall, and beyond the city the Pacific Ocean ran off into blue. Nanigen was miles away from this crater, and there was no way home.

Danny Minot lay in the rubble, holding his arm. He began to cry. His sobs echoed off the hangar and drifted into a sky shot with gray rolling clouds and wind.

Karen watched an ant hurry across the runway, carrying a seed. She turned her gaze up to the Great Boulder, and then past it to the horizon line and the clouds. Something moved against the sky near the boulder, and she suddenly realized it was the figure of a man.

# Chapter 39

How long the man had been standing there Karen couldn't say—possibly he had been watching them the entire time they'd explored the base. She saw his hair flash in the breeze, long, white. He wore armor of some kind, but she couldn't tell what it was made of. His eyes looked hard and cold, even at that distance. He lifted up an object, and she saw it was a gas rifle.

"Down!" Karen shouted, grabbing Rick.

He fired. There was a hiss, and glint of steel ripped past them and buried itself in the ground somewhere beyond, and exploded with a thump. Karen began crawling, dragging Rick behind her, but there was nowhere to hide. Another sniper . . . Drake had found them . . .

The man's voice came to them over the wind. "That was a warning. Stand up and show me your hands. If you have weapons, drop them in front of you."

They obeyed him. Karen held up the blowgun so he could see

it, and dropped it on the ground. She placed the container of darts next to it.

"Put your hands on your head."

Karen obeyed, and called out, "We have two injured. We need help."

He didn't answer. He moved toward them, keeping the gun raised. As he got closer, they saw that he was an older man, with a weather-beaten face bronzed by the sun, and deep-set blue eyes. He clearly had muscles, and he looked physically powerful. How old was he? He could have been anywhere from fifty to eighty, it seemed. His armor had been carved from the hard parts of a beetle. A scar ran across his forehead and wandered down his neck and ran under the breastplate of his armor. He studied them, searching their faces.

The man's eyes darted away, flicking around. Karen realized he was keeping alert for predators. He gestured at them with the gun. "Your names."

Karen gave their names and added, "Who are you?"

He ignored that.

"My arm—" Danny began, and fell silent as the man pointed the gun at his face.

Karen added, "We need medical treatment."

The man just stared. He poked at the blowgun with his foot. "Interesting," he said. He picked it up, then examined a dart, and sniffed it. "Poisoned?" he said.

She nodded.

"Where are your guns?"

"We lost our only gun. A bird attack—"

"Vin Drake sent you," he interrupted. "Why?"

Karen began to explain, "No, Drake tried to kill us—"

The man cut her off. "This is one of Drake's tricks."

Karen said, "You'll have to take our word."

"Where did you come from?"

"The arboretum."

"And you made it up here? That's impossible."

Karen walked up to him and pushed his gun aside. "Give me back my weapon."

The man's eyes widened, maybe in surprise, maybe in anger. After a pause, he pointed his gun at the ground, and broke open the firing chamber. A smile creased his face, exposing white teeth. "Somehow," he said, "you impress me." He handed her back the blowgun. "Welcome to Tantalus. My name is Ben Rourke. I'm the inventor of the tensor generator."

Karen eyed him. "How did you end up here?"

"Castaway by chance, a hermit by choice," he replied.

**Ben Rourke lived** in a warren of caves near the Great Boulder, about six feet above Tantalus Base. He led them upslope toward the Great Boulder; and he helped Rick along. The cave entrance was a hole in the soil at the foot of the boulder, with a tunnel that ran horizontally inward, like the entrance to a mine. They advanced through the tunnel, while the light grew dim. After some distance they arrived at a door carved from wood. It was shut and latched with an iron hook. Rourke opened the door, and they went through it into a pitch-black tunnel. He threw a switch, and a line of LED lights came on in the ceiling of the tunnel, trending inward. "Welcome to Rourke's Redoubt," he said. "As I call my little place." He closed the door behind them and slammed home an iron pin. "It's to keep out centipedes." He walked ahead, with a lanky, tough stride.

The tunnel went around a bend and sloped downward, plunging deeper into the mountain. It turned left and right, and they passed side tunnels going off into darkness. "This is an empty rat warren,"

Rourke explained. "Drake's people deemed the rats a threat to the humans at Tantalus Base, so they poisoned the rats and closed off the nest. I reopened the tunnels and moved in." At intervals on the ceiling, LED lights cast a blue glow.

"Where does the power come from?" Karen asked him.

"Solar panel. Up in a tree. The wire runs down here to a battery pack. It took me three weeks to drag the damn batteries over from Tantalus Base even with the help of a hexapod walker. Vin Drake has no idea what treasures his people left behind when they abandoned Tantalus. He thinks I'm dead."

"What's your relationship with Drake?" Karen asked him.

"Hatred."

"What happened?"

"All in good time."

Ben Rourke was a mysterious character. How had he ended up here? How had he avoided death from the bends?

Rick tested his limbs, rubbed his arms. He was covered with bruises, he could see them in the light. At least he could move. He wondered how much time he, Karen, and Danny had before the bends started to affect them, make them sick? How long had they been in the micro-world? It seemed like ages, but actually it had been only three days, he reminded himself. The symptoms start on day three or day four.

They arrived at another heavy wooden door. The doors functioned like the bulkhead doors in a ship, sealing off parts of the warren from other parts. Rourke barred the door behind them, explaining that you couldn't be too careful with some of the predators that lived around here. He threw a switch, and the lights came on, revealing a hall with a high ceiling, stocked with furniture, shelves of books, laboratory equipment, and supplies of all kinds. It was a living area.

"Home sweet home," he said. He began taking off his armor,

hanging it in a storage space. Side passages went off into additional rooms, and they could see electronic equipment in one room.

There was a desk with a computer sitting on it, several chairs made of twigs and woven grass. A circular fireplace hearth occupied the center of the hall. A rack near the fireplace held strips of smoked insect meat. Rourke had also laid in supplies of dried fruit, edible seeds, and chunks of dry taro root.

Rourke's bed was the shell of a candlenut packed with soft, shredded bark. A tall pile of cut-up candlenuts sat heaped against one wall. Ben Rourke carried several of the oily pieces of nutmeat to the fireplace, and he lit the fire using a gas torch. The fire caught, throwing light and warmth through the room, and the smoke went up through a hole in the ceiling.

Ben Rourke seemed to be a jack of all trades, clearly a brilliant man who knew a lot about many things. He seemed happy in his fortress; he seemed to have found a life he enjoyed. They wondered about his story. How had he ended up here? Why did he hate Vin Drake? What had Drake done to him? Karen and Rick both glanced at their hands and arms, and noticed the bruises there. It would be a good idea to persuade Rourke they needed to leave for Nanigen soon; or to learn from him how he had beaten the bends.

The first order of business, however, was for Rourke to examine Rick and Danny and tend to their medical needs. Rourke started with Rick. He rubbed Rick's limbs, stared into his eyes, and asked questions. He got out a small chest and opened it; it was a medical chest, rather like the kind that sea captains took with them on long voyages. The chest contained a number of items, including forceps, scissors, sterile compresses, a very long scalpel, a bone saw, a bottle of iodine, and a bottle of Jack Daniels. Rourke examined the puncture wound under Rick's arm, where the wasp's stinger had gone in. He doused the wound with iodine, which made Rick jump; and he said it would heal. He added, "You guys need a bath."

"We've been in the micro-world for three days," Karen said.

"Three days," Rourke said thoughtfully. "Actually you've been here longer than that. I suppose you've noticed the time compression?"

"What do you mean?" Rick asked.

"Time moves faster for us here. Your bodies are running faster; your hearts are beating like a hummingbird's."

"We had to sleep during the day," Karen remarked.

"Of course you did. And your time is running out. The bends are already affecting you; I can see it. The crash will come soon. The bruising, the pain in the joints, the nosebleed, the end."

Karen asked Rourke, "How did you avoid the bends?"

"I didn't. I damn near died from them. But I found a way to make it through; maybe some people can survive them."

"What did you do?" Rick asked.

"Right now we have to deal with this fellow's arm." He turned his attention to Danny.

Danny had seated himself in a chair near the fire. The chair was made of wicker woven from fern hairs and tiny twigs, yet it was massive and quite comfortable. He stretched out in it, cradling his arm. The sleeve had torn off completely, and the larvae under the skin made the arm bulge in lumps. Ben Rourke studied Danny's arm, poking it gently. "It was likely a parasitic wasp that egged you. She mistook your arm for a caterpillar."

"Am I going to die?"

"Of course." Danny opened his mouth with a frightened look, but Rourke added, "*When* is the only question. If you don't want to die right now, that arm has to come off." He drew out the long scalpel and handed Danny the bottle of Jack Daniels. "Anesthetic. Start drinking while I boil the tools."

"No."

"If you don't get that arm off, those grubs could migrate."

"To where?"

"Your brain." Rourke held up the bone saw and touched its teeth.

Danny leaped out of the chair and stepped backward, holding the bottle in front of him like a club. "Stay away from me!"

"Don't spill that whiskey. I don't have much left."

"You're not a doctor!" He took a glug from the bottle. "I want a real doctor!" He wiped his mouth, and coughed.

"You're not going anywhere right now, Mr. Minot," Rourke said, replacing his instruments in the chest. "Night is coming. At night, the wise stay underground."

# Chapter 40

ROURKE'S REDOUBT
31 OCTOBER, 7:00 P.M.

Ben Rourke loaded more chunks of candlenuts on the fire, and swung a metal cauldron over it. The cauldron was suspended on a hook and a hinged iron bar rooted in the floor—pieces of metal he'd scavenged from Tantalus Base. The water, a few teaspoons' worth, came to a boil almost instantly. Rourke dropped a smaller bucket into the cauldron, and carried a portion of the hot water over to a wooden tub, which sat in a niche in the wall.

It was a bathtub in a private space. He added some cold water to the hot water, taking it from a gravity-fed water tank.

Rick soaked in the water. The venom was still in his system, making him feel stiff, his limbs unresponsive, and he felt a little dizzy, too. There was a lump of soap, crude and soft. It was medieval soap: Rourke had likely made it from ashes and the fat of some insect. It felt great to wash his body after crawling around for three days in the muck. But he couldn't help noticing the dark shadows that had spread over his arms and on his lower legs. He tried to tell himself these were bruises he'd gotten from his encounter with the wasp. He felt strange, but it had to be the venom.

Danny refused a bath, afraid that the water might somehow stimulate the grubs. He sat in the chair, drinking from Rourke's bottle of whiskey and staring at the fire.

Karen luxuriated next in the tub of hot water. It felt so incredible to get clean. She washed her clothes and hung them to dry, then wrapped herself in a robe that Rourke loaned her, and sat by the fire, feeling refreshed. Rick wore a pair of Rourke's pants and a work shirt. The clothes were rough-hewn, but they were comfortable and clean.

Rourke, meanwhile, cooked dinner for his guests. He got a pot of water boiling, and added smoked insect meat, shreds of root vegetable, some chunks of leafy greens, and salt. The stew cooked rapidly, filling the hall with a savory smell. Rourke's insect-and-vegetable stew really was delicious, and it brought their strength back fast. They sat in Rourke's strange chairs near the fire. And they heard his story.


**Ben Rourke had** been a physicist and systems design engineer specializing in the most powerful magnetic fields. He had come across the data from the old Army experiments in Huntsville, and had decided to explore the method of shrinking matter in a tensor field. He had solved some of the seemingly impossible equations of turbulence in these fields. Vin Drake had learned of Rourke's work, and had hired him as one of the founding engineers at Nanigen. Working with other Nanigen engineers, he had built the tensor generator out of modified but standard industrial equipment, purchased largely in Asia. Drake had raised huge amounts of capital from the Davros Consortium; Drake had a magic touch, a way of making it all seem exciting and sure to lead to enormous wealth.

Ben Rourke had volunteered himself as the first human to be passed through the tensor generator. He had suspected it would be dangerous, and felt that he should be the first to take the risk. Living organisms were complicated and fragile. Animals that had been shrunk in the generator had frequently died, usually by exsanguination—by bleeding to death. "Drake discounted the risk," Rourke said. "He claimed there would be no problem."

Rourke had only stayed in a shrunken size for a few hours before he was returned to normal size. As more people were shrunk in the generator, and as they remained small for longer periods of time, they began feeling ill, bruising easily, experiencing mysterious bleeding. They were quickly returned to normal size and examined. The studies showed unexplained degradation of the blood's ability to form clots.

Meanwhile, Nanigen, swimming in investor money, raced ahead with exploration of the micro-world. The company decided to concentrate on exploring Tantalus Crater first. The crater had extremely high biodiversity, and offered riches of chemistry and biological compounds. Tantalus Base was constructed in modules. "We built each module as a scale model, at a 1:10 ratio, and the modules were then shrunk in the generator to make them the right size for micro-humans." Stocked with supplies and equipment, the modules were placed at Tantalus Crater.

At first, the field teams were allowed to stay at Tantalus Base for no longer than thirty-six hours, after which they were returned to Nanigen and restored to normal size. Then Nanigen installed the supply stations in the Waipaka Arboretum, down in the valley, and began staffing them with people.

It was difficult to operate the digging robots and to collect samples when the teams had to be rotated in and out so quickly. Vin Drake wanted to keep people longer in the micro-world despite the risks. Drake asked Rourke if he would agree to a longer stay at

Tantalus as a test—to see if the human body could adjust to the micro-world over time. "I had faith in Vin, and I had faith in my invention," Rourke said. "Nanigen patented my design, with money for me if it succeeded. So I was willing to accept the risks of a longer stay in order to move Nanigen forward."

Ben Rourke had offered to lead a team of volunteers who would attempt a one-week stay at Tantalus. "Since I had designed the tensor generator, I thought I should be the first person to try a longer stay. Take the risk myself." Rourke was joined by two other Nanigen volunteers, an engineer named Fabrio Farzetti and a medical doctor named Amanda Cowells, who would monitor the other two for medical changes. And so they had been shrunk in the generator and placed at Tantalus Base.

"Things went well at first," Rourke said. "We did experiments, we tested the equipment at the base. We stayed in regular contact with Nanigen through a special communication system—a video link with an audio frequency shifter, so that we could talk with big people." He indicated a wooden door in the living room. The door stood open, and beyond it they could see electronic equipment and a video screen. "That's the video link. I moved it here from Tantalus Base. Maybe someday Drake won't be in charge of Nanigen, and then I can call home. But as long as Vin Drake is running things, I don't use the system. Drake thinks I'm dead. It would be a fatal mistake to let Drake know I exist."

After a few days at the base, all three volunteers began to develop symptoms of micro-bends. "We developed bruises on our arms and legs. Then Farzetti got really sick. Dr. Cowells found he had developed internal hemorrhages. So she asked for an evacuation of Farzetti." Fabrio Farzetti needed to be hospitalized immediately or he would die.

"That was when Drake told us it wasn't possible to evacuate Farzetti. He said the generator had broken down," Rourke said. "He claimed he was trying to get the generator fixed."

Ben Rourke knew more about the tensor generator than anyone else. He began directing repair efforts from the micro-world, using the video link, while teams of engineers at the Nanigen headquarters followed his instructions. But somehow, the machine couldn't be fixed; it kept breaking down. And then Farzetti died, despite Dr. Amanda Cowells's best efforts to save him.

"I think Drake had sabotaged the generator," Ben Rourke said.

"Why?" Karen asked.

"We were guinea pigs," Rourke said. "Drake wanted to have medical data on us all the way up to the point of death."

Next, Dr. Cowells herself had fallen ill. Ben Rourke had cared for her, all the while begging for help on the video link. "I finally realized we were never going to get help. Vin Drake was determined to see his vile experiment through to the end—the death of all of us. He wanted to gain knowledge of the bends, but it was like a Nazi survival experiment. I tried to tell other Nanigen staff on the video link but nobody would believe me. I also think Drake enjoyed watching us die—the man takes pleasure in watching people suffer. It's as if when people are shrunk to micro size, Drake forgets they're still human. Nobody could believe that Drake would do this. People like Vincent Drake operate outside the bounds of normal morality. Their evil can become invisible to normal people, because normal people can't believe anyone would commit such evil. A psychopath can go on for years without being recognized, as long as he's a good actor," Rourke said.

Karen King asked Rourke if he thought Drake was working alone. "Does he have accomplices?" she asked.

"There are people at Nanigen who suspect the truth about Drake," Rourke said. "The Project Omicron people must know something."

"What's that?"

"Project Omicron? It's the dark part of Nanigen."

"The dark part?"

"Nanigen does classified research for the U.S. government. That's Project Omicron."

"What does Omicron do?"

"Omicron deals with weapons, somehow," Rourke said. "But that's all I know."

"So how do you know about it?"

"Employee gossip. It's unavoidable." He smiled and stroked his chin, and got up and went over to the pile of candlenuts. He took a big piece and carried it over to the fire. The fire flared up.

For a hermit, the man seemed kind of lonely, Karen thought. She stared at the fire, and found herself thinking about her life back East. She had been living like a hermit herself, in a cramped, seedy apartment in Somerville, spending long hours in the lab. All-nighters had become a regular thing. She didn't have any close friends, didn't go out on dates, didn't even go to the movies by herself. She had sacrificed a normal life in order to get a PhD and become a scientist. It had been more than a year since she'd slept with a man. Men seemed afraid of her, with her spiders, her temper, her drive in the lab. She knew she had a hot temper. Maybe it was just the way she was. Maybe she would be happier alone, the way Ben Rourke liked being a hermit. Right now her life in Cambridge seemed in another universe, almost. "What if I wanted to stay in the micro-world, Ben? Do you think I could survive?"

There was a long silence. Rick Hutter stared at her.

Rourke got up and threw another piece on the fire, and said, "Why would you want to stay here, Ms. King?"

Karen gazed into the fire. "It's dangerous here . . . but it's . . . so beautiful. I've seen . . . things I never dreamed of."

Rourke got up and helped himself to more stew, and went back to his chair, and blew on the stew to cool it. After a while he said, "There is a Zen saying that a wise man can live comfortably in hell. It isn't so bad here, actually. You just need to learn some extra skills."

Karen was watching the smoke go up through the hole in the

ceiling. She wondered where it went. She realized that Rourke must have dug the chimney himself. What a lot of work just to have a fire. What would it be like, trying to survive in the micro-world? Ben had done it. Could she?

Rick turned to Karen. "Just a reminder. Our time is running out."

Rick was right. "Ben," Karen said. "We need to get back to Nanigen."

He leaned back, looking at them through narrowed eyes. "I've been wondering if I can trust you."

"You can, Ben."

"I hope so. Come along and we'll see about getting you home. Do you have any iron on your bodies?" He made Karen leave her knife behind.

**The living room** had an alcove at the end of a short tunnel, closed off by a door. Rourke flung open the door. Behind it, a huge disc of gray, shiny metal lay flat on the floor, with a hole in the center, like a doughnut. "It's a neodymium magnet, two thousand Gauss," he explained. "Superstrong field. After Farzetti and Cowell died, I got sick. But I had a hypothesis that a strong magnetic field could stabilize the dimensional fluctuations that cause certain enzymatic reactions in the body to go wrong, like blood clotting. So I put myself inside this magnetic field and stayed there for two weeks. I was sick as hell. Nearly died. But I came out of it all right. Now I think I'm immune to micro-bends."

"So if we stayed inside this magnet, we might survive?" Rick asked.

"Might," Rourke emphasized.

"I'd rather get into the generator," Rick said.

"Of course. That's why I'm going to show you the secret of Tantalus," Rourke said. He led them out of the magnet room, down a long tunnel, through a bend, and up a sloping tunnel. They followed him, wondering where he was taking them. Ben Rourke seemed to enjoy mysterious revelations. They entered a wide, long chamber, sunk in shadow and filled with unidentifiable shapes. Drake threw a switch, and a line of LEDs blinked on. Parked on the floor stood three airplanes. The room was an underground hangar. Wide hangar doors remained closed over the mouth of the cave.

"Oh, my gosh," Karen said.

The airplanes sported an open cockpit, stubby, swept-back wings, twin tails, and a propeller at the rear of the aircraft. They stood on retractable wheels. "They were broken, so Drake's people just left them here. I fixed them up, added scavenged parts. I've flown all over these mountains with them." He slapped the cockpit of one of the planes. "Equipped 'em with weapons, too."

"Where? I don't see any machine guns," Rick said, inspecting the wings.

Rourke reached into the cockpit and pulled out a machete. "Kind of medieval, but it's the best I could do." He stuffed the machete back into the cockpit.

"Could we fly them to Nanigen?" Karen asked.

"It's a very long shot." He explained that the top speed of a microplane was seven miles an hour. "The trade winds average fifteen miles an hour across Oahu. If you try to fly into the wind, you'll go backward. If you get the wind at your back, you might get across Pearl Harbor. Or maybe not. It also depends on whether I decide to let you have my planes. These are solo-seaters, they carry only one person. There's three of you and there's three planes. That doesn't leave an airplane for me, now, does it?"

"Dr. Rourke, I would pay you a very large sum of money for one of your planes," Danny said. "I inherited a trust fund. It would be yours."

"I have no need for money, Mr. Minot."

"Well, what would work for you?"

"To see you bring down Vincent Drake. If you can do that, you can have my planes."

"Absolutely, we'll get Mr. Drake," Danny said.

Karen remained silent. Rick glanced at her. What was going on with her? Then he asked Rourke how Rourke would survive if he didn't have a plane.

"I'll build another one," Rourke said, shrugging off the question. "I collected a lot of spare parts." Then Rourke took charge. He had them sit in the cockpits, and he explained the controls. "It's very simple. Everything's computer-controlled. This is the stick. If you make a mistake, the computer corrects your action. There's a radio— here's the headset." They could talk to each other once they had gotten aloft. But there was no radar or navigation instrumentation.

How would they find Nanigen?

"Kalikimaki Industrial Park should be obvious from the air— it's a group of warehouses on the Farrington Highway." He gave them a course heading.

"Okay," Rick said. "So we manage to get into Nanigen, then what?"

"There will be security bots guarding the tensor core."

"Security bots?"

"Flying micro-bots. However, I don't think you'll have a problem. You're too small to register on the bots' sensors. They won't see you. You can fly past the bots without waking them up. There's a way to operate the generator from the micro side, if you're very small. I designed the control myself. The control is located in the floor of the room underneath a hatch. The hatch is in the center of Hexagon Three. It's marked with a white circle. You should see the white circle from the air."

"Is the control complicated?"

"No. Just throw open the hatch and hit the red emergency button. You'll get supersized—" He stopped talking and was staring at Rick. At his arm.

Rick had been leaning against a plane, his sleeve rolled up. Rourke stared at the bruises, lengthening up Rick's arm. "You're starting to crash," he said.

"Crash?" Rick thought he meant the plane.

"Once the bleeding starts, you're finished. Let's get you into the magnet," Rourke said to him sharply. "You're hours from a crash."

Karen looked at her arms. They weren't in such great shape either. It was going to be a race against time. Wait for dawn, and hope nobody's started bleeding by then.

Ben Rourke advised them to sleep inside the magnet. He couldn't guarantee anything, but the magnetic field might delay the onset of symptoms. The magnet room had a fireplace in it, too, and Rourke hauled in pieces of candlenut, and started a fire. Karen and Rick climbed into the hole in the doughnut of the magnet, wrapped in blankets, and tried to settle down for the night. Neither of them felt terribly relaxed. Yet they were so incredibly tired. Time ran more swiftly in the micro-world, and a day's rest could not come too soon.

Danny Minot refused to sleep in the magnet. He said he would prefer to sleep in the main hall, where he settled into one of Rourke's chairs and wrapped himself in a blanket.

Rourke threw another piece of nut on the fire, and stood up. "I'm going to the hangar to get the planes ready. You will need to launch at first light." Rourke went off down the tunnels into the hangar. He would service the micro-planes, test the instruments, and top off their electric charges, readying them for takeoff the moment daylight glimmered.


**Danny Minot found** himself alone in the hall, curled up in the chair. He couldn't possibly sleep. He drank the last of the Jack Daniels, and tossed the bottle away. His arm was stirring, moving on its own, the skin bulging and making crackling noises. He lifted the blanket and looked, and he could see the grubs twitching. He couldn't stand it. He began to cry. Maybe it was the alcohol, maybe the terrible state of his arm, maybe it was his general situation, but he lost it. He wept, and looked down the hall where Rourke had gone. How long would Rourke be gone?

And that was when his arm came apart.

There was a cracking sound, a sound like paper tearing. He didn't feel anything, but he looked down at the noise. And saw the head of a grub pushing out through a widening split in the skin of his arm. It had a glistening head. It was huge, and it was squirming, waving its head around, lengthening as it struggled out.

"Oh, God! It's hatching!" he whispered.

The larva began to do something strange and horrible. It spat liquid from its mouth, stringy, thin drools—no, actually, it was thread, it was silk. The larva, still partway inside his arm and more than halfway out, began to spin silk around itself. Rapidly waving its head around, it flung silk threads around its body, building up a covering of silk around itself, even while its rear end stayed rooted in Danny's arm.

What was it doing? It wasn't going to hatch! It was just going on to another phase. It was turning into a cocoon. But it refused to leave his arm!

Terrified, he tugged on the larva, trying to make it come free. It lashed angrily, spitting silk, threatening to bite him with little teeth, too. It didn't want to come out of his arm. It wanted to stay there, anchored in his arm, and build itself a silken case.

"Karen? Rick?" he said softly. The door to the alcove was closed. They didn't hear him. They couldn't help him anyway. "Ohhh . . ."

He stifled a moan of panic. What about that video screen in the next room? Rourke had said it was a communication system that connected with Nanigen. He glanced around. Rick and Karen were in the magnet room, a distance away. Rourke was in the hangar. He threw the blanket off, got up, and went into the communications room, where he inspected the video screen. He found a lens. It was a Minicam pointed in front of the screen. And there was a cover at the base of the screen. He flipped open the cover and discovered a power switch and a red button marked LINK. Simple enough. He pushed the power button, and in a moment the screen powered up, glowing blue. Then he pushed the red button, LINK.

Almost immediately a female voice came on, but the screen remained blank. "Nanigen security services. Where are you calling from?"

"Tantalus. Somebody help me—"

"Sir, who are you? What is your situation?"

"I'm Daniel Minot—"

Abruptly the screen showed the woman's face. She had a smooth, professional appearance.

"Put me through to Vin Drake, please," he said to the woman.

"It's late at night, sir."

"It's an emergency! Tell him I'm at Tantalus and I need help."

# Chapter 41

Vincent Drake was seated at the best table at The Sea with his current lover, Emily St. Claire, a surfer and interior designer. The Sea overlooked Waikiki Beach, and was one of the finest restaurants in Honolulu. The table was placed in a private corner of the room by an open window that looked along the beach toward Diamond Head. A breeze wafted over them and whispered through a palm tree near the window. They had finished dinner. Emily poked at a chocolate ganache tart and sipped a glass of Château d'Yquem.

Drake swirled a snifter of single malt scotch, a 1958 Macallan. "I have to go back East for a few days."

"What for?" Emily St. Claire said.

"To meet with some partners. Want to come?"

"Boston in November? I think not."

The lights of houses lined up along the base of Diamond Head twinkled, and the Diamond Head Lighthouse blinked and faded.

"We could do Paris afterward," Drake said.

"Mm," she answered. "Maybe if we go in the Gulfstream."

Just then, there was a buzzing sound and Drake touched his jacket. It was his encrypted corporate phone. "Excuse me," he said, taking the phone from his jacket. He stood up and placed his napkin on the table and walked over to an open window between the tables. On the screen of his phone he could see a live video feed; the face of Danny Minot looked back at him. "You say you're at Tantalus Base?" Drake said.

"Not exactly," Minot answered. "We're in Ben Rourke's fortress."

"What?"

"He's got all kinds of equip—"

"You're telling me Ben Rourke is alive?"

"Absolutely," Minot answered knowingly. "And he doesn't like you, Mr. Drake."

"Describe this . . . fortress."

"It's an old rat's nest. I need medical help—"

Drake cut him off. "Where is this, uh, rat's nest? Exactly."

"It's six feet up the hillside from Tantalus Base."

Drake was silent for a moment. They had climbed those cliffs. They had made it alive through unexplored super-jungle that should have rendered them dead in minutes.

"Mr. Drake! I need to get to a hospital!" Minot's voice went faster. "My arm. It's infected. Look—"

Drake watched on the screen of his phone as Danny raised his arm and peeled back the sleeve. The arm had been transformed into a bubbly sack dotted with . . . whiteheads. Enormous boils. The boils were . . . moving . . . twitching. Drake's stomach turned at the sight.

"They're hatching, Mr. Drake!" Danny moved his arm closer to the camera. The scene zoomed in, until Drake could see one of the whiteheads clearly. It was the head of a larva, struggling, pushing up through a hole in Danny's skin. The grub's mouth pulsed and it spat out a thread of silk. The camera moved, and he saw more grubs, waving and struggling, popping up through his skin. "Thank you, Mr. Minot, I can see very well—"

"It's horrible! My arm's all numb."

"I'm sorry, Daniel—" He felt his throat tighten. He glanced back at Emily St. Claire, who seemed impatient.

"For God's sake, help me!" the little face on his cell phone beseeched him.

"Who is with you?" Drake said sharply, holding the phone close to his ear.

"I can't see your face!"

Drake turned the phone so Danny could see him. "We will help you," he said gently. "Who else is with you?"

"I want to go to a top hospital—"

"Yes, yes, a top hospital. Who is with you?"

"Karen King and Rick Hutter."

"What about the others?"

"They're all dead, Mr. Drake."

"Peter Jansen is dead, too?"

"Yes."

"Are you sure he's dead?"

"He got shot. His chest exploded. I saw it."

"How terrible. Where are King and Hutter?"

"I don't care about them! Get me to a hospital!"

"But where are they?"

"Asleep," Danny said sullenly, jerking his head. "Rourke's in the hangar."

"Hangar? What hangar, Daniel?"

"Rourke stole some planes from Tantalus Base. He's a thief, Mr. Drake—"

So Rourke had micro-planes. How had he survived the bends? Rourke had learned of a way to deal with the bends. This was incredibly valuable. "How did Rourke escape the bends, Daniel?"

A shrewd look flickered on Danny's face. "That? Oh, it's simple."

"What did he do?"

"I'll tell you . . . if you help me."

"Daniel, I am doing my utmost to help you."

"Ben knows the secret," Danny said.

"What is it exactly?"

"Totally simple."

"Tell me!"

Danny knew he'd gotten Drake where he wanted him. He didn't trust the man, but he knew he was smarter than Drake. "Get me to a hospital, Mr. Drake, and I'll tell you how to survive the bends."

Drake's lips compressed. "All right—"

"That's the deal, Mr. Drake. It's not negotiable."

"Of course I agree. Now here is what I want you to do, Daniel. You must do exactly as I say."

"Just help me—!"

"Can you fly one of those planes?" Any idiot could fly one, even you, my little Daniel.

"Listen, get me help—"

"That's what I'm desperately trying to do."

"Just get me out of here—!" Danny was screaming over the cell phone.

"Can you listen to me for one moment?" Drake stepped to the open window and leaned out. He needed to get him out of there. Talk to him, pump him, get the information on Rourke . . . then take care of all the little people in short order. Drake looked along the length of Waikiki Beach. Little Daniel would need a landmark. He saw a light blink on, off . . .

Diamond Head Lighthouse.

To his left, inland, he could see clouds hovering over the mountain peaks. It meant that the trade wind was blowing. Blowing from Tantalus toward Diamond Head. That was important. "Daniel, you know what Diamond Head looks like, don't you?"

"Everybody does."

"I want you to take one of those planes and fly toward Diamond Head."

"What?"

"They're easy to fly. You can't crash. You just bounce off things." Silence.

"Are you listening to me, Daniel?"

"Yes."

"As you get closer to Diamond Head, you will see a blinking light near the sea. This is the Diamond Head Lighthouse. Fly toward the lighthouse. You can't possibly miss it. I will be in a red sports car parked as close to the lighthouse as possible. Land on the hood of my car."

"I want a medevac helicopter waiting for me."

"First we need to get you decompressed. You're too small for a helicopter."

Minot began giggling. "They could lose me in a helicopter, couldn't they? Ha, ha!"

"That's funny, Daniel," Drake said. "We'll take you to the best hospital."

"They're hatching!"

"Just fly to the lighthouse." Drake disconnected and pocketed the phone, and returned to the table, where he kissed Emily St. Claire on the cheek. "Total screaming emergency. I'm sorry."

"Oh, Christ, Vin. Where are you going?"

"Nanigen. I'm needed." He caught the waiter's eye; the waiter moved toward them.

Emily St. Claire shook her hair and took a sip of wine. She put the glass down. Without looking at Drake, she said, "Suit yourself."

"I'll make this up to you, Emily, I promise. We'll do Tahiti in the Gulfstream."

"That's so old. I'd prefer Mozambique."

"Done," he said. He reached into his jacket and lifted a thick wad of hundred-dollar bills from his billfold. He handed them to the waiter without looking at them and said, "Take care of the lady." He hurried out.

Vin Drake drove to a large discount store off Kapiolani Boulevard. On the way, he called Don Makele. "Meet me at the Diamond Head Lighthouse as soon as you can. Bring a micro communication radio. Come in the security truck. I will need the truck."

Drake emerged from the store carrying a plastic bag with something bulky in it. He placed the bag in the trunk of his car.


**Danny turned off** the video screen and went back into the main hall, and took a drink of water from a bucket. He felt unbearably thirsty. Fluid had been leaking from his arm as the grubs began to break out, wetting his shirt and dribbling onto his pants. And the horror was that the grubs were spinning silk around themselves: they were turning into cocoons! Stuck to his arm! His heart was beating too quickly; he felt terrified, but knew what he had to do. It was kill or be killed in this world. He curled up in the chair by the fire. When Rourke returned from the hangar, he closed his eyes and feigned sleep, snoring to make sure Rourke got it.

He watched through slitted eyes while Rourke added fuel to the fire and climbed into his bed.

Danny got up, began creeping toward the tunnel.

"Where are you going?" Rourke asked.

Danny froze. "Just the privy."

"Let me know if you need anything."

"Sure, Ben."

He went down the tunnel, past the opening to Ben's privy, and hurried down the corridor to the hangar. Once he got there, he turned on the lights. There were three micro-planes, which to choose? He selected the largest one, hoping it would have the greatest range and most power. A cable led from the plane's battery pack into the dirt floor. He unplugged the cable. He had forgotten to open the hangar doors.

The doors were held in place with metal pins. He pulled out the pins, and slid open the rolling doors, revealing a night sky studded with tropic stars, a waxing moon, and ghostly shapes of trees. He climbed into the cockpit and settled himself, buckled up, and touched the instrument panel.

At that moment, a terror struck him: he didn't have a starter key.

He searched the control panel, and found a button with a power symbol on it. He pressed it. The panel lit up and he felt the plane lurch as the electric motor turned over. Ready for takeoff. His left arm lay on his lap like a prop from a horror movie; the sleeve had shredded as the grubs chewed their way out. Two more grubs had broken through his skin and begun to spin cocoons around themselves. It was horrible; how could Nature be so cruel? It was so gruesome, so inhuman, and it really didn't seem fair.

He took the stick in his hands and moved it, and saw the ailerons waggle. He pushed the throttle forward. The propeller wound up fast, whining at the back of the plane. The plane began bumping along the floor. He slopped the stick around, cursing, and got the plane under control, and the plane shot out of the hangar and climbed into the voracious night.

# Chapter 42

Eric Jansen had gone out on Kapiolani late to get something to eat, and he walked back to the apartment carrying a styro box of kalua pork and rice. In the driveway he said hello to two guys, who were sitting on lawn chairs by the colorful pickup truck, drinking beer and listening to music. He went around to the back, and up a flight of steps to a second-floor apartment.

The apartment was a furnished one-bedroom. Eric sat at a tiny table and opened the box and began eating. He thought he'd better check the monitor, since he'd been gone for over an hour. He went into the bedroom, opened a drawer in the dresser. In the drawer sat the laptop computer, and next to it a metal box dense with electronic parts, along with an electric soldering iron, cutters, pliers, tape, and a roll of solder wire.

A light on the box was blinking. It meant that an emergency call had been made over Nanigen's intracompany network. Shit, he'd missed it.

The message was encrypted. He tapped the keys of the laptop, and ran the de-encryption program, the one he'd downloaded from Nanigen's VPN. It took a minute to unscramble the call, and then he began to listen as voices came out of the laptop.

"You say you're at Tantalus Base?"
"Not exactly. We're in Ben Rourke's fortress."
"What?"
"He's got all kinds of equip—"
"You're telling me Ben Rourke is alive?"
"Absolutely. And he doesn't like you, Mr. Drake."

Eric leaned over the dresser, listening more intently. This had been an emergency call made through the videoconference link with Tantalus. He couldn't get the image, but he could get the sound. The voices went on.

"What about the others?"
"They're all dead, Mr. Drake."
"Peter Jansen is dead, too?"
"Yes."
"Are you sure he's dead?"
"He got shot. His chest exploded. I saw it."

Eric gasped as if he'd been punched. "No," he said. He closed his eyes. "No," he said again. He made a fist and slammed it on the dresser. "No!" He turned around and pounded the bed with both fists, and picked up a chair and threw it against the wall, and sat down on the bed and buried his face in his hands. "Peter . . . oh, Peter . . . God damn you Drake . . . God damn you."

Eric Jansen didn't cry for long. He didn't have time right now. He got up and restarted the playback, and listened to the end of the message. "As you get closer to Diamond Head, you will see a blinking light by the sea . . . Fly toward the lighthouse."

He had been monitoring all the major intracompany data feeds, waiting, and hoping, for news of his brother and the other graduate students. He had felt pretty sure that Drake had dumped them somewhere, maybe at the arboretum, though he couldn't be certain. He had gone there in the truck and walked into the valley through the tunnel, and had listened with the equipment but heard nothing. Nevertheless, he had hoped that Peter would turn up sooner or later. He had had faith in Peter's resourcefulness. He had waited, hoping he could rescue Peter and the others.

He had made a terrible mistake. He should have gone to the police immediately, even if it had guaranteed his own death.

The call had come in almost an hour ago. Damn! He had taken his sweet time getting that food! Eric swore and dragged open the drawer, scooped up the laptop and a radio headset, and ran down the stairs. In the driveway, the two guys were sitting beside the parked truck. Eric didn't have a car. He had worked out a deal with one of the guys to rent the truck, paying fifty bucks every time he used it. Now, he handed the guy fifty dollars and got in, placing the equipment on the seat next to him.

"When you be back?"

"Don't know." He started it.

"You okay, man?"

"There's been a death in my family."

"Oh, sorry, man."

He swung onto Kalakaua Avenue and immediately realized he'd made a mistake. Kalakaua was the main drag of Waikiki, and the crowds had flooded the avenue, people going on foot and in cars. He should have gone the other way to Diamond Head. But that probably would have been just as bad. As he inched his way through the stoplights, past the major hotels, he began to cry again, and this time he let it happen. It's my fault, he told himself. My brother is dead and it's my fault.

. . .

**Drake had planned** the killing with extra layers of security, different ways to make Eric die. Eric wasn't sure exactly how Drake had done it, but Drake had made the boat stall in heavy surf, and he'd rigged something that had launched two Hellstorms at Eric. The killer bots flew out of the cuddy cabin after the boat stalled. At first Eric had thought they were flies or moths, but then he saw the propellers, and the munitions, too. After he jumped out of the boat with the killer bots flying after him, he had to keep himself under water, to avoid them. He had texted Peter just before he jumped, warning Peter to stay away, but there had been no time to explain things.

Eric was a strong swimmer and knew how to handle himself in surf. He had gone into the surf without a life jacket, diving deep whenever a breaker passed over him, in order to keep himself safe from the bots. He had considered the surf the safest place to be. Safer than anywhere else just then. He swam into a small cove, where there was a pocket beach known locally as the Secret Beach. The beach was tucked among the headlands. You couldn't see it from most places. It could only be reached by a hiking trail.

He had come out of the water at the Secret Beach only after he was reasonably sure no one had seen him swim there. He had bagged a ride into Honolulu from some local guys, who asked no questions and could not have cared less where he came from. Going to the police had not been a good option. The police would never believe his story, that tiny flying robots armed with super-toxin weapons had been sent by the CEO of the company to kill him: they would think he was schizophrenic. And if he went to the police, Drake would learn he was alive, and would send more Hellstorms, and he'd be killed for sure and very fast. In Honolulu, he had not returned to his apartment: Drake might have set a trap for him there. Instead, he'd visited a pawnshop, and taken his Hublot chronograph watch off his wrist and pawned it for several thousand dollars. He needed to go into hiding, and figure out how to bring Drake to justice. He had put down cash for a seedy, low-profile rental.

As Nanigen's vice president for technology, Eric Jansen knew a lot about the company's communication network. A degree in physics helped. After a trip to Radio Shack, he had tweaked up a listening device. He had begun scanning the Nanigen intracorporate channels, and learned that his brother had shown up in Hawaii immediately, then had disappeared along with the other students. He suspected Drake had done something with the students. He had not believed Drake would murder them; that would be too obvious, and Drake was a clever man. So Eric had assumed that Drake had made them disappear in the micro-world temporarily, and that they would eventually reappear.

Eric had been waiting for the moment when his brother would come to the surface, for he had faith in Peter. He had thought that Peter would get through this, and come to light, somehow, and that he, Eric, would eventually rescue him. If the two of them could go to the police, there would be two corroborating witnesses to Drake's crimes.

This was not to be.

He had screwed up massively. He should have gone to the police right away. Even if the police didn't believe him, even if it meant that Drake would kill him, because it just might have saved Peter's life. The whole source of the problem was Omicron. Eric had been very careful not to tell Peter what he had discovered about Project Omicron. Eric had been trying to protect his younger brother. None of this had done any good.

He swung through Kapiolani Park, picking up speed and weaving around the cars, hoping he would get to the lighthouse in time.

# Chapter 43

KOʻOLAU MOUNTAINS
31 OCTOBER, 11:10 P.M.

At an altitude of 2,200 feet, Danny Minot pointed the nose of his micro-plane upward, gaining height in order to be sure he would clear the sides of Tantalus Crater. The crater was lined with entrapping trees, black and menacing. He looked back, wondering if any micro-planes were following him. But he couldn't see anything. He headed upward, gaining altitude.

This was easier than a video game; the micro-planes had been designed to be almost crash-proof. Did the plane have running lights? He found a switch, and the running lights came on, red and green on the wingtips, white pointing forward. He turned them off so that the others couldn't follow him, but after a little while he switched the lights on again. It made him feel better, somehow, to see the familiar winking lights on the wings.

And he saw the city of Honolulu spread out below him. The hotels of Waikiki towered and seemed impossibly huge. Red-and-white lines of cars moved along the boulevards, and he saw a cruise ship docked in the harbor. The ocean was an inky expanse beyond the city. The moon floated over the ocean, casting a sparkling highway of light on the water. To the left of Waikiki Beach a dark mass spread out. It was Diamond Head, and he was looking down on it. Seen from above, Diamond Head was a crater, a ring. A few lights burned in the center of the crater. He could make out the shape of Diamond Head itself, a mountainous headland at the highest lip of the crater. But he did not see any blinking light. Just the dark shape of Diamond Head. Where was the lighthouse?

He increased the power and began to fly toward Diamond Head.

His plane suddenly flipped over and blew sideways, rolling over and over, and he yelled with fright. He had entered the trade wind as it burbled over the mountains. He swore and fought the stick while the plane tumbled in wind eddies. But then the plane stabilized, and began flying straight and steady in the wind, moving really fast. He had gotten into laminar flow. It was like getting into the main current of a river. He looked down. The forest was moving down there. Or rather he was moving over it. The altimeter showed he had gotten up to three thousand feet. In the moonlight he saw a magnificent view.

Behind him, upwind, the hollow of Tantalus Crater spread out. The crater was dark like a cave; no lights in the crater, no sign of Rourke's Redoubt or Tantalus Base. Directly below him, roads snaked up the flanks of the ridge. Lights burned along the roads. Ahead of him the towers of the city were coming perceptibly closer, until they seemed to burn with energy and rise to impossible heights. For a moment he felt as if he was flying into the capital city of an alien galactic empire. But it was only Honolulu. He still couldn't see Diamond Head Lighthouse.

The wind was carrying him toward the hotels that stood along Waikiki Beach. He wanted to go more to the left, more toward Diamond Head. He experimented with the control stick and with the throttle. He banked left and kept the power on high. He looked around.

He did not want to be blown into the city; that would be certain death. He would be crushed by traffic or sucked into the air-conditioning of a building. So he increased the power to EMERGENCY MAXIMUM, and kept his course toward Diamond Head. A screen flashed a warning: EXCESSIVE BATTERY DRAIN. Remaining flight time: 20:25 min . . . 18:05 min . . . 17:22 min . . . the remaining flight time was dropping like a stone. He would run out of power in minutes.

He checked his airspeed. The readout showed 7.1 MPH / 11.4 KPH. He found the radio panel and switched it on. "Mayday. Mayday. This is Daniel Minot. I'm in a small plane. A very small plane. Does anybody hear me? Mr. Drake, are you there? I can't reach Diamond Head . . . I'm being blown into the city . . . oh my God!"

A hotel loomed up like a first-order battleship from outer space. He saw two giants standing on a balcony, a man and a woman, holding drinks in their hands. His plane rushed toward them uncontrollably, carried in the wind. Their heads were bigger than Mount Rushmore. The man put his drink down and reached toward the woman, and pulled down the shoulder strap of her dress, exposing a colossal breast with an erect nipple standing out six feet. The man fondled it with a hand of horrifying size, and their faces closed in for a kiss . . . As his plane rushed toward a collision, he screamed and fought the controls, and passed between their noses under emergency power, propeller churning, and the plane was caught in an eddy of wind and swept around the corner of the building and out of sight.

The man jerked away from the woman. "What the hell—?"

She had seen something weird. A tiny man flying a tiny plane. Lights blinking on the wings. The tiny man had been screaming. She had distinctly heard his insect-like whine over the sound of a buzzing motor, and she had seen the open mouth, the staring eyes . . . it was impossible. One of those waking dreams. "The bugs are awful out here, Jimmy."

"It's these flying cockroaches they got in Hawaii. They got wings."

"Let's go inside."


**Danny regained control** of his aircraft as the wind seemed to decrease. He flew across Kalakaua Avenue, where he looked down on the nighttime crowds. He noticed that he had stopped being blown sideways. His plane was flying faster than the wind was blowing; he was making headway now. He banked and headed northeast, and flew along the length of Waikiki Beach, straight toward Diamond Head.

Now, as he peered at the famous shape of the headland in the moonlight, he saw a blink of light. On, off. Darkness. On, off. It was the lighthouse.

"I'm saved!"

He backed down the power a little, and left it at FULL CRUISE, because it would be a disaster if the battery ran out now. He was getting the hang of this. It was a matter of technique.

He gained altitude. He wanted to stay above the buildings, keep plenty of distance above them. It was funny how life could turn around so fast. One moment you think you're ruined and dead, the next you're on your way to the best hospital and admiring Waikiki Beach in the moonlight. Life was good, Danny thought.

A shape came out of the night. He saw a flash of wings—he threw the stick over, and just missed the thing.

"Stupid moth! Watch where you're going." That had been close. "Absolutely no brain," he muttered. A collision with a moth could drop him in the sea, and he could see breakers below him.

Then a peculiar noise reached his ears. Sort of an echoing *whish-whing* . . . He heard it again . . . *whish-whing. Whoom . . . Whoooemm*

... *eee* ... *eee* ... What was that? Something was making freaky noises in the dark. Then a drumming noise started up: *pom-pom-pompompom*. He saw another moth, and the drumming sound came from the moth ... and then the moth suddenly wasn't there.

Something had swept the moth out of the sky.

"Oh, fuck," Danny said.

Bats.

They were painting the moths with sonar. He had gotten himself into the middle of some kind of a bat situation. This was not good.

He advanced the throttle to EMERGENCY MAXIMUM.

He could hear the sonar pulses ringing in the darkness, left, right, above, below, nearby, far away ... but he couldn't see the bats. That was the worst thing. Above, below, on all sides, the predators were moving in three dimensions around him. It was like treading water at midnight surrounded by feeding sharks. He couldn't see anything at all, but he could hear them snatching prey. *Whoo* ... *whoom* ... *whooom* ... *eee* ... *eee* ... *eee/ee/ee* ... that had been a kill.

And then he saw it. A bat killed a moth right in front of him. He got a glimpse of a spiky shape as it swept by, and the plane shuddered and jumped in the turbulence of the bat's wake. Holy God. The bat had been far bigger than he thought it would be.

He had to get to ground. Just land, anywhere, even on top of a hotel. He pointed the plane into a dive, and went straight down, engines shirring at full power, aiming for the nearest hotel ... but he was headed for the beach ... oh, shit ... too far away from the building, too close to the water ...

The bat-sounds got louder. Then a sonar beam raked over him, and went away. There was a pause ... then the beam hit him full-force, making his chest flutter—*WHOOM* ... *EEEP* ... *EEEP* ... *EEE-EEE-EEE* ... The bat was painting him with a beam of ultrasound. The pings shortened and became focused. A chaos of sound enveloped him.

"I'm not a moth!" he cried. He threw the stick hard over and pulled sideways in a screaming dive-turn. With his good hand he began pounding on the outside of the cockpit, trying to imitate the drumming of the moths, thumping his hand on the plane. Maybe it would jam the bat's radar . . .

Too late he realized that by banging on his plane, he had told the bat exactly where he was.

He saw a flash of brown fur gleaming with silver-tipped guard hairs, a pair of wings flaring impossibly wide, blocking out the moon, and a wide-open mouth filled with a set of canines like chisels . . .

The micro-plane spiraled down, its wing broken, its cockpit empty, and landed in foam slick near the beach, where it vanished.

# Chapter 44

Rourke dozed for a while, but awoke when he became aware that Danny Minot had not returned from the privy. Time had passed; the fire had burned down. He got up and hurried down the tunnel toward the privy; Danny wasn't there.

The Redoubt was a sprawling warren, with many unused tunnels; perhaps Danny had gotten lost in a tunnel. Rourke went into a side tunnel, and called, "Mr. Minot! You there?" Nothing. Another tunnel yielded silence. Then Rourke noticed air moving in the tunnel. The hangar . . . he ran to the hangar, and found the doors open, a plane gone.

He closed the doors, then woke Rick and Karen. "Your friend has gone. He took a plane."

They weren't sure what had gotten into Danny. Perhaps he had become frightened, gone into a panic, with his arm in such bad shape, and had decided to fly to Nanigen on his own. It showed more courage than Danny seemed capable of.

"Maybe we should fly out and try to find him," Karen suggested.

Rourke forbade it. "He's gone. The wind could take him anywhere over the island." And he said it was too dangerous to fly after dark; the bats were out. "It's almost suicidal."

Danny might already be dead. And if he survived the flight, it wasn't clear how he planned to get inside Nanigen.

"It doesn't make sense," Karen said.

"Sheer panic," Rick said.

**Vin Drake sat** in his car. The beam from the lighthouse swung around above, shining through the branches of trees overhead. The moon washed the scene with silver. What a beautiful world it truly was. He felt almost placid. He was high above the world, walking on a tightrope and doing it well.

A black pickup swung in and parked next to Drake. Drake got out and climbed into the truck. He explained the situation to Makele. "He's in the air. He knows a cure for the bends. He's going to tell me when he lands."

"Then?" Makele asked.

Drake didn't answer. He put on the radio headset and began calling, staring up toward the mountains. "Daniel? Daniel, are you there?"

He heard nothing but a hiss of airwaves. He turned to Makele. "Watch for his running lights. Red and green, very small."

"What are you going to do with the kid?" Makele asked.

Drake ignored him. "Wind's blowing from Tantalus. He should be here any minute."

A car swung into the parking area. Drake snatched the radio off his head and stared. "Check it."

Makele edged closer to the parked car and saw a couple inside getting friendly with each other. He told Drake there was nothing to worry about.

Drake resumed calling, but with no answer. Cars passed, and

the lighthouse beam circled many times. The couple in the parked car went out of sight. The two men stared up into the sky, trying to see any lights against the backdrop of stars. "Little Danny was lying," Drake remarked.

"About what?"

"About a cure for bends." Lying to make me save him. Ha.

They listened for the whine of a micro-plane. Don Makele saw that the wind was blowing pretty hard. If they didn't see the kid, he'd get blown out to sea. Drake removed something from the trunk of the sports car and placed it in the back of the pickup truck. Then he said: "I'm giving you three more shares. Now you've got seven shares. That brings your net worth to seven million."

The security man grunted. Then he said: "What do we do with the kid?"

"Question him." Drake tapped on the radio headset. It could communicate with micro-humans.

"After that?"

Drake didn't reply for a bit. Then he leaned against the pickup truck and slapped his palm on the metal. Gazing into the sky, he murmured, "The bugs are bad tonight."

"I see," Makele said.

The two men watched a while longer. Makele backed up a few steps, moving alongside the truck, and glanced at the object Drake had placed on the bed of the truck. It was a plastic fuel container. He could smell the gasoline.

Drake called some more, finally ripped off his headset. "Mr. Minot had an accident. Or he changed his mind." He got into the pickup truck and handed the keys of his sports car to Don Makele.

"What do you want me to do with your car, sir?"

"Drop it at Nanigen. Take a taxi home."

Drake started the truck and it roared off on the Diamond Head Road. As he watched the headlights disappear, Makele shook his head.

# Chapter **45**

ROURKE'S REDOUBT
1 NOVEMBER, 1:00 A.M.

**K**aren and Rick were curled up inside the magnet, waiting out
the night.

"We're the last ones," Karen said.

Rick smiled thinly. "I didn't figure we'd end up together, Karen."

"What did you figure?"

"Well, I thought you'd survive. Not me," he said.

"How are you feeling?" she asked him.

"Perfect." That was a lie. His face had become streaked with
bruises, and his joints ached.

As Karen studied Rick's bruises, it made her wonder what she
looked like. I probably look like I've been mugged, she thought.
"You need to get into the generator, Rick."

He glanced at her face in the firelight. "You, too."

"Listen, Rick—" How to tell him about what she'd decided? Just
be blunt. "I'm not going back."

"What?"

"I'm going to be okay, I think."

"What?"

"I'm not flying to Nanigen. I'm going to take my chances here."

They were sitting shoulder to shoulder, wrapped in blankets and looking into the dying embers of the fire. She could feel his body going tense; and he turned and stared at her. "What are you talking about, Karen?"

"I don't have anything to go back to, Rick. I was so unhappy in Cambridge. I didn't even realize it. But here—I'm happier than I've ever been in my life. It's dangerous, but it's a new world. It's waiting to be explored."

Rick felt a kind of sickness take hold in his chest, and he couldn't tell if it was the bends or his feelings . . . "What the—? Are you in love with Ben or something?"

She laughed. "Ben? Are you kidding? I don't love anybody. Here, I don't have to love anybody. I can be alone and free. I can study nature . . . give names to things that don't have names—"

"For Christ's sake, Karen."

After a pause, she said, "Can you get back to Nanigen by yourself? Ben would probably fly with you."

"You can't do this."

The fire popped and crackled. Rick felt a disappointment grip his insides, like a fist closing. He tried to ignore the feeling. He looked over at her, saw the firelight shining on her raven hair, but couldn't keep his eyes off the shadow of a bruise on her neck. That bruise worried him. Had he done that to her? When he'd grabbed her around the neck? He couldn't bear the thought that he'd hurt her . . . "Karen," he said.

"Yeah?"

"Please don't stay. You could die here."

She took his hand and squeezed it. And let it go.

"Don't do it," Rick went on.

"I'll take my chances."

"That's not good enough for me."

She glared at him. "It's my decision."

"But I am involved."

"Like how?"

"By the fact that I love you."

He heard her take a breath. She turned away and her hair fell over her eyes, so that he couldn't read her expression. "Rick—"

"I can't help it, Karen. Somewhere along the way, I fell in love with you. I don't know how it happened, but it happened. When you got swallowed by the bird, I thought you were dead, Karen. At that moment I would have thrown my life away to save you. And I hadn't even known I loved you. And then, when I got you back and you weren't breathing—it scared me so much—I couldn't bear to lose you—"

"Rick, please—not now—"

"Well, why did you save me?"

"Because I had to," she answered in a tight voice.

"Because you love me," he went on.

"Look, get off this—"

He thought he had gone too far. Probably she didn't love him, didn't even like him. Maybe he should just shut up. But he couldn't. "I'll stay with you. We'll have the bends together. We'll get through it. Just like we got through everything else."

"Rick, I'm not somebody to stay with. I'm basically—alone."

He folded his arms around her, feeling her body trembling. He pulled her hair aside and found her cheekbone with his fingertips, and turned her head gently toward him. "You're not alone." He brought her mouth to his, and kissed her, and she didn't try to stop it. And then she was kissing him deeply, wrapping her arms around him. That was when he noticed how much it hurt to kiss her. Every part of his body hurt with a deep, unfocused pain, an ache in the joints and bones that seemed to be spreading everywhere, like a spilled liquid. Was he bleeding internally? She winced suddenly, and it made him wonder if she hurt the same way he did. "Are you okay?"

She pushed him off without answering. "Don't stay."

"Why? Give me a reason."

"I don't love you. I can't love anybody."

"Karen—"

Their talk got no further, because the ceiling lights went out, plunging the room into gloom except for the glowing fire pit. Almost immediately a weird odor began to filter through the tunnels. The room smelled like a gas station. The smell grew stronger.

Ben Rourke came running. "Gasoline!" he shouted. "Get out!"

## Chapter 46

A rumbling sound started up, making the tunnels shake like an earthquake, and then a glow of yellow light appeared in the ceiling smoke hole over the fire hearth. Rick and Karen jumped up, throwing the blankets off, as Ben rushed into the room. "To the hangar!" he shouted.

They began to run down the tunnel, but were hit with a blast of rushing air, hot and soaked with fumes. Karen fell; Rick picked her up and started dragging her, but she wrestled him away. But then she fell to her knees and collapsed. She seemed to have fainted or something. He couldn't see anything, and smoke had suddenly flooded the tunnels. He picked her up and slung her over his back and started to run, following Ben. He got dizzy and had trouble breathing, and realized that the oxygen was being sucked out of the tunnels. Ben was shouting, hauling him along, and he fell, dropping Karen.

This time Karen came around. She stood up and grabbed him,

and started hauling him along. "Come on Rick! Don't fall apart on me!"

Stumbling, choking, coughing, they ran through the smoke. It filled the ceiling.

"Get under the smoke!" Ben shouted.

They began crawling, keeping their heads under the swirling black smoke, while a horrifying deep roar made the ground shake. They made it to the hangar. Rick and Karen leaped into the planes, while Rourke flung open a hangar door. Just then, the door collapsed, revealing a curtain of flames blocking the mouth of the cave.

Rourke fell back, coughing.

"Ben!" Karen screamed. She saw him fall to his knees, then stand up, and he waved them on. "Go!"

But there were only two planes. Ben would not be able to fly.

Karen cried, "Ben! What about you?"

"Get out!" He was staggering backward toward the tunnel. Smoke poured from it, now.

Choking, her head spinning, Karen started her plane and waved at Rick. "Take off!" she screamed at him. They took off at the same time, flying side by side through the cave, while Rourke staggered backward. Karen looked back and saw him fall to his knees. He was crawling into the Redoubt. He couldn't breathe; he would never make it.

But now the wall of flames approached. She ducked, hunching herself in the cockpit, and the micro-plane burst through the flames and into cool night air. She looked over and saw that Rick Hutter flew next to her. He seemed okay.

She banked gently, testing the stick, and looked back. Rourke's Redoubt had become a sea of fire. The flames leaped up against the Great Boulder, painting its face with firelight, while the shadow of a giant man appeared outlined against the flames. The man held a red plastic gasoline container, and he was dumping it around Tantalus Base. The man stepped back, and tossed a match, and a burst of flames leaped up, revealing his face. It was Vin Drake. Bathed in the firelight, Drake's face radiated calm. He could have been staring into a campfire and thinking peaceful thoughts. He tipped his head from side to side, as if he were shaking water out of his ear or listening for something.

**Rick lost control** of his plane. He threw it into a barrel roll, and smacked into the Great Boulder. For a moment he thought he was dead, but the micro-plane bounced off the rock, corkscrewed, and stabilized, flying straight and level. These micro-planes were really tough. He looked around: he had lost sight of Karen. The trees extended upward in a tangled wall. He searched the trees but found no lights, nothing to indicate where Karen had gone. There was a radio in the cockpit, and he debated calling her on it. Just then, ahead of him, Rick saw a pair of lights wink on, green and red. Karen's running lights.

He switched on his running lights, then waggled his wingtips at her. She waggled back. Good: they could see each other. She flew into the crown of a tree, and Rick followed her lights. He could barely see the branches and limbs all around. He was flying through a dark maze, following Karen King.

Rick ran up the power and caught up with her while she circled inside the tree. Then he switched on his radio. What the hell. Drake couldn't reach them now, even if he could hear them.

"Are you all right, Karen?"

"I think so. What about you?"

"Doing okay," he answered. He realized that she had nowhere to go now except Nanigen. She couldn't stay at Tantalus since there was nothing left. He decided not to remind her of that reality.

They could see Drake through the branches as they circled. He walked downslope, and more flames leaped up. He was burning something else; whatever it was, he seemed determined to eradicate all traces of the base and of Rourke's Redoubt. The fires were burning in wet forest, and would probably die without attracting attention, leaving Rourke's Redoubt and Tantalus Base gutted ruins.

Drake moved off into the forest, his flashlight bobbing. They heard the sound of an engine, and they saw a pickup truck bouncing on the dirt road at the lip of the crater. The vehicle's lights vanished past the far side of the crater and darkness closed in. But the darkness wasn't total, for the lights of Honolulu sparkled through the branches. Karen flew up out of the top of the tree and into the open.

"Bats. Gotta land somewhere," Rick said to her.

"Where, Rick? We can't land on the ground." They would be exposed to ground-dwelling predators.

"Follow me," he said. He went past her and flew on ahead, while she followed. He could see branches, leaves, obstructions, and he flew around them, twisting left and right, always staying inside the crowns of the trees, where bats wouldn't be flying. Occasionally he looked back, and saw Karen's running lights behind him; she was staying on his tail. The light of the fires faded behind them, until they had gone down inside the depths of the crater, into a zone where the wind blew more gently, blocked by the walls and slopes of the crater. They could no longer see the fires at all.

"I'm going to look for a landing place," Rick said on the radio. He coasted along a branch, inspecting it: it was a wide, clean branch, free of moss, with plenty of taxi room. He settled down on the branch and came to a halt. These planes could land on a dime. Karen landed and taxied up next to him, until their planes were parked beside each other.

The branch rocked and bobbed: the wind played with it, threatening to pluck the aircraft off the branch.

"We need to tie these planes down," Rick said, and climbed out. He discovered that the planes had tie-down ropes in their noses and tails; surely Ben Rourke's invention. Rick secured both planes.

Karen King began crying softly, hunched in her cockpit.

"What's the matter?"

"Ben. He was trapped. He couldn't have survived."

Rick thought Ben might have stood a chance. "I wouldn't count that guy out." But there was no way of knowing if Ben had escaped or had died in the flames.

Then came the wait. The clocks in the instrument panels showed the time: 1:34 a.m. Dawn would not come for many hours, but they couldn't fly safely at night.

The trade wind was running strong, and the branch tossed and heaved like the deck of a ship in a storm. She could see the bruises on her arms, dark stains in the moonlight. The stains were getting larger. She wondered what the rest of her body looked like.

Rick became seasick as the branch pitched and bobbed, and he wondered if the micro-bends were getting to him. Or it might be lingering effects of spider and wasp venom. He thought about the distance they had to cover at dawn. Fifteen miles, including a long passage over Pearl Harbor, which was open water. He thought: It's not possible. We'll never make it.

# Chapter 47

When Eric Jansen swung into the parking area by the Diamond Head Lighthouse, the place had been deserted. There was no sign of Vin Drake's car. He had arrived too late. Or maybe too early? Maybe Drake hadn't shown up yet. He had parked in the corner of the area and debated what to do next. Wait for Drake? But Drake might have already been here. Should he go to the police? But that might cost the survivors their lives, because Drake knew where they were, and he might be heading for Tantalus to kill them.

Eric knew he had to go to Tantalus.

And so he drove up the Tantalus Drive, the truck roaring and misfiring, past expensive homes on hairpin turns. The road came to a gate with a rutted dirt track beyond it; the gate wasn't locked. He started driving up the track. It wound up the steep mountainside through guava forests, and came out at the lip of the crater, and it followed the lip down through dips and gullies, washed out in several places. This was a four-wheel-drive track only, and Eric was glad he had a fat-tire truck. Eventually he reached a turnaround; still no sign of Drake's truck. The place was deserted.

He did not have a flashlight; that was a problem. But he got out of the truck, leaving the headlights shining toward the Great Boulder, and stood there, listening. There was a reddish glow through the trees, and he began crashing through the undergrowth toward it. When he reached the Great Boulder he saw what had happened. Embers were dying down, the soil smoking, and the ground reeked of gasoline.

Drake had done the deed. He had killed everybody.

Regretting that he hadn't brought a flashlight, Eric got down on his knees and found the entrance to the rat warren: Rourke's hideout. "Anybody there?" he called.

It was useless. He waited for a while, though, poking his finger into the soil, wondering if there were survivors. It was too dark to see much, and they would be very small; he worried he might crush somebody by accident.

But there weren't any survivors, anybody could see that.

He stumbled through the woods back to the truck.

**Rick and Karen,** parked on the branch, saw the headlights of another vehicle bumping slowly around the rim of the crater. It was a truck.

Rick watched for a while, then said to Karen, "I'm going to investigate."

"Don't."

He ignored her. He untied his plane and started it, and taxied off. She heard it whining upward, toward the crater rim, toward the Great Boulder.

"Damn you, Rick!" Karen yelled. She wasn't going to be left alone, so she started her plane and followed him.

Rick saw a man get out of the truck. He circled through the branches, listening for bats, but he didn't hear any sonar, and he flew closer to the man. The man walked to the Great Boulder and got down on his knees in the darkness. His face wasn't visible. The man stood up from the boulder and walked away, crashing through the underbrush, a black silhouette. Rick followed him, dodging among branches and trunks.

The man arrived at the parked vehicle. It was a strange-looking truck with fat tires and a weird paint job. The man got in, and the dome light came on, revealing his face.

Rick had seen the man before. Where? He circled past the window as the truck started with a roar.

"Karen!" he called on the radio. "Who is *this* guy?"

She swooped past Rick and made a steep turn by the truck. She was getting the hang of flying; it was pretty easy. "It's Peter's brother!"

"I thought he was supposed to be dead. Is he in with Drake?"

"How would I know?" Karen answered testily.

The truck started and began rumbling off, moving along the dirt track.

Karen ran her engine up to EMERGENCY MAXIMUM. Running at full power, their planes could barely keep up with the truck, even though it bounced slowly along the dirt road. The moment the truck arrived at a paved road it would speed up and they would never catch it, and it would be gone. They had to get Eric's attention soon.

He was driving with the windows rolled up. Karen flew alongside the window, close to the man's face, and waggled her wings. No reaction. Then the truck sped up, leaving them behind in swirling dust.

"Get in the slipstream," Rick said. There would be a zone of dead air behind the truck's cab, he thought, so he dove for it, watching the back of the man's head in the glass. His plane flipped over and tumbled: the air behind the cab had gone turbulent and chaotic, and he nearly crashed on the truck's bed.

The truck came to a bad spot in the road, where rain had washed a gully. The man slowed, and rolled down his window and leaned out to get a better look.

Karen flew through the window into the cab. She circled once, and the man drew his head back in. She made a slow pass in front of his eyes, and rolled the plane, its lights winking.

He saw that. He jammed on the brakes. "Hey—!" His eyes followed her as she banked and turned and flew low over the dashboard. He held out his hand, palm upward, and she landed on his hand. She climbed out and stood on his hand, while he looked at her.

Rick flew in and landed on the dashboard.

"Which—ones—are—you?" he said, his voice rumbling. He held Karen delicately, and he tried not to breathe too much as he spoke. He didn't want to blow her off his hand.

Karen held up her radio headset and pointed to it. She remembered that Jarel Kinsky had said the radios could be used to communicate with full-size people. Maybe it would be easier to talk by radio.

"You—bet." He put her down on the dashboard, with her plane, and opened the glove box and took out a headset, and plugged it into a mess of electronic equipment sitting on the seat. "Go—to—seventy—one—point—two—five—gigahertz," he said.

Rick and Karen put on their headsets and tuned their aircraft radios.

The man opened his mouth and spoke words that rolled out: "Can—you—understand—me—now?" An instant later the same words sounded on their headsets in Eric's normal speaking voice: "Can you understand me now? This is a squirt radio. It collects my voice and speeds it up and squirts it at you. It also slows down your voices so I can understand you."

They explained to Eric what had happened. "We need to get into the generator as soon as possible," Karen said.

"First . . . about my brother."

They told him. As Karen described Peter's death, Eric's palms hit the steering wheel, throwing the micro-humans and the planes into the air. They came down amid choking dust particles, and waited. They gave him time. When he opened his eyes, his face had become set and calm. "I'm taking you into Nanigen. Then I'm going to find Vincent Drake."

# Chapter 48

CHINATOWN, HONOLULU
1 NOVEMBER, 2:30 A.M.

Dan Watanabe woke to the buzzing of his cell phone. He reached for it in the dark and knocked it off the bedside table, and heard it hitting the floor. He groped for the light, fearing bad family news: his seven-year-old daughter, living with his ex-wife; his mother . . . but the caller was the security chief of Nanigen: "Got a minute, lieutenant?"

Watanabe ran his tongue over a sticky mouth. "Yeah."

"There was a fire on Tantalus tonight."

Watanabe grunted. "What?"

"It was small, probably didn't get reported. Some people died in it."

"I'm not following you."

"Those students—they were murdered."

He sat up fast, instantly full awake. Take the man into custody, get a statement. "Where are you? I'll have a car—"

"No. I just want to talk with you."

"You know the Deluxe Plate?" It was open all night.

■ ■ ■

**He was nursing** a cup of coffee at a back booth, the only customer in the place, when Don Makele walked in. The man seemed . . . resigned. Makele eased himself into the booth.

Watanabe didn't waste time with chitchat. "Let's hear about the students."

"They're dead. Vin Drake has killed at least eight people. They were small people."

"How small?"

Makele put his thumb and forefinger half an inch apart. "Really small."

"Tell you what," Watanabe said. "Let's pretend I believe you."

"Nanigen has a machine that'll shrink anything. Even people."

A waitress came over and asked if Makele wanted breakfast. He shook his head, and waited in silence while the waitress walked away.

"Will this machine shrink another machine?" Watanabe asked.

"Well—sure," Makele answered.

"Will it shrink a pair of scissors?"

Makele squinted. "What are you talking about?"

"Willy Fong. Marcos Rodriguez."

Makele didn't answer.

Dan Watanabe went on: "I understand you want to tell me what happened to the missing students. But I also want to hear about the micro-bots that cut Fong's and Rodriguez's throats from ear to ear."

"How do you know about the bots?" Makele said.

"Did you think the Honolulu Police Department doesn't have microscopes?"

Makele sucked on his lips. "The bots weren't supposed to kill anybody."

"So what went wrong?"

"The bots were reprogrammed. To kill."

"By who?"

"I think by Drake."

Watanabe took that in. "So what happened to the students?"

Makele explained about the supply stations in Manoa Valley, and about Tantalus Base. "The kids must've found out something bad about Drake, because he's been pushing me to . . . get rid of them."

"Kill them?"

"Yes. They ended up in Manoa Valley. Drake wanted to make sure they didn't get out of the valley alive. They tried to escape. A few of them made it to Tantalus." He explained to Watanabe about Ben Rourke. "Drake torched the place. Also, I'm pretty sure he murdered our chief financial officer and a vice president . . ."

Watanabe's head was swimming. Vin Drake seemed to have killed thirteen people. If this was true, Drake was extremely dangerous. "Tell me why I shouldn't decide you're a nutcase?" he said to the security man.

Makele hunched over. "You decide what you want. I have to tell you the truth."

"Are you involved in these deaths?"

"For seven million dollars."

In his years as a detective, Dan Watanabe had witnessed many confessions. Even so, a confession never failed to give Watanabe a sense of surprise. Why did people decide to tell the truth? It was never in their best interest. The truth doesn't set you free, it sends you to prison.

"Last time we talked, lieutenant," Don Makele went on, "you said something about Moloka'i."

Watanabe frowned. He didn't remember . . . Oh, yes—Makele used the traditional Hawaiian pronunciation . . .

"You said Moloka'i is the best of the islands," the security chief went on. "I think you meant the people of Moloka'i, not the island."

"I don't know what I meant," Watanabe answered, and sipped his coffee, and sat back, keeping his gaze fixed on Makele.

"I was born in Puko'o," Makele went on. "That's a little spot on East Moloka'i. Just a few houses and the sea. My grandma raised me. She taught me to speak Hawai'ian—well, she tried to. She also taught me about doing the right thing. I joined the Marines, served my country, but then . . . I don't know what happened to me. I started doing things for money. Those students didn't deserve what we did to them. We left them to die. When they didn't die, Drake sent people to take them out. I will do a lot of things for seven million dollars, but there's some things I won't do. I won't take orders from Vin Drake anymore. I'm like *pau hana*." Work is done.

"Where is Mr. Drake right now?" Watanabe asked. The man was beyond dangerous.

"Nanigen, I think."

Watanabe flipped up his phone. "We'll get him."

"Not a good idea to just walk in there, lieutenant."

"Oh?" Watanabe said coolly, holding his phone away from his ear; you could hear his phone ringing. "Tactical deployments are pretty damn effective, I've noticed."

"Not with micro-bots. They can smell you, and they can fly. It's a hornet's nest in there."

"All right. Tell me how to get in."

"There's no way in unless Vin Drake permits it. He controls the bots. Hand-controller. Like a TV remote."

Watanabe got an answer to his phone call. "Marty?" he said, putting the phone back to his ear. "We've got a problem at Nanigen."


**Eric Jansen swung** the fat-tire truck into the entrance of the Kalikimaki Industrial Park, and cruised past the Nanigen building. Apart from a sodium light splashing the entrance door, the place seemed lightless and dead, in the early hours of a Sunday morning. Karen King and Rick Hutter stood on the dashboard of the truck next to their aircraft. Near them a plastic hula girl bobbled, stuck to the dashboard and swinging in a grass skirt. The hula girl loomed over Karen and Rick.

Eric drove the truck inside an unfinished building, just the frame of a warehouse and some concrete block walls, which sat next to Nanigen. He parked behind a wall, out of sight. He shut off the engine and got out, and listened for a few moments, and looked around. Time to move on Nanigen.

He put on the squirt radio headset, and spoke into the voice pickup. "Launch your planes and follow me."

Karen and Rick climbed into their planes and took off. Eric could hear the props whining near his ears as he crossed the lot, heading for Nanigen. He realized they were flying directly behind his head, to keep out of the wind.

"You okay?" he said on the radio.

"Fine," Karen answered. She didn't feel fine, she felt terrible, like a bad case of flu coming on. Every joint in her body ached. Rick probably felt worse, she thought, since he'd had loads of toxins in his bloodstream. That would accelerate the bends in him, probably.

The front door was locked. Eric opened it with a key. He held it open for a moment to let Karen and Rick fly through. Then he closed the door behind him.

He moved along the main corridor at a slow walk, hearing the mosquito-like buzzing behind his head. He glanced back and saw the two micro-planes, their propellers whirring, floating along under the ceiling tiles, bobbing in air currents generated by the building's air-handling system. His head created turbulence, and they bounced around in his wake as he walked. "Don't get sucked into a vent," he warned them.

"Couldn't we land on your shoulder? You could carry us—" Karen said to Eric.

"You're better off in the air. You might need to get away fast—if I run into . . . trouble." Eric glanced back at the planes, to make sure they were still behind him, and stopped at a corner, and peered around it. He was looking down a long corridor past windows covered with black shades. There was nobody in sight. He crossed this corridor and continued down a side hallway to a door, and opened it, and went in, the planes following him. "My office," he said on the squirt.

Eric's office had been ransacked. Papers were strewn about, and his computer was gone. Eric pulled open a drawer in his desk, rummaged through it, and said, "Whew. It's still here." He took out a device that resembled a game controller. "It's my bot controller. It should disarm the bots," he explained to Rick and Karen.

Then he led them back to the main corridor, and they flew along behind him past the darkened windows. Eric stopped before the door marked TENSOR CORE. He pushed the door.

It wouldn't open. There was no security pad, just a plain lock, he explained. "Shit," he said. "This door has been locked from the inside. That means . . ."

"Somebody's in there?" Rick asked.

"Could be. But there's another way into the generator room. We can get in there through the Omicron zone."

The bots in the Omicron zone might be programmed to kill an intruder. There was no way to know without entering the zone and seeing what the bots did. Eric just hoped his bot controller would work. He led the flyers around a corner, turned right, and stopped by a nondescript door. The door had on it only a small, unfamiliar symbol, with a single word: MICROHAZARD.

Rick flew past the symbol, a few inches from it, and said on the squirt radio, "What does this mean?"

"It means there are bots on the other side of the door that are capable of causing death or serious injury—if they're programmed that way. It could be nasty in there." Eric held up the controller where the flyers could see it clearly. "Let's hope this controls them." Then Eric tried the doorknob; it wasn't locked. But he didn't open it. Instead, he punched in a series of digits on the controller's keypad. "You see, Drake thinks I'm dead," he said on the squirt radio to the flyers. "I'm assuming Drake didn't bother to delete my PIN number from my bot controller, since he figured I'd never be using it again." He shrugged. "We'll see." He paused for a moment, pondering the danger on the other side of the door, and then thrust open the door and walked in. He stopped, holding the door open so that the micro-planes could follow him through.

They had entered the main lab room of the Omicron Project. The lights in the room were turned low, and the room was mostly dark. It was not a large space; it could have been a normal engineering lab. It contained some desks, some workstations, some lab benches with magnifying lenses mounted on them. Steel shelves held a myriad of small parts. A window made of thick glass looked into the tensor core; a door stood next to the window, an entry door that led straight from Project Omicron into the core.

Eric stood in the middle of the Omicron lab, holding the bot controller in his hand, looking around, listening. So far so good. He couldn't see the bots but he knew they were there, clinging to the ceiling. He listened for a faint hum. He might just hear their turbines if they sensed him and started dropping off the ceiling, coming for him. If the bots hadn't been disarmed, he'd only know when he started to bleed. But he heard nothing, saw nothing, and felt nothing. His controller still worked; he had disarmed the bots. He gave a sigh of relief.

"We're good," he said.

There were objects sitting on the lab benches, covered with black cloth. It was hard to see just what they were in the dim light.

"I'm going to show you," Eric said on the squirt radio to Rick and Karen, "why Vin Drake wanted to kill me. And why he killed your friends." Eric stopped in the middle of the room, and held out his arm sideways, bent at the elbow. "Land on my arm," he said. "You can get a closer look that way."

Rick and Karen landed their planes on his forearm. Moving carefully and shielding the planes with his hand so they wouldn't be blown off by a stray gust of air, he approached the closest bench. He removed the cloth from one of the objects. It was an aircraft, small, sleek, vicious-looking. It did not have a cockpit.

"It's a Hellstorm UAV," Eric said. "An unmanned aerial vehicle."

"A drone, you mean?" Rick asked.

"Exactly. A drone. No pilot."

It had a wingspan of ten inches.

Eric brought his arm close to the drone, letting Rick and Karen have a good look.

"This is a giant prototype of a Hellstorm," he said. "Once it's flight-tested, it will be shrunk down to half an inch."

Instead of landing gear, the Hellstorm had four jointed legs with what looked like sticky pads on the ends, just like the feet on the hexapod trucks. Under its wings it carried missiles: two glass tubes with long steel needles at their noses, fins, and what looked like a rocket motor in the tail.

"What does it do?" Rick asked.

"Indeed—what does it do?" Eric echoed. "It's a military drone the size of a moth. It can be used for surveillance. It can also kill people. It can evade any security system in existence. It can fly under a door or through a crack around a window. It can cling to a person's skin or clothing. It can also crawl, using those legs. It can fly along the electrical conduits inside a wall, then pop out and fly around inside a room. It can kill any person, anywhere, anytime. You see those rockets under its wings? Those are toxin micro-missiles. The missile is armed with super-toxins that Nanigen has discovered and extracted from life-forms in the micro-world—poison from worms, spiders, fungi, and bacteria. The missile has a flight range of ten meters. This means the drone has standoff-attack capability: it can fire toxin missiles from a distance. If one of those super-toxin missiles embeds in your skin, you'll die fast. One micro-drone can kill two people, since it carries two missiles."

"What are those scoops along the fuselage? Are they jet intakes?" Rick asked.

"No. Those are air samplers. They're used for targeting."

"How's that?" Karen asked.

"The Hellstorm can smell you. Every person gives off a unique fingerprint of scent. Each one of us smells a little different from every other person. Our DNA is unique, so naturally the combination of pheromones given off by our body is unique, too. A micro-drone can be programmed to seek out the odor of a particular person. Even if you are at a rock concert, the drone can find you in the crowd and kill you."

"This is a nightmare," Karen King said.

"The nightmare has no end," Eric Jansen said. "Think of a presidential inauguration. Think of a thousand Hellstorms released into the air, all of them programmed to seek out the president of the United States. If just one micro-drone gets through, the president dies. Micro-drones could take out the government of any nation— Japan, China, Britain, Germany—any nation could be cut down by a swarm of micro-drones." He turned himself around slowly, while Rick and Karen took in the scene from his arm. "This room is Pandora's box."

"So Nanigen isn't about medicine," said Karen.

"Nanigen *is* about medicine. It's just that Nanigen is working both sides of the street. Ways to save lives and . . . ways to end lives. This Hellstorm," he touched it lightly, "is a drug-delivery system."

"And you found out about it, so Drake had to kill you."

"Not quite. I knew about the Omicron program all along. Nanigen has a contract with the Department of Defense to develop micro-drones. The research went much better than the DOD people got told. Vin started lying to the government. He started telling them the micro-drones were a failure."

"Why?" Rick asked.

"Because Drake had his own plans for micro-drones. We had a problem with our patents on the micro-drone system. There's a company in Silicon Valley called Rexatack that actually invented and patented some of this technology. Vin Drake is an investor in Rexatack. He ripped off the patents and used them to build the Hellstorm drone. Then he decided he needed to sell the technology fast, because Rexatack was getting ready to sue Nanigen and get its patents enforced. What got me into trouble with Vin was when I discovered he was trying to sell the micro-drone technology to the highest bidder."

"Not to the U.S. government?" Karen said.

"No. Vin was looking for fast money, and there's more money overseas. Look—there are governments out there with money to burn—and it's dollars. Countries whose economies are growing faster than ours. They will pay anything for the micro-drone technology. *Anything.* I'm not saying that the U.S. government would necessarily do nice things with micro-drones. I'm just saying there are governments out there that would commit horrors with them. Some of those governments hate the United States, they have nothing but contempt for Europe, they fear their closest neighbors, and they hate and fear their own people, too. Those governments wouldn't hesitate to use micro-drones as a means to their ends. And then there are the international terror groups—they'd love to have micro-drones. I learned that Drake had gone to Dubai where he was talking with officials of several different governments about selling them the Nanigen Hellstorm technology. I protested to Drake. I said it was a violation of U.S. law. I said it was dangerous for the whole world. But I hesitated."

"Why?" Rick asked.

Eric sighed. "Drake had given me stock in Nanigen worth millions. If I went to the authorities, I knew Nanigen would crash and burn. My stock would be worth nothing. So I hesitated. Out of greed. I had gone into physics for the pure love of it, and I never thought, you see, that physics would make me a millionaire. Now millions would slip through my fingers if I blew the whistle on Drake, and it was my fatal weakness. Then Drake decided to kill me. I was in my new boat doing sea trials, and I'd told Alyson Bender I'd meet her in Kaneohe for lunch—it's on the windward side of the island. Alyson, or Drake, seeded my boat with Hellstorms. Prototypes, but they were loaded to kill me. My engines failed, and that's when I saw one of those damned things fly out of the front cabin. At first I thought it was just a bug. Then I saw it had propellers and needle missiles, and I knew it was a Hellstorm. Then I spotted another Hellstorm flying out of the cabin. So I texted my brother and dove overboard. The surf protected me. The micro-drones couldn't smell me, couldn't launch missiles at me because I was swimming under the waves. I made it to Honolulu and went into hiding. If I had surfaced and gone to the police, Drake would have hunted me down with more micro-drones. Vin Drake is drunk on the power of his bots." Eric sighed, and paused, and in the silence another voice spoke:

"That was an excellent description of me, Eric. I enjoyed it thoroughly." A small, bright light went on, and Vincent Drake stood up behind a rack of computers, the light beam swinging in front of him.

# Chapter 49

## KALIKIMAKI INDUSTRIAL PARK
## 1 NOVEMBER, 3:40 A.M.

Drake had been sitting on a chair in a dark space behind the rack of computers. He wore an earbud, and he was holding a gun in his right hand. It was a Belgian FN semiautomatic pistol with a tactical light attached to the trigger guard. The light dodged around. In his left hand he held a bot controller. He wore a black shirt, black jeans, mud-stained boots. He walked to the center of the room and pointed the gun into Eric's eyes, then toward Eric's forearm, and caught the two aircraft in the light beam.

"Peek-a-boo, I see you," said Drake.

The two micro-humans heard him perfectly on their headsets. He was using a squirt radio. Rick said to Karen, "Launch."

They powered up the aircraft and fell off Eric's arm, diving, the props ramping up.

Drake didn't seem to care what they did. He aimed the gun and light into Eric's eyes, standing with his body turned sideways and his gun arm held straight out. Drake held up the bot controller in his other hand. Its screen made his hand glow. He touched a button with his thumb and said, "Your bot controller doesn't actually work, Eric. Only mine does."

Rick banked his micro-plane and circled over Eric's head. He couldn't see Karen. He called to her on the radio: "Stay close to me."

"Rick—can Drake hear us?"

"Of course I can hear you," Drake's voice came on their radios. He swung the gun around suddenly, and the laser beam dodged around their planes, and they saw his vast, leering face. For a moment Rick thought Drake would fire the gun at them, but then he realized that the bullet probably wouldn't hit their planes. They were too small, dodging around too fast.

Drake kept the gun pointed at Eric's head. He held up the bot controller, pressed a button. "There," he said.

"What did you do?" Eric said, looking up.

Drake looked around and smiled. "I activated the bots." He took a step backward, waiting.

"You'll be attacked by them, too—" Eric said.

"I don't think so." Drake lunged forward and hit Eric in the face with the butt of his gun. Eric groaned and fell to his knees.

"What is it about you Jansen brothers? You seem to require beatings on a regular basis," Drake said. He kicked Eric in the ribs. Eric gasped and went down on all fours and began to crawl.

"Where are you going, Eric? Looking for something?"

"Go to hell."

Drake kicked him in the side of the head, viciously. Eric slumped down and curled up, and seemed to lose consciousness, while Drake's pistol light danced over him.

Eric tried to struggle to his feet, but couldn't.

"Well, Eric, there's something you don't realize. The bots ignore my body scent. They'll go after anybody except me." He chuckled. "They respect me."

Eric put his hand up to his face, then took it away. His hand was spotted with blood. A small razor cut had opened on his forehead.

"Too bad, Eric. Looks like one of them found you."

Eric crawled toward Drake, who darted backward and smiled. Eric began swatting at his hair, at his ears, shaking himself.

"Trying to get the bots off, Eric? Can you feel them crawling on your face? In your hair? Soon they'll be in your bloodstream. Don't worry, it doesn't hurt. You just watch yourself bleed."

**As Drake worked** on Eric, Rick flew toward the door to the generator room. That's where he and Karen had to go. He circled in close to the door, and he made a slow pass near it. He saw a small vent at the top of the door. It might be big enough for a micro-plane to pass through; he couldn't tell. He backed away and flew up close to Karen, until their wings nearly touched. He switched off his radio, and shouted at her: "He can't hear us when we shout. Fly toward the door to the generator room. Looks like there's a way through."

He got some altitude above the vent in the door, and ran up to full power, and dove at the slot. His wings clipped the slot as he went through, and he ended up inside the generator room, spiraling out of control. Karen followed him a moment later. Rick recovered, got his plane under control. He flew straight toward the center of the generator chamber, the pattern of hexagons below him. He picked out the central hexagon and banked, looking down. He could see a small white circle in it, far below: it marked the location of the control panel. He could see Karen King flying off his right wing. "I'm going to land by the circle," he shouted to her, hoping his voice carried over the rushing wind as his plane flew.

Just then Drake's voice came on their radio headsets. "I know what you're trying to do," he said. "I saw you fly into the generator room. However, you may wish to know that the bots in there can see you. Smell you, too."

They saw Drake's face staring in the window, now, his eyes

moving, tracking them as they flew. Drake held up the bot controller where they could see it, and he pushed a series of buttons. "I changed the sensitivity. Now they can find you," he said, and looked up at the ceiling of the generator room.

Karen followed Drake's gaze. She saw them: glittery specks, scattered across the ceiling. The specks were moving. Dropping and falling like tiny raindrops. As they fell, they fanned out, flying under their own power. She saw one of them turn toward Rick, and it began tracking him, flying after him. As Rick went into a dive toward the floor, the bot dove as well. It was powered by a turboprop fan in a housing, and it had a snaky neck, with knives on the end of the neck. As it flashed past her, following Rick, she saw the eyes: the bot had a pair of compound eyes like an insect's, but it was a machine vision system. A pair of eyes meant it had binocular vision, depth perception, she realized.

"Rick," she shouted. "Behind you!"

He didn't hear her. He was heading for the floor and the white circle. The bot closed in on him; she had to get that bot off his tail. Not sure what to do, she dove her plane, chasing the bot and Rick. Out of the corner of her eye she saw more objects flying, and she looked over her shoulder and saw dozens of bots, maybe more, flying behind her. They seemed to be converging on her and Rick. The bots shimmered as they flew, and some of them hovered, darting, seeking. "Rick, behind you!" she shouted.

He turned his head and saw the bot following him. He immediately pulled up and banked, getting out of the dive, twisting upward, trying to shake the bot off his tail. The bot flew at least as well as Rick did. It was closing in on him.

Karen accelerated and dove behind the bot that was chasing Rick. Maybe she could knock it out of the air by hitting it with the nose of her plane. Her propeller was in the tail of her plane, so the plane's nose could be used as a blunt weapon. She aimed for the bot and pushed the throttle forward. Just before the strike, she hunched down in the cockpit and tucked her head, bracing for impact. Her plane slammed into the bot.

There was a pinging sound and her plane ricocheted one way and the bot went the other way, both corkscrewing through the air. The crash didn't hurt the plane or the bot: they merely bounced off each other. The bot whirled around and stopped itself in midair, and hovered, and oriented itself, and then began to follow her plane. Karen regained control of her plane and peeled away, watching the bot. The bot accelerated toward her, putting on a burst of speed, and then, to Karen's surprise, the bot unfolded two jointed arms.

It grabbed hold of the wing of Karen's plane with the sticky pads on the ends of its arms. The bot clung to her plane as she flew. She tried to shake it off, slamming the stick around, banking left and right, but the bot had gotten a firm grip and wouldn't let go. It began cutting into the wing with its blades.

It was breaking up her wing.


**Rick turned back** when he saw the bot attach itself to Karen's plane. Karen was in trouble. He flew toward her, asking himself what he could possibly do to free her plane from the bot's grip. His plane wasn't armed. No guns, no fire control buttons, nothing. But wait—Rourke had armed the planes with machetes. There was one in here somewhere. He groped around and felt a handle, and swooped toward Karen's plane, holding out the machete like a cavalry rider. "Ayah!" he shouted and hacked through the bot's neck as he passed, severing it. The blades and neck spun off, squirming, and the beheaded bot released Karen's plane and zigzagged away, seemingly disoriented. Karen regained control of her plane.

The bots were hovering—dozens of them.

Rick circled through them. A bot darted in and clamped its arms on Rick's plane as he passed, and the bot began jerking his plane around. Then the bot began snipping through the wing with its scissor-swords while Rick struck at it with the machete, but he couldn't reach the bot. Rick's plane went into a spiral. Another bot grabbed his plane, and stopped its fall. The bots held Rick's plane in midair, hovering, as if they were quarreling over their prize while they cut it up.

Rick bailed out, taking his machete with him. As he fell, he flipped over on his back and saw Karen's plane above him. Bots clung to it; she was spinning out of control. One bot shredded Karen's propellers while another tore into the side of the plane. At that instant, Rick landed on the floor on his back, unhurt, still holding his machete.

He stood up. The generator room seemed enormous. He had no idea where the micro-control panel was; he couldn't see the white circle. The plastic floor, glowing with light from below, was strewn with golf-ball-size grains of dirt. Looking up and around, he tried to see where Karen's plane had gone. He couldn't see her. The floor was a mess.

He heard a sound like "Oof!" Karen King landed on both feet, like a cat, about a hundred yards away. She had bailed out, too. She was holding her machete and staring up at the bots. A dozen of them were bobbing high overhead, holding the planes and pieces of the planes, and chopping everything up. Debris from the planes rained down. For the moment the bots seemed distracted by the planes.

"It's this way!" Karen called, pointing with her machete.

Now he could see the white ring. He was surprised by how far away it was. They both started a desperate sprint toward the ring, jumping over debris, running an obstacle course through grit. Rick tripped while leaping over a human hair, and he sprawled.

He picked himself up. He had lost sight of Karen. "Karen?" he shouted.

Overhead, the bots had finished cutting up the planes and were now flying this way and that, hovering, swooping, fanning throughout the room, as if in seek mode. Rick wondered if the bots would be able to see them as they ran. Dozens more bots dropped from the walls and ceiling, until at least a hundred bots were flying back and forth, hunting for the intruders. Were they communicating with one another? It would be only a matter of time before the bots found them.

# Chapter 50

## TENSOR CORE
## 1 NOVEMBER, 5:10 A.M.

I t's not a bad way to die," Drake was saying. "You hardly feel a thing." He worked the controller.

Eric lay propped up with his back against the wall of the Omicron lab, by the door to the generator room, dizzy from the beating Drake had given him. Drake held the gun at his face, shining the light into his eyes. Eric could feel a bot cutting through his forehead. Blood had begun to drizzle down his face, getting in his eyes. He could see specks hovering in front of his eyes, their props whining like mosquitoes. Apparently Drake could direct them with the controller, because they all suddenly flew toward his face. He felt them landing on his cheeks, his neck, exploring his eyelids. A bot crawled into his shirt; he could feel it, and heard its engine buzzing.

"You see how they ignore me?" Drake worked the controller. "It's because I have the controller." Drake thumbed a joystick, and a bot crawled up Eric's cheek and stopped by the corner of his eye. "I can make them crawl into any orifice in your body."

"Why are you doing this to me?"

"Research, Eric."

Eric felt a slight sting near the corner of his eye. The bot had planted its scissors in his skin and was making a hole. It tucked its head into the hole, and began wiggling in, snipping through skin cells with the blades. A droplet of blood beaded up on his cheek.

**The police cars** closed off the access road to the industrial park and set up a security perimeter around the Nanigen building. The vans moved into position, and the hostage rescue squad deployed. The flashers on the police cars played across the metal building.

Dan Watanabe waited behind one of the cars, watching the building's door. He had made the handoff to the SWAT unit, so he didn't have operational authority now, but he wanted the op commander, Kevin Hope, to pay attention to him. "Where's Dorothy?" he said.

"She's on her way," Hope answered.

"What about the FD decon unit?"

In answer to his question, a yellow van came roaring in and ground to a halt. A squad of fire department people deployed from it, pulling on Tyvek protective suits. As soon as they'd put on protective gear, they began setting up a decontamination center, with a tent, washing equipment, and a processing line for victims.

"What's in the building, a virus?" Commander Hope said to Watanabe. He had gotten the call to deploy only twenty minutes earlier, and he didn't yet know what the investigation involved.

"Not a virus. Bots," Watanabe said.

"Say again—?"

"Tiny robots. They bite."

Commander Hope gave him a weird look. "Don't tell me this is gonna be a shooter with robots, Dan."

"Not a chance. You can't hit 'em."

"Any hostages in there?"

"Not that we know. Can't assume anything," Watanabe answered. Somebody handed him a tactical vest, and he put it on. Somebody else brought him a handheld multichannel communicator. He took the device and keyed it on, and said to Commander Hope, "You want me to make the call?"

Hope gave a wry grin. "You talked us into this deployment, Dan. You talk us out of it."

Watanabe shrugged and referred to a slip of paper upon which he'd written a phone number. He called it.

**In the Omicron lab,** Eric could feel a half-dozen bots entering his skin, pricking him as they burrowed, while Drake held the gun and light pointed into his eyes. Eric debated which way to go: to force Drake to shoot him in the head, or to wait a few minutes for the bots to open his arteries.

Just then a faint buzzing sounded in Drake's jacket. He took out his phone and looked at the caller ID. BLOCKED, it told him. He decided to answer it. He took a deep breath to get his heart rate down. "Yes?"

"Vincent Drake?"

"Who's calling?"

"Dan Watanabe, sir, Honolulu Police. Sir, is there anybody in the building with you?"

"Oh, my goodness, Dan. I'm by myself. Working late. What's this all about?"

"Sir, we have the building surrounded. Would you please walk out slowly with your hands placed on your head? You will be safe, I promise."

"Good grief, Dan! There's obviously been a mistake. I'll be happy to comply—just give me a moment."

"Sir, we need you to come out immediately—"

"Certainly. Absolutely." Drake switched off his phone and advanced toward Eric, his face contorted in fury. "You went to the police."

Eric shook his head. He was losing a lot of blood. His shirt was darkening in streams, he could feel warmth running down his neck.

Drake leaned over Eric and hauled him to his feet. "You're just like your fucking brother—sticking your nose into things." They were eye to eye. "Oops," Drake said, touching Eric on the cheek. "I think there's one in your eye."

Get the controller.

Eric had his left hand on the door handle, behind him, and he pressed it. The door opened, and Eric fell backward into the generator room, with Drake landing on top of him. He reached out with his right hand and felt his fingers close over the controller, and he ripped it out of Drake's hand as he fell backward.

Drake swore and staggered, sprawling past Eric into the generator room, and he fired the gun. Eric felt the impact in his leg, the bullet passing through his thigh, but oddly he didn't feel any pain. He was in shock. But he had the controller now, and that was the main thing. He knew what to do with it. He slammed the controller against the floor again and again, smashing it, feeling it break into pieces beneath his hand.

Now nobody could control the bots.

And then, to his surprise, he saw the gun lying on the floor right in front of him, while Drake was getting to his feet. Drake had dropped the gun. Drake and Eric lunged for it simultaneously.

**On the floor,** Karen and Rick saw the door open, and two gargantuan human figures fell into the room. The gun went off, and the shockwave of the blast rolled over the micro-humans. Moments later the two men fell with a floor-shaking impact, which hurled Rick and Karen into the air. A droplet of blood splashed, exploding into secondary droplets. They picked themselves up and continued to run toward the white circle.

One of the men rolled over on his back. He held the bot control-ler, and smashed it repeatedly on the floor. It broke apart, and pieces of electronic boards flew past Karen, knocking her to the ground. She saw the gun skidding across the floor toward her, and felt sure it would crush her. She dove away while the two men collided over the gun. A moment later Eric was holding the gun, pointing it at Drake, who was lying on his back.

Eric lay on the floor near Drake. He rolled over and propped himself up, blood running from his leg, and pointed the gun at Drake's face. "You move . . . I'll shoot you in the head."

Drake said, "Wait, Eric. We can get out. Alive. Together."

"Not going to happen. You killed my kid brother." Eric steadied his finger on the trigger.

"But Eric . . . you're completely wrong . . . I did everything to save him."

"You're insane."

**Rick and Karen** reached the circle. They could hear a deep thrum-ming sound—the pulse of robot propellers around them. They had lost track of what the big humans were doing. In the center of the circle there was a hatch like a manhole cover, with a sunken handle. Karen and Rick reached the hatch at the same time.

Rick got down on his knees and tugged on the handle.

Nothing happened.

The hatch seemed to be stuck. By now, several bots had con-verged on them and were hovering aggressively. A bot flew in and jabbed at Karen with its knives. She swung her blade, and, with a clang, knocked the bot away. It fell back.

Karen held up her machete. "Back to back!" she shouted.

Rick Hutter straightened up, and stood with his back to Karen King, his machete drawn. The bots surrounded them, and began darting in, flying and hovering, steel blades snicking. Rick slung a roundhouse blow with his machete and blinded a bot, shearing off its compound eyes. The bot hit the ground, its neck writhing, and it took wing, flying off erratically.

They continued to hack at the bots, but the bots had no fear, no sense of self-preservation. Whirling her machete, Karen said, "Open it. I'll cover you."

Rick bent over and tugged on the hatch again, while Karen straddled him, facing the bots, fending them off. But the hatch wouldn't come up. He began prying at it with the tip of his machete, then tried hacking at it. If he couldn't open it, he could cut through it. But the blade bounced off the plastic. "I can't get it open!"

"Listen Rick—ow!" She cried out in pain. A bot had slashed her. She swung her machete over her head. "Try again! Hurry!" She yelled.

That did it. He threw himself on the door, and wrenched it open. Inside was a single red button. He jumped on the button with both feet.

The floor shook. The hexagon began to descend into the floor, until they were swallowed in a hexagonal chamber.

A bot had gotten inside the hexagon with them. It seemed confused. Rick fended it off, banging at it with his machete as it bounced against the chamber walls.

The lights changed color, followed by a humming sound, and then a dreamy feeling came over Rick Hutter until he felt as if he was floating in space, and dancing with the bot, and dancing with Karen King, the three of them whirling around and around in a mad waltz.

**The tensor generator** powered up, and the fields crossed and recrossed, and wound up in poloidal loops, and the hexagons raised up and met the floor. Rick Hutter, Karen King, and a gigantic, enlarged bot were left resting on the floor. The people were full-size. The bot had been expanded to the size of a refrigerator.

Eric was lying on the floor, bleeding heavily from a wound in his leg and from several bot cuts, but he was conscious, and he kept the gun trained on Drake, who had started to crawl across the floor toward Eric, an expression of fear working on his face.

"Get Eric," Rick said to Karen. They scooped Eric up by the shoulders and feet and began dragging him out of the chamber. The gun slipped out of Eric's hands and hit the floor. Drake got to his feet, and made a mistake. Instead of going for the door, he went for the gun.

In that split second, Rick and Karen got Eric Jansen out of the generator room, and they slammed the door shut. Karen saw that it had a simple deadbolt. She threw the bolt.

This left Drake locked inside the generator room, in the company of a hundred flying micro-bots and one giant bot. The big bot sat on the floor, its compound eyes turning left and right, its gooseneck waving, its turbofan blades shrieking, but it couldn't lift off. It had become too heavy to fly.

Drake glanced at the big bot, then stood up, holding the gun. Rick and Karen watched from behind the bulletproof window as Drake picked up the bot controller: Eric had smashed it thoroughly. He tossed it away.

They saw Drake's lips moving, and heard his voice faintly through the glass: "Let me out."

Rick shook his head.

Drake fired at the window. The bullet starred the glass, but didn't break it.

Drake walked up close to the window. "Please help me. I'm very sorry." A bead of blood appeared, hanging at the tip of his nose. He backed up a few steps, and looked around wildly, and swatted at a bot circling his head. He cursed, and waved his gun around, the light beam crisscrossing the chamber. He caught a bot in the light, and fired the gun at the bot. Pointing the light around, he fired again.

And again and again Drake fired at the bots, until the tensor room filled with a haze of cordite smoke.

Then he took his cell phone out of his pocket; it was ringing again. "Hello, lieutenant. Would you please come get me? I'll tell you everything, of course. I'm in a bit of trouble in the generator room. The generator room. In the center of the building. Bots? There are no bots in here, Dan, it's perfectly safe . . ." The phone slipped out of his bloody fingers and clattered to the floor. A nosebleed drenched the front of his shirt.

Drake coughed, spraying blood. He staggered forward and pressed himself against the window and stared at Rick and Karen. "I will have you killed! I swear it—!" His eyes went wide, and a bead of blood appeared in the corner of his right eye. A bot emerged through the white of his eye and began crawling across the surface of Drake's eye, dragging blood along with it as it crawled. Drake seemed to be watching the bot as it crossed his cornea. "Get off me," he whispered, and dug a finger into his eye, and stared at his bloody fingertip, and screamed.

Then he turned the gun to his head and pulled the trigger.

Nothing happened. He had emptied the clip shooting at the bots.

Behind Drake's back, the giant bot had turned its eyes on Drake. It advanced upon him, dragging its arms. Its gooseneck lashed out and the blades thrust up through Drake's body cavity from below and burst out his chest. The bot raised him up, shook him on its gooseneck, and shrugged, slinging the body across the room.

**Rick and Karen** had turned their attention to Eric Jansen. Rick tore off his shirt and wrapped it around Eric's leg to make a compress. He took Eric under the shoulders and began half-carrying, half-dragging him through the Omicron lab. He was barely conscious, having lost a lot of blood.

Then they heard the humming sound of bots. Karen felt a stinging sensation on the back of her neck, and slapped at it. Her hand came away bloody.

"Room's contaminated! Move it, Rick!" Without thinking, she grabbed Eric with one hand and tried to sling him over her shoulder, but she couldn't do it. For a moment she thought, What's wrong? Her superpowers had vanished.

They managed to drag Eric into the hallway, and there they were met with a team of police officers, running, guns drawn, wearing body armor. Just behind came a slightly potbellied plainclothes detective. He wore a tactical vest but clearly wasn't a member of the SWAT team.

"Get back!" Rick shouted at them. "Bots!"

"I know," the detective said calmly. He turned to the men. "Get them out, quick." To Karen and Rick, he said, "Is there anybody else in the building?"

"Drake. He's dead."

"Everybody out," the detective said.

The officers bundled Rick and Karen along, and they scout-carried Eric, who had lost consciousness.

The last man out of the building was the detective. He came out through the door into the light of dawn, a trail of blood streaming from his forehead. The bots had found Dan Watanabe.

"Where's Dorothy?" he called out.

Dorothy Girt had arrived in her Toyota. She came forward.

"You brought your magnet?"

"Of course." She held up the industrial horseshoe magnet. She had grabbed it out of the forensic lab on the way over.

"Everybody into decon, hostages and officers," said Watanabe, as he took off his vest. "Dorothy will decontaminate you." An EMT squad brought Eric into the tent first, then loaded him into a mede-vac helicopter. Last of all, after everybody else had taken their turn, Lieutenant Watanabe walked into the white tent to have Dorothy get the bots out of him.

# Chapter 51

**THE PIT**
**1 NOVEMBER, 5:55 A.M.**

In the tensor generator room, the only thing that moved was the gigantic bot. It explored the room, shoving aside Drake's corpse, looking for a way out. It couldn't find a way out, so its program went into the drilling sequence. It bent its neck to the floor, and, using its knives, it cut through the plastic floor. When it had opened a hole, it broke through, crashing down into the pit full of electronic gear. There the bot continued to cut and chop, doing what it knew best.

Groaning, rending, crackling sounds came from below the floor of the generator room, the sounds mixing with blue and yellow flashes of electrical sparks. Suddenly there was a boiling hiss, and a cloud of vapor burst up through the hole in the floor. It was the sound and fury of superconducting magnets failing. The building shook as the magnetic fields in the generator went chaotic and relaxed. As the magnets failed they heated up suddenly, and the heat boiled the super-cooled liquid helium that surrounded the magnets. Helium vapor began pouring out of the pit.

Abruptly the lights in the building went out—circuit breakers had tripped. Meanwhile the giant bot still churned through the guts of Drake's machine.


**There was still** somebody alive in the Nanigen building. In the pit, while the big bot hacked at machinery, a slender man watched. He moved slowly, carefully, no jerky movements, nothing to attract the bot's attention. He removed a hard drive from a rack, pulling the data feed tapes out of their snaps. He slipped the drive into his jacket and left the pit quickly, climbing up a ladder, and from there he entered the fire escape tunnel. Behind him, he heard a thump, then a roar: the bot had started a fire.

The escape tunnel, lined with corrugated metal, went horizontally and ended at a ladder. Dr. Edward Catel, the liaison man from the Davros Consortium, climbed the ladder. The hard drive in his pocket contained five terabytes of data—all of Dr. Ben Rourke's designs for the tensor generator, along with priceless engineering data from test runs of the generator. When he had put two and two together and decided that Vin Drake had probably ordered murders of his own employees, he realized that Drake had become unstable and therefore could no longer serve effectively as a chief executive. He had gotten in touch with certain people, who for some time had been trying to discover what Nanigen was doing, and had told them that for a certain price he could get them designs of the generator. He had gone into the building that night. He hadn't realized Drake was in there, too.

Now, he stopped at the top of the ladder, below a hatch, and listened. What was going on above? He heard sirens, a helicopter thudding. Maybe he should wait here for a few hours. Give things a chance to settle down.

He felt something wet run down his cheek, drip on his collar.

He reached up to his face. Yes, a bot had gotten into his cheek. The escape tunnel had become contaminated. He could feel the bot burrowing through the tissues of his cheek. It would not be good if the bot entered a major blood vessel: it could swim to his brain and start cutting there, give him a hemorrhagic stroke. He would have to exit and take his chances.

He pushed open the hatch. It led to the middle of a patch of acacia brush by the parking lot. A fire truck was parked at the corner, but the crew's attention was focused on smoke pouring from the building.

He walked quickly into the underbrush, picking at his cheek with his fingertips. Had to get that bot out. He reached into his mouth with two fingers, pulled it from the tissues of his cheek, and pinched it between his fingernails, hard, until he felt it crunch. He kept walking. Thorns on the acacias caught at his clothing. He went from one empty lot to the next lot, and crossed behind a warehouse. He emerged from the business park and got on a sidewalk, and walked briskly along, until he reached a bus stop on the Farrington Highway, and he sat on the bench in the booth. Morning sun kissed the scene with a golden glow. It was a Sunday morning; the bus might not come for hours. He'd just have to wait. It gave him satisfaction and a sense of safety to be wearing a ripped jacket spotted with blood. He smiled. He could have been a homeless person, and very ill, the kind of person nobody wants to look at too closely. And he had the hard drive that contained the only complete set of Ben Rourke's plans for the tensor generator. The only plans.

A dark spot began spreading across the leg of his trousers. It was blood. This worried him. He opened his trousers, and felt around on his thigh, and got it. He held up the bot on the end of his fingertip and squinted at it. He could just see the little blades sparkling in the light. "Whither wander thou?" he murmured to the bot. This was quite good, he thought. He looked like a madman talking to his fingers. He was a free agent. Representing only himself, at the moment.

Catel crushed the bot between his nails and wiped his bloody hand on his pants. It was like crushing a tick. A fire truck rushed past, sirens screaming.

**A week later,** Lieutenant Dan Watanabe adjusted the angle of a laptop screen that sat on a hospital bed table; in the bed lay Eric Jansen. The screen showed an image of a bot cut neatly in half, with its insides laid open. "We got an ID on the Asian John Doe I told you about. His name was Jason Chu."

Eric nodded slowly. His leg was wrapped in bandages, and his face was pale and wan: anemia from loss of blood. "Jason Chu," Eric said, "worked for Rexatack, the company that owned the patents on the Hellstorm drone technology."

"So Mr. Chu organized the burglary of Nanigen to try to get information on what Nanigen was doing with his company's patents?"

"That's right," Eric answered.

"And you programmed these security bots?"

"Not to kill anybody. Drake reprogrammed them to kill." He closed his eyes and kept them shut for a while, then opened them. "You can charge me. My brother is dead and it's my fault. I don't care what happens to me."

"You will not be charged at this time," Watanabe answered carefully.

A nurse came in. "Visit's up." She checked Eric's monitors and said to Watanabe, "Can you guys take a hint or do I need to call a doctor?"

"I'm not a guy, ma'am," Dorothy Girt said politely, standing up.

Watanabe stood up and said to Eric, "Dorothy would really like a functioning Nanigen bot to analyze."

Eric shrugged. "They're all over the Nanigen core area."

"Not anymore. The place burned to crap. All that plastic. It took two days to put the fire out. There was nothing left. No bots. We found what we think is Drake. Dental records will tell. And that shrink machine—it's a charcoal briquette."

"Are you going to charge anybody?" Eric asked, just as Watanabe and Girt were leaving.

Watanabe stopped in the doorway. "The perpetrators are dead. The DA's getting pressure not to do any prosecutions. The pressure's coming from—let's say from government entities. Who don't want these robots talked about. My guess is this thing gets played as an industrial accident." His voice took on a note of disappointment. "But you never know," he added, and glanced at the forensic scientist. "It's the kind of conundrum Dorothy and I like to noodle with, don't we?"

"I enjoy conundrums," Dorothy Girt said rather primly. "Come along, Dan. The gentleman needs his rest."

# Chapter **52**

**MOLOKAI**
**18 NOVEMBER, 9:00 A.M.**

The rain over West Molokai had passed, and the trade wind had grown stronger, raking the palm trees along the beach and tearing spray from the surf. Set back from the water, a cluster of tents made of canvas and bamboo thumped and fluttered in the wind. The Dixie Maru eco-tent resort had seen better days.

Affordable on a student stipend.

Karen King sat up on the cot and stretched. The wind lifted a muslin curtain in the window of the tent, revealing a view of the beach, the palms, an expanse of blue water. Close to the beach, a white explosion burst from the sea.

Karen grabbed Rick Hutter by the shoulder and shook him. "A whale, Rick!"

Rick rolled over and opened his eyes. "Where?" he said drowsily.

"You're not interested."

"Yes, I am. Just sleepy." He sat up and looked out the window.

Karen admired the muscles across Rick's back and shoulders. In the lab in Cambridge, it had never occurred to her that Rick might have a decent body under those ratty flannel shirts he liked to wear.

"I don't see anything," he said.

"Watch. Maybe it'll happen again."

They observed the sea in silence. In the distance, across the Molokai Channel, the misty outline of the Koʻolau Pali of Oahu lay along the horizon, the mountain peaks capped with cotton puffs of clouds. It was raining on the Pali. Rick put his hand around Karen's waist. She placed her hand over his, and squeezed it.

Without warning, it happened again. First the head and then most of the body of a humpback whale appeared, breaching and turning in the air, followed by an incredible, bomb-like splash.

They watched the sea for a while longer, but it was quiet. Maybe the whale had sounded, or moved off.

Rick broke the silence. "I got a call from that cop. Lieutenant Watanabe."

"What? You didn't tell me."

"He says we're free to leave Hawaii."

Karen snorted. "They're hushing it up."

"Yeah. And we get to go back to boring old Cambridge—"

"Speak for yourself," Karen said, turning to him. "I'm not going back to Cambridge. Not now."

"Why?"

"Because I'm going to find a way back . . . there."

"The micro-world, you mean?"

She just smiled.

"But, Karen, that's impossible. There's no way—and even if there were, you'd be crazy to try it." He looked at his arms. The bruises still hadn't faded completely. "The micro-world kills humans like flies."

"Sure—every new world is dangerous. But think of all those discoveries . . ." She sighed. "Rick, I'm a scientist. I *have* to go there.

In fact, I can't imagine *not* going into the micro-world again. The technology exists—and you know as well as I do that with technology, once a thing is invented, it never gets un-invented."

"The bad things, too," Rick agreed.

"Exactly. Killer bots and micro-drones are here to stay. People will die in terrible new ways. Terrible wars will be fought with this technology. The world will never be the same."

A gust of wind shook the tent, and the canvas flapped against their duffels in the corner.

"What about us?" Rick asked, after the wind had died down.

"Us?"

"Yeah. You and me. I mean . . ." He tried to pull her back onto the bed.

But Karen was lost in thought. In her mind's eye, she saw the view from their camping spot on the cliffs of Tantalus: a mist-filled valley, cloaked in green, clear waterfalls trailing . . . a lost valley, not yet explored, or even truly seen by human eyes. "There has to be—" she began.

Something had caught her attention. A glint of metal, flying out of one of the duffels. A chill ran through her, the memory of bots whirling through the air like insects . . .

Whatever it was, it flew out the window, so small it passed right through the holes of the screen. It was nothing, she thought.

She turned to Rick. "There has to be a way back."

# Bibliography

This field is blessed by some of the best science writing for the general reader, as well as some of the clearest exposition for the college-level reader.

Agosta, William. *Bombardier Beetles and Fever Trees, A Close-up Look at Chemical Warfare and Signals in Animals and Plants.* Reading, Massachusetts: Addison-Wesley, 1995.

———. *Thieves, Deceivers and Killers, Tales of Chemistry in Nature.* Princeton, New Jersey: Princeton University Press, 2001.

Arnold, Harry A. *Poisonous Plants of Hawaii.* Tokyo: Tuttle, 1968.

Attenborough, David. *Life on Earth.* Boston: Little, Brown, 1979.

———. *The Private Life of Plants.* Princeton, New Jersey: Princeton University Press, 1995.

Ayres, Ian. *SuperCrunchers.* New York: Bantam, 2007.

Ball Jr., Stuart M. *Hiker's Guide to Oʻahu.* Revised edition. Honolulu: University of Hawaii Press, 2000.

Baluska, Frantisek, Stefano Mancuso, and Dieter Volkmann, eds. *Communication in Plants: Neuronal Aspects of Plant Life.* Berlin: Springer Verlag, 2006. (Technical.)

Beerling, David. *The Emerald Planet, How Plants Changed Earth's History.* New York: Oxford, 2007.

Belknap, Jody Perry, et al. *Majesty: The Exceptional Trees of Hawaii.* Honolulu: The Outdoor Circle, 1982.

Berenbaum, May R. *Bugs in the System: Insects and Their Impact on Human Affairs.* New York: Perseus, 1995.

Bier, James E., et al., and the Department of Geography, University of Hawaii. *Atlas of Hawaii.* Honolulu: University of Hawaii Press, 1973.

Bodanis, David. *The Secret Garden.* New York: Simon & Schuster, 1992.

Bonner, John Tyler. *Why Size Matters: From Bacteria to Blue Whales.* Princeton, New Jersey: Princeton University Press, 2006.

———. *Life Cycles: Reflections of an Evolutionary Biologist.* Princeton, New Jersey: Princeton University Press, 1993.

Bryan, William Alanson. *Natural History of Hawaii.* Honolulu: Hawaiian Gazette Co. Ltd., 1915. (Available on Google Books.)

Buhner, Stephen Harrod. *The Lost Language of Plants: The Ecological Importance of Plant Medicines to Life on Earth.* White River Junction, Vermont: Chelsea Green Publishing, 2002.

Chippeaux, Jean-Philippe. *Snake Venoms and Envenomations.* Malabar, Florida: Krieger Publishing, 2006.

Cox, George W. *Alien Species in North America and Hawaii, Impacts on Natural Ecosystems.* Washington, DC: Island Press, 1999.

Darwin, Charles. *The Power of Movement in Plants.* London: John Murray, 1880. (Available online at http://darwin-online.org.uk/.)

Dicke, Marcel, and Willem Takken. *Chemical Ecology, From Gene to Ecosystem.* Dordrecht, Netherlands: Springer, 2006.

Eisner, Thomas. *Eisner's World: Life Through Many Lenses.* Sunderland, Massachusetts: Sinauer Associates, 2009.

———. *For Love of Insects.* Cambridge, Massachusetts: The Belknap Press of Harvard University Press, 2003.

Eisner, Thomas, Maria Eisner, and Melody Siegler. *Secret Weapons: Defenses of Insects, Spiders, Scorpions, and Other Many-Legged Creatures.* Cambridge, Massachusetts: The Belknap Press of Harvard University Press, 2005.

Eisner, Thomas, and Jerrold Meinwald, eds. *Chemical Ecology: The Chemistry of Biotic Interaction*. Washington, DC: National Academy Press, 1995.

Fleming, Andrew J., ed. *Intercellular Communication in Plants, Annual Plant Reviews, Volume 16*. Oxford, England: Blackwell, 2005.

Foelix, Rainer D. *Biology of Spiders*. 2nd edition. New York: Oxford University Press—George Thieme Verlag, 1996.

Galston, Arthur W. *Life Processes of Plants*. New York: Scientific American, 1994.

Gotwald Jr., William H. *Army Ants: The Biology of Social Predation*. Ithaca, New York: Cornell University Press, 1995.

Gullan, Penny J., and Peter S. Cranston. *The Insects: An Outline of Entomology*. 4th edition. Oxford: Wiley-Blackwell, 2010.

Hall, John B. *A Hiker's Guide to Trailside Plants in Hawai'i*. Honolulu: Mutual Publishing, 2004.

Hillyard, Paul. *The Private Life of Spiders*. Princeton, New Jersey: Princeton University Press, 2008.

Hölldobler, Bert, and Edward O. Wilson. *The Ants*. Cambridge, Massachusetts: The Belknap Press of Harvard University Press, 1990.

Homer; Robert Fagles, translator. *The Odyssey*. New York: Viking, 1996.

Howarth, Francis G., and William P. Mull. *Hawaiian Insects and Their Kin*. Honolulu: University of Hawaii Press, 1992.

Jones, Richard. *Nano Nature: Nature's Spectacular Hidden World*. New York: Metro Books, 2008.

Kealey, Terence. *The Economic Laws of Scientific Research*. New York: St. Martin's Press, 1996.

Kepler, Angela Kay. *Trees of Hawaii*. Honolulu: University of Hawaii Press, 1990.

Krauss, Beatrice H. *Native Plants Used as Medicine in Hawaii*. Honolulu: Harold L. Lyon Arboretum, 1981.

Liebherr, James K., and Elwood C. Zimmerman. *Insects of Hawaii. Vol. 16: Hawaiian Carabidae (Coleoptera): Part 1: Introduction and Tribe Platynini*. Honolulu: University of Hawaii Press, 2000.

Magnacca, Karl N. "Conservation Status of the Endemic Bees of Hawaii,

Hylaeus (Nesoprosopis) (Hymenoptera: Colletidae)." *Pacific Science.* Vol. 61, no. 2, April 2007, pp. 173–190.

Marshall, Stephen A. *Insects: Their Natural History and Diversity.* Buffalo, New York: Firefly Books, 2006.

Martin, Gary J. *Ethnobotany: A Methods Manual.* Chapman & Hall, 1995; reprint London: Earthscan, 2004.

McBride, L. R. *Practical Folk Medicine of Hawaii.* Hilo: Petroglyph Press, 1975.

McMonagle, Orin. *Giant Centipedes: The Enthusiast's Handbook.* Elytra & Antenna: ElytraandAntenna.com, 2003.

Meier, Jürg, and Julian White, eds. *Handbook of Clinical Toxicology of Animal Venoms and Poisons.* Boca Raton: Taylor & Francis, 1995.

Moffett, Mark W. *Adventures Among Ants.* Berkeley: University of California Press, 2010.

Palmer, Daniel D. *Hawai'i's Ferns and Fern Allies.* Honolulu: University of Hawaii Press, 2002.

Perkins, R. C. L. "Insects of Tantalus." *Proceedings of the Hawaiian Entomological Society.* Vol. 1, pt. 2, pp. 38–51. (Available on Google Books.)

Perkins, Robert Cyril Layton. Author of various parts in *Fauna Hawaiiensis,* ed. David Sharp, Op. Cit.

Pukui, Mary Kawena and Samuel H. Elbert. *Hawaiian Dictionary.* Revised Edition. Honolulu: University of Hawaii Press, 1986.

Scott, Susan, and Craig Thomas. *Poisonous Plants of Paradise: First Aid and Medical Treatment of Injuries from Hawaii's Plants.* Honolulu: University of Hawaii Press, 2000.

Serres, Michel, with Bruno Latour. *Conversations on Science, Culture, and Time.* Ann Arbor: University of Michigan, 1990.

Sharp, David, ed. *Fauna Hawaiiensis, or the Zoology of the Sandwich (Hawaiian) Isles.* Vols. 1–3. Cambridge: Cambridge University Press, 1899–1913. (The principal collector and author of many of this series' parts was Robert Cyril Layton Perkins, op. cit. PDF facsimile downloadable at Karl N. Magnacca's website: http://nature.berkeley.edu/~magnacca/fauna.html. Also available on Google Books.)

Simonson, Douglas, et al. *Pidgin to Da Max Hana Hou. [Pidgin Hawaiian dictionary.]* Honolulu: The Bess Press, 1992.

Sohmer, S. H., and R. Gustafson. *Plants and Flowers of Hawaii.* Honolulu: University of Hawaii Press, 1987.

Spradbery, J. Philip. *Wasps: An Account of the Biology and Natural History of Solitary and Social Wasps.* Seattle: University of Washington Press, 1973.

Stamets, Paul. *Mycelium Running.* Berkeley: Ten Speed Press, 2005.

Stone, Charles P., and Linda W. Pratt. *Hawaii's Plants and Animals: Biological Sketches of Hawaii Volcanoes National Park.* Honolulu: Hawaii Natural History Association, 1994.

Swartz, Tim. *The Lost Journals of Nicola Tesla.* New Brunswick, New Jersey: Global Communications, n.d.

Swift, Sabina F., and M. Lee Goff. "Mite (Acari) Communities Associated with 'Ohi'a . . . " *Pacific Science* (2001), vol. 55, no. 1, pp. 23–55.

Walter, David Evans, and Heather Coreen Proctor. *Mites: Ecology, Evolution, and Behavior.* Sydney, Australia: University of New South Wales Press, 1999.

Ward, Peter D., and Donald Brownlee. *Rare Earth, Why Complex Life Is Uncommon in the Universe.* New York: Copernicus (Springer-Verlag), 2000.

Wilson, Edward O. *Naturalist.* New York: Warner Books, 1995.

Wolfe, David W. *Tales from the Underground: A Natural History of Subterranean Life.* New York: Basic Books, 2001.

Xenophon; Rex Warner, translator. *The Persian Expedition [The Anabasis].* 1949: Republished London: Penguin Books, 1972. (Pages 140–147: Xenophon's first speeches to the troops. An example of leadership in a survival crisis. Dramatic reading; served as a model for Peter Jansen's rallying speech to his fellow students.)

Zimmer, Carl. *Parasite Rex: Inside the Bizarre World of Nature's Most Dangerous Creatures.* New York: Simon & Schuster Touchstone, 2000.

Zimmerman, Elwood C. *Insects of Hawaii.* Vol. 1. Honolulu: University of Hawaii Press, 2001. (Reprint of volume 1, originally published in 1947, with a new preface.)

## ABOUT THE AUTHORS

**Michael Crichton** has sold over 200 million books, which have been translated into thirty-six languages; thirteen of his books have been made into films. His novels include *Next*, *State of Fear*, *Timeline*, *Jurassic Park*, and *The Andromeda Strain*. Also known as a filmmaker and the creator of *ER*, he remains the only writer to have had the number one book, movie, and TV show simultaneously. At the time of his death in 2008, Crichton was well into the writing of *Micro*; Richard Preston was selected to complete the novel.

www.michaelcrichton.com

**Richard Preston** is an internationally acclaimed bestselling author of eight books, including *The Hot Zone* and *The Wild Trees*. Many of Preston's books have appeared in *The New Yorker*. He has won numerous awards, including the American Institute of Physics Award and the National Magazine Award, and he is the only person not a medical doctor ever to receive the Centers for Disease Control's Champion of Prevention Award for public health. He lives with his wife and three children near Princeton, New Jersey.

www.richardpreston.net